AFRICAN WRITERS SERIES

The Healers

AYI KWEI ARMAH

an historical novel

HEINEMANN

Heinemann International Literature & Textbooks
a division of Heinemann Educational Books Ltd
Halley Court, Jordan Hill, Oxford OX2 8EJ

Heinemann Educational Books Inc
361 Hanover Street, Portsmouth, New Hampshire, 03801, USA

Heinemann Educational Books (Nigeria) Ltd
PMB 5205, Ibadan
Heinemann Kenya Ltd
PO Box 45314, Nairobi, Kenya
Heinemann Educational Boleswa
PO Box 10103, Village Post Office, Gaborone, Botswana
Heinemann Publishers (Caribbean) Ltd
175 Mountain View Avenue, Kingston 6, Jamaica

LONDON   EDINBURGH   MELBOURNE   SYDNEY
AUCKLAND   SINGAPORE   TOKYO   MADRID   PARIS
HARARE   ATHENS   BOLOGNA

First published in East African Publishing House 1978
First published in African Writers Series 1979

ISBN 0 435 90194 X (paper)

Set in 9 point Pilgrim

Printed and bound in Great Britain by
Cox & Wyman Ltd, Reading, Berkshire

90 91 92 93 94 95 10 9 8 7 6 5 4

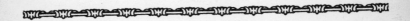

For Mkasafari Leweri
and Kokue Amegatcher

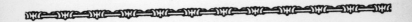

CONTENTS

PART ONE

1 The Whirlpool

In the twentieth year of his life, a young man found himself at the centre of strange, extraordinary events. Someone was murdered—a youth exactly the same age as himself. The killing was done in a particularly bloody, brutal way. Those who saw the victim's butchered body agreed on one thing: the murderer acted from a fierce, passionate motive, the kind of violent motive springing out of jealousy made hotter by pure, vindictive hate.

It seemed there were no living winesses to the murder. The victim was the heir in the house of power at Esuano, a prince named Appia. Those in a position to know said he was destined to inherit not only old power but, far more important, the possibility of fantastic wealth.

The prince and his mother were at the beginning of a journey when the prince was killed. Of the mother not a single trace was left. Among those who came to the scene of the murder, the most hopeful wished that in some mysterious way the mother could be found alive, able to tell the terrible truth about her son's destruction. But those who spoke from a more bitter exierence of life said something different. They said whoever had so destroyed the strong prince had certainly murdered the loving mother also.

Soon enough, the harsh certainty of the experienced ones scattered the hesitant wishes of the hopeful ones. Only two questions remained: how had the double crime been committed? And, above all, by whom?

In the absence of real knowledge suspicion became the guide to thought. Strange rumours flew fast and free. Some were light and wild, so light and wild they disappeared as fast as they were uttered. Their own incredible speed threw them beyond reach of even the most credulous minds.

But heavier rumours remained, turning round and round within easy reach. Speculation churned them into a circling whirlpool; and

1

skilful insinuation found a quiet, unsuspecting youth, and placed him at the exact centre of the dangerous, speeding vortex of suspicion. His name was Densu.

So in the twentieth year of his life, just when he saw the time perfect for planning how he would live his life, Densu was forced instead to open his mind to thoughts of death: the death of the prince Appia; the presumed death of the prince's mother Araba Jesiwa; and the impending death—if he found no way to fly free of the whirlpool of suspicion so inexorably trapping him—the impending death of his own self.

But now this tongue of the story-teller, descendant of masters in the arts of eloquence, this tongue flies too fast for the listener. It flies faster than the story-telling mind itself. Pride in its own telling skill has made it light, more than merely light. Pride has made this tongue giddy with joy. So the story-teller now forgets this rule of masters in the arts of eloquence: the tongue alone, unrestrained, unconnected to the remembering mind, can carry only a staggering, spastic, drooling, idiot tale. In such a story, told by an unconnected tongue, the middle hurls itself at the astonished ear before the beginning has even had time to be mentioned. The end itself is battered into pieces. The fragments are smashed against the surprised listener's ear, without connections, without meaning, without sense.

Let the error raise its own correction. The speeding tongue forgets connections. Let the deliberate mind restore them. Proud tongue, child of the Anona masters of eloquence, before you leap so fast to speak, listen first to the mind's remembrance.

Did you remember to tell your listeners of what time, what age you rushed so fast to speak? Or did you leave the listener floundering in endless time, abandoned to suppose your story belonged to any confusing age? Is it a story of yesterday, or is it of last year? Is it from the time of the poet Nyankoman Dua, seven centuries ago? Or did it take place ten centuries ago, when Ghana was not just a memory, and the eloquent ones before you still sang praises to the spirit holding our people together? Is it of that marvellous black time before the desert was turned desert, thirty centuries and more ago? Or have you let the listener know the truth: that this story now is not so old—just over a century old?

What of the place? Have you told the listener where the town Esuano was, beside which of the numberless rivers of Africa? Or have you left the listening ear without a guide, thinking confusedly of the twin Mfolozi, near whose banks Magolwane, the poet of the soaring silver voice, sang eloquence to the raging shaker of the earth? Is the listener to imagine such a river as the Sankarani, or the wandering Joliba, or the fierce Limpopo? Have you told the listener that of the sacred rivers of our land, the closest to Esuano was the Pra?

Let the listener know when. Let the listener know where. Then, Anona tongue, born for eloquence, continue your telling. And in the joy of your eloquence keep faith with the mind's remembrance, lest the teller's forgetfulness spoil the listener's joy.

*   *   *

Two streams flowed by Esuano. One was a calm stream. It flowed so gently there were places where its motion was barely visible. Its waters were extraordinarily clear. You could see all the way down to the bed of fine sand sprinkled with pebbles of many colours, from light yellows to deep, dark purples.

If your hearing was keen and your imagination alive, you could hear, deeper than the light breeze's sound, the sound of pebbles rolling forward under the water.

Along the clear river's right bank the fine yellow sand brought by this stream formed a narrow strand. Below Esuano, just before the confluence with the second stream, the strand widened into an open beach. Because the first was smaller and gentler than the second, and also because it was such a clear thing of beauty, people named it Nsu Ber, the female river.

The second river was wider and more turbulent than the first. Its bed was invisible; its waters were opaque with mud. In its flow past Esuano it carried a heavy load of leaves, twigs, and broken branches from its course upstream. Along both of its banks it deposited not sand but silt, a thick, muddy ooze. Partly because this second stream was heavy and physically forceful, and partly because it lacked the beauty of the first, people called it Nsu Nyin, the male river.

The male river flowed north for most of its course, but not far below Esuano it began a powerful westward turn, after which it held the new direction till it reached a greater river, the sacred Pra.

The female river had a more consistent course. It flowed steadily north-west, to meet the male river just past Esuano, a good morning's walking distance before the greater confluence with the Pra.

Between the female river and the male, below Esuano, lay a wide

3

strip of land cut off as if deliberately from other surrounding land. No one farmed it, though it was fertile, being river soil. A soft mat of grass covered it. It was entirely green, except that at intervals the green was broken by a flower, watery blue, bright yellow, or pale purple, raised a hand's height above the grass on a slender, quivering stalk. The grass was gentle, extremely gentle. Underneath it the soil was soft but firm, and the whole wide strip of land was innocent of thorns.

You could walk there in the early morning, lost in a quiet dream from the future. You could sit there in the total stillness of an afternoon yellow with sunlight, the silence one continuous sound just beyond your hearing, you could sit there thinking of the past and the present. Or you could run fast as your desire had strength to carry you in a breezy afternoon, and never feel a stone's harshness underfoot.

This was the field of rituals. Here the people of Esuano came at the end of every chosen year for the rituals of remembrance. Here on the grass, in the last two weeks of each chosen year, the generation of youths crossing into manhood ran races and played games of strength and skill.

The games had a power over the people of Esuano. For the two weeks that they lasted, most other activities stopped. In the final week the air grew sharp with tension. After the games were over everyone, participants and spectators, felt spent, exhausted.

How had these ritual games of remembrance begun? There had always been some talk of origins. But time had passed; the talk had grown vague. It grew a little vaguer every chosen year.

Those who cared to remember such things were few. They said the games had been entirely different in a different age. These people who remembered could talk of ancestors who had come travelling great distances, leading a people in pain. At Esuano, as at other places along the route, some had found clear water of life, flowing by good land. So they had taken root. In gratitude and in hope, they had enacted each chosen year the ceremonial games, the rituals of remembrance.

The way the people who still remembered talked of them, these had been festivals made for keeping a people together. They were not so much celebrations as invocations of wholeness. They were the festivals of a people surviving in spite of unbearable pain. They were reminders that no matter how painful the journey, our people would finish it, survive it and thrive again at the end of it, as long as our people moved together.

That was the spirit of the first rituals. But the hard realities of our scattering and our incessant wandering had long disturbed the oneness these festivals were meant to invoke, to remember, and to celebrate.

The truth was plain: among the wandering people some had chosen homes deeper in the heart of the land, and settled in the forests there. This was division. Some had pushed their way eastward till they came to a great, fertile river and settled along its banks. This was division. Some after coming south had gone westward; there they had seen deep, mysterious forest places answering their pained need for withdrawal, and they had settled there. This was division. Some had just moved south and south, till the sea told them they could move no farther, and they had settled there along the shorelands. This, too, was division.

That was how Esuano had been built. Other towns, other centres grew scattered over the land: Akropong, Domeabra, Techiman, Enyinase.

True, in the beginning each division kept for a while its fragmented remembrance of a past oneness, and still made hesitant invocations to a future unity: Achease, Odaso, Odumase, Edwinase, Afranse.

Yes, for a while each fraction continued in some form the ceremonies meant to remind a scattered people of our common origin. But in some places the ceremonies died with time. In all places the ceremonies changed. Their intended meaning had been wholeness. But the circumstances under which they had been played out had been circumstances of division, circumstances of fragmentation.

Time passed. Circumstance overwhelmed meaning. At Esuano the ritual games continued. But their meaning was no longer what it had been meant to be. In the circumstances of fragmentation, the meaning of unity had not been entirely destroyed, perhaps. But it had been torn to shreds.

The games had a kind of power over Densu. From infancy he had watched them every chosen year, and known his time would also come to take part in them. The games fascinated him. Yet in spite of his fascination, something about them disturbed him. In time this something made it impossible for him to look forward to the coming time with the clear, pure passionate enthusiasm of youth.

Before the young man's fourteenth year this something had not been definite. But in his fourteenth year it had grown into a question agitating his mind. He had been watching the end of that year's games. The question started like a spark in his head. It became a light, small but sharp, steady, insistent. What were these games for?

5

He felt the disturbance in his body also. There the question was a sort of warmth, a kind of heat that spread itself throughout his being: what was the purpose of these games? The agitation he felt grew so intense it became unpleasant. Densu wished the question would go away in time. It did not. Rather, it drew to itself more of his interest. It took more and more of his mind's energy, until he was driven to seek answers from people who might know.

The older people, most of them, had not given much thought to that kind of question really. When Densu asked them what the games were for, some said they did not understand the question itself. Others asked Densu a question to answer his: why had such a question become so important to him? They asked, because at Esuano the remembrance of a larger community had become a faint remnant from a forgotten past. There were people who knew stories of a time when the black people were one. But they were not easy to find. Even when found, they were rather silent, as if the question raised in their minds a regret that overwhelmed their tongues.

At Esuano the people, most of them, were content to know themselves as Fantse people. They knew of other people with ways and a language not really different from their own: Denchira, Wassa, Assen, Aowin, Nzema, Ekuapem, Asante. But they had not been brought up in the habit of thinking of all these as parts of a whole embracing themselves. The meaning of the ceremonies of unity had faded.

Something else. A few remembered the old ceremonies as rituals in which all the people of Esuano had done things together. These rituals had celebrated the struggles of a people working together to reach difficult destinations. But then that too had changed. The games were now trials of individual strength and skill. At their end a single person would be chosen victor, and isolated for the admiration of spectators and the envy of defeated competitors.

It was this that had, in his fourteenth year, so disturbed the young man Densu. The question that had troubled him then had not left his mind in his twentieth year: what was the purpose of these games? Why did they seem so purposeless to him?

A whole community gathered every chosen year to take part in rituals of wholeness. But at the end of the ceremonies of wholeness a single individual was held up to be glorified by the whole community. Where was the root of wholeness in such a strange ritual of separation? Densu searched his feelings for some possible affirmation, for some hope that the things going on around him could make sense. But his feelings rebelled at being forced to look for sense in nonsense.

The truth Densu saw was a sharp image: a single winner riding over a multitude of losers. Unwilling to accept the meaning of the harsh image, Densu searched his mind for reasons to soften the truth he had seen. But his mind refused to show him any of the smooth roads to self-betrayal. The only reason he found in the nature of the games was something monstrous, a perversion that repelled him naturally, powerfully.

2 The Wrestlers

Of the two weeks of ceremonial games the first was always an open time. Children still new to the power of motion ran races behind old men remembering irretrievable times when they too were swift. There was much laughter, none of the strife of competition, and no anxiety at all, in the first week, the open week.

In the final week all this changed. Children and nostalgic old men were driven from the centre of the field to the sides. They became spectators and watched the year's strongest youths compete for victory. The games began in the early mornings, before the sun was high. But the results were not celebrated then. Evening was the time of final victory.

The first day, Sunday, of the final week was set aside for wrestling. Children came early, carrying stools for adults to sit on. They themselves sat down on the still dewy grass. Or they stood, waiting for the judge to start the games. The judge was a muscular man in a blue and white hunter's smock over trousers of the same material. In a strong voice he called the competitors to come to him. Several young men stepped forward, and the judge went over them with his eyes.

The youth closest to the judge was rather tall. He had thin legs and long, thin arms. His hands ended in fingers which showed far more

7

delicacy than strength. Everything about his body looked as if it had been sharpened: the forward strain of his nose, the point of his chin; even his teeth gave the impression of having been carefully filed, each to a fine point.

After him came a copper-skinned fellow of roughly the same height. He had a hare-lip and his body looked decidedly awkward, no matter from which angle it was seen. The torso was twisted in such a way that at first glance an observer might expect it to relax presently. But the tension twisting it was permanent. Something in the shape of the legs extended this tension: the legs were bandy. The right thigh bent sharply inwards at the knee, and the lower leg bent as sharply outwards. Because the left leg was left unbent, it stood longer than its companion, so that when this fellow stood at rest he seemed to be leaning confidentially towards the person on his right.

On his right stood a short, slight fellow. His small size made him seem out of place in the group, the next shortest person being at least a head taller than he was. Otherwise there was nothing particularly remarkable about him. His face was handsome, and his expression calm.

Next to him there was a young man, not tall, not short, standing unshakeably on short, thick legs. He had a thick waist under a powerful looking paunch surmounted by a heavy, fleshy chest. His head rested most comfortably on an ample neck divided into three smooth cushions of fat. The fellow had a genial face. His cheeks were so enormous they looked arrested in a smile. His lips protruded as if in a pout, which was odd, because there was no suggestion of surliness on his face. The lips were permanently wet, shining softly as if he had taken care to keep them lubricated.

The fellow to his right was tall and handsome. His body was economically built, almost thin. His skin was smooth and black. His head was large. It had a bold, prominent forehead from whose gentle curve sunlight bounced as from a polished surface. He had his eyes half-closed against the morning light, though the sun was behind him. That made them look small; but occasionally he opened them wide, and then they were large, and had a beauty that came from a certain liquid clarity in them. His attention seemed concentrated on something, because though his body was quite relaxed, his look was intense. Whatever it was he was concentrating on was something inner; he was paying only minimal attention to the goings-on around him.

The next youth was just as tall. He was somewhat less handsome though. His body was more muscular. His attention was divided between watching the judge before him and the crowd beyond. This gave his eyes an eager, flitting look, as if he were impatient to have the fighting begin.

He who stood next was by far the most remarkable figure on the field. He was light-skinned. His skin had a reddish colour, not a smooth red but a sort of unfinished-looking red. This made him look somewhat like a clay pot prematurely snatched out of the kiln that should have fired and darkened it. Two things stood out about this one: his ugliness and his size. He was huge. He was not merely huge. He was a giant. Every part of his body gave an impression of overwhelming weight. His limbs were massive. The muscles on his thighs and arms were thick. They pushed hard against the skin, as if the covering it provided were not sufficient. His chest was enormous. It bulged forwards, backwards and sideways, the brawny upper arms mere gross extensions of the bulky body.

More remarkable than any other part of the giant's body, however, were his neck and the head upon it. With normal people the neck is something slender, the relatively delicate connection between two larger parts, the head and the chest. But the giant's neck had nothing delicate about it. It was a crude mass, immensely powerful-looking, and it grew directly from the torso. It seemed to have taken the whole expansive width of the giant's shoulders for its base. It was not a long neck, but in its short rise to the base of the head above it, it had time to taper somewhat. The head, far from broadening out from the neck, simply continued this tapering. The giant's head was therefore dramatically smaller and less impressive than the neck supporting it. The back of the head, as for that, it was quite flat. There was no rounding anywhere except at the top, and there the whole body ended in a blunt, brutal point.

As the giant stood now, his body seemed near to exploding. Every muscle bulged with some huge, uncontrollable tension. The inner tension was visible in the massive face. It seemed to have pushed all the giant's features outwards, so that his teeth, which were enormous, each yellow one separated from its neighbour by ample space, strained aggressively forward, forcing his slimy lips permanently open. His nostrils showed wide and open, as if they had run short of air, and were taking in gigantic draughts. The giant's eyes were small in themselves, pig-like. But they were subject to the same inner tension pushing his other features outwards. They strained beyond their

9

sockets from which they stared sullenly, uncomprehendingly at the world outside. They were bloodshot eyes, unclear, murky, utterly repulsive.

The youth next to the giant made an uncanny contrast with him. It was not a crude contrast, such as that between strength and weakness. It was subtler, and in a way more striking. The contrast was between two kinds of strength. One kind, the giant's, was crude, brutal. The other kind was full of grace.

This youth was not as tall as the giant, but he was tall, slightly taller than the tall, handsome one with the large forehead and the intense look, the third to his left. His build was slender. His skin was black, with a suggestion of depth and coolness in its blackness. The youth stood perfectly straight, without any effort to do so. There was no tension in any part of his body. When he moved, no matter how small the motion, it seemed to start somewhere deep in his being, and to involve the rest of his body, all of it, in a gentle, hardly perceptible wave of energy. Something about his eyes suggested an echo of the eyes of the tall, handsome one, the third to his left. His eyes were also clear, the whites luminous, the pupils dark and definite. He did not close his eyes but looked ahead, his body turned to the left so he could see the judge near the end of the line.

The last person in the line was in height like a twin to the last but one. His body was thicker, and he was powerfully muscled. His biceps and calves stood out most strongly. On his belly the individual muscles were tautly visible, each separated from the other, making a regular pattern. The young man had an easy smile on his lips. All in all, he gave the impression of having not only strength but skill, and enjoying immensely the confidence that came from knowing he had both.

The judge counted the young men ranged in front of him. There were nine of them. In a loud, clear voice, the judge addressed them. First, he reminded them of the rules governing the game of wrestling. Then he demonstrated the sign for conceding defeat—an arm raised, the index finger extended skyward. A victor must release his opponent the instant he made that sign. Continuing beyond that point would only damage the loser, perhaps maiming him. To win, a fighter would have to put his opponent down in three clean falls.

This said, the judge counted the young men one more time. He counted nine. The number disturbed the judge. An even number would have been easier. He paused thoughtfully, then raised his head. He seemed on the point of announcing a difficult decision. But just then one of the competitors caught his eye. This young man had his left arm raised casually above his head. The judge looked up at the hand and squinted. The index finger on that hand was extended skyward. The judge, his forehead creased with puzzlement, stared at the young man. He was the slender, relaxed one, the second from the end.

The slender youth had a sort of unfathomable, permanent calmness in the way he held his body, in the features of his face, in his every motion. He had stood completely relaxed as the judge announced the wrestling rules, and when he had raised his arm and pointed the index finger towards the sky the entire movement had happened without a single jerky motion. It was all one easy, continuous flow, as if the body executing it were a perfect extension of the mind that had decided on the action. The look in the youth's eyes was also calm, infinitely calm, a look beyond both humility and arrogance.

The judge stared hard at the slender youth and asked: 'What is it, Densu?'

'I'm making the sign of defeat,' the youth answered calmly.

'But you haven't fought,' said the judge.

'I don't wish to fight,' said Densu.

'You aren't going to concede defeat, just like that?'

'I am conceding defeat.'

The judge looked confused. He walked closer to the young man. He seemed about to try persuasion. But then he took another look at the slender youth and changed his mind.

'I suppose,' he said with an embarrassed smile, 'the rules don't prevent you from losing this way.' The smile broke into an uneasy laugh. 'But what is it, Densu? Are you afraid?'

The youth did not answer the question. He did not even seem to have heard it. He walked away from the line of competitors with that smooth, fluent, relaxed motion of his, and sat down cross-legged on the grass between two small groups of spectators.

Out on the field the judge cast lots to decide the pairing of the remaining eight. In a while he waved six of them aside.

In the centre, the first chosen pair prepared themselves for combat. One of the fighters was the one with the hare-lip. It made him look as if he were smiling with a weird, good-humoured menace at his opponent all the time. The other was the paunchy young man with the unshakable stance.

'Kweku Sipi will fight Yao Patu!' the judge announced. He gave the two fighters his final instructions, stepped back, and ordered them to begin.

The fight was short. On the surface the fighters may have seemed evenly matched. But as soon as the fight began in earnest the one with the hare-lip began to overpower his rival. Even the ambiguous smile of sinister good humour disappeared from his face. In its stead there was just a grim, controlled fury, a determination to beat the undisfigured one at least in this game. Only when it was clear the hare-lipped one had won did his face regain its smiling look. The menace was completely purged from it.

'The first winner is Kweku Sipi!' the judge announced as soon as the fight was over. 'Kweku Sipi, the first winner. Kweku Sipi!'

The triumphant winner strode over towards the spectators. Behind him the judge announced the beginning of the next fight.

'Kofi Antobam will fight Kobena Ampa. Kofi Antobam against Kobena Ampa!'

The youth with the hare-lip had been moving in a line that would have taken him directly where Densu had gone to sit. It seemed, in fact, as if there was something he was eager to share with Densu. But before he got close enough to say anything a man detached himself from the main crowd of watchers and came to stand directly in front of the seated Densu. The hare-lip hesitated a moment, then turned aside and looked for a dry patch of grass to sit on, leaving the intruder alone with Densu.

Densu stood up. It was clear the intruder meant to talk to him, and also that Densu owed him respect. The man was short and bald. He was not aged, but he was old, perhaps fifty. He moved gracelessly, but this awkwardness was not on account of age. The man was fat. Underneath all his fat it was clear his bones were small, and his natural frame was that of a small, slight person. But he had overwhelmed his natural frame with fat, and now he looked like a deformed sphere balanced unsteadily on thin legs. His arms were short. The upper parts were thick and heavy, but the lower arms turned suddenly thin a short way down from the elbow. The fingers, small and even dainty-looking, seemed on his bulbous body like something borrowed from a more delicate frame.

The intruder's face was like a gentler, somewhat pleasanter minia-ture of his body. It too was fat and round. Its roundness was made more noticeable by the total absence of hair on its shiny top.

In outline, the body and the head above it both suggested a full, overstuffed contentment. From a distance the man looked like someone who had spent more than sufficient time consuming an abundance of food and drink, and who, now more than sated, was groping unsteadily on his undeveloped legs looking for a place where he could rest for years and years peacefully digesting all he had consumed, a kind of python after feeding-time.

Yet something in the intruder's face, seen close up, contradicted the impression of round contentment. That something was in the eyes. The intruder's eyes were extremely active, in a quick, nervous way. These were not the eyes of a contented man. Had the intruder been thin and hungry-looking, these eyes would have given him the air of a restless, dissatisfied, voraciously ambitious man. But set as they were in this round face, above this rotund, satisfied body, the eyes hinted at something obscene. The eyes suggested someone already stuffed to bursting after having consumed everything within his reach, but so uncontrollably greedy that in spite of satiation he was still anxiously searching for more things to consume.

Densu greeted the intruder, but there was no reply. Instead, the bald man kept staring at Densu, examining him minutely as if the youth had something infinitely strange about him, something which had long baffled the older man's understanding but which he was bent on grasping. After a while the bald man smiled. It was a queer smile, as if his muscles were not used to smiling and the exercise hurt his face. At the same time as he was smiling, his eyes narrowed with a hostility impossible to disguise.

'You shouldn't have done that,' the bald man said.

Densu did not answer. His expression remained calm and his eyes were steady. He was looking past the bald head, listlessly watching the progress of the fight on the grass.

'Why did you do it?' the bald man persisted.

'Why did I do what?' Densu asked.

'Refuse to fight.'

'I don't like fighting for no reason,' Densu said.

'There's always a reason.' The fat man's voice was scornful. 'To beat the other fellow.'

'There's no reason I should want to beat him,' Densu said.

The intruder laughed. The look in his eyes became at once conspiratorial and unbelieving. 'Everyone likes to win,' he said, smiling a bitter smile. 'But I did not come to talk of winners and losers. I have come about something else entirely. I've had visitors from Cape Coast.

13

Important men. What they had to say concerns you. I want to talk to you in complete privacy.'

'Court affairs...' Densu started, his tone bored and irritated at the same time. The intruder cut him short.

'I know, I know. Court affairs don't interest you, Densu. But I'm talking of something more than the business of the court here at Esuano. Don't make up your mind before you know what it's about. That's a fool's way of doing things. Your future at least does interest you, does it not? Come to see me this evening.'

'When?'

'As soon as you've eaten,' the bald man said.

Densu nodded, and the bald man moved off, going back in the direction he had come from. He waddled into the crowd of spectators, and Densu lost sight of him. Now that the intruder was gone, Densu turned his attention back to the wrestlers out on the field.

The second fight was taking longer than expected. It was between the tall youth with the eager, flitting eyes and the short, calm one. The short fellow lacked skill. But he made up for it with a quite unexpected physical toughness and a stubborn determination not to yield. No matter how skilfully the tall one tried to throw him, the short one seemed incapable of losing his footing. Since the short one had not the skill to trip his opponent, and the other had not the strength to force him off his feet, the fight became a long, balanced test of endurance.

In time, stamina decided the issue. The tall one, in spite of all his skill, grew short of wind. The muscles of his legs and arms lost their resilience and speed. In the end the short one pressed him down with sheer conserved energy, three times, and the fight was over.

'Kofi Antobam has won this one!' the judge shouted. 'Ampa is the loser. The winner: Kofi Antobam.'

Winner and loser both walked off into the crowd.

'Now the third bout!' the judge announced. 'It's Kwao Buntui against Kwesi Anan!'

The giant walked heavily to the centre of the fighting area. He moved awkwardly, as if the huge muscles in which his body was bound did not belong to him and therefore did not obey his will. His opponent stood facing him. He was the tall, handsome one with the large head and the intense look. The judge reminded the wrestlers of the rules, briefly. Then he gave them the signal to begin.

From the beginning it was clear Kwesi Anan had no intention of grappling physically, brutally, with the giant Buntui. Kwesi Anan moved more like a dancer than a fighter. He circled around the giant, watching him, never for a moment taking his eyes off him and his massive body. Once he took a swift step close to the giant. Buntui's reaction was a powerful movement. He threw both arms out and drew them inwards, towards his body. His arms made a fearful noise against his chest. The movement was unco-ordinated, and so awkwardly executed that it failed in its aim. But the aim itself was clear enough. Buntui had simply wanted to grab his opponent and crush him bodily against himself. Had he in fact caught Anan, he would have done just that.

But Anan had only feinted with that swift step. As soon as he had taken it, he drew back, taking himself far out of Buntui's reach. So the giant had embraced and crushed the empty air. At that precise moment the dancer stepped in close again. Reaching behind Buntui with his left leg, he planted it firm as a sapling; then, putting all the rest of his weight behind his arms, he pushed the clumsy Buntui backward against his planted leg.

The entire series of motions had taken Buntui by surprise. He fell heavily backward, unable to make any attempt either to break his fall or to soften it in any way. The judge stepped near and took a look to see if Buntui's back had touched the earth. It had.

'One in favour of Anan,' the judge said. There was a species of wonder in his voice.

The fallen giant rose. The judge stood between the two combatants and asked them if they were ready to continue the fight. They said yes. The judge slipped backward from between them, giving them the sign to continue.

The giant's eyes had grown smaller. For moments he stood motionless there on the grass, staring at his elusive opponent. The dancing wrestler sensed the giant's anger, and moved more cautiously. He bent slightly forward from the waist and spread out his arms, as if he were searching for a place to get a hold on the giant.

The giant stopped all motion and stood quite still, watching his adversary with his small eyes now changed from their muddy colour to a harsher red. Now that the giant was immobile, the dancer was confused. He lunged forward swiftly with his left arm, then drew it back in the same instant. It was a feint, designed to lure the giant off the impregnable balance given him by immobility. But the giant simply stood there. He stood there, waiting with a massive, angry patience, staring malevolently at the youth who had felled him so easily with just a fraction of his physical strength.

Something made the dancing wrestler unwilling just to stand there doing nothing, and he closed with the gaint. Buntui made no move to defend himself. His gigantic arms simply reached out. The gesture was awkward and slow. But this time the giant's hands found something, and they held that something fast.

Buntui had caught hold of Anan's left arm. First he drew the dancer close to him, as though he meant to crush him against his heavy chest. But when he had his victim close enough, he adjusted his hold, slowly. Buntui's right hand travelled up Anan's body to grab him by the throat, just underneath his chin. The left hand sought the back of Anan's neck and head, and when Buntui was sure of his new grip he began to twist his opponent's neck.

On Anan's face there came a look of pure surprise. The aim of the wrestling game was not to maim the opponent. It was to put him down. But Buntui clearly had not the slightest interest in putting Anan down. He increased the pressure on Anan's neck. Surprise left Anan's face. Comprehension, a calm, ultimate comprehension, replaced it. He raised his right arm high overhead, and extended his index finger up towards the sky—the sigh of accepted defeat.

The judge moved forward towards the wrestlers saying: 'One each way now.' He expected the fighters to separate. 'Buntui and Anan are now even!' he said, raising his voice. 'One more fall to decide the winner.'

But the combatants remained locked together. Buntui would not let go of Anan's neck. Anan struggled with his hands, seeking some leverage to break the giant's hold. But pain weakened his knees, and they sagged. Still Buntui did not relax his grip. He now knelt awkwardly beside the fallen Anan, his biceps bulging with aroused power. Quite visibly, he was tightening his grip on Anan's neck.

The judge let out a frightened shout: 'Let him go!'

But Buntui did not hear him, and the judge stood above the fighters, utterly perplexed.

But from among the spectators a figure stood up and bounded towards the fighters. Densu brushed past the undecided judge. When he reached Buntui he hit him hard on the neck at the base of his head, a sharp, calculated blow to the right, near the ear. Involuntarily, Buntui's left arm relaxed its hold on Anan's neck. Densu seized the giant arm in both of his. Twisting it behind Buntui's back, Densu wrenched it upward so that it reached almost up to Buntui's left ear. The giant howled like a dying bull. But still he held on to Anan with his right.

Densu did not speak a word. He pulled upward on the arm in his hand till Buntui let go completely of Anan. Then he pushed Buntui off Anan's fallen body. The giant did not fall, however. Steadying himself with his right hand against the ground, he looked around in some confusion, then sprang directly upon Densu.

Densu was prepared. His left arm snapped out swift as a whip, rigid as a rod. The knuckles crashed against the bones in Buntui's throat. Buntui gasped, then took an involuntary step backward. The blow, so unexpected, had taken his balance away. His left arm reached the ground to give his body support; but that arm was infirm. It collapsed under the huge body. Buntui had lost all his recent aggressive energy.

Densu did not even look down at the fallen giant. He went over to the prostrate Anan and helped him up. There was no sign of pain in Anan's movements, but as he rose he brought a hand up to the side of his neck and pressed it, as if uncertain whether he had any feeling still left in it.

'Is it painful?' Densu asked.

'No,' Anan said. But immediately he felt a moistness on his upper lip, touched it and looked at blood that had flowed from his own nose. Densu took Anan's head and tilted it back. Then he led him slowly down the field, towards the beach below Esuano, by the Nsu Ber. Numerous spectators, seeing the morning's games so abruptly interrupted, stood around in confused knots seeking clarification. Densu walked past them, leading Anan.

Where the field merged with the beach there stood a young nim tree. At one spot on the beginning sand its leaves made a deep shadow. Densu asked Anan to lie flat on his back there, with his head in the darkest of the shade. Running down to the river he brought back a large, smooth stone, wet and cool from the water. He dug into the sand and laid the stone in it level with the surface, so that it made a kind of sunken pillow for Anan's head and neck. In a while the bleeding stopped completely.

'The fool was after tearing my head off,' Anan said musingly.

'He wanted to win,' Densu said.

'He could have won without murdering me.'

'I doubt it,' Densu said. 'Buntui has a huge body, and such a tiny brain to control it.'

Anan laughed, but in a moment pain turned the laugh into a wince, and he stopped. 'It's beginning to hurt now,' he said.

'Can you walk?' Densu asked him.

'Yes,' Anan said. 'It's just my neck that hurts.'

'Let's go home,' Densu said. 'You may be needing medicine.'

'Not yet,' Anan answered. 'Unless you're in a hurry to go back to the games.'

Densu just smiled.

'I like it here,' Anan said. He shook his head. 'Do you know why I agreed to fight?'

'Why, don't you enjoy it?' Densu asked him.

'Not as a rule,' he said. 'But today I became quite curious when I realized I'd have to fight Buntui. It was a queer feeling I had, almost a kind of happiness.'

'Happiness?'

'A very concentrated form of curiosity, at any rate,' Anan said, thinking. 'You know, the thing that makes me happiest is getting to know something I didn't know before.'

'What didn't you know about Buntui?' Densu asked.

'Whether I could deal with all that strength he has,' Anan answered. 'It's just curiosity. That's the only way I can think of it. When I don't know something, I have an urge to get into situations that will end my ignorance. Do you remember the bottom of the river?' A chuckle escaped him. 'It was just here,' he said, surprised.

Densu remembered. A year had passed, but his mind had not lost entirely the savour of that day. It had started out pleasant, warm and sunny but not hot, and it had stayed that way throughout the morning and the afternoon. It was a good day for Densu. An easy, pleasurable surge of energy throughout all his body had helped him finish the day's work so fast his speed astonished him. Finding himself with an excess of free time, he had gone to spend the afternoon on the field of grass.

He did not run that afternoon. He did not feel like running. He just walked up and down the field, pushed by no force outside himself, drawn forward only by his own desire. The warmth of the sun was under his skin, it was in his blood and in his very bones.

Then Anan had come running to him there in the centre of the field. In his hands he was carrying two long objects. They looked unfamiliar to Densu. Anan had come running so fast, and it seemed his spirit was in such a state of agitation that at first Densu wondered if it was bad news he was bringing. But as Anan came closer to him he saw his agitation came not from pain but from excessive happiness.

'We can see the bottom of the river,' said Anan at the end of a copious, bubbling flow of words.

'Which river?' Densu asked.

'The beautiful one,' Anan said impatiently. 'This one.'

'Tell me slowly,' Densu said. 'What are you talking about?'

'Have you seen the bottom of the river?' Anan asked.

'Yes.'

The answer surprised Anan, but he recovered quickly: 'I didn't mean just looking at the bottom for one moment and rising back to the surface. Did you ever stay in the river as long as you wished, so you could see the bottom?'

Densu admitted he had never done so. 'You can't go to the bottom of a river and stay there as if you were in the open air,' he added. 'You'll just drown.'

'Not necessarily,' Anan said. 'And try not to look at me so sadly.' He pushed one of the objects he was holding into Densu's hands.

'What is it?' Densu asked him.

'Look at it.'

Densu examined it. It was a long bamboo tube, bent at one end into a short loop. Near the other end, about a hand's length from the tip, the tube had been passed through a thick piece of cork. The whole was almost twice as tall as Anan himself.

'I still don't know what it's for,' Densu said.

'For breathing,' Anan said.

'At the bottom of the river?'

Anan nodded.

'I see,' Densu said, shaking his head. 'But Anan, if you keep talking this way to people they'll think you're mad.'

'Do you think I'm mad?'

'We know each other.'

'Just so. What makes you think I talk this way to anyone else? I know about madness.' He tapped his forehead. 'It's when you insist on talking to people who can't understand you. Don't worry about me.' Anan stared at the tube in his hand. It was identical to the one he had given Densu.

'You made these yourself?' Densu asked him.

'Not really,' Anan declared, shaking his head like a sage. 'The dwarfs, you know. They made them and slipped them under my pillow at midnight exactly.'

'People should hear you.'

'They won't,' said Anan. 'I'm quiet.'

Then Densu smiled and asked: 'Shall I tell you a secret?'

Anan had seen his smile. He said: 'No, keep it.'

'These are long bamboo tubes,' Densu said.

'Shocking news to me,' Anan said.

'Not yet,' said Densu. He made his smile more cruel. 'Bamboo tubes aren't hollow all the way, did you forget?'

Deep creases of sorrow disfigured Anan's face. His voice broke. 'If I were more than eight days old,' he said, 'I'd shed tears.' He turned his tube around and put the corked end to his lips. Taking a deep breath, he blew into the tube. A sound, long and low like the sound from a royal praise horn, came out of it. 'If this weren't hollow all the way,' Anan said, 'you know the music would have come from a different hole.'

Densu nodded. 'How did you do it?' he asked.

'An old spear with a heated tip, down both ends. Then I bent that end.'

'Now I'm anxious to see how it works,' said Densu.

On the way down to the river, Anan talked freely, excitedly. He talked about happiness: of the things that could bring him happiness, and of the things that could take it away from him. Densu asked him which one thing made him happiest. His answer was prompt.

'Seeing.'

'Seeing what?' Densu had asked.

'Seeing. Just seeing,' Anan had said.

'Talking in riddles again.'

'You understand me, Densu.'

'Just to sit and look at things?'

'That's not seeing,' Anan said sharply. 'That's just staring. Looking with the eyes only. Idiots can do that. If you look at things that way they're always separate and you never really see any sense in what you see. It's all right to look at things that way, separate. It's relaxing. But after that I always want to see what brings them together so they make sense. Then I understand. Seeing like that makes me happiest.'

'It's not a kind of happiness easy to understand,' said Densu.

'You understand it,' Anan said. 'I don't go about talking to people, explaining it to them. It's never that kind of happiness. It doesn't make me want to shout. I go quiet, enjoying inside me the under-standing I see outside.'

'The same thing makes you want to see the river bottom?'

'I may not explain it well,' Anan said, matter-of-factly. 'I don't like seeing the surface only and thinking that is the river. That makes me unhappy. I imagine I'd feel something like that if parts of me were missing when I woke up one day. And I don't like seeing only fugitive glimpses of the bottom when I can see the surface all day long. The surface isn't all. It's not even most of it. It's a rather small part, in fact. I like seeing the other parts too.'

As the two came to the river Anan did not try to contain his excite-ment. He flung off his cloth and, holding the bamboo tube high above his head, waded into the river. Densu followed him. Anan moved purposefully. It was plain he knew just where in the river he wanted to go.

'There's a root at the bottom,' he said. 'I'm looking for it.'

The water rose. Both of them started to swim and tread water.

'It should be somewhere here,' Anan said. He was looking not at the river but at the trees on the far bank. 'Before you go down, put the bent part in your mouth and hold it firm with one hand. The cork should keep it upright.'

He swam ahead. Densu followed close behind him. He swam so slowly that Densu kept up with him with hardly any effort. Then he stopped. Treading water, he put the tube in his mouth and nodded to Densu. Densu did the same. Anan slipped under the water, and Densu went in after him.

The tube in Densu's mouth jerked itself upward against his teeth as he went below the surface. With his right hand he held it more firmly and pulled it downward with him. It was beginning to need effort to go down against the water. In a moment Densu saw Anan come to a stop, and he went to his side.

Anan reached out with his free hand to catch hold of Densu's. He led the hand down till it touched his foot. Next he led the hand till it touched a thick tree root running across the river bed. Then he hesi-tated. Densu pressed his hand hard, three times, and Anan let go of him.

It was easy to see the bottom. Between the tree root and the river bed there were interstices where the soil under the root had been carried away. Anan had hooked his left foot into one of these spaces. In leading Densu's hand down to touch the root he had showed him how he'd done it. Densu did the same. That left an arm free. He used it to stroke the water, steadying himself. When he had found stability he looked at his friend, to see what he was doing.

Anan looked totally lost to the world. He was looking down at the bottom of the river, completely oblivious of everything else—so great was his concentration.

In all truth, the bottom was beautiful. Large pebbles, rounded by water and sand and time, lay quiet on the river floor, on sand so fine it was almost silt, except that it had such a pleasant firmness underfoot. There were yellow pebbles, black ones, white, purple, reddish brown pebbles, and pebbles streaked and whorled with many converging colours all at once, scattered over sand whose own watery colour shifted tremblingly from yellow to white, white to yellow. There were small boulders, also rounded and smooth, lying placidly among the pebbles on the sand. And the light of the yellow sun coming from above, because it had to pass through so much water to reach the bottom, shook and shimmered and vibrated like an audible note.

Occasionally an isolated pebble, pulled by the imperceptible current, leaned slowly forward as if it would topple over, but didn't. The invisible force proved a shade too subtle; the pebble relapsed to the bottom. Not in the same old spot, however. The pebble was shifted a fraction of its length forward.

Sometimes a smaller stone, also soundless but faster, left the bottom, rose suspended a tiny gap from the sand below, then fell gently back exhausted to the bottom lower down the river bed. Densu had to listen before he was sure: there was no sound there, just an immense silence, awesome in its depth. The absence was at first uncanny. Something like a feeling of panic flowed to him, not from any one direction but from the water all about him. But he did not let it overwhelm him, and in a while it passed him by. He looked at Anan.

Anan had his eyes closed. He looked asleep. The thought that he could be so relaxed in such a strange environment, under water, made Densu feel inexpressibly close to him. Almost without deciding to, he also closed his eyes.

The absence he had felt when his eyes were open now became something else entirely, a fantastic presence. Now he felt in direct contact with everything around him, with everything in existence. He could feel the universe gentle about him, its contact with him neither a pressure nor a suction, but changing from one to the other depending on how aware he was of the skin joining him to the world,

22

and it did not seem any more as if what was outside that skin was separate from the life within.

Even the air he was taking in was different. Breathed so deep, it had a distinct taste in his mouth, something clean and sweet, like water tasted slowly after the chewing of kola nuts. He did not feel his body as a hard, solid thing any more. It too had become a fluid form. Keeping his eyes closed he realized he didn't know or care which direction was up and which was down. He simply had no anxiety.

It must have been some time before he opened his eyes. He did not, at first, see Anan in front of him. He realized the current had turned him away from his old position. There was a subtle pain in his left foot, caused by the twisting of his body above it. He hadn't noticed it all the time he'd had his eyes closed. He looked for Anan, and found him.

Anan's head was now lower down. He was squatting, almost sitting, on the river bed. His knees were doubled, and his chin rested on them. He was leaning slightly backward, against the current. It seemed at that angle the current could not push him forward, and his own weight in the water was not enough to force him down against the current. His eyes were still closed. In that position he had such a calm look on his face, a look so far beyond ordinary life, that Densu felt a sharp alarm. He moved closer and looked at his friend's throat. In the slow water with its fugitive lights and shadows running constantly into and from each other he could not tell if what he saw was breathing or not. He reached out a hand and touched Anan on his cheek.

Anan, so slowly, opened one eye, then the other. He looked at Densu and smiled. Densu pressed his left wrist thrice, firmly. Then he unhooked his foot from the root at the bottom of the river, and let himself rise to the surface. Holding the breathing tube, he swam slowly to the beach, and when he got there he lay down in the sand and let the sun dry him.

He was already dry when Anan came out of the water and lay down beside him. He was in no hurry to go back to Esuano, so he just lay there with his eyes closed, watching the colours the sun made under his eyelids.

'When did you make them?' Densu asked Anan.

'What?'

'The tubes.'

'I finished them yesterday,' Anan said, then lay quiet. Densu could hear him breathe.

23

'You were kind, letting me use one,' Densu said. He was not only dry now; the sun had warmed his body. He rose, found his cloth and threw it over his body, and sat up on the sand. He reached out to give the tube to Anan.

'Keep it,' Anan said. 'I have mine.'

'Someone else might like to use it,' Densu said.

Anan shook his head. 'No one else. I could think of only one person here, and that was you.'

'I can't keep it,' Densu said. He held out the tube still. Anan reached up to take it. 'I'd like to borrow it some day. But keeping it . . .' He rose to go.

Anan nodded but said nothing.

Densu took one more look at him lying there in the warm sand. The look on his face was serene, far beyond happiness. It was much the same look that had touched Densu's mind with panic at the bottom of the river, before he had understood it.

* * *

'You were so quiet that day,' Densu said now. He looked and saw there was no longer any sign of bleeding on Anan's face.

'I'm usually quiet,' Anan answered. 'I can't talk of the things on my mind. Not with a lot of people.'

'You're still afraid they wouldn't understand?'

'No. I'm sure they'd understand if they were interested. But I don't think many people are interested in what interests me.'

'There must be some.'

'Not here,' Anan said. 'Perhaps you. But over there,' he looked across the river, east, 'I know there are people who understand.'

'Over where?'

But Anan merely laughed as if he'd caught himself doing something childish, and said: 'I feel fine. I may not need any medicine after all.' He stood up. 'I wonder who won the wrestling championship in the end.'

'We can find out on the way back,' Densu said.

They found out it was the short Antobam who had won the wrestling championship. Appia had been expected to win through to the final round. But something strange had happened to him also. His first and

24

as it turned out, his only opponent, was Kojo Djan, he of the long, thin, spidery limbs. Djan put up a determined fight. But after a while it became plain that he could match Appia neither in skill nor in strength. It would merely be a matter of time before he was forced to give in to his superior opponent.

But there was something in Kojo Djan pushing him to set his mind against conceding defeat. How stubborn this something was, and how potentially deadly it could become, the spectators and Appia himself were soon enough to see.

There are points in the wrestling game at which an opponent in difficulty has a simple choice: to yield, or to risk breaking a bone. Through the skilful use of force Appia manoeuvred Djan into just such a position. He had Djan at his mercy: only one thin arm supported him and kept his taut back from touching the ground. The arm was already twisted by tension, and the hand was awkwardly positioned. It's fingers pointed backward, away from the head, and the thumb was bent upon itself. Clearly, Appia had an advantage Kojo Djan could do nothing to counter.

Yet Kojo Djan would not recognize the truth of his position. The choice was therefore left to Appia—to press his advantage home even if it meant maiming his opponent, or to back away from him, giving up an obvious victory.

Appia seemed undecided. Later, of course, it became clear he was not so much undecided as determined to avoid a brutal victory. He kept the helpless Djan in that one position for the longest time, hoping perhaps that Djan would come to his senses and concede defeat. But Djan did not. So Appia quietly relaxed his grip, stood up from his opponent's contorted body, and walked away.

The judge could not award a foolish victory to Kojo Djan. So he declared the third and the fourth fights without result—Buntui having been disqualified already. It was left to Kweku Sipi, he of the hare-lip, and the short Kofi Antobam to compete for the wrestling championship.

Kweku Sipi fought no less well than he had fought in the first fight. But his height did not help him against Antobam's steady determination. Antobam tired Sipi and in the end had the great satisfaction, he the shortest of the nine, of emerging champion at the end of the first day, Sunday.

3 The Manipulators

In the late afternoon there was a possibility of rain. A swift wind blew from the south. But the wind passed and the rain did not fall. Clouds remained, however. They covered the face of the sun. They softened its afternoon heat, and they turned its remaining light blue and gentle.

The coolness calmed Densu and turned his thoughts inwards. After he had taken Anan home he returned to the Nsu Ber. This time he did not follow the river's flow. He walked upstream, following a path he knew well. It led towards the eastern forest.

There had been questions disturbing his mind, but now he felt almost certain he could see answers, and this near-certainty brought him a deep, calm clarity. He wished he could talk to someone older and more experienced, someone who would understand his mind's desire, and perhaps point out paths he wished to follow in his mind but could not yet see in the real world. The thought crossed his mind that he could simply walk on till he came to the eastern forest, looking for his friend, the healer Damfo. But he checked the thought. It was impulsive, unnecessarily so. There would be time to go to the eastern forest, to see Damfo and to listen to him. There would be time at the end of the games.

The thought that he would have to go to Ababio's house in the palace yard bothered Densu like an awkward burden, a burden not heavy but foolishly packed and therefore unmanageably bulky. Densu did not like Ababio. He had to remind himself often that he owed respect to the man to whose care he had been entrusted from the time his mother died, from birth. The respect due an elder from a youth Densu could give—as much as the outward forms demanded. But he had never been able to trust Ababio.

At first, when he was younger, he had felt merely an intense discomfort whenever Ababio was around. It was not a feeling he understood. It confused him.

But as he grew he thought much over this feeling, and he gained some understanding. He had, for instance, never known Ababio to leave anyone free to make a choice. Always, the man used force when he was in a position to. Otherwise he used trickery. Then afterwards he talked endlessly about how clever each new successful trick of his had been, and how wise he was in not trying to persuade people into doing what he wanted them to do.

Densu thought of a totally different man. He could not imagine Damfo ever using force or fraud to get anyone to do what he wanted him to do.

'Inspiration, Densu.' Damfo's favourite word, and the quiet smile with which he said it, no matter when or where, came to Densu's mind. 'For those who want to heal, to create what needs to be created, that's the best way. Inspiration.'

It had always been a joy to Densu to hear Damfo talk of medicine, of healing. Occasionally Damfo talked not of medicine but of poison. Just as he called inspiration healing medicine, he said the most damaging poison was manipulation. 'That is the most potent poison. It destroys people, plants, everything.'

Listening to Damfo had helped Densu climb into clarity. The uncertain, confusing, unpleasant but intense feelings Ababio had always roused in him became understandable after he had listened to Damfo talking of inspirers and manipulators. The world around him was the same. Only the way he saw the world was clearer. He now recognized certain people as manipulators. A few he also saw as inspirers. The distinction gave him knowledge of himself he had not had before: he did not like manipulators; he loved inspirers.

Something made Densu uncomfortable still. It was a thought that often threatened to bring back the confusion of the days before that first clarity. He felt in himself a natural, increasing urge to fly far from manipulators, seeking only to be with inspirers. Yet all the life around him belonged to the manipulators. It was not only Ababio. Everyone at court, and most of the people he had come to know outside the court also, seemed able to act only in manipulative ways. Force, fraud, deceit: these were the chosen methods of most of them. That this was the way of the world Densu had come to see with increasing sharpness. At the same time as he saw this, what he felt in himself was a great desire, a need, to put huge distances between himself and all such people and their ways.

Densu looked over his shoulder. He saw the last rays of a cool blue sunset disappearing. He had walked quite far along the path to the eastern forest. He turned back along the way home, walking faster.

4 Opportunity

When Densu knocked on Ababio's door it was opened immediately. Ababio did not waste time. He told Densu to sit. He gave him water. Then he came closer with his stool and sat less than an arm's length from him, watching the door.

'The king is old,' Ababio said in a rather strained voice.

It was an odd beginning to a conversation, and Densu did not try to respond. Instead, he simply looked at his host.

There was just one lamp in the room they were in. Its flame was fretful, and it chattered as if the oil under it had been mixed with drops of water. At unpredictable intervals its flame sent up a fitful tongue which lit up the room with a weird orange light, casting giant shadows on the walls. The largest of the shadows came and went on the wall opposite Densu. It was a huge, round, hulking thing, a blown-up silhouette of Ababio's hairless head as he talked.

'Very old,' Ababio said. He waited for a response.

'I know that,' Densu said. He felt uneasy.

'You know it,' Ababio said, his voice warming. 'But you don't know what it means. It means the time has come to see to a reasonable succession.'

'Affairs of the court . . .' Densu began.

'. . . do not interest you.' Ababio cut him short. 'Yes, I know. You have told me that before, and your father before you sang the same song. Ah, blood is amazing. How the son talks as if the father had lived for him to imitate. And he never even saw him.' He looked closely at Densu, with a look that might even have been affectionate. Then he said: 'Densu, you are no longer a child. You're a man, and I'm talking to you about just those things that make a man a man.'

Ababio leaned even closer. Densu felt the moist heat of his breath on his face. He was saying: 'I will not hide truth under riddles. I'm talking to you about power. The king does not belong with the living any more. We're talking about the succession.'

'Appia is the heir,' said Densu.

'Perhaps,' Ababio answered. 'Only perhaps. You see, Densu, there is a problem I haven't been able to talk to you about. Are you willing to listen?'

Densu nodded.

'The world has changed in ways some people do not yet understand,' Ababio began. 'Those born to rule must understand all these changes.'

'You don't think Appia understands them?'

'Appia doesn't want to understand them!' said Abio.

'What are these changes?'

'First, the white people. Appia still calls them strangers, visitors.'

'Isn't that what they are?'

'Not now,' Ababio said sharply. 'Not after so many generations. Look, the first of them came to the coast four centuries ago. Now all power comes from them. Whoever doesn't know that is still a child. That's what Appia is. A child!'

'I'm the same age,' Densu said.

'But you are willing to grow, to understand?' Ababio asked.

'To understand what?'

'There's a great change coming in this land. The whites have decided that, and what the whites have decided is certain. I've been to Cape Coast, and I know. Look, Densu, I know the whites. I know the whites like my own brothers. I have intimate friends at Cape Coast who are intimate friends of the whites there. That is how I happen to have eyes that see something of the future coming. I know this. The whites have decided it's time they took full control of this land. Not just the coast. The whole land, from the sea to the forests of Asante and beyond, right up to the dry Moshi grasslands.' He breathed in like a man who had run out of breath.

'These are big changes coming. They do not happen in every generation. You're lucky if such changes happen when you're young.' Ababio sighed. 'Because if you are also intelligent, and have courage, you arrange to place yourself on the right side of the changes as they come. Those who take care to place themselves on the right side of big changes, when the big changes have taken place, become big men. Those stupid enough to place themselves against such changes, of course they get crushed into tiny pieces. If they survive the changes at all, they survive as something insignificant, smaller than real men, infinitely smaller than big men.

'You're intelligent, Densu, that we all know. And you have courage. That's why I am talking to you about all this.'

'There's something I don't understand,' said Densu. 'Have you told Appia of these changes you speak about?'

'What if I have?' Ababio asked.

'It would be more natural to talk to him. He is the heir, after all, and I have nothing to do with the succession.'

'If you must know,' said Ababio, 'I have talked to Appia. I have explained everything, everything to him. At least he was patient enough to hear me to the end of what I had to say.' The last remark was pointed.

'I am listening,' said Densu.

'The whites are going to control this land, as surely as your father is dead. But they cannot control the whole land without help from people they trust. Black people they trust. Power comes from work, a lot of work. There will be fighting. War. We shall have to help the whites by finding men to fight for them, here and everywhere. We'll have to find carriers for the things the fighters need, and for the white officers. The whites will want to buy food for the soldiers. They'll need labourers to build roads. Don't you see? Once we agree to work for the whites, we put ourselves on the road to power. It is a road without end.

'If we do not help the whites, we shall be left by the roadside. And if we are such fools as to stand against the whites, they will grind us till we become less than impotent, less than grains of bad snuff tossing in a storm. That is the choice before every one of us. I myself, I have already chosen. And those who think like me have chosen. We shall be on the side of the whites. That is where power lies. We have chosen power because we find impotence disgusting. What I'm doing now is inviting you to be on the same side.'

'You say you've told Appia all this?' Densu asked.

'I have,' said Ababio.

'You invited him in the same way?'

'I did.'

'What was his answer?'

'The prince is out of his mind, I tell you!' Ababio shouted the words, then belatedly hushed himself up. 'The boy is utterly mad.'

'But what was his answer?'

'He refused!' said Ababio indignantly. As he talked now, it seemed the memory of his talk with Appia came back strongly, and his anger rose. 'He refused, just like that. Like a big fool he refused.'

'Did he give reasons?' Densu asked.

'I knew his reasons before he talked of them. It all comes from his mother. That prince worships his mother. His mother worships that mad healer, that homeless, wifeless wretch who lives in the eastern forest. The woman Araba Jesiwa is forever taking the prince to visit that lunatic healer, that Damfo. And that Damfo has filled the mother's head with that foolish talk of his against the whites. Would you believe it? The madman calls those who work with whites dogs. Dogs, I tell you. Dogs! Is that a name for human beings?'

'So Appia doesn't want to work for the whites,' Densu said.

'He doesn't,' answered Ababio. 'The healer has poisoned his mind. He says a king should work for all black people—to bring all the black people together. The boy's brain has been poisoned, I tell you. He, a prince, doesn't know there would be no more kings if some catastrophe brought all black people together. Kings belong to their tribes. He doesn't know that.'

'Appia is the heir,' Densu repeated. 'If you want his help you'll have to persuade him.'

'Densu,' Ababio asked, 'do I look like such a fool to you? A wise man persuades those who are open to persuasion, and I am no fool. I cannot persuade Appia against his own stubborn foolishness. All I see now is that he wants to stand against a force too powerful for him. He is asking to be destroyed. Densu, I'm not talking to you about any distant future. I'm talking to you about the present. It is necessary to put someone else in Appia's place. The position is more important than any one person.' Ababio paused. Again he drew breath, so intensely he sounded like a man in pain. Then he repeated the sentence: 'It is necessary to put someone else in Appia's place. The decision has been taken.'

Ababio let out breath—a long sigh. He was sweating, but there was no tension in his voice. He sounded as if he had just gone beyond a particularly difficult point. Now he began to talk ramblingly, repeating his ideas, talking almost to himself. 'In the past it didn't matter much to them what happened here. Now they want to control everything that goes on. From the coast to the forests, to the grasslands, even to the desert. And they will. If we help the whites get this control, we stand to profit from the changes. Those foolish enough to go against them will of course be wiped out. I'm among those who'd rather profit than be wiped out. Densu, have you ever seen those guns the white men have? The really big ones, not the little rifles men carry on their shoulders? Nothing will ever make me stand against those guns. The only place for me is firmly by the side of whoever possesses such powerful weapons. Appia doesn't want to understand this.' Ababio looked at Densu. He looked like a man appealing for help. He was sweating, and his bald head shone.

'I cannot be of any use to you,' Densu said.

'And why not?' Ababio asked.

'You know the reason. The work you talk of isn't what I want to do.'

'Don't be hasty with me, Densu,' Ababio said. There was something much like pain in his tone. 'I do not want you to decide anything now. Not just yet. This matter is important. Sleep over it. Sleep days, weeks, months over it, if you need time to realize what is good for you. Just remember this while you sleep: in this world there are those who thrive, and there are those who don't. Those who thrive, thrive because they respect power. They see where it comes from, and they take care to place themselves beside it, never against it. Densu, you are young. Nature has favoured you more than it has favoured all others of your age. You have strength of body. You have strength of mind. You belong by nature with those who thrive. You were born to win. What I'm giving you now is an invitation to your own future. Don't be hasty. Think about it.'

Ababio didn't give Densu a chance to speak again. He rose and walked towards the door. Densu followed him. Outside in the palace yard, Ababio said farewell, then turned to go back into his room.

The night was cool, and the air was now clear. Sounds of celebration drifted gently on the night air. But Densu had no desire to go in their direction, towards the centre of the town. Once outside the palace, he turned left and left again. He went past the palace wall, beyond the silent houses after it, towards the female river. He knew he would not be able to sleep now even if he went to bed. He needed to think.

An overpowering wish possessed him right then and there to go all the way into the eastern forest. But he brought the wish upward to his mind. There it lost its insistent, driving power, and Densu looked forward to going to the eastern forest but only when the time was ripe. The hope calmed him and he was able to think of sleep.

5   The Mind Game

Sunday, the first day, had been the day for wrestling. Monday was set aside for oware, a game of mental skill, not physical strength. This proved to be the longest day.

The elimination bouts began early in the morning, almost as soon as there was light enough. It was not until midday that the weakest players were defeated and obliged to join those merely looking on.

There was a break for the midday meal. Then the players and spectators came back, and the clash of champions began in earnest. There is no need to mention every detail, round after round. It is enough to say that near the end, to no one's surprise, the two players left undefeated were the prince Appia and Densu.

Before the final rounds the two were given time for rest. That taken, they greeted each other formally. Then they began.

Appia moved the counters first. He chose to start at the second hole. This was an unsurprising game. When, at the end of it, Appia, being the starter, took the last eight counters, Densu was left with two empty holes on his side. Appia had won the first game with the starter's advantage.

Densu started next. He began at the fifth hole. Answering, Appia in two fast circles first watered the beginning hole to fruition and then plucked the very first four to ripen. That too was expected. So was Densu's response: he captured two fours, one on his own side, the other from Appia. At the end of this game Densu in his turn had won with the starter's advantage—the same two holes.

That is how things went for the first thirty games. Then it was time to change the rules, since it was clear neither Densu nor Appia stood to defeat the other if the normal, easy rules prevailed.

After the thirtieth game the players were forbidden to count the counters before moving them. The time for thinking out each succeeding move was also cut in two. In addition, the starter's advantage was abolished: the starter would not get the customary eight counters at the end of a game. So now the result of each game would depend first on each player's skill, then on his judgment based on the strength of his memory.

The first six games after the rule change were even. But by the seventh a certain lack of sureness had begun to make Appia's game hesitant. Twice the judge had to prompt him to play before his time was up.

As for Densu, he played calmly, steadily. He played with such concentration that he looked like someone in a trance. The only indication his whole mind was present and engaged was the promptness with which he made each well-calculated move.

By the end of the tenth game Densu had an advantage of one hole, won entirely from skilful play. He did not lose it. By the fifteenth game his advantage had grown to two. The twenty-first game saw Densu holding an advantage of four clear holes. And it was just before the thirtieth game, precisely at the twenty-ninth, in fact, that Appia lost his last remaining hole. Densu had won the oware championship.

6 The Races

Tuesday was the day of the short races. Appia was the winner in each race. He ran with a firm explosive power of movement, enough to make any watcher marvel how so much energy could come out of a single human body in such concentrated spurts.

In each race Densu followed Appia closely, in second place. His running also had power in it, but there was nothing at all explosive here. Far more than power Densu's running had grace: a natural, unhurried smoothness that was a pleasure merely to look at.

Wednesday was the day of the longer races. It was Densu's day. The way he ran, it was clear his movement through the air was a joy to him. He leapt in long strides fleeing ahead of his pursuers, entering the forest and disappearing from view, emerging after unbelievably short intervals to climb up the crest of the exposed hill that marked the farthest limit of the race, circling a giant silk cotton tree, then plunging downward into the forest again on his way back and lost again from view before the runner closest to him had emerged in his turn to climb up the exposed hill—Densu ran as if air and earth both listened to him, and were happy to help him pass.

Again it was not power that marked Densu's running but grace, grace and a joy so pure it could not be hidden. It came out not only in the serene gladness of the runner's face; it came out in the motion of his arms, in the lifting of his legs, in every movement of his swift, flying form. Nor was Densu's joy mixed with tiredness even at the end of the longest race of all, the race to the edge of the eastern forest and back across the upper ford on the female river. So Densu won the long races. And always next after Densu was the determined Appia, somewhat winded but persevering to the end.

PART TWO

1 Decision Time

When the last of the long races was over, Ababio sought Densu out
and invited him to come and see him at home. 'It's important,' was all
the explanation he stopped to give, in an easy, conspiratorial tone.

Densu went to see him in the evening, at the time of the dances
celebrating his victory.

'You didn't expect me to call you again so soon,' Ababio said by
way of an opening. Densu just looked at him. 'But it had to be today,'
Ababio continued. 'Something has changed. It's important.'

Ababio halted. He seemed to want Densu to interrupt him, perhaps
to ask him a question. But Densu did not, so he continued. 'I thought
there'd be more time, but there isn't. Things have moved so fast at
Cape Coast we've all of us been taken by surprise. But we needn't
allow events to leave us behind. Do you know what has happened?'

Densu said no.

In the beginning Ababio had talked rather like a man unsure of his
ground. He talked out of breath, in a hesitant manner that seemed
strange indeed with him. But now, as if he'd finally decided to go
boldly ahead on a course he'd been hesitating to follow, his tone grew
crisp.

'You have to decide now, Densu.'

Densu looked more carefully at the man in front of him. Ababio's
eyes were extremely small, narrowed far below their usual size.

'To decide what?' Densu asked.

Ababio stared at him as if he intended to pierce him with the
intensity of his stare. 'I'll tell you. If the kingship of Esuano were
offered you, if the power came your way, would you be ready for
it?'

'That is not a serious question,' Densu said without hesitation.

'Never mind about its seriousness!' Ababio shot back. 'I've asked
you a question. Answer it. There are those who have the power to

36

make kings and unmake them. They would like to know. Now. If they brought power your way, would you have the courage to hold it?'

'Appia is the heir.'

'Do not exasperate me, Densu,' Ababio said. 'We know who and what Appia is. We were born long before you. We don't need you to tell us. All we want to know is: will you accept the power?'

'You know my answer,' Densu said.

'No, Densu,' said Ababio, very slowly. 'I don't know your answer.'

'I want to be left alone,' Densu said.

'You refuse the offer?'

Densu nodded.

Ababio let out a great quantity of breath. His shoulders sank lower where he sat. He just sat there looking at Densu, making no effort to move or to say anything.

'May I go now?' Densu asked him after a long silence.

Ababio did not open his mouth. But Densu, thinking he saw a nod and a sort of shrug, rose to go. As he reached the door Ababio called him.

'Come back, Densu.' The man's voice sounded infinitely weary.

Densu turned and walked back. When he came to Ababio he stood, waiting.

'It is not a simple matter,' Ababio said.

'What isn't a simple matter?' Densu asked.

'What you're involved in now.'

'I'm not involved in anything,' Densu said.

'Oh, but you are, Densu,' Ababio said. His voice sounded gentle, kind. 'You are involved. Very much involved. And it won't help you to seek to deny it at this point. You cannot, Densu, you cannot just walk away from people after they have bared their soul to you, and revealed their secrets to you. There is a bond between you and anyone who reveals himself to you. The bond is one of mutual protection. You must protect him, and he will protect you. If not, you walk away from a man knowing what he has revealed to you about his naked soul, about his ambitions. And the knowledge you have is like a knife in your hands, don't you see?'

'Are you thinking I want to use what you've told me against you?' Densu asked.

'Densu,' Ababio said patiently. 'I have nothing to say regarding what you want to do or do not want to do. I am saying something about what you must do, now that you know what you do know.'

'What is it I must do?' Densu asked.

'First,' Ababio said, 'stop dreaming idle dreams. Next, take up your responsibilities. When power is offered to you, the offer means the time has come for you to stop being a child, and to become a man.'

'Doesn't it matter what I've told you before?' Densu asked.

'What have you told me before?' Ababio countered.

'That I want to be a different kind of man?'

'Ah, that,' said Ababio. 'No. It doesn't matter now. Not after what you know.' Ababio talked in a tone of certainty, of unshakeable conviction. 'Densu, there is nothing to fear. All you need is courage, and you have that.' He spoke expansively now. 'And don't let Appia worry you. Yes, he is the heir. But power doesn't always go to those who most expect it. Those who decide these things have been watching you. They know, for instance, what everybody knows: that you'll be the winner of these games, and these things are important; you have no idea just how important.'

'Do you mean the games have something to do with the holding of power at Esuano?' Densu asked, surprised.

'More than you think.' Ababio laughed, a totally relaxed laugh. 'Far more than you think. You'll see soon enough. After you win the games, many a surprise will be waiting for you, along whichever path you walk. All you have to do is to be yourself, Densu, and win. I envy you.'

Densu felt bitter pain in his body, and a sudden dryness made his head ache. But he smiled. He asked Ababio the same question he had asked some time back.

'May I go now?'

This time Ababio answered promptly: 'By all means.' He even walked out into the night with Densu, his talk a gentle, good-humoured patter, cut now and then with a crisp chuckle. When he turned to go back he said to Densu: 'If anything new comes up I'll let you know. I don't expect anything much to happen yet. Not till after the games are over. But I'll let you know.'

There was something unpleasant in the night air, but Densu could not think what exactly it might be. It was not in the sky above him, and as for the earth below it still felt firm underfoot. He heard music, and in the faint lyrics floating on the small breeze he thought he could even hear his name. But he did not go towards the music. He could not.

He knew he would be facing another sleepless night if he found no way to clear his mind. In spite of the exertions of the day his body was not tired, and as for his mind it was alert with thoughts.

The thoughts were not new. But this night they had a sharpness that was keener than usual. In the past they had been more confusing, a mixture of feelings and thoughts, hard to grasp completely. Now they were comprehensible.

Densu thought of these games supposed to prepare the young for adult life. He wanted to go far, far from these rituals. The desire was powerful, steady. He felt no need to compete with those of his age. He felt no need to compete with anyone at all. He did not hate the games and the rituals. But he wished he had found rituals that could have given life a better meaning. The ceremonies, rituals, and games that could satisfy the yearning inside him would have to be ceremonies, rituals, and games of co-operation, not of competition. The present games made him uneasy. Nothing they offered gave an answer to his soul.

In his imagination he could see different rituals. In them it was not necessary to set apart a few active ones to run against each other, and to reduce the whole community to spectators. There would be no competitors, only participants. There would be a community whose members would be free to work together in the cool of the morning; they would be free to run, swim, jump, play, to celebrate health and strength in the late afternoon; they would dance to their own songs in the quiet of evenings. These things were good. Why should any of them be turned into competitions? What sense was there in excluding the whole community from the centre of the field, leaving only a few grim battlers? Why should everything have to end in a senseless victory for one isolated individual? What meaning could such a ritual give the community, turning it as it did into a defeated mass, all worshipping a lone victor?

Densu's uneasiness deepened into revulsion. The idea of a society separated into a small, active group of competitive fighters flying high above a passive mass of mere spectators with uplifted faces, brought ugly pictures to his mind: a very few lean, sinewy, strong champions dominating a soft, shapeless crowd beneath their feet.

Densu felt lonely. He felt an acute need for companionship whenever he thought of these things, of Esuano, of life. But in a community separated into dominant champions and passive spectators he could see no possibility of any companionship for himself. Every quality in him rebelled against the dumb passivity of the spectators, as well as against the wild vicarious frenzy of the celebrants of victories belonging to others.

And he did not want to have anything to do with the lone champion's stupid arrogance. There should be something better. But the night was half gone, and it would all slide imperceptibly away if he did not free his mind from thoughts of the sterility around.

2 Water Games

Thursday, the fifth day, was the first set aside for swimming. The day's races were short sprints across the Nsu Ber; one where it was narrowest, the other where it grew widest.

The strongest swimmer was Appia; but he did not prove to be the best. Across the Nsu Ber he raised a powerful trail of foaming water behind him. His hands hollowed out a trough in the river for his speeding body. It was a wonder to watch.

But behind Appia as he crossed the river swam a form so quiet it seemed to pose a deliberate contrast to Appia's robust churning. The form was Densu's. In the water it seemed to move with no overt effort at all. In place of a wake such as Appia raised, Densu left only a gentle ripple on the face of the water, barely visible beside Appia's tremendous foam. To tell the truth, Densu seemed to glide forward with the strength of a power not in his body alone but also within the water of the river itself.

The shorter race had a most puzzling finish. As the swimmers passed the middle of the river there was no telling which of the leading two would reach land first—Appia or Densu. From the middle of the river to the race's end their heads were level, always level, though the rhythm of their motion remained entirely different. Appia thrashed the river with undiminished power; Densu's limbs barely broke the surface as they left and re-entered the water, drawing it back for the smoothly gliding body to slip through. So two hands simultaneously touched the log marking the finishing point. For the first time in the memory of any living person, victory in the shorter swimming sprint had to be split.

The race across the wider part of the river took place in the afternoon. Appia swam as powerfully as before. At the start he took a slender lead. But by the middle he had lost it, and Densu was ahead. It was not a wide gap that separated them. But though there was a remarkable increase in the violence of Appia's strokes, the gap never grew narrower. Instead, it widened by infinitesimal additions, and Densu touched the wood several clear moments before Appia's flailing arm smashed powerfully against it.

The long-distance swimming race was held on the sixth day, Friday. It took place in the larger river, the male river Nsu Nyin. It was not a race across the river but along its length. It started from the landing for fishing canoes far below Esuano, where there was a hamlet of fishermen; then it went up the river's length all the way till the sacrificial rock of priests, a boulder called Akosombo. Around this the swimmers had to turn, then swim back to the fishermen's landing, this time not against the current but with it.

The long swim took place in the afternoon, after the noon-time meal had had a chance to go down. As for the swimmers themselves, this day they did not break their fast till late in the morning. They ate nothing at all at midday.

In the style of almost every swimmer there was a marked change from that of the day before. The day before had been a time of strong motions. But today the swimmers began with the knowledge that he who would last till the end must husband his energy, not waste it in a premature and ultimately useless display of potency. This change then, could be remarked in the way everybody swam this Friday afternoon.

Except for Densu. Between Densu's style of the previous day and his style this afternoon the difference was hardly perceptible. An exceptionally keen eye though, might have seen a kind of lengthening of every smooth stroke, a gentler glide through the water, and even less of an afterwake behind his body.

Up until the Akosombo rock the going was hard for all. And there was no great difference separating those in the lead from the swimmers following after them. The return swim was entirely different.

It was usual for swimmers to have tired themselves out by the time they reached the rock. Because of that the return swim, although aided by the current, was seldom as fast as the upward swim. But this day, as the leading group of swimmers rounded the Akosombo rock for the downward swim, one form glided forward and away from the others in a series of long, smooth, sliding thrusts, as if some force beneath, subtle but strong, were buoying it up and easing it forward ahead of everyone. The form was Densu's.

That amazing smoothness of motion was no passing wonder. Densu sustained it till the finish. He had already dried his lithe body before the second swimmer reached land. The second swimmer was Appia. So the sixth day, the day of the long swimming race, belonged to Densu. Once more the strong prince Appia was second.

3 The Captive Pigeon

The last day, Saturday, came, the day when the champion for the entire games would be chosen. In ordinary years the champion was known before the final day. But this year was extraordinary. The way the competitions had gone so far, no one could tell who would be the champion at the end of the final day. Between Appia and Densu the rivalry had been so close. Only the last day's competition could decide who would win the final victory.

The morning was sunny, the air clear. The world was quiet. Everything seemed paralysed with suspense, waiting for the final competition. This competition was to be in the exhibition of hunting skills. The ancient hunting tools—arrows, spears, knives—were not to be used. Ages had passed since the gun had replaced them.

The first test was simple: the competitors were to shoot bullets at a barrel set twenty tree lengths from the firing line. The first crack of gunshot relaxed the crowd a little, and some began to talk. The tension did not disappear, however. It turned into a sort of eager anticipation, a charge in the air. One youth, Kweku Sipi, failed to hit the barrel. He had to walk away from the line of competitors. The crowd did not even care to notice his shame.

The barrel was moved to thirty lengths. Again the gunshots blasted the air. Two youths fell out from the line: Buntui and Patu. Forty lengths. One more youth fell out: Djan.

When there were only five competitors left it seemed no one would miss the target and be dropped—all five shot with such consistent skill and care. But at ninety lengths one, Antobam, shot wide of the barrel. Another, Ampa, missed it at a hundred lengths. By mid-afternoon there were only three competitors left: Anan, Appia, and Densu.

The crowd showed signs of growing impatience, but the judges were patient. They moved the target just a little farther after each round of shots. Each time all three remaining competitors hit the barrel. The crowd was torturing itself with uncertainty.

Then an eager voice shouted: 'Bring the birds!'

At the sound of that call a look came over Densu's face as if there was something urgent he needed to tell the judge. He actually took a few steps in the direction of the judge. But before he came close enough to speak to him, he changed his mind and walked away again. He was smiling—a strange smile, as if he were smiling in spite of pain.

The birds were fated to die. The competitors would have to take turns shooting at them. If a competitor was successful, his bird died. If a competitor failed, his bird was pulled back down, then released for the next competitor to shoot at. The birds were brought. They were young pigeons, each tied at the end of a very long string. At a signal from the judge a bird would be let go. When it had flown as high as the tallest tree nearby, the judge would give the order, and one competitor would fire.

Anan was the first of the remaining three called to shoot. Three guns had been loaded ready for him, and he was quick in their use. He fired all three before the bird had flown the length of the string. The first shot was inaccurate; it missed the bird entirely. But the second grazed its tail and brought a feather spiralling wildly down in the startled wind. The third shot blasted the bird into a plunging mess of blood and bones and feathers.

But the success of his third shot affected Anan strangely. In his behaviour there was no trace of the joy of success. His arms shook slightly, and he seemed quite unable to look at the remains of the bird he had killed.

Appia shot next. He wasted just one shot—the first. The second brought down the bird. The bullet had pierced it straight through its body. Then it was Densu's turn to shoot.

Densu picked up the first gun. He stepped aside, leaving the two other guns on the ground beside him. The judge released the pigeon, and it flew. At first it hovered low, uncertainly, quite close to Densu.

Densu aimed the gun. The bird flew into perfect range, but Densu did not shoot. It seemed as if he intended to wait for the bird to fly higher. The flying pigeon rose. Its flight was now much stronger, much more certain now that the shock of sudden liberation had worn off. The bird flew forward, then up. The string holding it blew widely in the wind and formed a giant curve, lengthening still.

The bird had flown past Densu's aim, yet he did not seem disturbed. On his face had appeared a look of the intensest concentration. The judge frowned and looked impatiently at him. But Densu did not fire.

The judge coughed a rasping cough. People in the crowd began to murmur their bafflement. This wave of small noises brought Densu out of his concentration, back to some sense of where he was. He aimed more carefully in the direction of the fleeing bird. A smile relaxed his face as he tensed his fingers to pull the trigger. It was a smile of utter satisfaction, a smile too deep for any watcher's comprehension. Densu let the gun-sight rise to the pigeon. He hesitated a fraction of a moment. The pigeon flew a shade higher. Then Densu fired.

The bird, surprised by the sudden shot in the middle of such a profound silence, faltered in its flight then dropped from the height it had reached, as if the bullet had touched it. But in another moment the pigeon had recovered its speed and straightened out in steep, free flight. For just one more moment it hovered again in the still echoing air. Then it soared high. It soared high into the sky, far beyond the aim of any hunter's weapon.

The judge looked down astounded at the string which had so recently held the liberated bird. Left loose in his hand, it was now drifting foolishly back to earth. The judge looked up after the disappearing bird. Then he turned to look at Densu. The silence, the profound silence of the watchers echoed the judge's bewilderment. The judge asked the question agitating every mind there.

'What happened, Densu?'

'You saw what happened,' Densu answered. 'I missed the bird.'

'Deliberately,' the judge persisted. 'You shot to hit the string, not the pigeon.'

'I missed the bird,' Densu said again. He did not stay to hear what else the judge would say. Turning away from the scene of competition, he walked towards the river.

When the judge came out of his surprise, he walked over to the prince Appia where he stood and raised his right arm high above his head, the sign of final victory. He announced the coming night would be devoted to the celebration of Appia's victory. There would be feasting; there would be songs and dances. And the next dawn would see the birth of a new year.

4 Victory Song

The air was magical that night. The voices of young women sang of victory. Men's voices answered with the praise of strength. The aged invoked youth and the future. The very young sang remembered songs of a forgotten past.

Then there were dances. Appia danced first, alone. He danced the shy dance of the hopeful competitor. After that he danced new dances in remembrance of his own particular victories and defeats on successive days. His dancing was strenuous, but the happiness of victory gave him energy. It was not till after the end of his celebration of his final victory with the gun that he gave in to exhaustion and accepted rest together with the onlookers' praise.

Now came the time for the other young men to join in the dance. He who had known just once the pride of winners lived through his fleeting moment of glory once again. Those who had nearly tasted victory but had failed in the end, even they also danced and raised happy dust.

Densu watched the celebrations. He did not go to the centre to dance. He did not go to celebrate any of his own victories. His thoughts were far from this night's happenings. He was glad the competitions had come to an end, not only because he disliked the competitions themselves, but also because his mind was powerfully drawn to something far from them. He was eager to make the journey to the eastern forest. He was eager to see the healer Damfo again, eager to talk to him about the future he had already chosen in his mind, a life spent devoted to the work of healing.

Densu's inner calm was broken by a smooth voice speaking close to his ear. He had to make an effort to listen to what the voice was saying, and at first the effort was hard. The voice was not merely smooth; it was also patient. It repeated its words till Densu heard them and listened to their meaning.

'You threw away your victory.' The voice was Ababio's.

Densu did not answer, but Ababio sensed he had at least understood him. He did not repeat those words.

'It was unwise, a wasteful thing to do.' Ababio paused, as if in thought. 'It doesn't matter, though. You were born to win. You can't run away from that. It's in your nature. But answer me, Densu. Why are you afraid of winning?'

'Is everyone who loses afraid of winning?'

'Who loses deliberately, yes,' said Ababio. 'Do you deny that was what you did?'

Densu did not answer.

'Also when you refused to fight the others,' Ababio added, 'it was the same thing.'

Ababio fell quiet. He was not watching the dancers. He had turned the back of his head to them, and he was looking directionly into Densu's face. Because of the darkness outdoors he brought his face close to Densu's.

'I see you well, Densu,' Ababio said. 'Your disease is not fear. It's pride. You look down on victory. In a way that can be forgiven. You're a natural-born victor. So you don't understand defeat. You've never tasted its bitterness. That's why you want to play with defeat. You don't know as yet how necessary victory is for life. Or how useless, how stupid a thing defeat is. But you're young. You have power enough to waste. Don't waste too much of it, though.' His tone dropped and, as if in regret for something irretrievably lost, he sighed like an exhausted man.

Ababio put a hand gently on Densu's shoulder. 'However,' he said, 'that's not what I came to you about tonight. Come aside with me. I must talk to you.'

Densu walked with Ababio away from the dancers and watchers, away from the river. Ababio looked round to make sure there was no one near enough to hear him. Then he said, quite abruptly: 'You don't have time, Densu.'

'Time for what?' Densu asked.

'You have to make a decision.'

'What about?'

'About your future,' Ababio said.

'But I've made it,' said Densu.

'Densu, I am not talking to you as to a child.'

'I know.'

'I'm telling you again. Choose your future.'

'I've chosen,' Densu said.

Ababio brought his voice under control. It had begun to grow tense. Now its tone became patient, a little pained. 'Densu,' he said, 'I, Ababio, a man your father's age, I who knew your father and made a promise to him to help the child he never lived to protect, I came to you to ask you, to beg you even, to work with me and seize the only future worthy of you.'

Densu answered him: 'I have thanked you for the offer. But I can't accept it.'

'You refuse to.'

'I don't want to accept it, and I can't.'

'You can,' said Ababio. 'Listen to me, Densu. I came to you with the deepest trust. I showed you the way to the most important thing in a man's life, the thing every man who is a man works for. That thing is power. In life there is nothing else worth aiming for, Densu. I have shown you, so plainly, just what I myself am aiming at. I've invited you to make my aim your aim also. I've shown you just how we plan to reach this aim. You know my secrets, Densu. Do you realize what that means?'

'You still fear I will betray your secrets?'

'It's not what I fear,' Ababio shot back. 'It's just what happens to be true. You know my secrets. A man who shares your secrets is your friend. There is no other thing he can possibly be—except your enemy. He works with you. Or he works against you.'

'I have explained my choice of work to you,' Densu said.

'You have accepted my secrets,' Ababio answered. 'What you know commits you.'

'I did not ask to hear your secrets.'

'You heard them,' Ababio said. 'That's the important thing.'

'I'll keep them, then,' said Densu.

'Only if we work together!' Ababio had spoken these words with uncontrolled vehemence. He hadn't intended to. He repeated them, more calmly, more clearly, more deliberately. 'Only if we work together, Densu. A man who offers you his secrets puts a knife in your hand and bares his neck to you. He is offering you a choice. Friendship until death. Or enmity. Also until death.' Ababio peered closely into Densu's face. His eyes were shining in the dark, and there were beads of sweat on his forehead. Densu could feel the warmth of his breath against his shoulder.

'I like you, Densu,' Ababio continued. 'I would like to continue liking you. But you are setting yourself against me. I won't argue with you any more. I am your father's age, Densu. Does it not amaze you that I have come to you myself, so may times? I won't seek you out again. You haven't yet thought of your future. Not seriously. Go and do that. When you change your mind and decide we can work together, come to me at home. But there's not much time. I'll be there all day tomorrow. And, Densu, I won't seek you out again.'

There was no farewell. Ababio turned and walked away from Densu. He seemed in a great hurry.

All the way home Densu felt restless. When he arrived he could not stay indoors. He was tired, but he could not sleep. Thoughts he did not choose to think forced themselves on him. When he made the effort to push them out of his mindspace, a new swarm of similar thoughts took their place to worry him. The night was not warm. But the air felt heavy and wet on his skin. He decided to go and sit on the steps outside, to escape the feeling he was about to suffocate.

There were stars in the night. The moon too had been hidden, but now it was out. Around it a huge circle of pale light blotted out all but the brightest of the nearby stars. Densu gazed up at the stars away from the moon's haze, till his eyes relaxed and instead of separate stars he saw only connected streams of light in the sky.

A feeling of loneliness, intense and hurtful, came over him and threatened to overwhelm him. He tried again to find escape from it in sleep, but he failed. He turned his mind upon the feeling, determined to understand it. He knew inner pain was often a sign he had not understood something happening within himself. He knew also such pain would persist until he achieved understanding. Then it would vanish as pain, becoming just a calm awareness, the feeling of reality finally understood.

This loneliness, he knew, was not a desire for involvement in the public happenings at Esuano or beyond, at Cape Coast. He had been offered the chance of such involvement, but he had refused it. In the middle of all the activity of Ababio and his unseen allies from Cape Coast, in the middle of all the business of competitive games and rituals and dances and celebrations, Densu had always felt un-utterably lonely. Every moment spent near the men of power in the royal courtyard was to him time spent in alien territory. Not by accident, Densu had grown to think of relief in terms of distance from such people and such affairs.

Lately, this feeling that distance was necessary had spread to other areas. The celebrations and festivals, as he searched for their meaning, struck Densu as merely the customs and morals of the court being imposed on life outside the court. Competitions, struggles of individual against individual, faction against faction, the sharpening of knives, the search for allies, the deception of bystanders and enemies, the readiness of professed friends to betray those already used in the unending search for more power—from all this Densu desired only distance, a great distance.

Fortunately, the feeling did not end there. The sense of repulsion was strong. But beyond it there was a desire that was infinitely stronger. It was a potent urge to seek people whose ways were an antidote to all the petty poisons which were food to the men of power he had known. Densu desired a life lived with people who did not see other human beings only as material they could use and handle. He thought of Ababio.

Not a single instance could he remember of Ababio approaching anyone as a human being to be trusted, inspired, shown the truth of a situation, and left to make up his own heart and mind about it. In every case Ababio preferred to turn those he dealt with into blind victims—victims knowing only enough about the situation they had been forced into, to move just the way Ababio had planned they should move. In this way Ababio ensured that those he dealt with moved only in ways profitable to himself. A human being was to him nothing better than an obstacle to be tricked, lied to, manipulated and shaped by force or guile into becoming a usable ally in spite of himself. And if that failed, then a human being became simply an object to be destroyed.

The increasing knowledge he had come to have of Ababio's character had at first been a confusion inside him, strong, violent, agitating Densu. Time had turned the confusion into something clearer. It had become understanding, knowledge. That knowledge had helped create a great cold distance between Densu and Ababio, between Densu and all the people like Ababio, even when they touched him physically, between Densu and the manipulators.

In proportion as he gained a clear understanding of his repulsion, the opposite feeling, attraction, had grown stronger. Densu could think with increasing clarity of the people he desired to live together with, the ones he would like to spend a lifetime working with. This, too, the attraction, had started only as a feeling. It too had agitated him so strongly he had had to understand it. Good as it was, without understanding it too was capable of causing him pain. Understanding was always the first need.

Densu had examined the disturbing urge. Looking at it he had seen it as an attraction to ways and habits that were not lies. Could there not be festivals with meaning instead of the current rituals that could only blind a people who needed sight? Should it not be possible for people to know plainly why they did this and not that, why they moved and flowed this way and not that other way? Why would one not find, at Esuano, at Cape Coast, everywhere, people who had purposes they didn't need to hide because they were not ashamed of their purposes? Why could he not work with people not divided into factions and fragments? For what reason should he not find people who did not enjoy each other's pain? Why should he not search for people who did not waste life's energies trying to exhaust each other, trying to destroy each other, trying to outdo each other?

In himself Densu felt good possibilities. He felt great joy thinking of people who knew how to inspire others but had no wish to manipulate anyone. But always this joy turned to pain when his thoughts returned to Esuano and the present.

He could not sleep. He went out, crossed the courtyard and entered the kitchen. An oil lamp stood in a corner, faintly visible in the weak glow of the night fire. He took it, lit it, and returned to his room with it. He took his best cloth and, moving slowly to let time calm his mind, he placed on the cloth all the things he would need to take for the journey to the eastern forest. That done, he tied the whole up into a bundle he could carry easily. As the preparation for the journey absorbed his mind, the cold, heavy feelings of repulsion from a world he loathed once again dropped their hold of him. In their place the feelings attracting him to a world he desired brought a lightness into his heart, his mind, into the whole of his being. He was happy.

5 Early Death

The morning after the festival night marking the prince Appia's victory in the games of youth, the celebrated prince was found murdered on a little-used path leading from Esuano to the eastern forest. The way the prince had been butchered, it was clear as spring-water his murder must have been an act of violent hate. The corpse was found hanging, its wrists bound together above its head by rope woven for great strength. The rope was tied to the largest bough of a strong, supple guava tree. The body's weight had bent the branch into a gigantic bow.

Where the eyes had been . . .

Ah, Fasseke, words fail the story-teller. Fasseke Belen Tigui, master of masters in the arts of eloquence, lend me strength. Send me eloquence to finish what I have begun.

Where the corpse's eyes had been there were now two clusters of shiny green flies. The bluebottle flies were so close together that there were no visible spaces separating them. That morning was fresh. It should have been beautiful. The dew was not yet gone from the dark green blades of grass. On such a clean morning it should never have been possible to find flies abroad. But here was no deception. The flies were there, innumerable, heavy, drowsy, so sated with dead blood they could no longer even crawl.

Send me words, Mokopu Mofolo. Send me words of eloquence. Words are mere wind, but wind too has always been part of our work, this work of sowers for the future, the work of story-tellers, the work of masters in the arts of eloquence. Give me strength for this work, and give your own wounded soul reason to smile, seeing in the work of one who came after you a small, quick sign that your long, silent suffering was not meant, after all, to be in vain.

The prince Appia's eyes had been gouged out with some extremely sharp instrument. Two bizarre, nameless threads hung down from the sockets, invisible because more of the same motionless flies covered them completely. But that the eyeballs had been removed was clear. A line of blood had run straight down the right cheek from the right eye-socket. The neck had been cut in a deep gash across its right side. The cut left the head tilted sharply leftward, the ear touching the shoulder. In the wide open wound on the neck another accumulation of bluebottle flies, filthier than those caught in the eye-sockets and just as hopelessly drunk with blood, had gathered.

The corpse's mouth was encrusted with clotted blood. It seemed blood from the butchered throat had first spurted outwards through the mouth before finding its way down the newly hacked opening. There was a second, thicker line of blood. It was dry now, and strangely fibrous to look at. It ended under the left side of the corpse's chin, the last trickle of it trapped between the cheek and the tongue, which hung outside the mouth, limp, swollen, grotesquely elongated.

The prince's body, the trunk, was unmarked. But the arms also had been mutilated. There was a remarkable difference between the wounds on the head and neck, and those on the arms. The neck and head wounds seemed to have been inflicted in desperate haste. This was true even for the gaping eye-sockets. The right eye, for instance, had been gouged out so hurriedly and clumsily that when the flies were at last driven off, the naked cheekbones stood visible beneath the socket. And the neck wound, deep and brutal, seemed to have been inflicted with repeated, hasty, anxious, hacking blows. They had left a tangle of cut-up veins, sinew and bone. But the arm wounds were distinctly different.

Here were no hasty gashes. The arm wounds were cleanly cut, neat, precise. It was obvious the butcher, whoever he was, had not had to struggle against his victim in the making of these wounds. All signs showed these were wounds inflicted when the dead prince was already past any possibility of resistance. That was not all.

There were two cuts in identical places on each arm, half a hand above the elbow. The cuts were altogether strange. One thing was clear as mid-morning air: these cuts were not needed to kill the victim. They were not even needed to incapacitate him. Two slivers of flesh had been removed from the muscle tissue of each upper arm. Two very small slivers—but the space they left was definitely noticeable. There was no trace of the removed pieces of flesh anywhere in the area around the prince's corpse, though people searched long and thoroughly.

The legs had been similarly cut up. Behind each leg, two pieces had been cut out of the strong calf muscle below the bend of the knee. Again the cuts were clean, neat, precise. Again there was no trace of any of the flesh thus removed. People searched patiently and with great care. They found nothing.

*   *   *

When the horror of discovery began to subside, people came out of their stunned silence and asked the questions which had silently agitated their minds. What could the murder mean? For what evil purpose did the murderer remove the prince's eyes? For what uncanny sorcery did the killer need pieces from the strong prince's arms and legs?

These questions were asked in whispers. Before they could come out in the open and grow loud they were interrupted by a pressing need: the body must be cut down and taken home to Esuano for burial. The youths of the prince's age, those over whom he had achieved such recent victories, came forward to take down his corpse. A mat was laid between fresh stakes and tied securely to them. The body was laid on the mat, and covered with saffron cloth. Four youths, Djan, Anan, Ampa, and Densu, raised the bier with the fallen prince on it and led the march back home.

It was a slow, red-eyed march. A woman started a song in a fragile voice, a song of farewell. Of the marchers behind the body, few were able to open their mouths to chant the song with her. Most could only hum the melody. The words, carried by the woman's voice alone, rose unsteadily, painfully above the general hum. The dirge was a song of green fruit dying in a season that should have seen only growth: of the fall of young trees in the absence of any storm; of the unnatural cutting of the stream of life. And the chorus chant was of the unavailing search for a reason why.

Because the march homeward was slow the bearers tired on the way and were replaced, each tired one calling out the name of his replacement. All the youths of the prince's age took their turns, Densu twice because when Buntui's name was called it was found he was absent and someone else was needed to take his place as bearer.

The corpse was brought to the palace at Esuano. Women bathed it and cut its nails and perfumed it with herbs. They closed all the body's openings with dust of gold, ready for burial. In the dead prince's mother's room the grave was dug.

The day turned hot and fiery. Because the corpse had been so butchered and so much of its blood and flesh had been exposed to air and heat, it was decided to hasten the burial.

The entire palace had gone dumb at the realization that the prince Appia was dead. Those who had sung the song of death along the way fell silent when the body was laid down. The mourners and criers themselves lost their voices. Beyond a rising wind no sound was heard, till Ababio came in and brought a violent commotion.

Ababio had been away from the palace that morning. He had gone north and east, he explained, along the big river with Buntui to cut stakes for a new barn he wanted built. As soon as he arrived the silent courtyard grew loud with his questions.

'Tell me, someone, why is there such a crowd? What has happened?'

Ababio was brought to the body of the murdered prince. He stood staring at the corpse, his eyes gathering wildness, his face the face of a man struggling to contain unbearable passions, and all at once words broke strangled from his throat.

'Where was he found? How? But who? Which animal has done this? Where is he?'

Still the silence.

'Did you let him escape?' Ababio's voice was anguished. No one answered him. No one could answer him. But the silence angered him, and his passion exploded more violently.

'Are you all dumb and deaf?' No answer.

'What have you done to my prince? Who killed him?'

Ababio asked for kola and it was brought to him. He chewed it till his eyes and lips were an angry red. The women who had prepared the body for burial asked the young men of the prince's age to come forward again and move it. It was time to bury the prince.

But as the youths lifted the dead prince Ababio placed himself directly in the corpse's path. He shouted for a servant to go into his room and bring the strongest drink there. The servant went and came with a bottle of schnapps. With an impatient gesture Ababio struck off the neck of the bottle with a stone. Standing beside the dead prince's head, Ababio poured out the crystal liquid and swore a long oath:

> Here is drink for the dead.
> Fathers, grief has cut my breath.
> Here is drink for the dead.
>
> Here is drink for one just dead:
> Fathers, your grandchild, Appia.
> He died against nature,
> A noontime death,
> A fresh morning death.
> He died against nature.
> Here is drink for him,
> Here is drink for you.
>
> Fathers, here is drink for you.
> Drink, and listen to a survivor's sorrow.
> Receive our prince
> And welcome him, fathers,
> And soothe him in his pain.
>
> Such a bitter death he died,
> A death against nature,
> Death before his time.
> Drink, fathers,
> And listen to our sorrow.
>
> A death like this calls vengeance.
> See my eyes, fathers,
> Note their redness.
> See my tears, fathers,
> And taste their bitterness.
>
> My eyes will not sleep—
> They cannot sleep;
> My hands will not rest—

Where would they find peace?
My mouth will not eat—
What would not taste bitter to these lips?
Until your grandchild is avenged.

I, Ababio, promise you, fathers.
I promise days without food,
I shall spend nights without rest,
My eyes will be tortured with sleeplessness
Till the killer lies beneath my hand
And Appia's soul can stop
The painful wandering of the murdered
And find peace with your spirits.
Drink, fathers,
And remember this promise of a sorrowing survivor.

Ababio paused for breath. The intense prayer had exhausted him. He looked at the bottle in his hand. A quantity of the drink of ancestors was left in it. He swallowed it, grimacing. Thus refreshed, he shaped his mouth to continue his incantation. But a voice, gentle yet firm, stopped him.

Nana Esi Amanyiwa, the dead prince's grandmother, had been standing ready since before Ababio stormed into the palace yard. She had left her sickbed because she wanted to be with her favourite grandchild on this his final journey. She had stood there in the yard, patient, wordless, her sorrow running unchecked down her cheeks. The day was burning.

'The sun has been fierce,' Esi Amanyiwa said. 'The burial must be done now.'

So Ababio swallowed the words he had been preparing to speak. Reluctantly, he made way for the carriers of the bier to pass. The carriers took the prince Appia's body into the room of his mother, Araba Jesiwa.

The grave-diggers had done their work well. They had dug a hole so deep it hid them completely when they were down in it. Then they had dug sideways into the wall of the hole farthest from the door, to make the prince's final resting place.

Gently the carriers lowered Appia's body into the grave. The grave-diggers received the dead prince and placed him seated, his knees drawn high up towards his face, in the space prepared for him.

Weeping, the prince's grandmother Esi Amanyiwa approached the grave and said her last farewell. The words she used were inaudible— she did not raise her voice, so intensely was her sorrow focused on the departed prince.

Esi Amanyiwa had brought the most precious of her possessions with her. She had brought a fertility doll, something from her own departed days of womanhood and fruitfulness. She had brought also two silver rings, a bangle made of red, unmixed gold, and two long chains of the same metal at the end of which hung one locket of a ram and another of a dove. Esi Amanyiwa placed the ornaments of gold and silver in a small urn, also shaped of gold. Then she gave the urn, together with the image of fertility and return journeys, to the diggers in the grave to place beside the prince's body.

Nana Esi Amanyiwa took earth in her hand and threw it in a spray into the grave. She let it fall close to the prince, but could not bring herself to make it actually touch him. Then she stood there immobile, unable to make the final move from the boy who had been the joy of her life, unable to say a word.

It was then that Ababio rushed into the burial room. He came energetic, like a hurricane. The wind he brought after him was strong enough to lift Esi Amanyiwa's saffron headscarf slightly, forcing her to raise a hand to make sure, in her absent-minded way, that it was still in place. Still she could not speak. Ababio's entry was not merely stormy. It was loud. The grave-diggers were ready to climb out of the grave and to shift earth back into it, covering the prince. Ababio halted them.

'Let me go with my prince!' he shouted. 'I shall not let him go alone!' So saying, he rushed past the silent Esi Amanyiwa.

One grave-digger was on the lip of the grave, hoisting himself up to climb out. Ababio fell upon him and took him back down to the bottom of the grave. The astounded grave-digger picked himself up. Together with his partner he began trying to persuade Ababio to climb out of the hole.

'With all respect,' said the first grave-digger, 'life goes on.'

'With all respect,' said the second grave-digger, 'let's help you up again.'

'Leave me alone!' Ababio cried. 'Today I go with my prince!'

The grave-diggers were baffled. They had been on their way out when Ababio hurled himself into the grave. Now Ababio had moved towards the corpse and, clasping its feet, had begun an incantation to

57

the spirit of the dead prince. Uncertain about what to do, unable to force the tearful, grovelling Ababio out yet unwilling to leave him in the grave, the grave-diggers stood undecided beside him in the hole.

Then Nana Esi Amanyiwa's voice was heard.

'Let him go with him,' the voice said, 'since that is his wish.'

Esi Amanyiwa had spoken calmly. She had not raised her voice. But the effect of her words was instant. Where before the room had been filled with the noise of Ababio's loud lamentation, now there was the profoundest silence, a silence like the sound of forests on a starless night.

Ababio stopped weeping. He turned and looked for the grave-diggers. He did not see them. They had already climbed out of the hole, and were standing above him. Ababio raised his arms above his head and brought his hands hopelessly to rest on the edge of the grave nearest the doorway. It was clear he was incapable of raising himself up unaided. Mutely, from his station in the hole, he looked up into the downturned faces of the grave-diggers, those whose help he had so magnanimously spurned only moments previously. Ababio could not find his voice, so he spoke no words. The look in his eyes was eloquent enough. It begged the grave-diggers to raise him up into the world above. They helped him up.

Esi Amanyiwa had already turned to go. She did not look in Ababio's direction. Had she done so she would have seen the redness of his eyes subtly changed, from the sad redness of a mourner's eyes to the angry redness of the eyes of a resentful, mortally humiliated man.

On rising, Ababio had fallen into a bottomless silence. He walked past the crowd waiting wordlessly outside the house. Of all the prince's relatives he alone forgot to throw into the grave the customary handful of earth before the unfortunate Appia was finally covered over with soil in his mother's room.

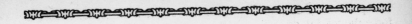

6 Whispers

After Appia's burial there was a lull. The questions and whispers that had been floating around the day the body was discovered were not heard for one day, two days. But on the third day after the burial rumours began again to whirl around.

One whisper said Ababio had had a dream. The dead prince had come to him in spirit while he slept, and promised he would reveal to him a sure way of trapping the murderer. The curious sought Ababio to confirm the rumour. They could not find him. But they found a friend of his willing to talk of the strange dream Ababio had had.

Ababio's communicative friend was the court priest Esuman. Esuman was certain the dream would point the way to the truth about Appia's murder, and reveal what had happened to his mother Araba Jesiwa also. But Ababio had yet to receive all the necessary instructions from the dead prince's spirit. Esuman counselled patience.

PART THREE

1   The Inspirers

The discovery of Appia's murder had interrupted Densu's preparation
for the journey to the eastern forest. The suddenness and the brutality
of the prince's death had knocked against Densu's brain with enough
force to stun it. He had helped carry the body back to Esuano, taking
two turns when the giant Buntui could not be found to do his share of
the carrying. But that whole day he had remained barely conscious,
unable to see meaning in anything that was happening. Till evening
he walked like some headless animal. The feeling of hunger had deserted him, and he felt no thirst though his mouth was dry.

At night he did not sleep. One after another, bizarre thoughts took
turns turning themselves into weird images to haunt him. He saw a
fierce, nameless beast, half serpent and half forest cat. The beast had
coiled itself around the body of the prince Appia, still alive, and
Densu saw it bare its fangs to destroy Appia. In the half-awake nightmare state he was in, Densu had only seen the body of the prince. But
at the moment when the beast was on the point of sinking its fangs
into his neck Densu saw Appia's face. It was his own.

Densu got up from his bed, went out and walked into the night,
trying to free his mind of the images of terror rushing into it. But the
images followed him no matter where he walked. He returned to his
room and abandoned himself to them. Once, exhausted in this abandonment, he almost succeeded in losing himself in sleep. But at the
moment between wakefulness and sleep he saw himself shoot a gun at
something running towards him. The thing fell and he moved to it. A
voice like the voice of the dead Appia called out to him. He turned his
head so sharply he felt a twinge of pain at the base of his neck. The
pain woke him fully. He had not seen the one who called him.

In weeks gone by Densu had felt the desire to reach the eastern
forest as something much stronger than the wish to leave Esuano.
Now the two were growing indistinguishable, and the total feeling

they produced had gained a hallucinating intensity. He would have gone the next morning. But he was weak from sleeplessness and hunger, and after he had eaten in the morning a huge wave of sleep covered him over and did not leave him till the day and most of the night had passed.

When he woke again Densu felt inordinately strong. His body was rested. A new calm had replaced the anxious confusion of the time before. He did not wait for dawn to come before starting on his journey to the eastern forest. He picked up his bundle and walked out into the cold, sharp air.

He had not meant to walk fast. But by the time the first rays of sunlight came towards him he was already past the last arm of the Nsu Nyin and far beyond the place where the prince Appia's murdered body had been found. Distance, even mere physical distance from Esuano, calmed Densu's mind. He would not have been able to name anything specific, but the very air of Esuano had become for him charged with hostility, and the slightest contact with it agitated his mind.

The forest was not hostile. It could have been friendly, except that as yet Densu did not really know the forest. He felt happy walking under its trees, on the soft humus of its earth, hidden under fallen leaves. And he felt good breathing in its quick, changing, surprising, humid scents. But when he really looked at the trunks coming towards him and up at the roof of leaves softening the sunlight above, he did not know what particular kind of tree he was looking at in every case, what it was like, in what way its spirit differed from that of other trees, and in what ways it was similar. Around him were all the small, subtle sounds of the forest. But there were few he recognized without a doubt, and he felt his own ignorance like an aching hollow within his being.

Once he took deliberate note of all the trees he knew, and it depressed his spirit to see they were so few and far between. He wished for time—time in which to open his eyes and ears and nostrils and the taste-buds of his tongue to the whole world about him. He wished for time in which he and the universe would grow familiar with each other.

* * *

As Densu walked through the forest, his mind shifted. It left the sights and sounds around him, and returned to the days of his first contact with the man he had looked forward so long to going to see, Damfo. Something about his remembrance disconcerted him: the first contact had been merely accidental. Something in Densu's mind wished it had not been so. He would have found it satisfying had there been something inescapable, some rock-solid necessity, at the bottom of that meeting. Because before it happened he had been thirsting for just such an encounter, without suspecting how very close he had been to it all the time. The cause of that first meeting was roundabout. He wondered what made it so hard for him to accept the idea that something so good, so perfect, should have come to him accidentally.

Damfo the healer did not come often to Esuano. Living in the eastern forest together with a small circle of others dedicated to the art of healing, he seldom had reason to come. Densu had seen him from time to time at Araba Jesiwa's home, but that was not where he had first spoken to him and begun to know him.

Damfo had married a woman from Esuano in his youth, and had lived with her in the eastern forest together with a few other healers. The woman's name was Ama. They had had a child, a girl called Ajoa. After her they had no other child. The love that had brought Ama to Damfo and the forest of healers did not survive the years following Ajoa's birth. In the child's sixth year her mother separated herself from Damfo and returned to live in the wider world at Esuano.

Ama's estrangement was not from the man Damfo himself. She respected him still, more than before, according to herself. But the life she found in the forest of healers left a large part of her soul unsatisfied. It was a quiet life, and Ama was the kind to miss the commotion and the festive business of the wider world. As the years passed the unsatisfied part of her soul grew bigger and bigger. In the sixth year after Ajoa's birth, Ama's dissatisfaction completely overwhelmed any remaining desire of hers to stay on in the eastern forest.

Damfo understood his wife. He did not block her desire to return to Esuano. What at the time he had only considered likely he found out a little later to have been the naked truth: Ama did not leave the eastern forest alone. Returning to Esuano with her was a companion called Esuman.

Esuman had entered the profession of healers at a time when he was very young, and his spirit was still involved in the exciting brightnesses of the wider world. For several years he had sulked in sullen impotence in the eastern forest, wishing he could make some triumphant return into the world outside, perhaps as a much sought after doctor, or a priest, a respected sage among ordinary men. Only the grim prospect of a lonely life among people he had lost touch with kept him together with the healers in the eastern forest.

When Esuman found out that Ama, Damfo's wife, was depressed with life in the eastern forest and yearned to return to Esuano, he knew he had found the companionship without which he would not have dared make the desired move. Esuman went with Ama back to Esuano, to begin a new life. With them they took the child Ajoa.

Densu, then in his eighth year, had first seen Ajoa then. He had seen her the very day she came with her mother and Esuman to settle at Esuano. She was then a small, fragile-looking child, but already her skin had that darkness that was a promise of inexhaustible depth, and her eyes were even then liquid, clear windows into the soul within. She was beautiful.

The second day of Ajoa's stay in Esuano Densu had gone to her and offered her a gift. It was a guava nearing ripeness, a little thing quite perfect in its oval shape.

Ajoa had not accepted Densu's offering of the fruit. She had run away from him, not like one afraid, but like a veritable woman-child overwhelmed by her own shyness. She had run till she reached her father. Then hiding behind him as if he were no mortal man but some huge, safe wall, she had peered from between his legs at the uncertain Densu holding his gift in silence. Those eyes of hers had such strong clarity. Whether for rejection or for pulling the admiring onlooker, those were always powerful eyes. Densu did not, even then, feel pushed away by Ajoa's eyes. She had run from him, but a power in her eyes beckoned to him with a strength whose source he felt within himself.

For three days Densu kept the unaccepted fruit, hoping to give it to Ajoa when he should find her again. In his mind the fruit was hers entirely, hers only. He could not have thought of giving it to anyone else. As for eating it himself, that was impossible.

Densu looked for Ajoa, and did not find her. He decided to save the fruit till they met again. But next morning he saw the first faint, ominous beginnings of wrinkles on the fruit, and he knew he should not wait. He did not stop to think about what he should do. He took the fruit and went straight to the house Ajoa's mother had made her new home. As soon as he saw the mother he greeted her. Then he asked her directly:

'Mother, where is my friend?'

The mother's answer was most unexpected. Ajoa's mother wept. When, in spite of the woman's tears and his own bewilderment, Densu finally heard the mother's message, he cried with her. The new child, the friend for whom he had so lovingly found and kept the gift, was lost.

The hunchbacked crier beat the gong all day asking anyone who had seen or heard the absent child to come and share the news. In the evening the sorrowing mother accompanied the crier, searching for the lost child in every house at Esuano. She was not found.

The day following, weird stories swirled around Ajoa's disappearance. The idlest said she was no human but a spirit child gone back home to the land of spirits. Some swore she had been carried off by some monstrous beast of prey. Strange old stories were remembered about sinister priests who went about catching virgin children and sacrificing them to cruel gods in exchange for horrific, occult powers.

That same day Densu took the fruit gift and in despair went and buried it behind the house where the girl had lived. In his mind nothing was certain. He had no idea why he was burying the fruit—whether he was hiding it in a safe place, preserving it from decay, or planting it for future growth. The sight of the guava fruit had begun to bring him too much pain and he was confused. Densu suffered from Ajoa's absence. Strangely, it brought to his mind a renewal of the sense of loss which from time to time overwhelmed him when he thought of the parents he had never known in reality, whom he had been aware of only as a painful absence from his incomplete universe.

In the morning of the third day after her disappearance from Esuano, Ajoa came back. Damfo brought her. The child had gone off alone, into the eastern forest, searching for her father. She had spent the greater part of a day going along the path leading to the healers' village. Part of the way she remembered, but after that fraction of the journey her direction had grown uncertain and she had wandered around in circles lost, but quite unafraid because she did not know it. One of the healers, out gathering herbs, had heard a child's voice in that far place and found Ajoa there, singing to herself, walking along a path that would only have brought her endlessly to the same point. He took her home to the healers.

When Ajoa saw her father again she went quietly to him. It seemed then to occur to her for the first time that she had been lost, and she cried, her body shaking as she asked her father over and over again: 'Why did you leave me? What did I do?'

Damfo explained to Ajoa that she had done nothing, and he had not abandoned her. He had taken her to live with her mother in her new home at Esuano because he knew she needed to be near her mother, and also because life at Esuano would be easier and more enjoyable for her than the difficult life of the forest. She would have companions there of her own age to grow with. In the evenings she could play and dance and listen to stories and tell her own stories together with all the other children.

Damfo asked her if the life she had had at Esuano these few days had been pleasant. Ajoa said yes, it had been pleasant. He reminded her how hard life in the forest could be. She listened and said nothing.

Damfo brought Ajoa back to Esuano. He spent a day there with her, mostly talking to her. He held her on his knees as Ajoa's mother told her how she and her new husband Esuman had missed her and how long they had looked for her. As for Esuman, he was anxious to know if anything he had done had upset the child.

At first Ajoa just sat silent, unable to answer the adults' persuasion. When all the grown-up explaining was over and the adults assumed the child would now agree with them, Esuman walked over to where Damfo sat and reached out a hand to take Ajoa. It was a friendly gesture, but Ajoa shrank from it. She pushed herself hard against her father, holding on to him with a desperate need. The revulsion she had expressed against Esuman, and the preference for her own father, were so strong that the adults said nothing further about separating her from her father.

The next morning, before Damfo and Ajoa set out on the return journey to the eastern forest, Densu sought Ajoa and found her at home. This time she did not run away from him. She listened as he tried to tell her about the fruit he had wanted to give her, how he had saved it, how he had feared it would spoil, and how finally he had planted it for her. And he showed her just where he had planted the guava fruit.

Ajoa listened, but she seemed much too disturbed to understand. Her eyes, those eyes, were restless, full of a nervous energy. Even when they came to a momentary rest, they did not rest on Densu. They looked far away. Still, those eyes did not reject him. It was just that they seemed drawn to sights far beyond the present moment. And Densu himself, drawn to those eyes, felt no need to resist the power in them, or to resent the desire that turned them away from him.

It was this power of Ajoa's over his spirit, this attraction against which he neither needed nor wanted to struggle, that had first brought Densu close to Ajoa's father, Damfo. The more Densu tried to understand this the more he found it strange—that his relationship with Damfo had begun through Ajoa, and in such an accidental way. Yet sometimes he could see the accident was only on the surface. Deeper than the surface he could see connections; he could sense natural links between his love for Ajoa and his long search for understanding and knowledge, the search that had brought him, all alive with conscious purpose, to Damfo.

The search had begun long before Densu was aware he was involved in it. Quite early in his life he had found himself almost playfully looking for his future self in the adults around him:

'Shall I be like this one when I grow up to be a man?'

In his head there had passed constantly a kind of procession of the grown-ups he knew, the adults of the world at Esuano. Some he liked; some he had no feelings about. He was most curious about what each person did, what work he spent the greatest part of his time on. He asked the grown-ups about the different kinds of work they did, and in spite of discouragements from some of them in the end he got answers. Mostly the knowledge he thus gained satisfied his curiosity and so left his mind free to think of other matters. But when he asked about Damfo and his work, the answers he got, though they told him something about the man and what he spent his time doing, did not end his curiosity. The answers left him still curious, wanting to know more.

It was not possible for a long time to ask Damfo himself about his work, though Densu sought persistently to see the healer and ask him. Damfo, after the first chance encounter when Densu had seen him while searching for Ajoa, never stayed a whole day in Esuano. Densu might see him of a late morning when he had work to do. By evening the healer was gone and another chance to talk to him was lost.

There was, however, one person at Esuano who knew something of Damfo and his work, and was happy to talk about both. For her Densu did not have to search. She was Araba Jesiwa, the mother of the prince Appia. Araba Jesiwa knew more of Damfo than anyone else at Esuano did, apart from the woman Ama who had been the healer's wife. Whenever Damfo came to Esuano, no matter how short the visit, he paid Araba Jesiwa a visit. In return, every harvest time and at the time of every important festival, Jesiwa would make a long journey to the eastern forest, to see the one man who was to her something of a father and a mentor—a great friend.

Jesiwa, to look at her from the outside, should have been one of those women born to be fortune's favourites. Nature had given her body beauty. She was not born to poverty: her mother was Esi Amanyiwa, the queen-mother at Esuano. Araba Jesiwa, to look at her from the outside, should have been fortunate from birth. But the way she looked was deceptive. Araba Jesiwa had suffered. For years her soul had sunk into a deep, horrifying hole and stayed trapped there at the bottom, unable to crawl out. How she had found strength and help to climb out of the long depression—that was something that stirred her mind with gratitude and wonder.

Densu never tired of listening to Araba Jesiwa. Strangely, he never went to her as though she could be for him the mother he had lost at birth. She was to him someone without specific age, just a friend of his soul. Sometimes he went to her when his friend Appia was also home. Often he found Araba Jesiwa alone, and sat before her listening to her talk about her life.

To the boy Densu, Araba Jesiwa talked freely, as if he were to her already an adult. She talked to him of anxiety—the terror clutching at a woman's entrails at the thought that she might go through life and die at the end without once seeing a single new life spring out from her. She talked of the pain, of the fear of barrenness, of the distress of the mind ceaselessly asking itself: 'What have I done, what is wrong with my soul, that I, a woman, should be stone-hard, unable to conceive?'

She talked to him of waste—the discouraging experience of great efforts all reduced to nothing. She talked of huge inner energies of the heart and body brought up in preparation for creation, only to be burned up, utterly destroyed.

She talked to him of despair—the bottomless loss of hope that could turn a vibrant human being into something less than inanimate flesh and bones, a trembling mass afraid to rise because it knew the attempt to rise could only be a foolish invitation to the constant, shattering, crushing blows of fate.

Araba Jesiwa loved to talk to him of hope, and of the unexpected coming of a friend bearing potent knowledge to help her soul liberate itself from traps it had entered only half aware.

She talked to him of change—how a life lived to the dull, flat rhythms of despair picked up energy, changed speed and found its ruling sound turned from a self-pitying moan to an endless song of love.

She talked to him of renewal—of the purging of falsehoods out of the abused self, of the flushing out of poisons from body and soul. She talked of the regaining of contact with a truer self abandoned in the past because false selves had offered the illusion of greater convenience. She talked of the incredible joy of the rediscovery of the authentic self, when the self too long exposed to lies was set free at last to roam along the paths to truth. She talked of remarriage, the finding of a soul closer to her own, and the quickening discovery of the body that held that soul.

Araba Jesiwa talked to Densu of conception—the first explosion in the mind at the understanding that she carried new life at last at the end of so much despair. She talked of the joyful nausea brought on by the welcoming of strange life within her hopeful being.

She talked then to him of fear—the fear that she would have to do something more definite than just waiting, otherwise the life growing within her would die once again and the long spiral of hope and despair prove endless after all.

And she talked to him of that indescribable bursting out of joy which had made her laugh when she felt the actual pain of childbirth.

Araba Jesiwa talked of the pride of a mother.

She talked of the fear that continued in spite of joy—the fear that some accident would extinguish the fresh new life that was fruit of her own.

She talked of fullness—of the gaping emptiness of life now filled with the sweetest activity; of her discovery of the tremendous need of the child for the mother's presence, a need as great as her own for his. She talked of life flowing in a stream that was full and good and sweet, because Araba Jesiwa had found the fulfilment of her soul, the child Appia.

And she talked of gratitude, of something greater than gratitude. It was a calm, bottomless love for the awakener of her true self, for the friend of her life, the healer Damfo.

Again and again, excited by Jesiwa's remembrance and her emotion, Densu asked her to tell him specifically about Damfo's work.

'What exactly,' he asked her, 'did he do to you?'

'With me!' Jesiwa started, then hesitated. She was baffled. She was baffled, not like a person lacking an answer to the question asked. She was baffled in the restless way of someone filled to overflowing with the answer but unable to find a way to communicate it to the questioner because the experience she wants to explain is too intense for words, and the questioner lacks the experience.

'What can I say? I was destroying my life. I wasn't living. Every day was just one long streak of pain, and I didn't know why. Damfo stopped me from destroying my life. He changed my life.'

Glimpsing knowledge beyond experience, Densu asked her: 'Did he force you to change?'

The question touched a nerve in Jesiwa. It energized her.

'No. No force at all. That is a quality of Damfo's which makes him what he is. No deception, no force. He said to me: "Things go wrong when we do violence to ourselves. Yes, we have more than one self. The difficulty is to know which self to make the permanent one, and which we should leave ephemeral. You set one of the passing selves above your permanent self: that's doing violence to your self. Things will go wrong then, and you'll never know why as long as you remain in the same situation and don't move out of it."

'In time I understood what I had to do. I had been false to myself. I had to start being true to my self. It wasn't easy. In my blindness I had almost killed my true self. I had embraced false selves and set them up to dominate my real self. They were not even of my own making, these false selves. They were pieces of other people, demands put out by others to whom I used to give respect without stopping to think why.

'Do you understand, Densu? I had been told it was the right thing to do, that I should marry one of the royals because I was one myself. Had I listened to my real self, I might have wondered why. But I was not in the habit of listening to myself. I feared I would go wrong. I did what the others said was right. That was the source of my troubles, the violence, as Damfo said, that I had done to myself.'

Araba Jesiwa would not fight back her tears at the remembrance of her long nightmare. But the tears were no longer bitter, being now just a part of something sweet. The bitterness belonged to memory.

For years it had seemed Araba Jesiwa was fated to die childless. It was not conception she did not conceive. At least four times she welcomed man-seed in her womb and gave it space to grow into new life.

Every time she had held the seed inside her with anxious care and a heartbreaking abundance of hope. But every time the new spirit she sought to welcome had refused flesh. The spirit had fled the world untried, and the abortion had turned the full hope in the would-be mother's eyes to vain water, impotently flowing.

Jesiwa sought help from a veritable procession of doctors promising cures. They stuffed her stomach with scrapings from the barks of innumerable trees. They fed her scratchings from snakes, rhinos, lizards, spiders, and scorpions, a most impressive array of beasts. Each doctor promised with his concoctions to give Araba Jesiwa the key that would unlock her love-gift and open her to fruitful life.

Araba Jesiwa was not a foolish woman. Her mind was subtle, and her heart, left to itself, was good. But after the glowing promises made by so many doctors had failed her, she began to cast a quickened eye around her in too many directions. She became suspicious of people, and her world became the playground of numberless, hidden enemies. Worse, she no longer cared to look for hope. She had reached the point where she saw hope merely as a fugitive illusion, and was glad to give it up. Now she looked instead for people and objects against which she could hurl her despair. So the usual casual talk of idle, feeble-minded people, the talk of witchcraft and the sinister doings of strange people, began to constitute for her an increasingly valuable source of comfort in a harassing world.

Then, in the twenty-eighth year of Jesiwa's life, Damfo the healer from the eastern forest came to her.

When the healer Damfo came to Araba Jesiwa, he talked to her exactly as if there was nothing at all she need fear from people or from the world outside. He told her there was nothing she should fear from her body itself either.

The healer Damfo asked Araba Jesiwa to talk to him of something she had forgotten: how exactly she had come to lose her first promise of a child. Jesiwa remembered an accident. It was an ambiguous event, terrifying to think of, because she could not swear she was entirely blameless in its happening. That accident, if that was what it was, had snuffed out the first promise of life in her and left her bleeding and in bodily pain. But at the time, riding high above the pain, there was this horrifying memory of a feeling within herself—a kind of glad relief.

'Did you want the child?' Damfo asked Araba Jesiwa.

'I wanted a child, very badly,' Araba Jesiwa answered.

'Araba,' Damfo said, 'answer me without fear or secretiveness. Did you want that child? The child of the man you married?'

Araba Jesiwa did not, could not answer the question Damfo asked. Damfo did not press her for an impossible answer. He asked other questions, and she found she could answer those. She told him she knew the cause of the loss of the first child; it was the second, the third, and the fourth losses of a possible child that had no direct, understandable causes.

In the end Jesiwa had come to feel she was gripped by a power too strong for her. She felt herself the impotent prey of an evil power beyond her understanding, able to reach into her being to constrict her love-gift and make it impossible for her to give a home to new life, to be a woman.

The healer Damfo spent time with Araba Jesiwa, patient, unhurried time. He spent a quarter, a third, half a day, sometimes a whole day listening to her, and he never tired, never lost patience. Men sometimes pointed to the healer and asked in indiscreet whispers why a grown man spent so much time listening to a woman's talk. The healer heard them, but the words slipped off his mind like water off a duck.

At times the healer disappeared back into the eastern forest for days. On his return he brought a small bundle of herbs, some leaves, perhaps a strip of healing bark, nothing much more. He prepared medicine for Jesiwa and told her to take it for her body's comfort. But always he reminded her to understand it was not really her body that needed healing work, not her body but her violated soul.

'You talk of a constricting power that has reached inside you to strangle your love-gift,' the healer said. 'And you are right. There is such a power. But where does it come from?'

'How can I know such a thing, Damfo?'

'Think about it. Do you feel it, as you said, coming from outside you?' Damfo asked.

'Not always,' said Jesiwa. 'Not entirely. Not outside. Here.'

'Where?'

Wonderingly, like a person still surprised by a discovery, Araba Jesiwa placed her palm just below her navel. 'Could it really be inside me?' she asked.

'Is that where you feel it?'

'Yes. Inside me.'

'So it isn't something reaching into you from outside to destroy you?'

'But it is so strong. How can it come from inside myself?'

The healer let Araba Jesiwa rest. He sensed her mind had, for the moment, exhausted her energies in reaching for that question. He never pushed her forward. The speed of her progress was what she herself needed and could sustain. Sometimes, in the enthusiasm of a good moment, she wanted to push forward even though she was tired. At such times the healer let the conversation slide quietly past the question agitating her, and waited for a fresher day.

'Why do you say it's so strong?' the healer asked Araba Jesiwa.

'It's too powerful for me,' she answered. 'It makes me helpless.'

'Yet you see it's all yours to do with as you wish,' the healer said.

'How mine?'

'It exists inside you, you've said. So it can't exist without you.'

'Still, it's stronger than I am.'

'If, as you say, it's inside you then all the strength it has, it has to borrow from you, yourself.'

'That's what makes me so helpless,' Araba Jesiwa said. 'It weakens me.'

'Have you thought of denying it strength?' the healer asked.

'How?'

'By refusing to co-operate with it,' the healer said.

'It controls me.'

'Only if you let it,' the healer said. 'You could control it instead.'

'I'd have to be strong,' Araba Jesiwa said.

'What persuades you you aren't strong?' the healer asked.

And Araba Jesiwa laughed. The healer looked steadily at her.

'If you bring together all your scattered energies,' he said, 'then you can see your own strength. After that you can judge whether you really are weak or strong. But have you done so yet? Have you brought all the parts of your self together?'

Jesiwa was slow to believe in her own strength. She was tempted again to take sour comfort in total disbelief; but the healer in all his dealings with her had treated her honestly. She decided to keep faith with him. He had never made her false promises. He had never spoken mere empty words to her. His words, all ordinary, possessing none of the flashy fire she had come so bitterly to associate with doctors and priests, made it impossible for her to judge him with the cynicism of her days of despair. She listened to the healer. All that was best in her understood his words; understood them, and began to act upon them.

Araba Jesiwa found it hard to talk about her marriage. Whenever her conversations with the healer approached that subject, she turned the course of her talk determinedly away from any mention of the husband she had chosen. She did this quite gently, quite subtly at first. But when her husband's name began to intrude more often, she fell into the habit of breaking off her conversations with the healer explosively, always to the accompaniment of hurt tears. The healer let her take her own time observing her own explosions of rage. When she was ready to understand what she was doing she calmed down and talked freely to him.

Araba Jesiwa had married a man from one of the royal houses, a man called Bedu Addo. She did not marry against her will. But there was no love in her choice. What she had thought at the time was what those she then respected had told her: that in marrying Bedu Addo she had done what was right for a person in her place.

Bedu Addo, the man Jesiwa accepted for a husband, was a man entirely without any energy of his own. Left to himself, he never expressed anything—nothing good, nothing evil. He did act at times, but always in compliance with influences and suggestions pushed upon him by those who surrounded him. As a result, all he ever did was what was expected of him by the royals at Esuano. His character was not like a young river, its rushing waters refracting light, mixing with the sun and air. His character was a becalmed pond, placid, dumbly reflecting the limited fragment of the universe around it, a stagnant little pool, going nowhere.

This was what, through the years of silent, uncomprehending frustration following her marriage to Bedu Addo, had revolted Araba Jesiwa's soul and knotted up her entrails with a quiet, hopeless, desperate disgust. Araba Jesiwa's spirit was lively. It was playful. It was like a turbulent young river. The natural motion of her soul was dynamic, effortlessly so. Her spirit in its lightness was endlessly capable of flying higher and higher provided only she could find a life companion able to fly with her. In infancy and early youth Jesiwa had known such a companion, one whose mind kept time with hers, and whose spirit helped hers in a period of swift painless growth. His name was Kofi Entsua.

Kofi Entsua grew to become a craftsman, a carver among carvers.

He was a creator of windows, doors, and mortars not only strong for the work they were meant to do but also beautiful just to see. He was a man who, when he had finished the heavier work of a day, could put a knife to wood and from the wood draw out a soaring song of love.

Araba Jesiwa loved Entsua. Entsua loved Jesiwa. When his heavier work was done for the day, it was his pleasure to take a piece of dark wood and to coax images of Jesiwa out of it. Sometimes he used clay, not wood. Sometimes he worked on stone. Out of the hard substance he brought out Jesiwa's head, her face, her breasts, occasionally her whole body. He saw her beauty in everything he touched. He loved her.

Araba Jesiwa grew to ready womanhood. The time came for her to accept a husband. Acting on the earnest advice of people who talked knowingly of the responsibilities of married life, Araba Jesiwa over-looked Entsua, who loved her and whom she loved, and married in-stead the royal Bedu Addo.

Jesiwa's choice hurt Entsua. He did not understand it. In time he stopped trying to understand it. He did not for that reason stop his work. But he put less time than before into the heavy work of carving mortars and doors and canoes for his living. The time thus freed he used for carving figures.

These figures were still beautiful—whatever Entsua worked on turned out beautiful. But their beauty now was a new, frightening sort of beauty. It was not a soft, happy beauty but a harsh kind of beauty, mixed with pain, frustration and suffering, a kind of beauty crossed with evil. The figures Entsua made were strange, tortured shapes. He kept them to himself. Whenever he finished one he began another immediately. It was as if the pain was something he could not contain alone even for a day.

Meanwhile Araba Jesiwa tried to make something good out of her marriage to Bedu Addo. The wedding had been something to remem-ber. It was a huge affair to which guests came from Cape Coast, An-omabo, Mankesim, Manso, and even from Kumase. There was glittering gold to be seen, rich, oily food to be eaten, and an overflow of drinks to heighten the spirits of the crowd of revellers.

Afterwards Jesiwa reminded herself daily that she had done nothing at all she need regret; that she had chosen wisely in preferring the royal Bedu Addo to the craftsman Entsua; that this new depression of her spirits was bound to be merely temporary; that all she needed now was patience to endure a short stretch of seeming emptiness. After that she would begin having children, and the children would fill the remainder of her days with song.

But Araba Jesiwa deceived herself in vain. Months turned years yet the sad emptiness of her life did not end. It deepened itself. It spread itself. The children she hoped for refused her womb.

Worse, throughout the time of her marriage Jesiwa did not feel her spirit take a single step forward in growth. If anything, she felt herself being pushed steadily backward, into states of mind she thought she had left behind forever in her infancy. This feeling was vague. It remained vague for a long time, because Jesiwa had no wish to turn it into definite thought. It remained vague; but it did not vanish. In a way nearly secret even to herself, Araba Jesiwa's soul began to dread annihilation, to fear the reduction of herself to a nothingness equal to her husband's royal emptiness.

Jesiwa had numberless waking dreams. In these dreams a companion she could hardly recognize travelled with her up a long, swift river. The sun and wind played over their naked bodies. Thirty thousand exquisite plants, flowers, animals, rocks, and stones flowed past in long, unhurried conversations with their eyes and ears. But at night Jesiwa had no dreams. What she had were nightmares. In these nightmares she had no companions. There was no one save herself, and she was surrounded by a voracious, menacing void whirling inexorably toward her, intent on absorbing her utterly. Throughout the years of Jesiwa's marriage the dreams coloured her days and the nightmares terrified her nights, while she struggled vainly to contain the pain of childlessness and fought a losing war against despair.

Then the healer Damfo came. The healer Damfo came and listened patiently to Jesiwa as she talked of her waking dreams and of the fears tormenting her nights. The healer asked her if she herself had tried to see any meaning in her dreams and nightmares.

'Why are they so frequent?' the healer asked.

Araba Jesiwa laughed at the question—a high, shrill sound—before she answered sharply: 'How should I know?' The healer did not insist. He let Jesiwa talk about whatever came easiest to her. In time Jesiwa confided to the healer that when she allowed herself to think closely about it, she could see her life like fine river sand. It was so fine, this sand, that it was passing through her fingers, and she could do nothing to retrieve it. This saddened Jesiwa.

'Why does that make you so sad?' the healer asked her.

75

'My hands will become empty,' she answered.

'They can be refilled,' he said.

'Who is there to refill them?' Jesiwa's voice rose with the question, and she began to cry.

The conversations between the healer Damfo and Araba Jesiwa were numerous. Damfo did not push Jesiwa to a decision. He asked questions but gave no answers, not even when Jesiwa insisted he do so. Whenever he found the conversation had tired Jesiwa, he looked for a way to end it, then waited till a fresher day. And always, he held open to Jesiwa the knowledge that she could change the direction of her life . . . if she decided to do so.

This is what Araba Jesiwa did in the end to save her soul. First, recognizing that in marrying the royal Bedu Addo she had violated her best self, she decided to break from her husband. The break was not violent, not even very hard. For months Araba Jesiwa secluded herself and allowed her mind to wrestle with the matter. Then at the end of her conversation with her soul she went to her husband and, in the presence of the same people who had been witnesses to their marriage, she requested a final separation.

Bedu Addo was disappointed, in his own numb way. Following the advice of those around him, he went away from Esuano to live at Cape Coast where he had friends among the princes at the court.

After the separation Araba Jesiwa spent three months of much needed solitude and rest. Then she began finding strength in the renewal of an old affection. Entsua spent time with her, and it became harder and harder for her to remember why it had seemed so reasonable when relatives and friends had advised her to marry only someone of royal blood.

In three more months there was a marriage between Araba Jesiwa and Kofi Entsua. Here was no loud ceremony of immature bodies hastily driven against each other. Here was a quiet understanding between two people whose spirits needed unity. Within a year Araba Jesiwa and Kofi Entsua had brought a child into the world.

But first, what care, what gentleness was not lavished on the pregnancy that became the child? This food was evil—it might poison the precious man-seed in the womb; that liquid was impure—it could contaminate the coming child's blood; such and such a breeze was ill-mannered—the way it blew, it was likely to give the unborn child a cold, or at any rate to injure it in some unsuspected way. What unseen dangers did the aspiring mother not avoid in those nine months of her suspended hope? She carried her belly like an egg, like the only egg, the egg containing all the tomorrows of the universe, an egg the loss of which would mean the loss of everything. Jesiwa suffered the sweetest agonies looking up into the rafters of the most solid roofs under which she slept those nine months, wondering if there was enough strength up there to keep the weight of the roof from coming down to crush her precious burden.

As for Entsua he spent hours just gazing, gazing at the fullness of Araba. His spirit went great distances beyond caring what other men would call him seeing him so absorbed in the contemplation of one woman—a fool or a madman? He carved thirty female forms, one a week, all bearing life, each one closer to birth.

The child was born. He stayed beyond the seventh day. On the eighth he was given a name—Appia.

After the boy's birth Damfo's visits to Esuano grew infrequent. At intervals Araba Jesiwa travelled to the eastern forest to take gifts of gratitude to Damfo, and just to sit with him and talk of her soul's desires and fears. When Appia grew old enough, she sometimes took him with her on these visits. On her return she always brought back a calm, peaceful contentment, except once, when she came back from the eastern forest to face a death in her family.

Kofi Entsua had died in a cruel accident. A tree being felled for hollowing out to make a giant canoe had twisted in its descent and crushed him. No one, not even Damfo, could comfort Araba Jesiwa for this loss. Only time helped soften the pain of remembrance, time and the consolation of Appia's continuing life, his growth to strong youth.

Near the end of Araba Jesiwa's remembrance the spellbound Densu asked her again: 'What did Damfo actually do to you?'

'He didn't do things to me,' replied Jesiwa. 'He never pushed me. The opposite was the way he treated me. Sometimes I was in a hurry to do something. He would urge me to hold back a bit and think of the thing I wanted to do, to make sure that was really what I needed to do. He never pushed me. And he never deceived me.'

'You say he showed you things you hadn't known before.'

'Things I hadn't let myself see,' Jesiwa corrected. 'What I understood because of him I must have known before, because when I saw it clearly it never seemed strange. It seemed a natural part of myself, something I had known in my self all along but which I had somehow hidden from myself. He showed me I had many selves. He helped me see which self was deep, and which selves would merely float on the surface for a passing season and then disappear. You know, I had chosen the wrong self, one of the ephemeral selves, and set it up as myself.'

'Why?'

'I was afraid of my true self. I feared the disapproval of my relatives and friends. They wanted the ephemeral self to be my self. I listened to them, and grew deaf to my own needs. I lost the desire to listen to my own soul, and almost lost the ability. I wanted to be right in the eyes of others. So I did myself wrong. I suffered till I saw I had to change. Of course I was frightened when I saw what I had to do—to accept the desires of my own soul and to know they were not wrong just because others might disagree with them. I had to do what was natural to me, and leave others to do what was natural to them.'

'Why should that have been frightening?' Densu asked her.

'I wasn't used to doing what was natural,' Araba Jesiwa said. 'But Damfo was there. He helped me see my nature and follow it. Then I saw all the crippling fears of my life had been unnecessary. But listen to me talking this way to a boy. Don't let my talk confuse you, Densu. All I wanted to say was that what he did for me was beautiful. He let me see my nature, and he let me see it was good.'

Of his conversations with Araba Jesiwa, Densu kept sweet memories. They were memories of the search for the true self, the natural self; the attempt to let the true self reveal its nature and follow its own path in life; the avoidance of force, deception, and manipulation in relationships with close ones; the constant reliance on inspiration to do the work of the spirit. Beyond all that, there was a final, mysterious statement from Jesiwa, a statement that stayed in his mind:

'You know,' she said, 'one thing I never understood: Damfo always says his real work is not the healing of sick individuals.'

Even after Densu had heard the whole of Araba Jesiwa's remembrance, he still questioned her about Damfo's work and the way he did it. No matter how fully she tried to answer him, his desire to know was not diminished. It grew.

In his fifteenth year Densu asked Araba Jesiwa to help him see Damfo long enough to talk to him about matters agitating his spirit. Araba Jesiwa laughed at him for the earnest tone of his request, but the next time Damfo was in Esuano she told him about Densu's desire. And Damfo had time to talk to him.

That time Damfo had come without Ajoa. That disappointed

Densu. But the disappointment was not as strong as his excitement at having a real meeting and a long conversation with the healer.

Damfo had seemed undecided between puzzlement and amusement at the beginning. But after Densu had asked the first question on his mind he looked neither baffled nor amused. To Densu's surprise, Damfo talked to him not like an adult to a child, but just like one person to another person: seriously, plainly, honestly.

'What really is a healer's work?' Densu asked.

'You may say it's seeing. And hearing. Knowing.'

'I don't understand,' Densu told Damfo.

'Take any place, the forest, say. Men walk through the forest. They see leaves, trees, insects, sometimes a small animal, perhaps a snake. They see many things. But they see little. They hear many forest sounds. But they hear little.'

'A healer sees more?' Densu asked.

'A healer sees differently. He hears differently,' Damfo answered. 'Yes, he hears and sees more.'

'How?'

'Say the snake bites a child. Those who walk through the forest with their ordinary eyes see the child near death, lying there helpless in the middle of all the leaves of the forest. The healer sees not just a mass of leaves. He can recognize the different spirit in each kind of leaf. He can see the leaf that has a spirit opposite to, and stronger than the snake's poison. He can squeeze its juice for the spirit contained in it and use it to save the child. You see, it is as if the spirits of all the leaves of the forest were talking to the healer, telling him what it is they each contain, what it is each can do, and what they cannot do. The leaves, animals, even stones, say much, and they show much, to any prepared to see and hear.'

'Why can't others see and hear?'

'They could if they prepared themselves to see and hear.'

'Can't people see and hear naturally?'

'What do you mean, naturally?' the healer asked the boy.

'Without preparation.'

'No one sees without preparation. Not the healer's kind of seeing.'

'Yet you made seeing sound very natural.'

'It is,' agreed the healer. 'And preparation isn't unnatural. It is also natural.'

'But children, no one prepares them to see anything.'

'Adults do that,' the healer said. 'A child has eyes for seeing light and shade and colour. But seeing for ordinary people isn't just that, is it? It's knowing what the light and shade and colour go to make. Recognition is what people call seeing. What healers mean by seeing isn't just that.'

'Is hearing the same?'

'More so. The ear hears sound. When a child understands language, he hears more than sound. The meaning is in the arrangement of sounds.'

'What is the healer's preparation for hearing and seeing?'

'The answer is a matter of years. Three years to start with. But in truth the preparation is endless.'

'Does a healer know languages others don't know?'

'You may want to understand it that way. You know how full of sounds the world is. Some of these sounds we are taught to understand. Most we don't understand, ever. In the universe there are so many signs. A few we understand, the way farmers know what clouds mean, and fishermen understand stars. But most signs mean nothing to us because we aren't prepared to understand them. The healer trains his eye—so he can read signs. His training is of the ears—so he can listen to sounds and understand them. His preparation is also of the nostrils—life and death have their smells. It is of the tongue, and the body's ability to feel.

'After his training the healer walks through the same world every person walks through. But he sees signs others don't see. He hears sounds others don't hear. The same tree that just stands there dumbly to everyone, to the healer its leaves have things to say. The healer learns the meaning of the river's sound, of the sounds of the forest animals. And when he needs the curing spirit from a plant, if his eyes are well prepared, he may see from a great distance some small sign of the leaf that is ready to be taken.'

'Can everyone become a healer?

'Few ever want to be healers.'

'But could everyone be a healer?'

'No.'

'Why not?'

'The healer must first have a healer's nature.'

'What is that?'

'I can't tell you what it is, just so,' said Damfo. 'But for a beginning he who would be a healer must set great value on seeing truly, hearing truly, understanding truly, and acting truly.' The healer laughed at himself. 'You see why healing can't be a popular vocation? The healer would rather see and hear and understand than have power over men. Most people would rather have power over men than see and hear.'

'What gives the healer his nature?'

'The same that gives him life,' the healer said.

'What is that?'

'I do not know,' the healer said. Densu looked at his face and knew he was telling the truth.

'You said for a beginning.'

'Yes,' Damfo said. 'It's not enough for the one who would be a healer to have a healer's nature. Beyond that he needs training, preparation.'

'Is it hard?'

'Infinitely so.'

'What does it consist of?'

'We don't talk about it just to talk,' said Damfo evenly. 'The only people who need to discuss a healer's training are those actually undergoing it.'

'What makes it so hard?'

'Many things. For one thing, the healer devotes himself to inspiration. He also lives against manipulation.'

'I think I understand inspiration,' Densu said. 'But manipulation?'

'It's a disease, a popular one. It comes from spiritual blindness. If I'm not spiritually blind, I see your spirit. I speak to it if I want to invite you to do something with me. If your spirit agrees it moves your body and your body acts. That's inspiration. But if I'm blind to your spirit I see only your body. Then if I want you to do something for me I force or trick your body into doing it even against your spirit's direction. That's manipulation. Manipulation steals a person's body from his spirit, cuts the body off from its own spirit's direction. The healer is a lifelong enemy of all manipulation. The healer's method is inspiration.'

'Why did you say healing people isn't your real work?'

'Did I tell you that?' Damfo asked, puzzled.

'You didn't tell me, but . . .'

Damfo laughed and looked at Araba Jesiwa. She looked ready to say something in self-exoneration, but Damfo spoke first: 'We heal people, individuals. That's part of our work. But it isn't all. It isn't even the greater part of it. It's just a part. The whole of it concerns . . .' the effort to find a word threatened to exasperate him, but he breathed deep, smiled, and said with an air of giving up: '. . . whole-ness. Those who learn to read the signs around them and to hear the language of the universe reach a kind of knowledge healers call the shadow. The shadow, because that kind of knowledge follows you everywhere. When you find it, it is not difficult at all. It says there are two forces, unity and division. The first creates. The second destroys; it's a disease, disintegration.

'It is the first, unity, that gives healing work its strength. Think of it. Healing an individual person—what is that but restoring a lost unity to that individual's body and spirit?

'A people can be diseased the same way. Those who need naturally to be together but are not, are they not a people sicker than the indi-vidual body disintegrated from its soul? Sometimes a whole people needs healing work. Not a tribe, not a nation. Tribes and nations are just signs that the whole is diseased. The healing work that cures a whole people is the highest work, far higher than the cure of single individuals.'

'Are health and unity the same, then?'

'To healers, yes,' Damfo said. 'There's health when everything that should work together works together. Take the single person. If body and soul are working together the mind thinks: I should do this; the will decides: I will do it; the muscle tenses itself to help the will; and the hand does what the mind has thought. Everything works together. But say there is a bone broken in the body. The mind may think some-thing; the will may desire it; but when the muscle tries to move the hand, there are two pieces of the broken bone pushing against each other, fighting each other, instead of working together. That is dis-ease. The cure of that kind of disease is one of the first steps in healing.'

'Only the first steps?'

'Only one of the first steps. There is disease which comes from conflict between body and soul in the same individual. That is more serious. It takes much longer to cure. Years, usually.'

'That is high work,' Densu said.

'Not the highest, though,' the healer said. 'There are worse diseases needing healing. When one person in a community—body and soul—clashes with another individual in the same community, that too is disease.'

'But is that also work for healers?'

'The ending of all unnatural rifts is healing work. When different groups within what should be a natural community clash against each other, that also is disease. That is why healers say that our people, the way we are now divided into petty nations, are suffering from a terrible disease.'

'What do you say caused the disease?'

'You do ask some heavy questions,' Damfo said. He looked at Densu, then turned to look at Araba Jesiwa as if he needed her help in answering the question. But he continued: 'The events that have shattered our people were not simply painful events. They were disasters. They were strange, unnatural catastrophes. Those who survived them could only survive in part because they found ways to forget the catastrophes. When you're still close to past dangers that threatened to wipe you out, even remembrance pains you. Our people forgot a lot of things in order to survive. We even went beyond forgetfulness. To forget thoroughly the shattering and the dispersal of a people that was once whole, we have gone so far as to pretend we have always been these silly little fragments each calling itself a nation.'

'Is forgetfulness natural?'

'It is natural, but only for a while, not for all time. Forgetfulness helps the diseased cross over the time of greatest pain. It is a sort of sleep, like the sleep brought on by herbs to help a sick man rest when his disease has exhausted him. In that case forgetfulness works towards health. But when the period of forgetfulness is prolonged unnaturally, then it doesn't work towards health. It works towards death.'

'But if forgetfulness is natural, what is there for healers to do?'

'They can be ready to help in the awakening to life, when the time comes. Learn the signs of life. Learn how to work with life, against death.'

'If forgetfulness is natural, what good will it do to work against it?'

'Sleep is natural,' the healer said, 'even when it comes after unnatural disasters. But waking is even more natural. Healers are just awakeners of a people who have slept too long. The awakening is natural. Healing work is part of nature. Very much a part.'

'How long will the work of healers take?'

'There will always be work for healers, even when the highest work is done. That highest work, the bringing together again of the black people, will take centuries. You, Densu, growing up, have been told you belong to the Fantse people, like everyone else at Esuano. No one told you the Fantse people are no people at all but a single small fragment of one community that misfortune blew apart. Of that exploded community the Asante are also a part. The Denchira, the Akim, the Wassa, the Sewhi, the Aowin, the Nzema, the Ekuapem—all these are merely scattered pieces of what once came together.

'Not only that. The Akan community itself was just a little piece of something whole—a people that knew only this one name we so seldom hear these days: Ebibirman. That was the community of all black people.

'The disease—the breaking-up of that community—has taken centuries and centuries, thousands of years. Most of our people do not even wish to imagine any such possibility of wholeness. If you talk to them now of the unity of all the earth's black people they stare at you like idiots. Some can understand, but even they are confused. The healers are also confused, not about the aim of our work, but about the medicines we may use and about what may look like medicine but may end up being poison.

'Often, our confusion comes merely from impatience. The disease has run unchecked through centuries. Yet sometimes we dream of ending it in our little lifetimes, and despair seizes us if we do not see the end in sight.' Damfo laughed, the laughter of a man amused first at himself. Then he added: 'A healer needs to see beyond the present and tomorrow. He needs to see years and decades ahead. Because healers work for results so firm they may not be wholly visible till centuries have flowed into millennia. Those willing to do this necessary work, they are the healers of our people.'

Densu was unable to open his mouth. He was looking at Damfo's eyes. Even after the healer had stopped speaking, the boy kept looking at his eyes, just looking. Then he recovered the desire to speak.

'How does a person become a healer?' the boy asked.

Damfo laughed: 'You're much too young to ask such a question,' he said. Unaccountably, the healer's voice now sounded strained, very tired. His manner took on a sudden, forced brusqueness. He seemed to be avoiding Densu's eyes. The boy saw something glimmer in the healer's right eye. He never found out if the tear was from pain, or from the healer's recent laughter.

Damfo's words had come as sweet music to Densu's soul. The boy's soul had been thirsty for just such music. That first conversation had been long. It had kept Damfo at Esuano beyond the time he had planned to leave. But the change did not irritate the healer. Densu understood he had made him late, and asked for forgiveness. But Damfo just smiled at him.

'Can you tell Ajoa I greet her?' Densu asked at the end.

'Shall I mention your name, Densu? Or will she know if I just say her admirer?'

Densu felt his back go suddenly warm. The wave of heat passed up his spine and reached his head and face. He saw sweat beads form at the tip of his nose. He murmured his thanks to Damfo and Araba Jesiwa, and turned to escape from the two adults who meant so much to him.

That evening and that night, Densu could not stop thinking of the work of healing. When sleep came after a long inner conversation, it came with dreams. In one dream Densu was with Damfo, Araba Jesiwa and Ajoa. All four were on the bank of a huge river, powerful in its flow, threatening to look at. Across that huge river lay a single precarious log. Over the log four people were crossing the river. The first three were far ahead of the last, and at every step they left him farther behind. All three leading figures were indistinct, but as they reached the far bank Densu lost sight of the fourth one also. He turned, meaning to say something to Damfo and Jesiwa and Ajoa about the disappearance of the fourth figure. But a wave of abandonment overwhelmed him—the three were no longer by his side. He tried to see if they were the three who had crossed over to the other side of the river. But the river's flow had accelerated into a wild, tempestuous torrent sending so much spume into the air that Densu's sight was misted over. In the sheer anxiety of the dream he woke up.

When morning came, Densu knew his life had changed.

2 Change

At first the change inside Densu made him see the world outside as if it too had changed. In his mind a great distance had come between him and life at Esuano. He thought of a complete break with the old life, and an immediate initiation into a new life, the life of healing. But in the passage of days, weeks, and months, Densu understood he would have to contain the change within himself, at least for some time. The dream inside himself could not produce an instant answer from the world outside. It would take time and care before it could grow to reality.

From that time on, whatever Densu did at Esuano, he saw himself in a kind of double vision. In spirit he had long decided to say farewell to the world there around him. But as yet he had not found a welcome into the world his soul desired. So he went through the motions of living in the old world, as if he were still involved in it. But always, no matter what he did in the old world, there was a second, detached self which stood apart and watched the involved self.

That did not mean Densu began to do things badly. On the contrary, the double vision gave him a strange kind of heightened consciousness of his own actions, and an increased sensitivity to the how and why of everything he found himself doing. So he found out there were things he could do well with practically no effort because he found joy in doing them. And there were things he did not even care to attempt, no matter what the inducement. He liked his work at the time, especially the work of planting and tending. After work he liked to play. He liked running, and he liked swimming. The feel of water and air on his body excited him, and speed exhilarated his whole being. But he did not like running races against people. He could get no enjoyment out of victories in such races, only a sad feeling of frivolity whose full meaning escaped him at first but whose strength was unmistakable.

He had waited long. In the time of waiting he had come to know more about the eastern forest and the life he aspired to. Sometimes, when there was no pressing work at Esuano, he went alone to seek Damfo and to talk to him. There were numberless questions on his mind. Sometimes he went with Araba Jesiwa on her journeys of gratitude and love, either together with her son Appia or, when Appia was caught up in some lively pursuit at home, just with her. Damfo always answered his questions plainly, never hiding what he knew, never pretending to know what he did not know. And he constantly reminded Densu it was important to take seriously the normal life at Esuano.

In the time of waiting Densu also came to know more of the ways of Esuano and the wider world it belonged to. Men seeking to be his mentors had explained to him, without perhaps intending to, the common passion for turning everything into a fierce competition. The explainers told him this was all a preparation, the one real preparation, for life in the real world of adults. This life they saw as a kind of game, but a serious, deadly game. Between the life Densu desired and the life available around him the distance grew immense.

He had needed patience. It took patience to wait through the months and years before the start of adulthood. It took patience to wait through the games, to participate in the rituals of competition in which he saw nothing worthy of his respect, in which he saw nothing good. It took patience to listen respecfully to Ababio talking about the necessity of power, convinced he would make a convert of his young listener. The wait was long and hard. But, in spite of everything, Densu had survived it. He was ready for the eastern forest and the future he had already chosen.

3   The Eastern Forest

He walked all day through the forest, not noticing his speed. He stopped at three streams and a spring to drink, but he felt no hunger, nor did he feel any need to stop and rest on the way, so cool and restful was the forest. It was night when he reached the eastern forest, but the night was not yet deep and he found light in Damfo's house. When he knocked Ajoa opened the door for him.

87

She was surprised. She had been expecting Damfo himself, she told him, as she gave him a stool to sit on.

'Why, where has your father gone?' Densu asked her.

'Let him tell you himself when he returns,' Ajoa said.

Ajoa went to the corner where the lamp stood, took it and brought it where Densu sat. She did not put the lamp down. She squatted before Densu, holding the light close to his face, and looking intently at his face.

'Welcome,' she said at length.

Ajoa brought him water and told him he would not have to wait long for supper. That was when Densu realized he was hungry. 'When did you start?' she asked him.

'This morning.'

'Did you fly?'

'I was eager to get here. I started very early, before the sun.'

'Still . . .' Ajoa said. 'What could have made you so eager?'   –

Densu did not see her smile. He said: 'Questions on my mind. I have to talk to Damfo.'

'You'll have to be patient,' Ajoa said. 'The Asante people have him now.'

'What's happened?'

'I don't understand yet,' Ajoa said. 'People from Praso and Kumase came to see my father with some message. He's been with them all this time. I don't know exactly when he'll be back. But that's my gain.'

'How so?'

'You can tell me what's been happening at Esuano,' Ajoa said.

'The news isn't good,' Densu said.

'About Appia?'

'You knew?' Densu asked, surprised.

Ajoa nodded in answer, but added no explanation. 'Have they found out who the murderer was?'

'No,' Densu said.

Ajoa shook her head, then said: 'I think the royals did it themselves.'

'Why?' Densu asked her.

'Who else would want to kill Appia? The royals have their power games. People are nothing to them. Just things to use. Or obstacles to break down. You're lucky they never tried to involve you.'

'One of them tried,' Densu said. 'Ababio.'

'What did he want?' Ajoa asked.

'He had a faction. He wanted me to join him.'

'What did you tell him?'

'No.'

'He won't forgive you,' Ajoa said. 'Did you explain?'

'He wouldn't listen,' Densu said. 'I told him often enough I wanted to be a healer.'

'You've decided finally then?' she asked him.

'I've decided.'

'That is so good,' she said. Then she grew quiet.

When it grew darker Ajoa decided not to wait for Damfo. She went to the kitchen, prepared food, and brought it. She was quiet during the meal, lost in thought. When it was over and she came back from washing the pots and bowls, she said to him: 'You must be careful, Densu.'

'Of what?' he asked.

'Ababio,' she said. 'If he's asked you to work for him and you've refused, he has to be afraid you might expose him.'

'He told me I shared secrets with him. He thought that would persuade me to work with him.'

'Either that, or he'll have to do something to you.'

Densu had no answer. He sat looking at Ajoa. His gaze made her uncomfortable.

'My father isn't coming,' she said finally. 'We shouldn't sit up waiting for him. He'll be here tomorrow.'

'Is he safe?' Densu asked.

Ajoa laughed: 'That he is. Don't worry about him.'

She showed him his mat. Before she turned to go she said: 'Be careful, Densu.'

When he woke up in the morning he saw that Damfo had come in during the night. He was sitting on his bed, not lying down.

'You didn't sleep,' Densu said, after greeting the healer.

'I did,' Damfo said. 'Not much, but well.'

'Ajoa said you were with people from Kumase.'

Damfo nodded. 'Some of our people. Healers. They want us to go there.'

'To Kumase?'

'Not all the way,' Damfo said. 'To Praso. We have a healers' village there also. Not far from the river, on the right bank. They think there's work for us there.'

'Will you go?'

Damfo smiled. 'Perhaps. I slept over it. I think we'll go.'

Deliberately Damfo changed the subject. He asked Densu the news from Esuano. Densu told him about Appia's death and burial. Damfo was dead quiet while Densu talked. When he finished he asked: 'Has there been any news of the murderer?'

Densu shook his head. 'But Ababio has sworn to find him.'

'Ababio?' Damfo sounded puzzled.

'Yes, Ababio,' Densu said.

Damfo grew quiet again, as if he were trying to remember something that kept slipping just under his memory. Then he seemed to give up the attempt to catch the elusive thought.

'You came in a hurry,' he said to Densu.

'I wanted to come even earlier,' Densu said. 'Before the games.'

'Something you wanted to talk about?'

'I wanted to come and stay,' Densu said.

'To stay?' The healer's voice was troubled.

'I've made up my mind,' Densu said.

'To be a healer?' the healer asked him.

'To learn.'

Damfo was thoughtful. 'How long ago did you reach this decision?' he asked Densu.

'I can't say,' Densu answered. 'It seems to me I've always wanted to come.'

'You haven't taken leave of Esuano yet,' the healer said.

'I don't understand,' Densu said.

Damfo spoke with a certain unwillingness, and this worried Densu. 'You say you've decided to learn,' Damfo said. 'That's good. But whoever wants to be a healer must take leave of the world he's grown up in before his mind is free for learning.'

'I have left Esuano,' Densu said.

'Your body has.'

'My spirit also has.'

'That is difficult to know.'

'I'm sure of it.'

'I'm not trying to discourage you,' Damfo said. 'But I must let you know the things a healer turns his back on are innumerable. These are things of the world. Not only things of the flesh, but also things touching the spirit. There's comfort. Wealth. There's also love, the respect of close ones. Even fame, the respect of distant people. Power among men. The satisfaction of being known wherever you go. These are the things that sweeten life for men. The healer turns his back on all of them.'

'Do you think I have not understood that?' Densu asked.

'It's hard to go away from the things everyone is going toward. It's lonely. It's hard to live the way a healer must necessarily live. It's hard to live without respect in the world.'

'Does a healer have no respect?' Densu asked.

'Not in the world as it is now.'

'But he does have respect.'

'Only from those who know the value of his work. Those are always few. Sometimes only one or two.'

'Is such respect not enough?' Densu asked.

'It's good to have you ask that,' Damfo said.

'I think it,' Densu said.

'I believe you. Only . . . has anyone ever told you what the learner has to do and not to do?'

Densu shook his head.

'There are rules,' the healer continued. 'Many who thought they'd like to be healers ended up hating the rules alone. They found them hard. Some found them unnatural.'

'What are they?'

'In the beginning, there are seven.'

'Will you explain them to me?' Densu asked.

'Another day we can begin. The custom is to talk about one rule a day.'

'Why only one?'

'To give all the time necessary for complete understanding.'

'Are the rules that complex?'

'Some find them so. Then they need all day to examine their implications. Some understand them easily, like breathing.'

'Can we begin tomorrow?'

'We can begin tomorrow,' the healer said. 'Now I have to go.'

'Where?' Densu asked.

'Questions, questions,' Damfo said. Smiling, he went away.

4 Conversations with the Healer

This was the first day's conversation between the healer Damfo and the novice Densu.

The healer said: 'The learner does not drink or smoke intoxicants.'

Densu smiled.

'The rule amuses you, I see,' the healer said.

'I don't like alcohol,' Densu said. 'And smoke makes me uncomfortable, even outside my body.'

'Dislike without knowledge is not firm,' the healer said. 'Do you know these things you dislike?'

'I have tasted alcohol,' answered Densu. 'I don't like its taste.'

'Few drink an intoxicant for its taste,' Damfo said. 'It's what it makes you feel. The happiness it brings. Alcohol stimulates people.'

'I'm not stimulated that way,' said Densu.

'What does stimulate you?'

'Different things. Thinking of someone I love. Being with someone I love. Something I like doing. The highest stimulation I get comes from doing something I believe in, together with people I love.'

This was the second day's conversation.

'The learner wishing to be a healer does not use violence against human beings. He does not fight.'

'The principle sounds good,' Densu said.

'Would you obey it all the time, under every circumstance?' the healer asked.

'When the circumstances are reasonable,' said Densu.

'Could you make yourself clearer?' the healer asked.

'If the healer is attacked, surely he defends himself.'

'The attacker is a human being,' the healer said.

'Is a human being human under every circumstance?'

'When is a human being not human?'

'Suppose a man turns killer. Is he not more like a beast then? Or if he invades your house, flashing a weapon?' Densu asked.

'As one learning to be a healer,' Damfo asked, 'what would you do in such a case?'

'I would stop him.'

'Violently?'

'Violently.'

'Without killing him?'

'If that's possible.'

'If it's impossible?'

'I would kill him,' said Densu.

'That goes against the rule,' the healer said.

'Not against its meaning, I don't think.'

'What do you think is its meaning?' the healer asked.

'Respect for life.'

'How can you kill out of respect for life?'

'If what I kill destroys life,' Densu answered.

This was the way the healer Damfo began the third day's conversation with Densu.

'The learner should never call upon his god to destroy anyone.'

'I have no god to call upon,' Densu said.

'You have no faith, no belief?'

'Faith I have,' said Densu, 'and belief. But not in gods.'

'You find nothing good in life?'

'Whatever is not evil I find good.'

'What do you see as evil?'

'Whatever lowers the quality of life.'

'How?'

'By pushing life closer to death.'

'Do you consider anything sacred then?' the healer asked.

'Everything that lifts life higher.'

'Do you worship what is sacred?'

'I worship nothing.'

'Is that not impious?' the healer asked.

'Doesn't worship come out of fear?' Densu asked.

'You do not fear what is sacred?' the healer asked.

'I love the sacred,' Densu answered him.

'Is fear, awe, not an expression of love?' the healer asked.

'Never,' Densu said.

'What attitude do you think expresses love?'

'Respect,' said Densu.

This was the fourth conversation.

'The learner does not go to the king's court,' the healer said. 'The learner avoids going to any place where men go to seek power over other men.'

'What if someone falls ill at the court?' Densu asked.

'A healer goes when asked to save life. He does his work and leaves when it's finished. That's different from going to the centres of power to flatter those already powerful in order to catch droppings from the powerful. The nature that knows how to flatter the powerful is an inferior nature. He whose nature is inferior cannot remain a healer.'

'I have never felt at ease at court,' Densu said.

'Perhaps because you hate the people there?'

'I don't hate them,' Densu said. 'I just feel distant from them. What interests them does not interest me. What interests me does not interest them. Still, there must be some circumstances under which healers should seek the ears of the powerful, even at the king's court?'

'Can you think of any such circumstances?' the healer asked.

'If a disease strikes many people at once, an epidemic. Surely then the healer needs royal power to support the necessary measures for restoring health?' Densu asked.

'This has always been difficult for healers to think about,' the healer said.

'Why so?' asked Densu. 'Is the dislike of royals greater than the love of life?'

'It isn't simply dislike,' the healer answered. 'It's understanding. Healers see royalty as a disease affecting the people. Does it make sense to seek the help of one disease to fight another?'

'Can healers live and work without social power always?' Densu asked.

The healer said: 'Healers need to work with social power, but that power must not be diseased.'

'Does any such power exist?' Densu asked.

'It may not exist,' the healer said, 'but it should be possible.'

'What kind of power would that be?' Densu asked.

'A power based on respect. Royal power grows from contempt. The kind of power we see now grows from contempt. It comes from the abuse of human beings and things.'

'It will take ages for the kind of power healers want to grow against what is there now,' Densu said.

'Yes,' Damfo agreed. 'The worst kinds of power grow most easily.'

'Meanwhile, isn't it advisable to work with royal power?' Densu asked. 'It's all there is.'

'Healers have tried that before. But it's never been fruitful,' said Damfo. 'Healers will find their true support only from a healthier source of power.'

'But you say that's a matter of the future,' Densu said.

'The distant future even.'

'Meanwhile?'

'Meanwhile the healer heals the individual sick,' Damfo said.

'That is all?'

'Healers work to create a power based on respect.'

'Where?' Densu asked.

'Wherever they see possibilities.'

This was the fifth conversation.

'The learner hoping to be a healer must not gossip. Neither must he quarrel,' Damfo began.

Densu merely looked at Damfo without batting an eye, then, unable to help himself, he smiled at the solemnity of the words. The smile infected Damfo. He did not pursue the matter this day. Or any other.

This was the sixth conversation.

'The learner does not waste the night,' the healer said. 'He spends the time of early night thinking over the work he's done for the day, and about what he will do the morrow. The remainder of the night he sleeps, to rise early as his spirit wakes.'

'That's not difficult,' Densu answered. 'It seems reasonable and natural.'

'There are other ways of spending the night,' the healer said.

'I know,' said Densu.

'Pleasanter ways.'

'Not to me.'

'You never liked the dances at night?'

'I loved them,' Densu said. 'Years ago, whenever I had nothing pressing on my mind, and no work drawing me. But the dances don't call my spirit any more.'

'You have entirely lost the desire to dance?'

'How can a human being lose that?' Densu asked. 'I would like to dance. But only after a lot of work done.'

This was the seventh conversation.

'The learner respects those older than himself,' the healer Damfo said.

Densu asked him: 'Only those?'

The healer's only answer was a laugh.

*　　*　　*

The day following the seventh day's conversation, Damfo was away. He returned in the afternoon of the next day and after he had rested, Densu went to greet him.

'I didn't know the visitors from Asante were still here,' Densu said.

'They're gone now,' said Damfo.

'What did they want from you?'

'Someone is ill,' Damfo said. 'They think I can help cure him.'

'Is the illness rare?'

'It's not rare,' Damfo replied. 'Not the illness itself. But it doesn't usually strike important people. And this person who's ill is important.'

'An important man from Kumase?'

'From the court.'

'Is that where you'd have to work if you went?' Densu asked.

'No. He'd come to Praso. There's a village of healers not far from the river.'

'Will you go?'

'The other healers think I should.'

'Why?'

'They think the work could be good healing work. I think they see possibilities of a new kind of power growing.'

'From this important man?'

'From his disease,' Damfo said.

'What kind of disease is it?'

'Would it make sense to you if I said despair?' Damfo asked.

'I'll need some explanation. Would I know the person's name?'

'His name is Asamoa Nkwanta,' Damfo said.

'Oh!' Densu's exclamation came by itself. 'He's the commander of the armies of Asante.'

'He was,' said Damfo. 'He was. But he no longer is.'

'What happened to him?' Densu asked.

'The royals killed his favourite nephew.'

'As a punishment?'

'No,' said Damfo. 'I see you haven't heard. For their royal pleasure.' Damfo told Densu of the root of Asamoa Nkwanta's sorrow.

5   The Root of Asamoa Nkwanta's Sorrow

Among the Asante it was unthinkable to have the king travel anywhere alone. A king, after all, must have slaves and attendants to ease his passage through the world. It was beneath the king's dignity to do anything for himself, and yet the king must always be comfortable.

When the time came for a king to go on the last of all journeys, the journey into death, the royals thought it necessary to provide him with slaves. Just as slaves had made his days on earth easy, so slaves should be sent with him to death; they would ease every passage of his spirit; they would give the spirit all the luxury the body had grown accustomed to.

So whenever a king died, the royal youths were permitted—it was a duty some turned into a pleasure—to raid Kumase after dark and to slaughter anyone they found. The murdered victims would serve as slaves of the dead king in the underworld.

'Do you remember when Nana Kweku Dua died?' Damfo asked Densu. 'He was the king before the present one, Karikari.'

'I heard about his death one Saturday night five years ago,' Densu answered.

'Yes,' said Damfo. 'It's always terrible news, the death of an Asante king, and it travels fast.' He continued his story.

97

When Kweku Dua, the first king of that name, died, the young princes at Kumase went for their guns and swords and rushed around the city looking for victims to send after the dead king. They were just following the custom. Had they killed only the powerless, people without relatives to avenge them, the killings would have been forgotten soon enough in the usual indifference of habit. But one of the princes, Boache Aso, took advantage of the murderous excitement of the time. He went looking for a young man he hated for his own reasons, and murdered him. That young man was a nephew of the commander of all the armies of Asante, Asamoa Nkwanta. Not just a nephew—his favourite nephew.

Asamoa Nkwanta was already the greatest of Asante generals. He was more than a general—he was the teacher of generals. Edu Bofo and Amankwa Tia were mere novices compared to him. They were both his pupils. The highest title for bravery among warriors, Osajefo, was already his. If the worth of a man depended on his deeds and not on his birth, Asamoa Nkwanta would easily have been the most important man in the whole land.

The killing of his favourite nephew plunged Asamoa Nkwanta first into a terrifying rage. He sought immediately to destroy whoever had destroyed his nephew. But Boache Aso the prince had disappeared, and Asamoa Nkwanta turned the fire of his fury against the royals. He, the chief defender of Asante, commander of Asante armies, threatened war against the royal family. The soldiers under Asamoa Nkwanta loved him. Many would have followed him anywhere, even if he had decided to attack the city of Kumase itself. Then the threat of civil war would not have remained a mere threat.

The royals found a sacrifice to pacify Asamoa Nkwanta: Opanin Kwamen, an uncle of the prince Boache Aso, was that sacrifice.

But Asamoa Nkwanta's anger did not disappear. It turned into sorrow of such depth that he vowed not to touch arms again in defence of Asante.

The vow became something like a curse upon the Asante army. After Asamoa Nkwanta's refusal, the armies of Asante wasted themselves in one foolish adventure after another. Altogether they were like a powerful beast with its head cut off. The remaining generals lacked the skill of Asamoa Nkwanta. Of his vision they had none at all. So they could only exhaust the armies without achieving anything.

The soldiers of Asante kept calling for Asamoa Nkwanta to return to lead them. But the murder of his nephew had pushed him far from any desire to serve the royal power.

'That murder sickened his soul,' Damfo continued, 'and he can do nothing till the disease of his soul is cured.'

'You intend to heal him?' Densu asked.

'I'll try, I think,' said Damfo.

'Isn't it strange?' Densu asked, almost musing. 'A warrior in the service of royalty is to be healed by healers who have no trust in royalty. When Asamoa Nkwanta is healed, he will go back to being a general, will he not?'

'That would be most natural,' Damfo answered.

'A general in the Asante army?'

'Of course,' agreed Damfo.

'Serving Asante royal power?' Densu asked.

Instead of an answer he got a question: 'You think so?'

'I don't know,' he said to Damfo. 'I'm asking you.'

'I'll tell you the truth,' Damfo said. 'I have no idea what purposes Asamoa Nkwanta will wish to serve after he's cured. I intend to find out. A healer always seeks knowledge.'

'What I'm trying to ask you is, is there a possibility of Asamoa Nkwanta working for something other than royalty after he's cured?' Densu asked.

'There are always possibilities,' Damfo said, a bit too calmly.

'Shall I understand that you're thinking of healing work—the kind that transcends the healing of individuals?' Densu asked.

'Shall I understand that to be a question or a realization?' Damfo asked. He was smiling.

Densu smiled back at him and nodded: 'I see a bit of something now. Dimly, but I begin to see this general Asamoa Nkwanta.'

'What happened to him is important,' Damfo said. 'He was treated like a slave. That shattered him. If the pieces of his life are to come together again, he must understand what shattered him and conquer it. He'll have to understand slavery. Not on the surface, but deeply. It isn't often men like Asamoa Nkwanta have to rethink their whole lives. It takes a catastrophe to push them to it. Usually the catastrophe is stronger than the man. It wipes him out. But I don't know this Asamoa Nkwanta myself. From all I hear, he's a strong man: physically, morally, mentally. Strong in every way. If he's able to survive this catastrophe he'll come out better than just strong. He'll be wise, in addition to being strong. He'll see the world around him differently.

He'll also see the way he wants to fit into that world differently.'

'You sound like you think he'll become a healer,' Densu said.

Damfo laughed out loud. 'Better than a healer,' he said, 'better than a healer. You know, it's not healers who heal a sick body. The body has its own healing energies, which fight the poisons of disease. A healer merely recognizes these healing energies. Then he works to multiply them, and to reduce the poisons of disease.'

'You think Asamoa Nkwanta is such a healing force?'

'I intend to find out,' Damfo said.

'When will you go to Praso?'

'I don't want to wait too long. Within a month, I think. I have work here I can't leave behind. But as soon as possible I'll move.'

6   The Frailty of Generous Decisions

The following morning Damfo was in a restless mood. A few times he seemed about to say something to Densu, but then he drew back. When at length he held himself from drawing back, what he said to Densu was: 'I expect you'll be going back soon.'

'Where?' Densu asked.

'Home. To Esuano.'

'I don't understand,' said Densu. 'I came to learn to be a healer.'

'Yes, I've understood that,' said Damfo.

'But you still want me to go away?'

'It is necessary to go back.'

'You doubt my sincerity then,' Densu said.

'No,' answered Damfo. 'Not your sincerity.'

'You are rejecting me,' Densu said.

'It's not rejection,' Damfo said. 'You've reached a generous decision. You want to spend your life doing healing work.' Damfo took his eyes off Densu and stared at the ground in front of him. 'There's something strange about generous decisions. They ought to be the best kinds of decision, but they aren't. A generous decision often lacks strength, firmness. A decision to be a healer must be firmer than any other decision. It shouldn't be made out of the generosity of a young spirit alone.'

'You don't believe me?' Densu asked.

'I believe you,' Damfo answered. 'But do you know what you are choosing and what you are rejecting?'

'You yourself have told me what I know about healing work,' Densu said. 'What I know convinces me it's what I want to spend my life doing.'

'And what you're rejecting—the life at Esuano and in the great world beyond Esuano and Cape Coast?'

'That life holds no attraction for me.'

'Not now,' agreed Damfo. 'I believe you. But time may change your mind. Especially time spent facing difficulties. Healing work is hard. To learn to be a healer, you go through three years of rigorous training. After that you begin work. The work is hard, harder than the training. There is no comfort in it for the body. Occasionally healers get thanks. More often there is suspicion and hostility. Always there's the contempt of those who'll never understand the work we do. There are many of those in the world. Very many.'

'I thought of that before I made up my mind,' Densu said.

'The decision is still only in your mind. When it becomes part of your feelings also, you'll be ready.'

'How can I show you it's already part of my feelings too?'

'It takes time,' said Damfo.

'How long?' Densu asked.

'A year, at least.'

'What am I expected to do in that year?'

'It's the time of farewells,' Damfo said. 'Taking leave of the world you've known.'

'Do all healers have to go through such a period?'

'Normally, yes,' Damfo said.

'What use is it?'

'If a learner has made a hasty decision, the year gives him time to reconsider.'

'And if the decision is genuine?'

'It gets firmer.'

'Why this distrust?'

'I wouldn't call it distrust,' said Damfo. 'Do you know Esuman?'

'The witch-doctor at court?'

A smile, rather sad, came to Damfo's lips. He suppressed it. 'Is that what they call him at Esuano?' he asked. 'He was a healer once. When he began, his enthusiasm was higher than the sky. In the end he had to leave the work of healing. He went back to Esuano. We here were left to worry about the reason. We found it. Esuman's spirit had never left Esuano in the first place. He thought of healing work as something that should make the healer personally important. The work itself was not enough for him. He needed satisfactions outside the work. He expected rewards from the world. Fame. Wealth. Power. We don't have those things here. So Esuman had to leave.'

'Do you think I will repeat Esuman's mistake?' Densu asked.

'I don't know,' Damfo said. 'I just hope you see that healing requires sacrifice. Sometimes the sacrifice may seem too much.'

'Are you afraid I can't make the necessary sacrifice?'

'I am afraid your decision to accept the necessity of sacrifice is too early yet. The fruit of premature acceptance of sacrifice is regret.'

'I wish I could make you see,' said Densu, 'that for my nature, the things you say are necessary are not sacrifices.'

'I hear you,' Damfo said. 'But then are you afraid your nature will change within this coming year?'

'I don't fear that,' said Densu.

'Are you afraid you can't resist the rewards and attractions of Esuano and Cape Coast?'

'No,' Densu said. In spite of pain, he smiled.

'What is it then?' Damfo asked.

'I've told you already. That life repels me.'

'I see,' said Damfo. 'Your unease comes from disgust. That's understandable. But it's not the best of signs. Disgust can turn the mind in perverse directions. It can make us do things not because we want to do those things but because we're disgusted with something else. Disgust clouds the mind. The best choice a healer makes is not a choice against anything. It's a choice for the healing vocation.'

Densu asked Damfo: 'Do we love something and not hate what goes against it?'

'You're right,' Damfo said. 'But for healing work love must be stronger than hate. Much stronger.' The healer looked at Densu, then said: 'I see you're angry.'

'I didn't expect to have to go back to Esuano,' Densu said. 'I didn't come prepared for that.'

'It's necessary,' Damfo said. 'All of us, no matter what we do, have moments of regret. These are the times when we wish we could return to what we were before we took a particular decision that changed our whole lives. These kinds of regret a healer must avoid. They are fatal to his vocation. If a man changes his mind before his initiation into the profession of healing, there's no harm done. But we have to make sure every healer has a genuine chance so to change his mind. Otherwise an initiated healer may feel he was trapped into a disappointing life. Because the naked truth is a healer's life is no entertainment.

'There's power in healing work. But it isn't personal power. It cannot satisfy an individual's craving for self-importance. It's a real power that has nothing to do with our small, selfish dreams. It's the power to help life create itself.

'All power has a negative side. Learning about ways to give life, a healer also comes to know ways that kill. The healer with no regrets about the life of healers turns his back against the negative power he knows about. But the healer whose soul is filled with regrets and ambitions to be great in the outside world, when he finally enters the world again, re-enters it knowing a lot about this negative power. He will use it eventually. From healing he will descend to killing.

'Power in the world is such that the negative work of killing yields faster results than the slow, endless work of healing. The healer who re-enters the world dreaming of glory and power and wealth must seek power among the powerful. He joins the manipulators. They will quickly enough urge him to use all his knowledge, the good and the bad, as long as it yields them more power, the faster the better. Do you see a bit more clearly why we have to try hard to avoid regret?'

Densu nodded, then asked: 'This Esuman, the one who went back from the healers: has he done anything evil with his knowledge of life and death?'

Damfo shook his head. 'That I don't know. I haven't sought to find out. I don't say he's done evil. I say he may, because now he's surrounded by men of power and he depends on them. Men of power have one aim in life: to maintain themselves in power. Neither good nor evil is an end to them. Both are means. Evil to them is just another unavoidable means they use to maintain their power.

'Esuman wants to share power with the men of power. Or at least the crumbs of power. They'll use him for their own ends. In return they'll give him the power he seeks.'

'Is Esuman the only one who left?' Densu asked.

'No,' Damfo answered. 'This is not the only village of healers. They are not many, but they are spread all over the land. From time to time a healer departs. Esuman isn't the only one.' Damfo's voice was sad. He continued: 'And perhaps it will ease your mind if I tell you you aren't alone. There's someone else your age, from Esuano, who has chosen healing for his life-work. He came last year. I told him to go back to the world he wanted to leave, for a year, then come back if he still believes in becoming a healer. He still has a few months to go.'

Densu was surprised. 'Who is it?' he asked.

But Damfo did not give him a direct answer: 'I'm not supposed to tell you. Since you both want to come the same way, you'll find out in time. It's natural.'

Densu did not answer.

Damfo continued: 'A year is long. But not too long. Don't just go away, Densu. Come when you wish to talk. Come as often as you wish. When the time comes for us to go to Praso, I'll come to Esuano and say farewell. When we return this way I'll let you know.'

In the evening Damfo was away again. Ajoa brought supper, but Densu could not eat. He had lost all desire. Ajoa watched him and saw he was suffering. She could think of no way to soothe him, so she was quiet. In the end, unable to remain quiet any longer, she asked Densu: 'My father has upset you?'

'I must go back to Esuano,' Densu answered.

'You sound like it's the grave. Is it so bad?'

'I'd set my mind on staying here,' Densu said.

'Does he say you can't?' Ajoa asked.

'After a year.'

'The healers call it leave-taking time,' Ajoa said. 'You have to. Especially you.'

'Why especially me?'

'They say those who have the whole world open to them need a long farewell. In a year you may well decide the charms of Esuano are too many to give up for life here in the forest.'

'What charms, Ajoa?' Densu asked. 'I remember you left Esuano happily enough yourself.'

'I'm not Densu,' Ajoa said. 'The world is not offering itself to me.

Tell me truly: how many beautiful women have made you see how much they like you?'

'I don't understand you, Ajoa.'

'Perhaps not, Densu. Since you don't wish to talk of certain things let's talk of something else. From what you said, Ababio is offering you a piece of the earth. A large piece.'

'You're laughing at me,' Densu said.

'A little,' Ajoa said. As she looked at him the playfulness went out of her voice and her eyes. 'Come back often. And be careful. Be careful of those who want to make you powerful.'

Her eyes were taking on a heightened brightness. She hid them. 'Come back often,' she said, moving towards the door in haste. 'Often, Densu. Will you promise me that?'

Densu's soul was a battlefield. His thoughts fought his desires. Peace was far. He told himself there was no reason to resent Damfo for the hard decision he had made, but the pain of resentment still burned him.

He closed his eyes. He saw a figure left standing alone in a tree-less, shelter-less wilderness, cold and windy. The figure approached him. When it reached him it became himself.

He thought of the coming year he would have to spend at Esuano and tried to imagine it as time usefully spent. But the only images that came to his mind were images of devastation.

Only when it was almost dawn, after the first cocks had begun crowing, was he able to sleep at last. He slept a short sleep, broken three times by anxious starts.

*   *   *

When he woke the sun was already high. He said his farewells and did not let Ajoa walk with him as far as she wanted to. He was quiet as she repeated her call to him to come again and often. Then she turned to go back, and he walked on west, towards the town he had left hoping he would not have to return.

The air should have been warm but he felt cold. Around him he saw leaves, branches, trees. But they communicated nothing at all to him today. He had been half blind to the forest on his way from Esuano. Now on his way back there, he was totally blind. The forest was already alive with moths and butterflies, but their scattering flight at his approach held no fascination for him. Now and then a solitary bird cut the air with its sound, and some larger animal of the forest screamed. These sounds were now mere noises to Densu. Between him and the universe around him the connection that hung on desire had been broken.

He did not stop to rest but his pace was slow. He did not even think of his direction. Only habit guided his feet. Occasionally, when he let the pain of awareness overtake him, he was surprised to recognize a part of the forest much closer to Esuano than he wished to be. Night came upon him with less than half the journey done. It did not matter to him. The forest was quiet, and the path back to Esuano was not difficult to follow. It was a narrow line, paler in the darkness than the earth beside it. In spite of the coolness of the night, whenever his mind broke from its numbness it found no comfort, only pain. He did not turn to see the dawn when it came. He saw it colour the leaves and the high tree trunks in front of him. The dark reds and oranges of the beginning turned with smooth rapidity into the white light of day.

At the ford crossing the Nsu Nyin the river was rising. The water had already covered the smaller stones, but the larger ones were still visible. In crossing, Densu wet his feet and was surprised the water felt so cold on his soles. After the ford the path climbed upwards from the bank, a narrow passageway between overhanging bushes.

Ahead of Densu a bush quivered. The movement was odd. The morning had grown dead still. The sounds of the deeper forest had stopped at the ford. As for the river's flow, it was a constant, even murmur, a part of the general silence. In this stillness the movement in the undergrowth ahead caught Densu's attention and he slackened his step. Near the top of the rise a second bush shook with a more violent motion. From the green cover above him something heavy and swift hurled itself upon Densu.

More by instinct than by conscious effort, Densu had anticipated the danger. He stepped back, letting the bundle he was carrying slide to the ground behind him. That freed his arms. The hurtling object could not check its own momentum. It came straight at him. Densu bent his left leg at the knee, then straightened it out hard just as the attacker reached him. The impact jolted Densu's thigh and sent his attacker crashing to the ground.

The attacker screamed in pain, and Densu recognized the voice. He bent down, surprised.

'Buntui,' he called the man on the ground. The answer was an angry groan.

Densu was bending down over Buntui, his mind flooding with questions, when he saw the forest around him come alive.

'The ford!' a voice shouted. Ababio's voice. It was followed by a wild whirl of motion. When the whirl resolved itself, Densu saw four men behind him at the ford he had just crossed over. Ahead of him other men came out on the path. He counted three, five, then he stopped counting. There were men on his left, men on his right, men before him and men behind him crowding the small path. All were closing in slowly upon him now. In front of him one of the men was Ababio.

Densu looked at the men around him. Buntui still lay on the ground beneath him. Apart from him, all the others he could see were older than himself. On their faces was something Densu could not understand. It was a terrible grimness, clearly growing out of a kind of fear. But what did they fear?

Ababio called out to the men: 'Who has the rope?'

From behind Densu a voice answered: 'I have it.'

Another voice, from the side: 'It's here.'

Two ropes: Densu looked at the faces closing in on him. There were so many questions on his mind, but for the moment he would have to leave them unanswered.

He thought of fighting his way out. But out of what? And into what? There was no more time anyway. The circle around him had grown tight. The men were no more than three steps away from him now.

'Tie him up!' Ababio shouted.

'There's no need to,' Densu said. Then he addressed Ababio directly. 'Eja Ababio, what is happening?'

Ababio laughed a short, nervous laugh, rather like a whimper. That was his only answer.

As Ababio's laugh ended one of the men behind Densu threw himself upon him in a desperate leap. He caught Densu before he was ready to defend himself, but there was something strange in his hold. It was a tight, urgent grasp, but it was oddly lacking in hostility. That leap excited the others, and their shouts filled the air.

The leaping one bore down heavily on Densu's back. In all that commotion he brought his head closer to his, and whispered harshly: 'Don't fight. He'll get you killed that way.'

A combined feeling, part surprise, part an instant awareness that he should not betray this sudden friend, made Densu continue with the motions of resistance. But he put no great force into the effort to break free of the leaping one's friendly grasp. Instead, he threw his weight forward and down, and the leaping one went down with him. The fall made him roll sideways, and Densu saw his face. Anan.

Anan kept his hold on Densu. The other men were an excited, disorganized little crowd now, each moving forward to hold some part of Densu, unaware there was no need of force.

'Tie him up!' Ababio shouted again.

Anan said nothing. Getting up from the ground, he turned to one of the men with the ropes and ordered him calmly: 'Give me the rope.' As if he had been taking orders from Anan all his life, the man complied.

Anan worked swiftly, in silence. He bound one end of the rope around Densu's right wrist. Then he handed the loose end to the man from whom he had got the rope.

'Tie it around my wrist,' Anan said, holding out his left arm. It was done.

'That's nothing!' Ababio shouted. 'He will escape.'

The others stood around, uncertain what to do. But Anan answered Ababio:

'The rope is tight. He'd have to drag me with him to escape.'

〰〰〰〰〰〰〰〰〰〰〰〰〰〰

PART FOUR

1   The Captive

There were not many people in the streets of Esuano when the men
returned with their prisoner. The town looked half deserted. A few
saw Densu being led towards the palace. They darted quickly back
into the safety of their homes, as if they had run into some creature of
evil omen.

Densu was taken to the palace. Inside the courtyard Ababio led the
way, left from the entrance, and all the way to the end of that wall. A
hut was there, built so that two of its walls made up the corner of the
long palace wall. Ababio took a key hanging from his neck and
opened the low door.

'Put him in there,' he said.

Several hands pushed Densu from behind. He felt a gentler pressure,
and found Anan beside him, in the hut.

'Someone help me undo this!' Anan shouted through the doorway.
A man came, and in a few moments the knots were loose.

'Take this to Eja Ababio,' Anan said to the man who had helped him
untie the rope. As the man went out, Anan whispered to Densu: 'Wait.
I'll come. But don't eat the food.' In a hurry, he turned to go to the
door. At the entrance he looked out, then turned and repeated: 'Don't
eat. I'll come.'

In a little time Densu's eyes became adjusted to the light in the hut.
The hut was small inside. From the smell of it, it had not been lived in
for a long time. It was dank. There was rot in its air, but it was not
heavy. There was nothing in there—not a stool, no pots, not even a
mat.

Densu felt tired. His reluctant farewell from the eastern forest had
brought unwelcome thoughts to ravage his mind, exhausting it and
finally numbing it. The journey itself had been heavy on his soul.
Every step of it had taken him in a direction he knew was wrong for
him. Then the sudden apparition of Ababio and his strong men on the

path back had pushed his weary mind against sharper puzzles. He knew he would be foolish to try and understand this day's events, since he knew nothing of their beginnings yet.

He took off his cloth and spread it on the floor where he felt it driest underfoot. Lying on his back on one side of the cloth, he wrapped the free length over his body. From his toes to his eyelids and the skin on his skull, he let every muscle in his frame drop loose, so that his body felt like a boneless mass pressing softly into the earth below. Deliberately, he closed his eyes and refused mind-space to the swarm of thoughts trying to worry their way in. When his mind was as clear of tension as his body, he slept. He slept a deep, peaceful sleep innocent of nightmares. When he woke up he could see it had already turned dark. Time passed.

Densu heard voices outside the door. The voices died. The door was unlocked and two figures entered. Densu gave no sign or sound of being awake. Of the two men one held a weak lamp, more smoke than light. The other held two bowls, one in each hand. The man with the bowls placed them on the floor near the doorway. The one with the lamp took two hesitant steps towards Densu, stopped and tilted the lamp forward as if that would help him see better. Then he gave up the futile effort and told his companion in an uncertain voice:

'He's asleep.'

Densu did not stir.

'It's impossible,' his companion said.

'He is,' the light-bringer insisted. 'I'm told it happens. A murderer sleeps soundly.'

'I haven't known many murderers,' the other said.

'Nor have I,' said the light-bringer, rather sharply. 'I only heard it said.'

The two men left. When the noise they made locking the door died out, Densu went to the food they'd brought and smelled it. It was chicken, fried and stewed in palm oil, with mashed yam in the second bowl. Densu felt an involuntary smile coming. Whoever had had the food prepared knew what he liked. He was hungry. He felt weak. It took effort not to return to the food, but he made the effort and lay where he was. In a while the effort lost the edge of pain, and took on a faint taste of pleasure from the knowledge of control achieved.

The words Anan had spoken came to his mind so sharply he could hear the urgent whisper again: 'Don't eat. Don't eat.' Densu turned the sound over and over again in his mind. He wondered if in the confusion of his capture he had heard the words wrongly. But he remembered the sound clearly, as clearly as the fierce, friendly embrace after Anan's desperate leap. He did not touch the food.

He felt a little surprised that he was still so calm. He wished he had a way of finding out more about the situation he was in. There was some mistake. Of that he was certain. But as he thought of it he was less certain the truth, whatever it was, would be allowed to surface. The little he knew so far increased his doubt: Ababio's active leadership in his capture, the two men calling him a murderer, and the strained, desperate words from Anan. The longer he considered it, the clearer it became: the mistake was no accident.

Because he knew so little about things in which he was inextricably involved, he became anxious. He was trying to clear this anxiety from his mind since he had no power to do anything about his situation, when he heard the door open, softly. It remained ajar. Whoever was coming in had brought no light and the night behind him was dark. Densu could not make out his shape.

The intruder came closer. He chuckled softly: 'Densu.' Densu did not answer.

'You aren't asleep,' the intruder said with perfect confidence. 'Listen, I've only come to ask you how you are. If you want to talk, we can talk. If you don't want to talk, you can continue pretending to be asleep.' He sat down near Densu. As if it were something he had forgotten to say, he added: 'My guards are outside.'

'Why do you tell me that?' Densu asked. 'Is there something you're afraid of?'

Ababio laughed. 'In this world a man needs protection, at all times.'

'Why would you need protection from me, Eja Ababio?'

'When you offer a man friendship and he refuses, you must fear him.'

'Did you arrange this?' Densu asked Ababio.

'Did I arrange what?' Ababio asked in return.

'My being brought here,' Densu said.

'Ah, that,' Ababio said, sounding relieved. 'Let's just say the people of Esuano are still mourning their prince. They're hunting for the murderer who killed him. I'm one of those most eager in the hunt.'

'Am I suspected of having killed Appia?' Densu asked.

'Do you imagine you were brought here in preparation for a dance of love?' Ababio asked Densu.

'Do you believe I killed him?' Densu asked.

Ababio chuckled again. 'Densu, if you live to be as old and experi-enced as I am, you'll learn that beliefs are quite unimportant in the affairs of adult men.'

'What is important?'

'Events,' Ababio said. 'Things that actually happen, not what should happen, but what does happen. Events don't respect beliefs. They happen. If you've learned how to live well they happen for you. If you haven't, they happen against you. That's all.'

'What's happening now?' Densu asked.

'You've been away,' Ababio said. 'I almost forgot. A lot has hap-pened. Those interested in hunting down the prince's killer have thought of the killing, the way it was done. Do you remember, certain parts of the prince's body had been cut up and removed. That could only mean one thing: juju.'

'So I'm suspected of being a juju man?' Densu asked.

'Patience, Densu, patience,' Ababio said. 'Whoever killed the prince needed the missing parts of his body for some purpose. We have met and decided what kind of purposes these might have been. Consider this: the prince was the strongest fighter in the games. He didn't win the wrestling match, but everyone knows why he didn't win. He was too kind to win. Now the murderer cut pieces of muscle from both the prince's arms and took them away. Another thing. The prince was fastest in the races—at least in the short ones. The murderer took pieces of muscle from his strong legs. One more thing: the prince won the final competition, the shooting match. So the murderer took out his keen eyes. Why, Densu? Why do you suppose the murderer took out only those parts of the prince's body?'

'I don't know,' said Densu.

'Well, the people know,' said Ababio. 'The people are clever, Densu. From the evidence, they know the murderer was jealous. He was a defeated rival, humiliated by the prince's strength, his speed, his as-cendancy over him. In this world there are people who wish to come first in everything, no matter by what foul means. If someone proves superior to them, do you think they agree to stand in his shadow? No. They remove him.'

'And I'm supposed to be that kind?' Densu asked.

'Who knows what kind you are, Densu?' Ababio asked. 'Who knows? Do you think I should know? It is known you're capable of many things, some of them amazing indeed. Everybody says you're strange. That means no one is ever sure what else you may be capable of. Anything, possibly.

'I'd have liked to speak for you, Densu. To say to the others: Listen, I know this boy. He can do this, and this, and that too. But murder is beneath him. I would have loved to say that for you. But do I know you? Have you let me know you? I wanted to know you. I let you know me. I let you see what I was doing and planning. I showed you my secrets. I invited you to be my friend. You refused. When people began suspecting you of having killed the prince, I couldn't pretend I was such a friend of yours I knew your secrets.'

'Eja Ababio,' Densu asked, 'Why are you telling me all this?'

'Don't be suspicious,' said Ababio. 'I'm not trying to make you my friend now. That's all over. You rejected me. I've accepted that rejection. If I talk to you now, perhaps it's only for entertainment. To relax myself. Because I don't really have to talk to you to try and find out who the murderer was. I have my own ideas.'

'About the murderer?' Densu sat up.

'About the murderer,' Ababio said. 'I can tell you who I think did it. Don't think I'm telling you out of generosity. I've never suffered from that disease. There's no softness in my head. If I tell you now, it's only because your knowing it won't make any difference. In the situation you've got yourself into, even if you stood in the market-place and howled you were innocent and could name the murderer, no one would believe you. The best they could say about you would be that not being satisfied with being a murderer, you'd decided go to mad in addition.'

'Do you really know the murderer?' Densu asked.

'Do you think I'm just playing with you?' Ababio asked.

'You are doing that,' Densu said.

'I'll stop playing then,' Ababio said with a smile. 'You want to know who killed the prince Appia. Buntui killed him. Kwaio Buntui.'

'How do you know?' Densu asked. 'Not even Buntui would walk up to you and say: "Eja Ababio, I've just murdered Appia." '

Ababio laughed. 'That he didn't say. But there were signs.'

'What signs?' Densu asked.

'The prince and his mother were carrying things. Jewels, cloth, all sorts of rich stuff. Jesiwa was taking them as gifts to give Damfo, that healer in the eastern forest. Araba Jesiwa had an amazing amount of respect for that man. But you'd probably approve of that. She loved him as if he were her own uncle. The world is full of foolishness,' Ababio sighed. 'But anyway, Buntui is a thief, you know.'

'He killed the prince just to steal those gifts?'

'That, I suspect, is what happened,'' Ababio said. 'Buntui can't resist anything that shines. It's a disease.'

'What did he do with the jewels?' Densu asked.

'I don't know,' answered Ababio. 'I only saw him with one of them by accident.'

'I see,' Densu said. 'Did he explain how he got the brains to trap someone like Appia and kill him?'

'I didn't ask him,' Ababio said.

'What happened to Mena Araba Jesiwa?' Densu asked. 'Did you ask Buntui what he did to her?'

Ababio's voice grew involuntarily grave. 'I did ask him that. But I've never understood his answer. He said she disappeared.'

'What did he mean, disappeared?'

'Just that,' Ababio said. 'She disappeared. Araba Jesiwa disappeared.' Ababio had lost his laughter. His voice did not carry even a trace of a smile. Clearly, this was something that made him uncertain, robbing his tone of its buoyancy.

'Why don't you tell people what you know?' Densu asked.

'That would be such a waste,' said Ababio.

'Why a waste?' Densu asked.

'Buntui has quite the strongest body anywhere around,' Ababio said. 'You, Densu, could beat him in a fight any time. But that's not because your body is stronger. You mind is faster, that's all. Thirty thousand times faster than his. The poor boy has such a small brain. But, do you know? Sometimes that defect makes a person a valuable ally. All the powerful body needs is a friendly brain willing to command it. Can you think of a better servant? A perfect servant.'

'A slave,' Densu said. 'A zombi.'

'Call him what you will,' Ababio said. 'Should I waste such an ally? This brainless Buntui is a treasure. If a wise man finds a treasure, he doesn't go and waste it, does he?'

'So you've decided to make me the murderer in Buntui's stead,' Densu said.

'You misjudge me, Densu,' Ababio said. 'No one has decided you're a murderer, least of all me. All of us are hunting, just hunting. In a few days we should know the truth.'

'Is anyone else suspected apart from me?' Densu asked.

'Everyone in the prince's age group may undergo the trial.'

'So there's to be a trial?'

'Yes.'

'When?'

'Saturday.'

'Why am I the only one kept here?' Densu asked.

'When the decision was taken to have the trial, it was discovered that everyone in the prince's age group was in town, except one. You. No one knew where you'd gone.'

'Eja Ababio, you knew I'd gone to the eastern forest.'

'No, Densu,' Ababio said. 'The world isn't like that. Did you say farewell to me when you went off? I could have proved to be a liar if I'd said I knew where you were.'

'What kind of trial is this to be?' Densu asked.

'I can't really talk about it now, but it's sure to reveal the murderer.' His tone turned pensive, and a bit sad. 'We could have worked so well together, Densu. Why did you refuse? Why did you decide to waste your life?'

Densu heard Ababio stand up. In the darkness the older man sighed heavily, like a man oppressed by weariness. He walked over to the door. In the doorway his shape was faintly visible. He stooped over the food.

'I myself had this food prepared for you,' he said. 'Chicken in palm oil, with yam. At least eat your food. You'll need strength.'

Densu did not answer him.

2 Friendship

After Ababio left, Densu found it harder keeping his mind clear of anxiety. Thrice he came close to sleep. Each time his eyes closed over fierce images of predatory beasts hunting someone he could not see.

The chase was so vivid, so intense, it disturbed him each time, and so he stayed awake.

Time passed. The night did not grow lighter. But because Densu could not sleep, his open eyes got more accustomed to the darkness. Then unexpectedly the door opened and a shape slid into the hut. Densu would have recognized that shape anywhere. It was Anan's lean form.

Anan came carefully towards Densu where he lay:

'Are you awake?' he asked softly.

'Yes,' said Densu.

'I'm your guard now,' Anan said. 'But I brought you food. You can call for water any time.' He took out a covered bowl from under his cloth.

'Are you alone?' Densu asked him.

'No. We're three.'

'Where are the others?'

'Outside,' Anan answered. 'I shouldn't stay long. Eat. When you finish, call for water. I'll come. We have to talk when we can.' He went out.

He had brought boiled ripe plantain and a peppery stew of fried herring. When Densu finished eating it he called out and Anan brought him water.

'The others are tired, so we can talk,' said Anan. 'We have some time.'

'I'm supposed to be a murderer?' Densu began.

'Ababio and Esuman are saying so,' Anan said.

'What trial is there going to be?'

'Who told you of a trial?' Anan asked.

'Ababio.'

'So he's been here. It's the poison-bark trial,' Anan said. 'Someone is suspected of a crime. They make him drink this poison. He dies. That proves he's guilty.'

'Isn't it supposed to be that only the guilty will die?' Densu asked.

'The poison isn't well known, but I've asked around,' Anan said. 'All those who know it say the first person to drink the poison always dies. Now they say you'll have to be the first to drink it on Saturday.'

'Who says?' Densu asked.

'Ababio and Esuman. Esuman is the one who brought the poison bark. He's also talked about a drug put into food to make people admit crimes.'

'A truth drug?'

'I doubt it,' Anan said. 'It sounds like something that simply weakens you. Makes you agree to whatever you're told. Don't eat what they bring you here. I'll make sure you get food with no funny drugs in it.'

'Doesn't anybody realize Ababio is lying?' Densu asked.

'They don't know,' Anan said. 'They don't care, really. People are confused. Ababio is the only one who isn't. He tells them something definite, so they cling to whatever he says.'

'I can't defend myself then.'

'Not at the trial,' Anan said. 'The trial is designed to kill you. You'll have to escape. That's the only way.'

'How many guards in all are watching this place?' Densu asked.

'You can't escape from here,' Anan said. 'There are thirty guards taking turns. Ten at a time. Three around the hut, the rest guarding the way out. No, that's impossible. Ababio has told all the guards you'll definitely try to escape. The farthest guards have guns. He's told them to shoot you if you run.'

'Still, I intend to try,' Densu said.

'Yes,' agreed Anan. 'But not the way you plan to do it. That's just the way Ababio wants things to go. He'll be happy if the guards shoot you. He wants you to try and escape. Give me time. I'll find out how the trial is to be conducted. I know where already: the open space outside the palace. I think the time of the trial itself will be the best time to act.' He rose to go. 'I have to go now. Give me time, and we'll see.' He stopped at the door, came back, and repeated his warnings: 'Don't eat what they bring you. Try and rest. Sleep well.'

The town was told the trial had been fixed for the third day following Densu's capture. There was a fear, started by Ababio and spread by whispered rumours, that Densu, suspected of the murder of the prince Appia, would somehow outwit all his guards and escape, never to be found again. So the quicker the trial was held, the better. The day would be a Saturday.

3 The Trial

Early on Saturday morning the master drummer began to beat his drums. He beat only the heaviest male drums. He beat them slowly. Even a complete stranger to the language of the drums could have understood the master drummer was beating out a message to the dead.

The message warned the dead ancestors of a coming death among the living. This would be the death of a dangerous one, one who had spilled human blood and cut short a human life. The drums warned the dead to expect a birth among themselves: the birth of a dangerous one leaving the living to roam unloved among the dead.

While the master drummer standing firm as a forest tree, the veins on his forearms prominent as lianas and the sweat running freely down his sides, beat out his message to the dead, the crier roamed through the streets of Esuano crying to the living.

The crier was a hunchback. He was dressed in the tunic of a warrior, and his small, dense body was covered with white, brown, and red talismans and amulets. The crier's voice was high. It came through his nose, but its sound had an odd, tingling clarity, so that even when he spoke fast it was easy to understand everything he said. Whenever he came to an open space where people had gathered for any purpose, he stopped and chanted his message to the living:

> Leave your food to flies
> Let the sun drink your water
> Remember the prince who died
> The strong one who died green
> The green one who died without fruit.
> A man has died before his time
> Another will die tonight.
> The trial will end in death
> Outside the palace gates tonight
> Leave your food to flies
> Let the sun drink your water.

The crier cried out his message to the living, not counting the number of times. The veins stood out on his neck. One single vessel in his forehead seemed about to burst free of the skin. His eyes stared upward into the universe. He looked like a frog with something heavy pressing on its neck. His mouth was hot and dry. But he did not stop crying out his message to the living till long after the sun had passed its highest point and everyone at Esuano had heard him.

*   *   *

The poison-bark had boiled over a slow fire at the palace for three days. As the sun went down on the day of the trial the fire and the poison-bark boiling on it were moved from inside the palace court-yard and taken to the open meeting place outside. The fire was made hotter. The water holding the poison-bark boiled fiercely. It sent wavy vapour trails into the darkening air.

Night came moonless, and very nearly starless. The fire under the boiling bark made an intense, bright circle that in all the darkness drew the eye irresistibly into itself. Four guards with guns stood near the fire. The crier's voice, normally pitched so high, had gone incred-ibly low this night. Already there was a crowd. It stood expectant, in a dim semicircle occupying the side of the open space farthest from the palace. It was a crowd obviously stunned by the weight of events to come.

The members of the murdered prince's age group had yet to appear, but space had been left for them near the fire. Densu would be the last to be brought. He would come from the palace, under a strong guard.

The crier told the assembled listeners about the coming trial. He kept his voice low, as if he were himself physically oppressed by the seriousness of his words. But the silence was deep, and the night air carried his voice easily. The crier said the coming trial was not really new; it was among the most ancient of our people's rites. For obscure reasons it had fallen into disuse, and knowledge of the fatal drink of truth had become a rare secret. But extraordinary events had hap-pened at Esuano recently. They had made it necessary to search for extraordinary answers to extraordinary questions. In that search the wisdom of the palace had discovered the ancient trial rite.

The crier said the rite of the fatal drink of truth had unbreakable rules. Among these rules, the first was that in any case of murder the fatal drink of truth must be swallowed in turn by those closest in age to the murdered one. The second rule was this: if there were many close in age, the first to drink should be the one tied to the murdered one by the keenest rivalry—whether this rivalry was in the wiles of love, in the search for power, in the exhibition of physical strength, or in the exercise of mental skill.

The members of the dead prince's age group arrived as the crier finished speaking. They were arranged not far from the fire in such a way that they stood facing the silent crowd of watchers. The fire with the liquid boiling on it was between the youths and the crowd. The youths stood in a line, as if some uncanny memory had arranged them this night: Djan was closest to the fire. After him came Sipi the hare-lip; the short Antobam; the paunchy Patu, his lips glistening in the firelight; the tall, handsome Anan, the fire dancing on his bold fore-head; the muscular Ampa, just as tall; and the giant Buntui.

Esuman, the healer who had quit the hard life of healers in the eastern forest to savour the rewards of life at Esuano, stood near the fire. He stood near the fire as if he owned it. From every action of his it was clear he was the one who had found the poison-bark on the fire.

Esuman was not dressed in the simple style of healers. He wore a flowing silken robe. Its many colours crowded busily against each other in the leaping light of the fire under the boiling liquid. Esuman moved slowly. He moved like a man who had at last realized a long elusive dream of his soul, so that now his head, his heart, his whole being was filled with the sweetness of each moment. This was a man who knew that this night, whatever happened would happen because of his power to make it happen. It was he who would know when the fatal drink was ready for the trial. It was he who would tell the attendants around the fire what to do and when.

The attendants came. One carried a large brass pan. Another carried in his right hand a smaller container, a cup made of tin. In his left he brought a ladle. A third attendant brought a heavy, greasy clay pot. He set it down close to the fire, and looked greatly relieved after he had done so.

At Esuman's bidding, the attendant who had brought the large brass pan moved it closer to the fire. Next it was filled with water. The crier raised his voice to tell the world this was pure, fresh water, brought straight from the female river. Esuman ordered the attendant with the tin cup to place it in the brass pan. The tin cup floated in the water in the pan. Firelight bounced upward from the brass pan, from the water in it, and from the shiny white cup floating on the water.

Esuman gave a command. Two men came forward from behind

him. They had thick pads of cloth in their hands. Going to the fire, they lifted the boiling pot off it and set it close by the brass pan, almost touching it. Esuman took the ladle from the attendant holding it, and began to fill the tin cup in the brass pan with the steaming liquid from the pot.

The tin cup had been bobbing up and down in a lively way. Now it danced a slower dance in the water in the brass pan. It moved less freely with each added ladleful of the boiling poison. Finally it settled immobile in the centre of the pan. The fire burned free. Now and again it threw a clear flame into the air, a single flow of light shading from dark orange at the bottom to pale blue near the vanishing tip.

Esuman held the back of his left hand above the tin cup to test the coolness of the drink of death. It was not ready. He walked over to the third guard and held a solemn, whispered conversation with him. Then he returned to the brass pan. This time he dipped the little finger of his left hand into the tin cup. The liquid did not burn him. He withdrew the finger, called to an attendant to pour water on the hand, and after he had washed it wiped it with a corner of his robe.

Then Esuman walked over to the fire. He made a sign. An attendant handed him the ladle. Another held up the heavy, greasy clay pot, and Esuman scooped up a ladleful of oil from it. Holding the ladle over the fire, he let the oil drop in a slender stream into the fire, then stepped back. The fire flared up, the yellow of it overwhelming every other colour. The flame rose in one bright column, shivered, then steadied itself. The colours of Esuman's robe burned brilliantly in the high light. Esuman's face of itself seemed to radiate its own strong light.

'It is ready,' Esuman said. 'Now we shall begin.'

He called out to the crier. The crier emerged from his silence to speak again. Standing beside the fire and looking skyward, his head thrown back above his massive chest, the crier reminded the waiting crowd of the power of the poison drink. He called it the drink of truth. It would, he said, kill the guilty but leave the innocent untouched. It was deadly to murderers, but to the clean of heart it was harmless as water.

The crier remembered one rule he had forgotten to mention before: before each drinker drank, it would be necessary to tie up his genitals with strong string. Otherwise the wily guilty one would force the drink out in urine, and mock the power of the drink of truth.

The drummers began to play. They beat out a multiplicity of

rhythms. Each man, after he had drunk the drink of death, would find the special pulse that called his body to movement and dance to it. Thus dancing he would die, or live.

Esuman threw another ladleful of oil upon the fire. When its light was highest he declared: 'Let the first among those of the departed prince's age come and take the drink of truth! He will walk away a living man tonight if he is innocent of the prince's murder. If he is guilty, he will die the painful death of murderers. His body shall be thrown unburied far from the paths of men. Animals will shun the poisoned corpse. The vultures themselves will stay away from it. Bring him forward now, the first of the prince's age.'

Densu was brought from the palace into the light of the fire in the centre of the open space. The four guards with guns stood around him. The guards formed a square, so that Densu stood in a kind of closed human box.

In spite of the terror of his situation, Densu looked calm in the firelight. He had nothing of the wild, restless, alternating look of a creature aware it has fallen in a trap. He looked most like a man awaking to full strength after a long, calm, restful sleep. In the lowering light, now red and gold, he looked serene. A man might have such a look if he knew there was no trap in the universe capable of holding him. Or he might have such a look if he had seen himself in a trap, and reached the final conclusion that nothing he could do would change his doom.

Esuman gave another command. The two guards behind Densu stepped forward and held his arms behind him. The precaution was unnecessary. Their victim seemed far from any thought of resistance. He stood dead quiet as the first of Esuman's attendants came to him, knelt in front of him, pushed his cloth aside, and tied his penis with strong string, starting at the base and ending just below the tip. That done, the attendant rose, walking backward like an enchanted being, to join his companions. The two guards who had pinioned Densu's arms behind him let go of him. They also stepped back to their positions.

A figure came from the palace. It did not stop till it came within range of the firelight. It was Ababio. He stopped behind the guards in front of Densu. He said nothing. He just stood there looking at Densu. Then he hung his head and brought a palm up to his eyes, like a man in great sorrow, and turned away from the light.

Esuman walked to the fire again. Once more the first attendant held out the pot of oil to him and the second gave him the ladle. Esuman took a ladleful of the oil and raised it above the fire. When the ladle came level with his head he let the oil drop, this time in a thick stream. The flames shot up violently. Esuman dipped the ladle into the oil pot a second time, emptied it into the fire, dipped the ladle a third time, emptied it. The flames reached high above Esuman's head, and the heat forced him to step back.

'Bring the drink of truth!' he commanded, and his voice shook with a passion audible in spite of the effort he made to control it.

The second attendant raised the lethal cup from the centre of the brass pan. Water fell in slow drops from the side of the cup into the pan. In the high firelight the drops of water looked golden and orange, like beads.

The attendant gave the cup to Esuman. Esuman walked forward with the deadly drink. He walked like a devotee obeying some infinitely remote god. He walked past the two guards in front of Densu. When he came to Densu he stopped. In a gesture that was like an act of worship Esuman held out the cup of death to Densu.

Densu took the cup. He looked into it like an initiate in a trance. He looked into the cup like a diviner searching holy water for secrets long forbidden human eyes.

'Drink!' the voice of Esuman commanded, a cold, clear voice piercing the night.

Densu raised his head and looked in the direction from which the voice had come. Then, still holding the cup of death in his hands, he began to walk. He walked towards Esuman as if the voice had called him to walk, not to drink.

The fire was still high and bright, though it was falling. Esuman's face was plainly visible. At first he looked simply perplexed, unable to decide what the condemned man's uncommanded movement could mean. Densu drew closer. He walked steadily, without haste. When Densu was less than three steps from Esuman, Esuman too began to walk—backward. He walked backward silently, like a creature hypnotized, till he bumped against one of the guards behind him. The jolt released his voice.

'Stop him!' he screamed.

The two guards behind Densu moved towards him. The two in front stood firm, holding their guns ready. Apart from Densu, Esuman and the four guards, no one moved. Everything around was caught in a kind of suspense; everything, except the still active flame of the fire behind the condemned victim and his pursuers. As for noise, there was none at all.

Then a violent motion, surprising, breath-taking, cracked the stillness that had fallen over everything. From the group of the dead prince's age-mates a figure, lithe and tall, sprang forward towards the fire. In a single flash of motion he had reached the brass pan by the fire. In the same headlong motion he lifted the broad container and hurled it straight into the fire. The flames roared angrily, once. In an instant they were gone. All that was left of the fire was a sound—the long hiss of fire and water devouring each other.

Water triumphed. The circle of deadly light went out completely. In its place there was now the deepest darkness, and in the darkness voices. The voices screamed panic:

'Ao, he's killed me!'

'My eyes! My eyes!'

'Help me! He's killing me!'

Then above the confusion of voices in panic rose another command from Esuman: 'Shoot him!'

In blind obedience there came a loud report, then another. A guard shouted: 'My gun won't fire!' There was a third report, followed at once by a terrified shout from the voice that had complained about the defective gun:

'Oh god! Someone has shot me!'

In the wake of that shout, the once silent crowd came alive. The noise was immense, a huge murmur of amazement mixed with the sound of the confused movement of a multitude of feet and bodies.

Two friends found each other in the confusion and plunged into the protective darkness. They held hands so as not to lose each other. Gently they made their way forward through the lost crowd. Anan led Densu past the palace wall, beyond the town, into the night. When they had left the town behind them, they turned left in a half-circle and walked swiftly till they left the grassy open field behind and came among the trees near the bank of the Nsu Ber.

'Shouldn't we stop to untie that string?' Anan asked Densu.

Densu felt the string wound around his penis. 'That would help,' he said. 'It's tight, but the end may come loose easily.'

He stopped to work at the string, in silence. In a moment a small, triumphant breath escaped him. He threw the string away. Then he felt his friend thrust something at him, and he took hold of it. It was a long, slender tube.

124

'You think of everything,' he said.

A distant voice came over the night air. Its message was indistinct but the friends understood it. They ran towards the river. In the darkness another voice called out. There was nothing indistinct about this one. It was a shout of encouragement from one pursuer to the others.

'Bring the lights! Towards the river!'

The hunt was on. The voices grew closer, more insistent. Their sound was mixed with that of footsteps in a hurry. The steps became a rapid pounding against the earth, and overwhelmed all voices.

'Over there! I see them!' As soon as that shout was uttered a fusillade of gunshots shattered the air.

'They're firing blindly,' Densu said.

'One hit me,' Anan said, almost in a whisper.

'Where?' Densu touched his friend's neck, as if he expected to find the wound there.

'In my shoulder,' Anan said. 'I don't think it's bad. Just a flesh wound. I feel no pain. Let's go in. They're coming.'

The two reached the river and plunged in. They swam quietly but fast, and reached the middle before the first pursuers carrying torches reached the bank.

'They'll swim across!' one pursuer shouted.

'They're not far,' another answered. 'I saw them.'

From the bank there was the repeated splash of heavy bodies hitting the water. Anan asked Densu if he had the tube in his mouth. Densu said yes. Taking hold of Densu's free hand with his own, Anan pulled him under the water with him. Beneath the water all was darkness and silent motion. Occasionally Densu could feel Anan's form gliding evenly just ahead of him, and he almost thought he could see him. But when Anan came to a stop Densu bumped softly into his body before he realized what had happened. Anan had reached the area of tree roots on the river bed. He waited till Densu steadied himself beside him. Then, taking his hand, he guided it till it touched a curved root, and Densu held it.

First the water was dark and still around them. Then it began to feel denser, as if some heavy force were compressing it. The heavy feeling soon gave way to a rocking motion. This was gentle at first, but gradually it grew quicker, till it reached a wild, agitated pitch. Now the water became noisy. The noise was strange—a rapid metallic beat, like a crowd of small pebbles and tiny stones hitting the iron blade of a hoe one after another, so close together there was only the smallest of intervals between the sounds they made.

Light followed. It too was strange—a diffuse change in the water's dark mass so subtle it made it impossible to say just when blindness gave way to hazy sight. The light could not have been very near. In the water it was a dark yellow vagueness, but it was enough to let Densu see his friend. What he saw made him grow cold with anxiety.

Anan's form had lifted off a little from the river bottom. He had lost his grip on the root. He steadied himself, and Densu saw him reach down with his right hand to catch hold of the root again. But the hand seemed incapable of motion. Slowly, Anan turned round in the water. He turned till he was in a completely upright positon. Then he pushed a foot down against the root, worked it till it was firmly wedged between the root and the river bed, then rested again.

In Densu's mind anxiety became knowledge. Knowledge brought fear and a foretaste of regret. He shifted his position, then hooked his left foot under a humped root. He clamped the bamboo tube in his mouth hard with his teeth. It stayed steady when he removed his hand. Both hands were free. From his own shoulder he untied his cloth. He folded it so that it formed a thick pad in the middle, with two long, thin wings.

He moved towards Anan, reaching out to feel the wound in his shoulder. It was slippery. A lot of blood must have flowed from it. Densu laid the padded cloth on the wound, pulled the two ends under Anan's shoulder and wound them about the upper arm. He tied the final knot as securely as he could, but the fear of what could happen made his body cold and his hands weak.

The light had disappeared. The water was still agitated, though less violently now. The noises decreased, then ceased altogether. Densu waited. The wish to break surface again was strong. He was afraid for Anan. But he was not sure the disappearance of the light and the cessation of the noise in the water meant the searchers had finally returned home. So he waited.

It took a long time, but the light came back. It came back faint, sickly and eerie. Then it grew stronger as its source drew closer. Densu wondered how much closer it would come this time. The noises also came again. But this time they were different. The sounds were fewer, and the frantic speed was no longer there. The light grew so strong Densu was able to see Anan's face in the water, hazily. It was just a glimpse, but it was enough to give him some hope. Anan's eyes were open.

The light retreated. Before the water got completely dark again the sounds died down altogether and the river resumed its normal flow. Densu did not wait any longer. He groped for Anan's face, made sure the bamboo tube was still in his mouth, unhooked Anan's foot from under the root, then gently but swiftly rose with him to the surface. It was still a dark night. But up on the surface there was a little more light than there had been below.

Anan had managed to keep the bamboo tube in his mouth under the water, but the moment he broke surface the tube drifted off and Densu lost it. He let his own also go. Without it he found it easier to swim, carrying Anan. He swam directly to the right bank. He rested to get his wind, then climbed up the bank on to firmer earth. Taking the cloth covering Anan's wound, he squeezed it dry and wiped Anan's body with it. Nearby, he could see the faint line of a path leading east. Carrying Anan bent double over his shoulder, he started along that path.

He walked steadily, conserving strength by avoiding quick, jerky movements. The night air had grown cold, but after he had been walking a while his skin began to feel warm. He did not tire easily. He did not tire at all, but at regular, frequent intervals, when he reached a patch of soft grass, he laid Anan down and stretched out beside him. Closing his eyes and breathing in deep draughts, he rested his whole body, and tried his best to rest his anxious mind.

By the first light of day he could recognize the path he was on. Few used it. He continued along it, stopping frequently to rest, to give Anan a drink, and to drink himself when he came to good water. At the first such stop Anan drank a few drops. After that he could not open his mouth to swallow anything. When night fell again Densu was not far from the village of healers. But the tiredness and hunger he had not felt all this time descended on him with a brutal fierceness, and his steps became painful and slow.

Now that he was within reach of shelter, thoughts he had had no time to think crowded into his mind. He thought of the closeness of death, of the absence of justice in the world, and a huge weariness overwhelmed him leaving him so weak he wondered how he had found the strength to keep moving this past day. Sadness invaded him. He wanted to find out if his friend on his shoulder was still breathing; but even when he stopped to rest he did not dare find out.

Then he thought he could see a house ahead of him. It was Damfo's house. But the house was mocking him. The faster he walked towards it, the farther it moved off before him. Then the house disappeared altogether, and all Densu could feel about it was that it did not even matter any more.

4 Loss

Densu had no idea how long he'd been asleep. He thought, vaguely, that he would like to get up. But when he tried to rise pain seared its way through the left side of his head and he lay down again, exhausted. He looked around. He was in a room. Somewhere in the back of his mind something said the place was familiar, but he could not remember why. There was light, but it was outside, and not much of it reached into this room. He thought it could not be far past dawn, early morning probably, because he could smell the air, and the smell was so fresh it made him glad in spite of his exhaustion. He fell asleep again.

When he woke a second time he was not alone. There was a face above his, looking down. The eyes looked extremely sad, and Densu's first impulse was to give some comfort to whoever was looking at him through those eyes. But the one standing by him smiled in spite of the infinite sadness in her eyes.

'Don't try to get up,' she said.

Densu wanted to raise a hand to touch her. She saw his desire, and placed her left hand on top of his right. He did not try again to get up, but he asked her a question.

'Where's he?'

'Your friend?' Tears came into those eyes, and the eyes failed to hold them. She had no answer to complete her question, and for the moment Densu lacked the strength to ask her other questions.

She brought him bowls of food in a basket, and water, and sat silent on the bed beside him while he tried to eat. He gave up the attempt, washed his hands and thought of a walk outside. But when he took the few steps to the door he felt as if he had climbed a mountain. His knees were weak. Every joint in his body was quick with pain. He returned to his bed.

She brought him some liquid in a calabash. It felt warm.

'Medicine?' he asked her.

She nodded. 'My father says it'll do you good.'

'Do you know what it does?'

'Many things. He says it helps the body relax, and the mind. That way a person isn't fighting against his own cure.'

He drank the medicine. In a while he felt a peaceful warmth spreading over his body. He welcomed it.

When he woke up he was alone. Ajoa was gone. He was not sure if he had simply dreamed of her. He could see there was light outside still, but it was weak, and even as he looked it grew darker. He closed his eyes but did not go back to sleep. Someone entered, moving softly. He thought it would be Ajoa, but when he looked he saw it was Damfo. He greeted him. Damfo answered him, went out and came back with the basket. He set it beside the bed.

'Where's Ajoa?' Densu asked.

Damfo did not give a direct answer. He looked preoccupied, as if he did not want to think of an answer.

'She has work to do,' he said finally.

'I asked her about Anan.'

'Densu, try and rest now,' Damfo said.

'I've been resting all this time.'

'You haven't had enough rest.'

'But my friend . . .'

'Tomorrow, Densu.' Damfo turned to go. At the door he reminded Densu: 'Eat as much as you can. And drink the medicine. It's the best.'

Again the medicine put him into a warm, dreamless sleep. The warmth remained in his body when he woke, but after a while it turned cold, and he felt as if a fever could be coming over him. Then the feverish feeling also passed.

Damfo came and asked him if he felt strong enough to take a little walk.

'More than just a little walk,' he said. Damfo smiled.

Damfo led Densu up along a small stream to its source. He stood there a while with him, then turned to go back, not having said a word. Back inside, he said nothing till Densu asked him the question that had been troubling his mind.

'Where's Anan?'

The same preoccupied look came into Damfo's eyes.

'He bled too long from the wound in his shoulder,' he said.

'Where is he?' Densu asked.

Damfo did not answer the question. He sat staring straight ahead. In front of him there was only the wall behind the bed.

'I'm going to have some heavy work to do,' he said, rising. 'I'll come back as soon as it's finished.'

'I'll come with you,' Densu said.

'You're too weak.'

'I feel strong enough.'

'A deceptive feeling. It happens. That's the nature of the illness.'

'I want to come with you,' said Densu. He got up.

Damfo did not try any more to dissuade him. He let him walk all the way to the grave, and he did not block him when he took a hoe and worked at the other end.

'It wasn't the wound itself,' Damfo said, as if his thoughts had been a conversation. 'It shouldn't have been possible for him to die from such a wound.'

'We had to hide in the water,' Densu said.

He felt no fatigue as he dug into the earth. He felt no pain. He could not feel the sun on his skin, or the sweat running down his body. No sound from the hoe reached his ears. The sight of his own hand moving the metal at the end of the wooden handle was something remote from him. He was aware of Damfo's presence, but Damfo too was a figure in a faraway place.

After the grave was dug Densu held Anan's body and with Damfo placed it in the grave. The body had to be slanted because it had grown stiff before it could be made to sit. Densu helped Damfo fill in the grave again. He did not feel a single prick of pain. His body did not belong to him.

Damfo watched Densu anxiously, but did not stop him. After the burial the two walked back. They washed the sweat and dirt off their bodies, and Damfo saw Densu back to his room.

The numbness left Densu. A sense of loss he had been unable to feel all morning descended upon him in a wave that took him and whirled him helplessly in an unending spiral of pain. He had felt no tiredness all morning, but the moment he reached his bed all energy deserted him and he knew he would not have made it had he had to take another step. The terrible distance that had insulated him from the world had disappeared. Now the universe pressed in on him, and it was a chilly universe, with no refuges he could recognize. His body was cold. It was cold in his room.

Sleep did not bring relief to his tortured mind. Instead, the descent from consciousness became a slippery plunge into nightmares. A river flowed over him and a friend. The friend was drowning though he was holding on to Densu's shoulders. He tried to raise his friend's head above the water to help him breathe, but the water had a viscous strength and against it he was powerless. The friend's hold slipped. The current took him, not downstream but upstream. Densu swam after the friend, but the same current that was taking his friend away was flowing against him. If he could reach his friend he knew he could save him from drowning. But he did not seem able to move against the water's force. He went through the motions of swimming but nothing changed. Around him the river turned to air. Ahead of him it remained water, strong water bearing his friend away.

Densu felt lifted with an unexpected surge of power. It brought him so close to his friend he could almost touch him. But the river held his friend and kept him always just beyond reach of Densu's extended hand, till his fingers ached with stretching. Then the river flowed away and disappeared completely. The swimmers did not fall on land, however. Both rose, the air bearing them with as much force as the river had. The friend rose high. He rose higher than the tallest trees. The wind carried him far, far up into the air. Densu rose after him but his rise was slower, so that he lost sight of him, then found him, and lost him again.

From below a gun was thrust at Densu. He did not see who was giving him the gun. He did not think why the gun had been given him. He took it, aimed it at his flying friend, and shot him. A river flowed from the wound and carried the dead body past a large crowd of people standing in single file, all wearing saffron. No mouth was open in any of the silent faces below, but a voice that belonged to all of them wailed the funeral song the woman had sung for the dead Appia. What the voice wailed was not the whole song but a single sentence of it, over and over again. The wailing swelled in loudness and Densu woke.

Beneath his back the bed was soaked with sweat. The cloth

covering him was also wet. He got up and changed positions, searching for dry parts of the bed and cloth. There were none.

In the days that followed, the difference between night and day became unimportant. The passage of days did not matter. Food became an irritation, then a pain. Densu stopped eating. Neither Damfo nor Ajoa forced food on him, or tried with words to persuade him to regain interest in survival. He continued to drink, and they gave him in addition to water the juice of fruits and vegetables and occasionally the weak broth from boiled meat. They brought fruit and left it with him. What he did not care to touch they removed after a few days.

By the time Densu felt like eating fruit again he had lost count of days. That day Damfo was in the room with him. He saw him taste a tangerine and not spit it out in disgust. He peeled a second and put it within Densu's reach.

'What day is this?' Densu asked.

'Tuesday.'

'Where's Ajoa?'

'She's working.'

'Where?'

'Not too far from here.'

'She's never here when you are.'

'No, she isn't.'

'What I mean is, why is that?'

Damfo laughed. 'What a lot of questions all of a sudden,' he said. He went off laughing.

The next day Ajoa brought Densu more fruit and he was able to contain it. The day after that it was Damfo he found when he woke. After washing he tried to eat, but the fruit tasted bitter on his tongue and when he swallowed some of it he vomited.

'You've spent a long time struggling against life,' Damfo told him.

'There's nothing in it,' Densu said.

'Is that what you believe, or just the way you feel now?'

'I can't make sense of anything,' Densu said.

'Can you make sense of a refusal to live?'

'The way he died . . .'

'Sometimes you look as if you think you killed him,' Damfo said.

'He was helping me. That's why he died.'

'It's hard. But that's not saying you killed him.'

'I was the cause.'

'Would you have helped him if he'd needed your help?'

'He was my friend.'

'That he was,' Damfo said. 'More than that. His soul looked in the same direction as yours. It was an accident that he died. Don't make it a matter for self-blame. Would it have made more sense if you'd both died?'

Densu was quiet.

Damfo continued: 'You feel diminished by his death. It's natural. What's not so natural is the wish to die. It helps no one. Not you, and certainly not him.'

'I can't help the feeling when I think of him.'

'Think of him. But if you give in to despair, his life is wasted. Just wasted.'

* * *

The will to live returned slowly. In the beginning Densu's mind troubled itself with thoughts of the necessity of destruction in life. Even the plucking of ripe fruit was an act of violence whose justice escaped him. Would not fruit so ripe it fell on its own be better food? Meat was simple murder. For a long time he could not forget that and the thought made his throat reject even broth.

Then it became easier to forget such thoughts. The taste of food, even the taste of meat, grew familiar again. Still, the thought of living did not lose its hollowness. One thing only remained capable of bringing a small, immediate, quickening joy to him: the presence of Ajoa. This was more than a pleasure to Densu. It was a beckoning that said life should be worth surviving for, in spite of everything.

Ajoa was absent on alternate days at first. As Densu got better her absences grew longer—two, three days at a time. Then for a week she did not come.

'Where is she?' Densu asked Damfo.

'When you're stronger, we can go and I'll show you where she is,' Damfo answered.

The question Densu had asked was still unanswered, but the way Damfo had smiled at him he could not feel the evasion had been sly. His curiosity grew. His energy increased. His strength returned.

He began by walking around in his room. Then he went out and walked around the house. He ended up taking long walks in the great forest around. Everything was new to his eyes emerging from the partial death of illness. Now again the air some mornings was so fresh it left a taste of clear water in the back of his mouth, and his lungs opened themselves insatiably for the sweet air. The earth under the forest trees was firm underfoot, springy, pleasant, gentle, not hard. Sunshine reached eyes open to rejoice in its light. Muscles and skin and bones too long ravaged by extreme shifts between sweating fevers and paralysing chills now welcomed the steady, comforting warmth that reached them filtered through overhead leaves covering peaceful paths.

Densu walked far along the paths of the forest. He walked fascinated days in a part of the forest where healing herbs had been planted for watching and use. Once more the future stopped being a mocking thought. He walked in a different direction every day, and his legs regained their old joy in movement. Remembrance still brought pain. The thought of Anan's death still filled Densu's mind with the taste of ashes. But there was a difference: now there were other feelings in a day beside pain, and despair did not rule every moment.

One day he walked beyond a point where before he had always turned back. There was a small stream across the path he had taken. Beyond the stream the path was definite for just a few steps, then it turned a corner and was hidden from view. Densu crossed the stream this time and followed the path into the bend. He would have gone on, but something in the air above him caught the edge of his sight and he stopped.

Where he stood, he was surrounded by tall, slender saplings all thrown together in this part of the forest, near the path. There was no wind, not even a breeze from anywhere, but one of the saplings had seemed to sway in all that stillness. Densu turned his eyes the better to see the particular sapling. It had not swayed. It was bent. What had struck Densu was the way it stood out from all the others, which remained straight and quite immobile in the stillness.

Densu followed the young tree with his eyes all the way down from its leaning top to the bole and the beginning of its roots. At first he saw nothing. He looked again, more carefully this time, from roots to crown. Almost till the very crown there was nothing to see. But two branches below, Densu saw the rope. It was a liana, hanging loose, and so slender that even an eye searching for it might have missed it. Densu's eyes followed it down to the ground. It disappeared in the undergrowth close to the path.

Densu looked around him for a branch he could use. He found a stumpy log lying on the ground beside the path. The log had been partly eaten by termites. He took it, hurled it hard against the ground to shake off the earth and the termites, then picked it up again. Then he edged forward slowly, stamping the path ahead of him with the log. At the third step the log was jerked from his hand with such violence that one end of it knocked against his right forearm and numbed it. The stump shot upward at the end of the liana. It was flipped half-way up the straightening sapling, then it fell down again and stayed bobbing at the end of the trap, turning and quivering in the air like something nervously alive.

Densu examined the path. The trap had been so well laid that before it was sprung he could not have guessed there was anything but soil and grass on the path. He looked farther up the path. Everything seemed ordinary enough, but then everything had seemed ordinary enough before he'd come to the trap. He looked up and searched for the sun. It was time for him to go back.

5   The Woman

When Densu told Damfo of the trap he'd seen, Damfo was not surprised. Densu wanted to know what was there—was it just some strange hunter's chosen ground?

'That trap was one of many,' Damfo said. 'They were set for a purpose. If you're strong enough to walk that far, you're ready to find out. We'll go tomorrow.'

The promise was vague, but it gave Densu an energy he hadn't known was there. He felt he was about to do something he had wanted to do for a long time. A great part of the night he spent thinking. He did not sleep till dead of night, and he woke long before dawn, yet he did not feel at all tired.

As soon as they had eaten Damfo led the way along the path Densu had followed. But when he came to the small stream he did not cross it. He walked along the left bank till the stream turned left. That was when he crossed it. Densu followed him. There was no real ford, but the stream was shallow.

Once on the other side, they came to a path that ran straight ahead, as if it were a continuation of the stream that had turned. Damfo followed that path. But soon he abandoned it. The journey became more difficult. There was no visible path to be followed, only a rough passage through thick undergrowth. Damfo pressed forward with such sureness however, that Densu stopped worrying about the difficulty of the passage. He followed Damfo in what appeared to be a huge, swinging semicircle through the forest. Then quite unexpectedly the forest lightened into an open space cleared of all vegetation, leaving only grass.

In the shade of five great odum trees, three houses stood across the open space. Two, near the middle, looked ordinary, except perhaps in the sense that they were smaller than most houses. The third was bigger, about the size of the other two put together. It was also higher, rising above the ground on stout poles almost twice a man's height.

Before he reached the edge of the open space Damfo looked around casually and picked up two sticks from the ground. Each was about the length of a child's forearm, and no thicker. Damfo beat the two sticks together at a slow, deliberate speed. At the fifth clack he stopped and waited. He walked slowly, past the houses, to the opposite side of the open field. There he stopped and again beat the two sticks together. This time he stopped at the third clack. He recrossed the field, knocked the sticks against each other once only, then dropped them a short throw from the path.

In the nearest wall of the house on stilts, a door, till now imperceptible, opened. A ladder was lowered gently till it touched the ground, its upper end remaining within the house above. Densu had time to see the one who had lowered the ladder. It was Ajoa. Damfo nodded to Densu to follow him. When they reached the ladder Damfo climbed up first, waited for Densu to climb after him, then drew the ladder in after him and closed the door. The incoming light was cut off, and Densu could see nothing. He closed his eyes, kept them shut the space of ten breaths, then opened them again.

The light inside was faint, but it was enough to see by. The house was not divided into rooms. It was all one room. To the right of the doorway Densu saw two guns. On the other side there lay an animal, a sheep. It had not attempted to rise even when Densu passed close to it. He wondered why. But before the sheep's immobility could pre-occupy him, something else drew his attention. On the far side of the room here was another being, this one a human being.

Damfo had stopped about half-way across the room. Densu also stopped, but Ajoa went directly to the figure on the far side of the room. From where he stood Densu focused his eyes, trying to see clearly the form in front of him. It took a great, hard effort, but at last recognition spread relief over his mind and a new, happy knowledge quickened his blood. A fantastic joy animated him. In pure astonish-ment he leaped forward in spite of himself, unable to suppress a little sharp cry of infant, inarticulate happiness.

'Mena Araba Jesiwa!' he cried.

But even in the fullness of his ecstasy, something checked his for-ward motion. He felt alone. The sense of joy was his exclusively and this was strange. Around him everyone, everything, was dead still. He turned to look at Damfo. He looked backward, at the silent, motion-less sheep by the door. He looked forward again, and saw Ajoa. Her face was invisible, because she was looking down. Only the top of her head showed. Beside her lay the figure Densu had recognized. Densu looked hard, struggling against the rising feeling that he had made a cruel mistake. He took two steps forward, then a fear stronger than himself halted him again.

He was not mistaken. The woman lying there was Araba Jesiwa. But there was such a strangeness about everything now, and her being here was so incomprehensible. There was such an oppressive silence: Araba Jesiwa's silence, such a terrifying, unexplained silence; the silence of Damfo and Ajoa. Even the silence of the sheep. Why did it not bleat? There was such a strangeness about everything.

Densu could feel his whole body. Every nerve in it was raw, as if he were just that very day climbing back into life from the nadir of some devastating disease. He felt unutterably weak. Yet the weakness did not come from doubt. It was Araba Jesiwa he had seen. He had looked at that face he'd known so well. He had looked into the eyes.

He had looked into the eyes, and the eyes had been open but they had given him no sign of recognition. No sign of energy, not a single sign of life. Nothing. Had the eyes been closed, he would have taken the form before him for a corpse—so still, so bottomless was its immo-bility. But they were open, those eyes, open, not even staring, just open, changeless, open. Those eyes that had been so active, so quick, so alive in the past, were now totally passive, completely still, fixed in their unchanging openness like some staring image of death.

Damfo said nothing. Ajoa did not speak. Densu could not open his mouth.

Araba Jesiwa lay supine on a low bed. A large sheet of cloth covered her body, but the outline of her limbs was visible under the cloth, and they gave a pronounced impression of heaviness. In time Densu saw the cause: each arm was covered tightly in a massive clay cast wrapped round with thick cloth. Each leg was similarly sheathed, only the leg casts were much heavier. Something about the casts made Densu turn to look again at the sheep by the door. Its immobility reflected exactly the unnatural stillness in which Araba Jesiwa lay. Not only that. The animal's limbs were also encased in clay.

Densu heard Damfo speak. His voice was low. Otherwise there was nothing unusual about it. His tone was casual, friendly as always. But his words themselves were out of the ordinary. He was talking to Araba Jesiwa, taking extreme care to repeat each statement a number of times before making another one. He called out his own name, and told Jesiwa he had come again to visit her and to find out how she was. He had brought a friend, someone she knew and liked. Here Damfo hesitated, then repeated the part about a friend, but said nothing further about her having known Densu. Everything he told her was designed to reassure her. But she gave no sign of having heard anything.

Damfo told Araba Jesiwa she would be well. He told her she was already much better than she had been in the first days.

'Look at the lamb,' he said repeatedly, 'Look at the lamb. He will walk, just as you saw the hen walk. It will take him longer, only because the lamb has bigger bones, and they take longer to heal when broken. The lamb will walk as surely as the hen walked. You will walk as surely as the lamb will walk. Don't be afraid.'

There was no response, no sign of life from Jesiwa.

The live pain that had possessed Densu's body after the shock of seeing who the body on the bed was had died. In its place had come a numbness shutting off all feeling. For a while his mind held no thought. It was an empty space ignorant of suffering or joy, dead to life. Then feeling and consciousness came back and made him giddy with impulses fighting against each other.

The realization that Araba Jesiwa was alive could have maddened

Densu with joy. There was a natural surge of all the juices of life in him eager for a celebration of that knowledge. But the promise of celebration was crushed under the heavy weight of what he had seen.

This was brutal knowledge. Araba Jesiwa was alive, but was this life? In what way was this her life different from death? Here was her form, but what did it contain? Consciousness? How then could everything about her—her body, her face, everything—have become so inert? The knowledge she was a person wrecked might have proved bearable. But the doubt in Densu's mind was heavier: was there a living being left in that wreckage?

His mind strained to give itself hope in a possible answer: yes, there is life, there is consciousness in the ruin here. But that hope itself ran straight into more desperation. Suppose, in spite of all the destruction of her frame, suppose Araba Jesiwa still had consciousness, what horrific suffering for a soul born to fly, this heavy, painful, earthbound impotence! Suppose she had consciousness and choice. Would she perhaps not prefer real death to this merciless survival?

The giddy swing brought Densu back to wild, raw pain. He found no more solace in elusive hopes. His mind stayed stunned. He saw Jesiwa, Ajoa, Damfo, saw the lamb again. But he did not try, he could not try to contact any of them. He did not understand anything.

On the way back he walked with Damfo, but knew nothing about where he had been, or where he was going. They came to the last little stream, and this time they walked up along the right bank till they were near the area of the traps. Even when Damfo pulled him hastily down among the bushes, Densu's mind could not tell him what might be happening. He simply obeyed the urgency in Damfo's motion, and stayed where he had knelt on the soft soil, hidden by the tall reeds and thick bushes on the bank.

'Don't move,' Damfo whispered to him, repeating the command until he was sure Densu had at last understood it. 'Don't make a noise. I'll be back.'

Damfo walked forward, stepping so carefully along the bank that his progress was noiseless. His figure had almost disappeared from sight when he came to a halt. There had been vague noises to which Densu had found it hard to give a meaning. Now they became clearer. They were human noises. The noises rose in a shout. There was the sound of relief in the voice, but it was so strained it sounded as if it were coming from a strangled throat.

'Cut me down!' the voice groaned.

Damfo's voice, much softer but quite distinct, said: 'Who are you?'

'Cut me down, I beg you!' the hoarse voice groaned again.

'Who are you?' Damfo repeated his calm question.

A huge cocoyam leaf was blocking Densu's view of the full scene. Now that his interest in what was going on in the world around him had been aroused, he pushed forward slowly, reached the big, fleshy leaf and bent it gradually till its thick soft spine was crushed near its base and it fell flat.

The hole the fallen leaf left was not large, the tangle of reeds and leaves ahead was thick. But through it Densu was able to see more of Damfo, and a little bit of the man with the strangled voice. The man was hanging head down. One of the traps had done its work.

'Set me free, I beg you!' the upside-down man pleaded. His voice was frantic.

Damfo's remained calm: 'Tell me who you are. Where are you from?'

'Esuano.'

'What do they call you?'

'Ackon.'

'What brings you here?'

'Set me free, I beg you.'

'What brings you here?' Damfo repeated

'I'm a hunter.'

'A strange hunter you are,' Damfo said. 'You bring no gun, not even a knife. What do you use for a weapon? Magic?'

The upside-down man laughed through his pain: 'Heh, heh, I told you a lie.'

'Tell me another,' Damfo said.

'This is the truth. I was looking for someone,' the upside-down man said.

'A relative, no doubt? Perhaps your mother?'

'Heh, heh, heh. Not my mother,' the upside-down man said. 'Don't make me laugh, heh, heh. In this heh, heh, position, it heh heh heh hurts so badly. Cut me down.'

'I'll help you down,' Damfo said clearly. 'But you'll have to tell me the truth first.'

'I've told you the truth.'

'You're not from Esuano,' Damfo said.

'Ah, that's true. I wasn't born there. But that's where I came from today.'

'Where do you come from?'

'Oguaa. Cape Coast, that's what we say these days.'

'What did you come this way for? Lost the road to Cape Coast?'

'Heh, I said I was looking for someone.'

'The relative.'

'Not a relative.'

'Who then?'

'A murderer.'

'A murderer? Is he your friend, this murderer?'

'No. Two murderers, in fact. There's been a murder at Esuano.'

'When?'

'Some time ago. But the murderers escaped.'

'You know them?'

'No.'

'How come you're searching for them?'

'I'm not the only one. There's a reward.'

'I don't believe you,' said Damfo.

'I've told you the truth, this time.'

'You were going empty-handed to catch two whole murderers?'

'Not to catch them, hehehe, I'm no fool. Just to find out where they're hiding. No man can catch them.'

'Are they wizards?'

'Perhaps that too. But I hear they're very strong and cunning, altogether dangerous. They're murderers, after all.'

'And what would you do after finding out where the murderers were hiding?'

'That wouldn't be my concern. It's the big man who wants to know.'

'Which big man?' Damfo asked.

'The one they call Ababio. He's the one offering money just to know.'

'Don't tell me you decided to risk your life in a strange forest just for the promise of money?'

'I'm telling you that, friend. Haven't you heard? Money is life,' the upside-down man said.

'Would Ababio then go after the murderers himself?' Damfo asked.

The upside-down man chuckled: 'That he wouldn't do. He doesn't have to be brave, and I hear he's no fool. He's gone and got thirty guns from Cape Coast. Thirty men are to go hunting for those two murderers, just as soon as they know where to look for them.'

'Who said they'd be here?'

'No one. People are trying all over the place. Some say they're dead. Drowned. But no one has seen their bodies. So others say they're still alive.'

'There are no murderers here,' Damfo said finally. 'We're all healers. We have our farms here. The traps we set are for thieves. If you come this way again, there won't be anyone to cut you down. You hear me?'

'I hear you,' the upside-down man said.

Damfo walked over to the trap sapling and pushed it till it bent enough to bring the upside-down man back down to earth.

'Free yourself,' he told the trapped man.

The man struggled with the trap knot on the liana. It took him some time, but finally he worked himself free. So great was his happiness he forgot to thank his liberator. He simply leapt into the stream, slipped and fell in the shallow water, picked his wet self up and was gone, slithering like a greased snake through the undergrowth.

It had happened fast. So fast that when it ended, it left the watching Densu with a vague sense it had not been real. Still, it had punctured the numb forgetfulness in which he'd been drifting after leaving the raised house and Araba Jesiwa's shattered, near-lifeless frame. Pain now came to him in small, sharp shocks, then went away again into the feelingless void. All the way back, he could not talk; he could not think about any one thing. Even when Damfo told him they were home again, he did not really know where he was and he was not capable of caring.

He did not eat, but he was hugely thirsty so he drank a great deal of water in one breathless draught. What followed was not sleep. It was a weird, uncontrolled consciousness in which a multitude of nightmare images crashed against each other in a mind-space grown too small to contain them all. Even singly, the images could have raised thoughts frightening to their thinker. Coming together so riotously, they devastated not only Densu's peace of mind but also, in the end, each other. Their result was not fear. It was exhaustion.

The morning following, Densu was weak but his mind was peaceful. Damfo brought him medicine and food and sat by him to talk to him.

'Eat well,' Damfo said. 'You shouldn't fall back into the illness.'

'I thought I was well,' Densu said.

'You are. But big surprises weaken your spirit.'

142

'I don't understand anything,' Densu said.

'There's time. We'll talk,' Damfo said. 'Whenever you're ready.'

'Now?'

'If you feel up to it.

'Will she recover?'

The look on Damfo's face was sombre. His eyes looked for a moment as if they were searching for a hiding place, but in a moment they discontinued the search and looked plainly at Densu: 'A healer always hopes,' he said.

'But the way she is, that's enough to kill all hope.'

'Not to kill all hope, no,' said Damfo. 'You didn't see her the day I found her.'

'Where?'

'There, where Appia was killed. On the old path leading this way from Esuano.'

'The day he was killed?'

Damfo nodded: 'There are nights when I don't sleep. It isn't that I'm worried. I think about something new—some herb whose healing spirit we are still unfamiliar with, some new way of setting broken bones, thoughts of that nature. Thinking like that gives me energy. When I get up the energy urges me, and I go searching. I don't always find something new, but occasionally I do. That morning was like that.

'I'd spent the day thinking about a plant I'd seen near Esuano. It's a green climber with fruit—little yellow and white berries. I'd never had time to stop and examine the plant, but I'd seen a bird pecking at the berries once. The bird's behaviour interested me. He was sucking juice from the berries, a peck at a time. After each peck he leapt upward, bright as a straight flame, and flew with a wild, unusual kind of energy. I remember wondering if the energy was something in the bird himself, or something he was absorbing from the plant.

'I forgot about the plant and the bird, but one day they came back to me and thinking of them made me restless all day long. I felt the urge to search for the plant, so that same night I went along the way towards Esuano. I must have travelled fast, because I came to the last ford before Esuano and still the dawn hadn't come. It was not far off, though.

'The coming morning seemed likely to be good. The air was clean and crisp. While waiting for light I walked in circles, large at first, so I could spiral in towards the area of my search when the sun rose. It was such a pleasant time, I practically forgot what I had come to do and was simply enjoying the sense of being alive on such a night, when the dawn came and surprised me. I stopped walking in circles and began to move directly towards the place where I'd seen the plant.

'That was when I heard the wail. It was a woman's voice, so powerful and urgent I was already moving towards it before I had actually thought to do so. I was still rather distant from the place itself. The voice had carried far, but it was in the direction I'd been aiming for.

'I had some difficulty finding her. After that great wail no other sound came, and I lost the exact direction. Even after I reached the place I could see no one at first. There was no sound. But something moved above me and I looked. There was Appia's body, hanging head down from a guava tree. Do you know what Jesiwa and Appia were to me?

'I did not try to cut Appia down. He was dead already, though not long dead. His neck had been slashed deeply on the right side. That wound was sufficient to kill him. The blood was still coming from it, but thickly, in remnant drops.

'I could see nobody else. But I had heard a woman's voice, and now I'd seen Appia's body I knew the voice had been Araba Jesiwa's voice. Yet she was nowhere to be seen.

'Then I looked beneath the hanging corpse and I saw signs. Crushed grass, dew shaken from leaves, the earth badly bruised in spots. There had been a struggle. There were things scattered around: food, new cloth, some jewels. They'd fallen from a basket which itself had been trampled on.

'I followed the signs. Where they ended I found Araba Jesiwa. I couldn't tell whether she was dead or alive. I reached down trying to feel her breath on the back of my hand. I felt nothing. But finally I bent low enough to bring my eyelids under her nostrils. Then I thought I could feel breath. That gave me hope.

'I could see no sign of the attacker, whoever he was. First I thought of taking Jesiwa with me, carrying her back here. But I was greatly afraid the attacker might return. If he did, and did not find Jesiwa, he would look for her. Would he be alone or would he have helpers? Carrying her, I could only have walked slowly. I thought it better to hide her.

'I knew the area well. It wasn't the first or the tenth time I had come walking there. There are large trees, many of them the odan type, with large hollow boles, in the area.

'I chose one tree suitable for the purpose I had in mind. It was hollow, with ample space inside the bole. But from the outside it looked as solid as any other tree. The entrance to it was overgrown with bushes, and imperceptible to any passer-by. That is where I hid Araba Jesiwa. You might pass by that place thirty times and never suspect there was space where I hid her.

'Something else I hadn't known. As I raised her, all her limbs hung loose. The bones in them had been broken. That gave my own body unbearable pain from just thinking how painful it must have been for her, and I was thankful she had lost consciousness.

'I came back as fast as I could. I needed help, first to put together a light bed to strap Jesiwa firmly on, and then to share the load in bringing her back here. Ajoa and two healers who were here at the time, Kwao Tweneboa and Kojo Mensa, helped me. Another night had almost turned morning when we took her from the hiding place for the trip back here. She was conscious again when we found her, but I had brought some medicine to give her, so she went to sleep again all the way back. The next day we moved her to the raised house where you saw her. It's the best place. Of the two smaller houses, one covers a well, and the other is for keeping food and charcoal.'

'But can she recover?' Densu repeated his despairing question.

'We're setting her bones,' Damfo said. 'They will set, though they were broken badly in many places. It'll take time, but they'll set.'

'It's not just her bones, though,' Densu said.

'No,' Damfo agreed. 'It's her spirit. To see her son killed before her eyes, to know the killer, but to be unable to do anything, even to speak . . .'

'When you saw Appia's body, you say it was hanging upside down?' Densu asked.

'Yes, upside down,' Damfo answered. 'A trap had caught his right leg.'

'He was hanging by his wrists when we went and found him,' said Densu.

'Someone tied him that way then, after he died.'

'Were his eyes cut out?' Densu asked.

'No.'

'Had any bits of muscle been removed from his arms?'

'No.'

'Or from his legs?'

'He was whole when I saw him,' said Damfo, 'except for that one wound in his neck. That's the thing that killed him. It was huge. It bled him to death.'

'The things—the gold jewels, the cloth—did you leave them there?'

'I didn't touch them,' Damfo said. 'Why, didn't people find them there when they took down Appia's body?'

Densu shook his head. He sat there listening to Damfo, his head nodding gently, involuntarily, with increasing understanding. Again he heard Ababio's voice offering him a sweet future filled with riches and the honours powerful men could give, then turning the promises to threats when he had refused to be enchanted. He thought of the trial with the drug of death, misnamed the drug of truth. He thought of his escape from death, of the friend who helped him, and of the death he needed to forget.

'We'll have to move sooner than planned,' Damfo said. 'That upside-down fool said he wasn't the only one. Ababio's men will be coming this way to search for their murderers soon.'

'Where shall we go?' Densu asked.

'Praso,' Damfo answered. 'There's work waiting for us there.'

'You've decided to help Asamoa Nkwanta then?'

'I've decided to look into the matter more closely,' said Damfo.

'Will it be possible to heal him?'

'A good question,' Damfo said. 'I don't know the answer. But the other healers think I can heal him, and that I should.'

'Why should?'

'Some see the future in Asamoa Nkwanta. They believe the man could be the start of something new among our people, just as men like Okomfo Anoche have started new things but in a different way. Something new, and good.'

'You agree?'

'I don't know,' mused Damfo. 'I'm willing to find out.'

'But you seem eager to go to Praso.'

'The decision was taken by all of us healers through discussion. We work together. Even if I disagree with a decision, once we've made it I work with it. And I don't disagree with this particular decision. I just don't know how things will go. I'm willing to try.'

6 The Voyage on the Sacred River

The preparations for the move to Praso went smoothly, swiftly. The trip would be by water, up the river Pra. It would be necessary to take Araba Jesiwa along, and travelling over water would be a way to keep her healing bones in place within their casts. It would be a slow way, but the best. Bamboo poles were cut to make a bed on which Araba Jesiwa could be held securely. It was narrow enough to fit into the bottom of the canoe to be used. In a few days the preparations were complete. The start was set for the night following a day of rest.

The night was not starless, but it was dark enough. Two other healers went with Damfo and Densu to take Araba Jesiwa down to the canoe. She had been tied securely to the frame of her bed, so that when the bed was tilted for lowering down to the ground from the raised house she did not fall or shift from it. The bed-frame was tied fast to the bottom of the canoe, together with all the clothing and covering necessary for the trip.

Ajoa brought the food she had prepared to the canoe. She and Densu sat in front, at the foot of Araba Jesiwa's bed, each with an oar. Damfo sat at the end, near Araba Jesiwa's head. His was the long steering pole. The canoe slipped down the side stream cutting through the eastern forest, moving fast and smoothly with the current. Soon it reached the Nsu Nyin.

Esuano slid by, just a few flickering lights falling back in the distance. The Nsu Nyin broadened and flowed a little faster, turned left below Esuano, grew turbulent at the meeting with the Nsu Ber, then quietened down towards the confluence with the great river Pra. Damfo steered the canoe away from the bank, standing upright to get greater leverage. In front, Ajoa and Densu added speed, driving the water behind them.

At the confluence with the Pra the canoe lost direction. The current from the Nsu Nyin shot it forward past the middle of the Pra. Then it was turned upstream by an eddy, turned sideways and carried back down the left bank to the turbulence at the mouth of the Nsu Nyin again. The canoe was sent through the circle once more before Damfo steadied it and steered it between the river's middle and the left bank, going up. The work was harder now, but the sun showed signs of rising, and it would soon be possible to see clearly up the big river.

Damfo steered the canoe away from the middle of the river—the pole did not push against firm ground there. He steered it along the left bank. The canoe went right, following the turn in the river-bed. The current grew stronger near the left bank, forcing the canoe to stall till Damfo turned it into the centre and leftward, almost all the way to the right bank. There the current was calmer.

In a while the canoe was pointing in the direction of the rising sun. Gentle light, its colours not yet overwhelmed by the white glare of full day, came through a basket of openings in the trees on the left bank. Again the river turned away from the sun, northward, past a small stream whose mouth turned contrary to the Pra's flow at the confluence.

The canoe went up the valley in a half-circle past the foot of a long, low hill rising to the right, past three swift, boisterous little rivers emptying into the Pra, when Damfo pushed it to a gentle halt on the left side. Upriver the water changed colour. It was not a sheet of brown water any more, but a boiling turbulence flecked with froth, throwing up white spray at irregular intervals into the broadening light.

'Rocks ahead,' Damfo said. 'We'll have to get off and carry the canoe. It's only a short walk round.'

It was slow work bringing the canoe to the bank, untying Araba Jesiwa, carrying her while Ajoa carried the things from the canoe, then coming back to lift the canoe to the far side of the rocks, but it was done.

After the rocks had been skirted the left side was too shallow and rocky to take the canoe. But not far ahead, a stream making its way into the Pra gave easier access. Once back on the Pra, Damfo turned the canoe left and upriver again. More rivers ran towards the Pra, the swifter ones coming from the right. Ahead lay more spray and spume, but this time the thing troubling the water was an island, not rocks. The more peaceful channel lay to the right. Damfo guided the canoe into it, past the island, steadily upstream. Along the rib of this first island there appeared a second, smaller one. Now it was the channel between the two islands Damfo chose, a gently curved opening which turned near the middle into a cool, dark tunnel covered by leaves. Then the larger island was alone again, lying to the left. The canoe went up leftward, past two more islands close against each other, past another, and left a pair of close twins on the right. Two more small islands slid by. For a while there were no more visible.

Slowly the canoe persevered against the river, up, then right till the sun shone in the voyagers' eyes, then left again and up, keeping the sun on the right. The heat rose. Ajoa raised a cloth cover above Araba Jesiwa to keep her cool. Another great bend to the right, and the sun came overhead. Across on the river's left bank higher land brought an overhang of shadowy bushes to the water, but the tired travellers could not take the cool invitation: the current there was fierce, and the voyage had merely begun.

Damfo looked out at the passing land sliding by and named places he could recognize. Around the next bend came a new island. Beyond the island rose the sound of troubled water. This time the canoe was brought to a rest on the left bank: a wild stream too near the rapids made landing on the right bank impossible.

'Let's rest a while,' Damfo said.

Past the rapids the travellers rested the canoe in the water in the shade of a great tree to which they tied it, and lay down to relax on dry grass on the bank. Ajoa poured out some of Araba Jesiwa's liquid food for her. As usual, she absorbed only a little quantity of it. The other three ate, and drank water taken from the river. They rested just long enough to let the food descend, then they resumed the work of going against the river. Two islands, twins again, then a whole cluster around one big one. The heat grew intense. Under the awning raised by Ajoa the silent Jesiwa's face ran with sweat.

A large branch of driftwood swept down so fast there was no time to avoid a collision. The canoe shook but stayed afloat. The impact turned it half left, but that was all. The branch raced off down the river. Damfo tried to coax the canoe along the right hand channel, but there the current was too strong. He turned the canoe left. Before long it had reached another barrier of rocks stretching from the island to the right bank. Around a bend in the river more foam from yet another barrier could be seen.

'We'll have to carry it beyond that,' Damfo said.

A spit of land jutted into the river at that point. The travellers carried the canoe over it and found an easy place beyond the second cataract from which to get it back into the river. On the opposite side the bank was steep, coming to the river in a small cliff. Now it became impossible to keep count of the islands passed. A loop up and to the right, and the afternoon sun came against the travellers' backs. At first the heat was pleasant, but along this stretch the river valley went west to east for longer than at any other point before, and the heat grew intense. Sweat ran down the small of Densu's back in a warm rill, and the back of his neck burned.

Then the canoe turned left, and the heat and brilliance were left behind. Here the river's course was dark, and the air was abruptly cool as if the trees lining the river had reached over from both banks and formed a tunnel with their leaves.

Evening on the river was cool. At the front end of the canoe, Ajoa and Densu both rowed with a vigour that made Damfo ask them if it was just the air's freshness that had so energized them.

'We have a week of rowing ahead of us,' he said. 'Why be in a hurry to exhaust yourselves?'

The two rowed more gently and the canoe's forward glide became hardly perceptible. Once it drifted too close to land. A swarm of mosquitos burst upon the travellers, and stayed with them till Damfo called for more speed and the frail insects fell behind with the breeze.

Night came. Ajoa suggested they take turns sleeping, one rowing, another steering while the third lay beside Araba Jesiwa. Ajoa herself was the first to sleep. She covered Jesiwa with a blanket to keep her warm. Then she lay down beside her. Soon her breath could be heard in the night's silence, even, calm, and deep.

For the remainder of the night neither Damfo nor Densu spoke. Nothing broke the silence on the river. Ajoa woke after a deep sleep and asked who wanted to be relieved. Densu continued at the oar, Damfo slept, and Ajoa steered. The morning started with a cold wind. It came from the north, a dry wind. Damfo woke then, and Densu took his place. Before the sun was up, he was lost in long-deferred sleep.

It did not rain. For eight days the canoe climbed gradually north against the current of the Pra. It was a slow voyage but the river was calm and peaceful, and even the difficult work of lifting the canoe and the shattered woman, Araba Jesiwa, past rapids gave the travellers a welcome change from the dreamlike placidity of open stretches of water. On the afternoon of the eighth day the canoe turned east after the last great bend in the river.

'That last village on the left was Awisam. These are the last rapids we'll have to go round,' Ajoa called out to Densu from the front.

There were more rapids just ahead, but a channel to the left gave the canoe free passage and the voyage stayed smooth and easy. Ajoa pointed out villages as they crawled by the canoe. Koshia, Hwidiem, Domeabra, Bremang, Nyame Bechere; then the two Praso's, Assen Praso on the left bank, Adanse Praso on the right.

Not far beyond Adanse Praso a small stream joined the Pra, coming from around a hill that lay between it and the big river. Damfo was again at the rear. He steered the canoe up the little stream. The stream spread out into a pond a short way off the Pra. On the bank of the pond closest to the foot of the hill there was a rough sort of beach. Damfo guided the canoe there and gave it a last strong push that grounded it gently. He untied Araba Jesiwa's bed. Densu took one end of it, and followed Damfo along a path leading up the hillside. Ajoa, carrying her bundle, overtook them when the path broadened out, and led the way up the gentle slope. The slope rose more steeply, took a right turn as if it would double back upon itself, straightened out again, and then there was a clearing on the side of the hill with seven houses making a sort of circle on the edges of a central open space.

Ajoa stopped at the third house on the right. She put down her load, opened the door and stood just outside the doorway, looking towards the other houses. Damfo motioned to Densu to set Araba Jesiwa down when they came to the door. He went into the house, and Densu followed him. It was dark, but the air within the house was fresh as if someone had recently been there to air it out.

There were two beds, spaced far apart, one on each side of the big room.

'We don't have enough beds,' Densu said.

'Jesiwa and Ajoa won't be staying here,' Damfo said.

Densu was about to ask Damfo where they would go, but an excited shout outside the door broke the beginning conversation. Something as dynamic as a wind blew into the room and did not stop till it reached Damfo and practically knocked him over.

'Ah, Damfo,' said the voice of the wind, 'it's been so long since you went. Welcome.'

The wind was a woman. In the gathering darkness her face was indistinct, but she had a small, neat body. She wore a simple piece of cloth tied primly above her breasts, and though her voice said she was an old woman, her motions were quick, like a girl's. Ajoa had followed her, and stood just within the doorway.

'Hold me, my brother,' the old woman said, 'hold me well. You did well to come. I was afraid you wouldn't.'

'Ei, Nyaneba,' said Damfo, 'you grow stronger every time I see you.'

'And Ajoa is a woman already,' Nyaneba said, turning to look at her. 'Come here, let me see you.' Ajoa went to her. The old woman looked at her, then shook her head. 'My eyes grow weaker all the time.'

'It's not your eyes, Nyaneba,' Damfo said. 'It's getting dark.'

'I don't know the young man,' Nyaneba said. 'Who is he?'

'They call him Densu,' said Ajoa.

'I hear a smile in your voice, Ajoa,' Nyaneba said.

Unable to find an answer to that, Ajoa ran outside, doing her best to muffle her laughter.

'I see where the drizzle slants,' Nyaneba said. 'Densu, where are you from?'

'Esuano,' Densu answered.

'That is the son born to Maanan and Kwame Ansa,' Damfo said.

A gasp escaped Nyaneba, but she controlled herself. She sat silent a space, then, letting the words out as if she did not trust her voice, she said to Densu: 'Come and sit by me, here.'

She went over to the bed on the right, and sat on it. Densu sat beside her.

'And has he come for healing?' she asked.

'He has long wished to be a healer,' Damfo answered.

'Ao!' the woman's voice shook. 'Sometimes the world is so good. Maanan's son, Kwame Ansa's son, and he would want to be a healer.'

Something in the words brought a complex feeling of sadness to Densu. It was a feeling made up of regret that things that should have been were not, but the nature of the things themselves whose absence so saddened him escaped Densu.

'Are Tweneboa and Mensa here?' Damfo asked Nyaneba.

'They've gone to Kumase to get Asamoa Nkwanta. They should be back any day. I thought they'd be here before you.'

The old woman began to ask Damfo for news of Esuano, but suddenly she caught herself. 'What a woman I've become, to forget to give travellers water and food!' She rose immediately and rushed outside, calling out: 'Ajoa, Ajoa my child!'

Araba Jesiwa was taken to Nyaneba's house. There she was fed and given a mild potion to help her rest. Nyaneba gave Damfo and Densu warm water to wash with, and after they had eaten at her house she walked back with them and wished them sound sleep.

The day following, the travellers spent resting. Their bones and muscles, now that the constant exercise of the last eight days was over, felt raw and sore, and Nyaneba cared for all of them like a mother for her children. The second day was also a day of tiredness. But on the third day each felt renewed and strong.

Densu went with Nyaneba to the top of the hill. There was farming work to do—a little hoeing—and Densu finished it before the morning had had time to turn warm. He sat down on a bald rock on the west side of the hill, and looked down at the scene below.

Below him was the immediate greenness of the forest, covering the earth with its quiet, unending softness. Into this the broad line of the river cut at the foot of the hill. The river flowed almost straight, past the twin villages called Praso and nearly the same distance beyond, then it disappeared under the eternal green roof of the forest raised above it. Far, far in the distance, to the left, an occasional bright glint gave a sign that the river flowed there, searching its way south.

Nyaneba bade him good-bye and went down the path home, but he did not feel like stirring. He sat there lost in the peace of the scene, and was aware of nothing beside the great beauty of the sky and the leaves and the string of water below him, till something cold and sly crawling over his right ear made him start.

'You were asleep to the world,' said Ajoa. She stood there behind him, pulling a single blade of grass slowly across her tongue, wetting it.

'How long have you been here?' he asked.

'Ages,' she said. 'But you didn't see me.'

'You hid behind me all the time,' he said.

'I wanted to find out,' she said.

'Find what out?

'They say a person can sense your presence, even if he doesn't see you. But he has to like you truly.'

'Will you come and sit by me?' Densu asked her.

'Will you let me?' she asked him.

'You always ran from me. Do you remember?'

'That was so long ago,' she said.

'You know, the fruit I planted for you, it never grew.'

'That was a sign,' she said.

'Of what?'

'That you didn't really like me even then.'

He was quiet, then he said: 'What would be a sign of love?'

'That is difficult,' she said. 'The lover must go to the land of the dead and fight three battles against three monsters. If he survives and comes back he must give the tails of the three monsters to the beloved. That is the sign.'

'Terrible,' he said. The river drew his eyes again. She wet her blade of grass and tickled the back of his neck with it. He tried to catch her hand, but she was already up and beyond his reach. He sat quiet as a cat, then lunged backward aiming to catch her legs. But though he touched a foot she eluded him and stood just out of reach. He got up and saw her flying away from him.

She ran fast and delightedly, but her speed was slower than his, and his delight when he reached her over the crest of the hill was infinite. She was running down a slope, and the grassy path she was following turned too sharply for her speed. She would have fallen flat on the grass but her pursuer had caught her, and pulling her against her own momentum softened her collapse into a gentle fall that brought her rolling on top of him.

She did not try to escape him any more. She did not resist him. She only reached out to touch the grass beside him, seeking to take her weight off him. He understood her movement, though she had said nothing.

'Your weight isn't a burden,' he said, his hold becoming firmer. Lying beneath her, he looked at her face against the sky, and he had no desire at all to stop his desire for her.

She did not resist him. He touched her chin, her neck. He let a finger find its own space between her collarbone and her neck, then the hand came down, touched a nipple and found it hard with the desire she was not hiding. As if they had passed this way before, she parted her cloth and took off the band joining her beads, but she could not touch him or even look at him any more.

He turned her so that she lay on her side, then more on her back than on her side. Her cloth was below them, adding its thin softness to the comfort of the grass. He took his own cloth and covered both of them with it, and then he groped between her thighs and let her wetness guide him into her. He slid in gently, and she made room for him till she could make no more.

He looked at her again. Her eyes were closed, and a vein in her forehead stood out so strongly he could almost see it beat. He said nothing to her, but passed a hand behind her so that her back was cradled. He felt her unopened, and hesitated. Then he looked at her face and saw not fear but a determination to go beyond fear, and he let his desire answer hers. Tears came, but she did not cry out, did not

154

give any sign that the pain had touched her joy, or even come close to it. She was the reluctant one when the time came for separation.

'The pain is now,' she said when he was out of her. She was laughing through her tears.

PART FIVE

1   Memories

The river, the forest, and the sky all drew Densu to the top of the hill with a power he had no need to fight against. He asked Nyaneba if there was any more work he could do on the farm up there. But at that time there was nothing really, and Nyaneba almost scolded him when he asked once more if there was anything to do.

'Densu,' she said at the end of her patience, 'the animal that does not rest gets so angry and unhappy it spreads destruction wherever it goes. A human being works fully when there is work to do. A human being rests fully when the season comes for rest.'

Densu did not importune Nyaneba about work any more. Almost every day he climbed up the hill and sat on the warm rock looking at the river below, and the forest above the river, and the sky above both the river and the forest canopy. From where he sat, the river looked thin and completely still. Seeing it in the distance, he had to think before it became in his mind a moving thing, not a dead, flat sheet shining passively in the sun.

So he knew the river's motion in his mind though his eyes perceived only stillness. Once the motion was clear in his mind, it did not stop. It flowed in a thoughtstream that could take him from the present all the way back to moments so far in the past his remembrance surprised him.

Some of the memories he would never understand. He had known a great happiness during a time about which he remembered nothing but the feeling itself. This remembrance took his feelings back to a time when he was helpless but feared nothing because there was a presence around him that made fear a stranger. He had told people about this feeling and always left them puzzled. They said he could never have had such a time, because his father died before he was born, and his mother also died in childbirth. Yet the feeling was part of his memory, and it was so strong he knew it was true in spite of what others saw and said. And often, as he grew up, he had found himself searching, sometimes in anguish, sometimes with sheer desire, for a return of that time and of the feeling.

Yet life at times became an argument saying that presence, that wholeness he remembered so mysteriously and sought so naturally, would never be possible in the world outside the wishing mind. He had known people at Esuano, and begun to see life clearly, but most of the people and most of the life he saw led his mind far astray from the peace he sought.

This too he remembered: in his twelfth year something strange had happened. A white man had arrived at Eusano. He was not an official from the castle at Cape Coast, so people were astonished to see him there at all. They were more astonished when he told them he was a trader on the coast but had grown tired of trading. He said he wanted rest. People shunned him. They were afraid of him, and they had reason enough. He lived as if he and water had quarrelled bitterly. He did not like food. His sustenance was drink, and when he was really hungry he would look for fruit, like a child at play, and that would be his meal.

Densu went to him and sat watching him. He still went to him long after the other children had fled in fear. One day the strange white man stopped singing his drunken songs, pointed to his heart and shouted something:

'Collins!' He repeated the name, stabbing his breast repeatedly with an extended finger.

When he stopped Densu pointed to himself and said: 'Densu.'

The white man roared happily. He seemed immensely pleased with himself that Densu had understood him, as if he had actually taught him to speak. He began a game of names, teaching Densu English words and learning Akan words from him.

In less than a month the game of words changed. It became uneven. Densu went to Collins whenever he had time. The idea of learning the strange language of the white man excited him, and he worked hard to make free time for his new passion. Collins taught him willingly. He seemed to live for the hours when the eager boy came to talk to him. But Collins stopped asking Densu the Akan names of things. With an eagerness answering the boy's he taught him as fast as he could absorb new knowledge, and his yellow-red face exploded with joy when Densu began at last to speak to him in his own language. The solitary white man then gave up all pretence of wishing to learn

Akan. He was happy enough to have a person to talk to, and teaching Densu to read and write gave him something to do when he was not drinking.

Densu asked him why he had left Cape Coast to come to Esuano. The white man's answer was quite incomprehensible to him. All he understood was that the mention of Cape Coast made the white man violently angry. Once, later, Densu asked him why he did not go home. The drunken white man wept tears at the question. From then on Densu did not ask him any such questions again. In his first months at Esuano the white man Collins sold a few things to the few who had any money. But after his third month at Esuano he sold nothing. Knowing adults predicted he would die in a matter of weeks. They were disappointed and embarrassed when in spite of the way he drank and starved himself, he remained noisily alive.

Collins lived two years at Esuano. When he died it was not from drink or starvation. He died the week another white man, this one a priest called Warner, came to Esuano. The priest Warner was a heavy, red-faced white man. He was at the palace, a guest of Ababio, for most of the first week he was at Esuano. On his fifth day he went to Collins and passers-by heard the two talking loudly all that evening. The next day the priest again spent with his host Ababio at the palace. As for Collins he was neither seen nor heard that whole day. Densu went looking for him, but found his door closed and his windows shuttered. He heard no noise, so he went away.

It was the following day that Densu found Collins's body. He had never known his strange friend to stay in all day like that, so he stood outside the door and called his name. There was no answer. He touched the door and it opened. He saw a body bent double in a chair. In the light coming from the doorway he saw the left side of his friend's face was missing. A long pistol lay between the door and the corpse.

The new white man, the priest Warner, surprised everyone by moving into Collins's house straight after the burial. Ababio sent Densu to him, and he said he wanted Densu to teach him Akan. Densu did not like the priest but he agreed to teach him Akan, the better to continue learning English. His friend's death saddened him, but when he talked to the priest about Collins his answer was unvarying, gruff, and brutal: 'Serves him right!'

Densu taught the white priest for three months, then stopped going near him at all. The priest had a book of stories he wanted to translate into Akan. Densu read the stories, but when he told the white priest how interesting he found them, the priest exploded at him:

'They aren't stories!' he shouted. 'The Bible is the truth!'

Soon enough Densu understood the white priest saw him not as a teacher teaching him a language, but as a servant whose duty it was first to help him translate the Bible stories into Akan, and then to help him persuade people that the stories were the truth. One day he told Densu he expected him to work for him the rest of his life.

Densu did not go to the white priest after that. Ababio tried to make him go, but he refused. Something in the way the white priest had tried to use him reminded him strongly of everything he disliked about Ababio and he found himself avoiding both the priest and Ababio, and seeking conversations with Araba Jesiwa more and more often.

There were also good memories, but now even those made him sad. The memories of the friendly, playful but always rather mysterious Anan, now gone forever, upset him with regret so that his mind fled from them. Memories of days spent with Araba Jesiwa and the prince Appia brought a vanishing taste of joy, then the crushing hopelessness of harsh knowledge.

There was hope in the future. The presence of Ajoa, such a total acceptance of his own, drew his mind forward from the deadnesses of the past. And there was Damfo. Damfo was always opening his mind to a future that went far beyond single lifetimes, or even the lifetimes of single tribes and nations. The vision was terrifying even in its hopefulness, but with greater understanding the terror of his own impotence dissolved in the knowledge that if he worked well he would be part of the preparation for generations which would inherit the potency that should bring people back together.

And the woman Nyaneba, he did not know her but her presence was always good, and she gave his belief in healing work even greater strength. She had told him not to be afraid of rest, and heeding her he had sat on the hill, sometimes alone, sometimes with Ajoa, looking again and again at the flow of his life, drawing closer to its meaning. Her advice had been good.

2 The Sacrifice of Victims

One Monday morning Densu had gone again to sit on his favourite rock. The distant view of the river had absorbed his thoughts, and he was lost to the present. A movement across the river caught the periphery of his vision, but he did not bring his mind to it and it passed. Then he heard a sound he could not ignore. It was a sound fit to wake ancestral corpses from the sleep of ages. A terrified cry, impossibly loud and prolonged, it was eloquent of a victim's understanding that all hope had fled. Carried on the clear air across the river, the eerie sound destroyed the morning's calm.

Densu, roused by the sheer power of the sound, sat still and listened. He could not, at first, tell from which part of the other bank the cry had come because it filled the entire sky so that the air, which had before been quite motionless, sounded suddenly violently alive.

The first cry died, but hard after it came another, longer, even more desperate wail. By its sound it must have come from a different throat. But its message was the same final loss of hope, only more intense. More sounds followed. The loudest were more victim cries of despair, but there were other sounds: the noises of an excited crowd of men approaching the river. The first to come into view were the victims.

They were on the other bank, just across from the cliff. They were bound, each of them. Even from a distance Densu could see the ropes not only tied their arms together but also bound them each to a separate, heavy stone. A small crowd of men, led by three priests in white, their faces painted with death's white clay, accompanied the victims. There were two drummers beating drums carried on the heads of drumboys, drumming a slow death call to the spirit of the sacred river Pra. Densu heard the message and knew its meaning.

It was a message pleading shame and guilt. The drummers, on behalf of the king of Assen Nyankomase, accepted the guilt of people who had neglected their gods in happier times. Now, surprised by danger, they had come to ask forgiveness. Yes, the sacred river had sent its waters and the waters of its children to bring life to the lands and people of Assen. The Subin, the Kunkum, the Brupae, the Fomso, all the children of the Pra, had brought their blessings year after year. The people of the bank had consumed these blessings and forgotten to give fit offerings of thanks to the river. Now the people, awakened by impending disaster from their forgetfulness, had come with gifts, multiple gifts. The drums asked the river to believe the people's promises of increased respect and mindfulness in future. They asked the river not to turn its long-nursed anger against the neglectful worshippers. Instead, they asked the river to raise its anger against the Asante army which, the drummers said, would be coming soon to cross the river, bringing death to the river's worshippers. The drums alternated, repeating their prayers. After each prayer the refrain was beaten:

Accept, O Bosom Pra,
Accept this offering, sacred river,
Accept, accept.

A new victim was pushed to the edge of the water with each such prayer. At the words 'Accept, accept', strong men cast him down forcibly and a sword slashed his throat. His blood poured out to redden the river. His weighted body was flung into the water where, dragged down by its heavy stone, it disappeared from sight. Densu found himself standing tensely upright.

A desperate urge, less thought than feeling, agitated Densu. He wished he had the power to snatch the victims from their executioners. He looked at the river beneath, and the urge dissolved into a question. Should he also leap into death's jaws, what would that mean to the victims? The urge disappeared. In its place a heavy weariness possessed Densu, and he had to sit down, so oppressive did the air itself feel on his body. He could not look away.

There were three women among the victims awaiting death. Of the male victims nine were still left after five long hopeless wails had ended in death. One of the priests, holding in his left hand a whisk and in his right a bottle from which he poured a libation to the river, kept giving instructions to the drummers and the executioners also. Behind the crowd at the river's edge sat a king under his umbrella, surrounded by his courtiers. To him the priest with the whisk went after each new death. But whatever message the priest carried, Densu could not hear it.

Densu could not remember why he had come to the cliff. He wondered why he had been so full of energy and the joy of being alive this morning. The sight of the river's surface brought a feeling of nausea into his mouth. The way back seemed so long now. The taste of the day had turned bitter. Densu knew the impotence of the living soul when faced with triumphant death and the knowledge made him weak. In his mind there was a powerful image: death looming hugely over life. He turned to go back.

When he arrived at the clearing he stood outside in the sun like a man with a fever coming on. Damfo came to him and asked him several questions. But if he heard the words, he could not understand their meaning. Ajoa came to speak to him, but he did not understand her either. He was quiet the rest of the day. Night was one long night-mare repeating itself. It always began with him playing happily with a friend of his youth, Anan. It always ended in death by drowning or murder along the banks of rivers.

The next day Damfo took him to a distant farm where in between mounds of yam, rare herbs had been planted the last time before Damfo had returned to the forest east of Esuano. There was work to do clearing weeds and firming mounds. Densu worked like a man possessed by all the demons of work. When he returned he was exhausted enough to sleep that night. In spite of everything, he couldn't resist the impulse to return to the hill. The sight of the river brought pain. But, paradoxically, it seemed the only thing capable of easing that pain.

That night harsh, ominous noises broke the peace of the air. Morning came, a Wednesday morning, and the idea occurred to Densu to go down to the river to see about the safety of the canoe.

'Where are you going?' Damfo asked him, looking steadily into his eyes.

'To the river, Damfo,' he answered.

'You aren't well, Densu,' Damfo said. 'Try and rest today.'

'I don't feel bad,' Densu said, a bit distantly.

'The unwell don't always feel bad,' Damfo said. 'I wouldn't go so far if I were you, not today.'

But Densu continued, and Damfo did not follow him with mere arguments. He did not climb up to the cliff-top this time. Instead, he took the same path they had used on the day they had arrived, and he walked slowly. When he had crossed the long hind-spur of the hill and was descending the gentle slope which took the path to the river, he saw the cause of the voices he had heard in the night.

On the Pra's northern bank a great stream of people were now gathering. It was plain they came from Asante and were bent on war. They spread along the bank of the Pra, warriors in their thousands upon thousands. Some groups trailed their women, their attendants, their slaves. The multitude seemed altogether irresistible, yet at the river's edge this mighty stream of people had been forced to halt. For all their war-like, impetuous haste, the army had to obey the river. From where Densu was, he could see clearly enough how eagerly the soldiers wanted to cross over to the far bank. He left the path, found a fallen tree and sat down on it, because he was beginning to feel tired. He could hear the morning breeze hoarsened with the sounds of warriors in a hurry.

Some of the warriors broke off from the main mass and searched all along the bank. They were looking for canoes to cross over in. A few were found, but they were tiny things built to carry one person only and his load. At most each of these frail canoes might have carried four men squeezed together. But then any sudden movement would have meant drowning for all four. The small canoes were left aside, and the search continued.

Some of the searchers beat the bushes coming close to the spot where Densu was sitting. The canoe was not far. The searchers went out of sight. In a little while a great happy shout went up from where they had disappeared. In a moment they came again into view, heading back towards the main mass. They had found the healers' canoe and, happy at the discovery, eight strong men had raised it high above their heads and were running with it towards their friends.

A great crowd of warriors gathered round the canoe when its carriers set it down on the bank. Whether because its construction attracted their curiosity, or because the interest in crossing the river made the canoe an object of special attention, it seemed everyone was trying to reach it all at once. The hum of interest with which the crowd had greeted the discovery of the canoe was in time replaced by a more definite noise, a rising shout of wonder. It seemed as if the crowd was stretching itself, a part of it extending into the water. Densu wondered what was happening. In a moment he knew.

They had pushed the canoe afloat, and two men were brandishing the oars above their heads. The canoe seemed immobile. No part of its surface was actually visible: the warriors had clambered on to it in such hasty numbers that there was no empty space on any part of it. It stood uncertainly there near the bank. Then several people on land stooped and gave it a strong awkward push. It moved heavily into the stream. An excited shout arose from those on the bank. The canoe moved only a short distance and stopped. It was clear it had become stuck. No one seemed to have any idea what to do.

'Get down!' shouted a man from the bank.

Those in the canoe looked inclined to obey, but they hesitated at the idea of jumping into the water. One of them shouted back, almost pleading: 'We shall die.'

The frank admission of fear was not greeted with laughter. All had grown uncannily quiet. The speaker on the bank said: 'You will not die. The bottom is shallow. The thing cannot move at all if you stay on it.'

When the wisdom of this statement was accepted those nearest the bank, pushed eagerly by those farthest, started the descent into the water. The first to accomplish it waded gratefully to land. Their safety gave the remainder courage so that instead of the slow, cautious descent of their comrades, they leapt with excessive boldness into the water as if to tell the world they never had had any fear at all of the river. Here and there some of those who had remained on the bank could be seen shaking hands with those who had been the few steps into the water and back, as if they were brave heroes returning from dangerous journeys into the unknown.

In their haste to disembark, all had abandoned the canoe to the river. The pressure of the large number of people on the shore end had caused the other end of the canoe to rise a little distance out of the water. When the last man leaped into the river, the raised end dropped back all the way into the water. The motion was not violent, but it had enough force to loosen the stuck part of the canoe. Thus freed from silt, it commenced to float gently towards the middle of the river, going downstream.

One brave warrior dashed into the water after it. He was rather short, for all his courage, so the water rose up to his armpits before he had even gone within touching distance of the playfully bobbing canoe.

'Come back!' shouted a female voice, with an urgency that could not have been greater had she been calling a lover back from the underworld. The fellow was brave but he was also wise: he heeded the advice of the female voice and regained the bank. The canoe turned in a tight circle upon the water, gathered speed, then settled into a steady drift westward, down the river. In time it disappeared round a bend.

The men on the bank searched anew for canoes. A group searching farther from the water than others raised a shout for help. More of the warriors went to assist them and after some exertion three canoes, longer than the first, were brought to the bank. These were strange river craft. How long these hollowed tree trunks had lain useless on the humid soil would have been hard to tell. Two of the three, after they had been brought in triumph to the river, had to have their bottoms scraped free of dirt and vegetation. Two huge lumps of red earth—termite mud— fell from them. Whoever had left the canoes in that state must have been in flight, or completely ignorant of river craft: they had been left sitting directly on the earth. Termites had built their homes between the soil and the canoe bottoms, merging earth and wood.

From one of the canoes a piece fell right out of the bottom, leaving a hole bigger than a grown man's fist. It seemed as if some attempt was made to repair the damage, but the attempt was over fast, too fast. Now the war captains, impatient for the crossing to begin, taunted those who stood looking with fear and hesitation at the canoes, and called them cowards. The taunts had a sharp effect. The three canoes were bravely launched upon the water. The boldest warriors, making a point of being among the first, waded two, three steps into the water, then climbed into the canoes. Densu counted forty-five men squeezed into the first canoe, forty-five in the second, forty-three in the third, apart from six oarsmen in each, two in front, four at the back.

'Twenty would be too many for those old canoes,' Densu thought. He could not take his eyes off the happenings on the bank.

Now that the canoes were ready for the crossing, the anger of the Asante war captains gave way to an equally noisy show of good humour. The general chant was picked up again. It grew more forceful, more powerful. Several warriors, in sheer enthusiasm, waded into the river a step or two and helped give each canoe a lusty push into the water. All three canoes were steady enough at the start. The oarsmen guided them slowly, gliding low in the water, towards the river's centre. What exactly happened next was uncertain. Did one man suddenly panic in the leading canoe? Had some man feared he was about to fall, and in his anxiety destroyed the general balance trying to save his frightened self?

In the leading canoe something happened that looked like a sudden slide of all the warriors backward. For several over-long moments the canoe's front end was raised clear of the water. The men in it, shouting, confused, now clearly unable to hide their fear of the water beckoning them below, every moment added to the craft's giddy imbalance.

Three men from the very front were thrown clear into the air, their desperate fingers clutching air. As they hit the water they each clawed frantically reaching for their lost canoe, but all were strangers to the swimmer's art. They were not immobile. Motion they had, motion so strong and frantic it turned the dark water into froth around them. It was wasted motion. The bodies remained caught the same distance from the bank. If they moved at all it was to the right, with the slow, inexorable force of the current.

A few still in the boat, made forgetful of their own safety by the urgency of their comrades' danger, lunged forward trying to help. They too were thrown into the unfamiliar water. Now the leading canoe stood bolt upright in the water. Then, in a slow, awkward, oblique turn, it slid under the surface with all the panic-stricken warriors clinging on to it.

Those taken first by the river knew a calmer death than these. For these the going down was a furious, clawing struggle of men turning on each other in their common fear. Their cries were terrible, cries of men who had left home bent on the conquest of others merely to run into death with this unexpected swiftness before they were even close to the enemy they sought. For Densu, there were wild echoes in their cries, echoes from the cries of a previous day, the cries of the victims on the other bank.

The second canoe went all the way to the middle of the river before it too began to capsize. It was not any particular person's panicky motion that first destroyed its equilibrium. Water had seeped in through the patched-up hole in the bottom; for a time the warriors had bailed it out with their hands, faster than it entered. But perhaps the water had softened more of the rotten bottom. Quite without warning, there was a fantastic upward rush of water. In a moment the canoe was no longer visible. Here too there was the desperate, close struggle of men afraid of water. It was briefer than the first. In very little time the water at the river's centre had swallowed up even the most energetic warrior thrashing around in it. Only bubbles told of their passage. Soon the bubbles also disappeared, dancing downstream, blowing up like so many winks.

The third canoe was still only steps from the bank.

'Don't go!' shouted the living from that bank.

'Return!' the living shouted again.

In fear the oarsmen in the third canoe turned it slowly round and brought it back to land. Now the war captains who had been so loud in their impatience and humour fell quieter than the stricken thousands waiting upon their decision. Seven priests approached the water's edge to look at the bodies it had been possible to recover. To these priests a man was brought. Whether he was a prisoner or a voluntary bearer of news it was hard to tell—so completely was he surrounded. But it was clear he had a message. In its telling he pointed several times towards the bank opposite.

Even while the men talked to the priests those looking for the dead brought up a new body. This was no drowned companion of Asante warriors, though. This was the headless body of a woman in early youth, one among the victims from a previous day. This body had already lost its stone.

A wail of fear rose from the beholders of that sight. The priests ordered the body to be brought to them. It was brought. Between the priests and the man who could have been either a prisoner or a willing informer there was a long conversation. After it the priests went aside to talk earnestly and just as long with the war captains. The captains then dispersed immediately, disappearing among the clusters of warriors.

But in a while they returned. With them came small, strong groups of warriors driving before them other human beings, men and women, not warriors but people bound ready for sacrifice. There were twenty men and ten women thus bound and led to the river. Of the women two looked like mere children. The distance to the place of the coming sacrifice beside the river should have been too great for Densu to see anybody's face at all, but as he looked at the priests and warriors with their victims, the conviction possessed him that there on the bank were faces he could recognize. They were faces from a past that was still fresh as a wound. He saw Appia, he saw Anan, he saw Jesiwa the destroyed mother, and his body moved towards them, its speed entirely its own.

He did not decide anything. What did he hope to do? He did not hope, he did not think. All he was aware of was the unbearableness of what was happening. He felt no difference between his body and the air around him at that moment. So it was not any conscious decision of his that made it happen: he ran down the hill, his motion free as wind.

He ran free as the wind, and did not stop even when he came to the sacrificial crowd, the executioners and their victims, on the bank of the river. One of the executioners, a huge one so fat his breasts came down in folds like a woman's, raised a short barbed arrow skyward. He asked the blessings of his god on the weapon in his hand and on the job he was going to use it for. His prayer said, he beckoned to his companions and they pushed forward three victims, the slaves destined for sacrifice.

The executioner with full breasts drew back his right arm, ready to skewer the first victim's cheek with the little arrow that would stop his tongue from cursing his killers at the moment of death. He almost reached his aim, but at the point of impact something hit him in his left side with a force not even his fat frame could resist. The executioner's barbed arrow flew from his hand and struck a companion in the leg. The fat killer himself fell, howling oaths and clutching as much of his side as he could hold. Those holding the victims ready for sacrifice, astounded at the suddenness with which Densu had struck, and unable to understand just what was happening, panicked and let go of the first three slaves.

Densu shouted with all the power in his lungs: 'Run!'

The first slave seemed to have heard the shout the moment it was uttered. He ran directly away from the mass of captors behind him straight into the river. He did not hesitate at the water, but plunged into it and swam with strong, desperate strokes, making for the other bank.

The warriors, priests and executioners, all astounded by the unforeseen turn of events, stood as if petrified the space of a few breaths. Then their astonishment gave place to angry, violent activity. The warriors were the first to act. A number of guns barked, and the river around the victim swimming to escape death sent up small, agitated columns of water into the air. The swimmer continued in spite of the hail of bullets, but he did not get to the middle of the river. There was no sudden sinking—his strokes became feebler, then there were no strokes at all, just a hand reaching from water to air, closing over emptiness before the current pulled it down, slanting it to the left.

The second victim also rushed towards the river after his moment of pure astonishment. But he was no swimmer. When he reached the water he hesitated, looked back at the executioners behind him, and turned again to face the water. He reached a decision but it was a despairing one, and the jump he took into the river was forlorn.

No warriors wasted bullets or powder on him. They stood and

watched him struggle forward in the water, until his movement could not take him anywhere. Then their anger turned to amusement. Some laughed so loud they cried tears to see the frantic victim drown in his own efforts.

There was the third victim. The commotion had left him also free, but he stood just where he was. He did not move as much as an eyelash. All he did was look at Densu with a look at once kind and calm. It was a look of infinite pity and it said, more eloquently than words could ever have said, that it was too late. The amazing thing was, it was not self-pity in his eyes, but pity.

Densu saw the third victim's look, and the sense of himself as a separate body returned to him, bringing him a torrent of sharp and heavy pains. He could hear the anger of all the warriors and priests and official killers concentrated upon him in an endless, massive howl of rage. Beyond that, he felt the sheer brute power of this rage against his body, and in a few moments he knew his own attempts to protect his body were doomed.

Then he heard as if through a haze a strangely familiar voice. But the voice was confusing. The voice of a friend, it spoke like an implacable enemy's:

'Bring him here, here!' the voice commanded angrily. 'Bring him!'

He knew he was not mistaken about the voice. He wanted to call out its owner's name, but his mind could not decide which name it should be, Damfo's or Anan's. It came to him vaguely that one of the two was gone. As he tried to remember which one, he felt something slide into his mouth, something at once insistent and gentle. Then he lost all feeling of pain.

3 Sympathy

Densu woke up feeling exhausted, thoroughly beaten. There seemed to be no one around, and it was dark. But he knew the smell of the air where he was, and the knowledge reassured him. He stayed awake a short time, then slipped back into sleep. When he woke again it was clear morning. Damfo came to see him after he had cleaned himself and eaten a little porridge.

'How did you bring me here?' he asked Damfo.

'It was Asamoa Nkwanta who took us to the river,' Damfo answered.

'Is he here already?' Densu asked.

'He came yesterday, in the morning. Something seemed to be obsessing him. He heard the noises from the river and insisted we should go with him. We found the Asante army trying to cross the river,' Damfo chuckled ruefully, 'and you, Densu, trying to stop the army.'

'I couldn't stop myself,' said Densu feebly.

'No, you couldn't. But you should. I was just lucky Asamoa Nkwanta was with me. He said nothing, but when the warriors saw him with me they moved aside for me.'

'So it's true they worship him,' Densu said.

'No. What I saw was respect, not worship. Those warriors love that man. You should have seen the way some looked at him. There was no fear at all. He's very ill, these days, and looks weak. Some of those warriors seemed close to tears, just looking at him.'

'I'd like to see him, and thank him,' said Densu.

'That you'll do,' Damfo said. 'I didn't think you were suicidal, but that's what you were going to do yesterday—kill yourself.'

'I know now,' admitted Densu. 'It wasn't my intention. I saw those people killed the other day across the river. I did nothing, and I was sick. Then yesterday it was going to happen again, and something turned inside me.'

'An impulse. You should have thought about it before acting on it.'

'Would thinking reconcile me to all the killings?' Densu asked.

'Not to the killings. But thinking would reconcile you to what's real: that you can't stop people from being brutes. Not all at once. Not in a lifetime. Not in centuries.'

'So nothing is to be done?' Densu asked.

'I don't say that,' said Damfo. 'What's your mind for if not to find out what can be done, how to do it, how long you'll have to work in the direction you see, and how paltry the results will look to your impatient eyes?'

'It's hard.'

'Yes, it's hard. But suppose you saw a huge, wild fire and you wanted to put it out. How would you go about it? Would you throw your single physical self into the fire? Would that be a way to stop the fire?'

Recovery from physical wounds was quick. But the pull away from despair took longer. Damfo was a steady presence always keeping open a vision of the future still to come.

Strength returned to Densu, and in time he moved from being a burden on Danfo to being his helper in the work he had come to do. Sometimes he sat with Araba Jesiwa and watched her, ministering to the needs of her healing body when Nyaneba and Ajoa had work elsewhere. Most often he was with Damfo, just watching the healer at his work.

The first day of work with Asamoa Nkwanta, the healer called the clearing of the ground. Asamoa Nkwanta did not come alone to the village of healers at Praso. Apart from Kwao Tweneboa and Kojo Mensa, the two healers who had gone to Kumase to bring him, there was Okomfo Tawia, the priest. A priest from the palace at Kumase, Okomfo Tawia always followed Asamoa Nkwanta, like a shadow ignorant of night.

In the centre of the healers' village was a large odum tree. Under it Damfo would spread a mat and sit with Asamoa Nkwanta, holding his healing conversations with the warrior. The first day, the priest Okomfo Tawia came to sit under the tree, taking a position near Asamoa Nkwanta, across from Damfo. When Densu had brought all of them water, and given Damfo the herbs he had prepared against this day, he also sat, taking a position on the healer's left.

The first thing Damfo did was stare evenly not at Asamoa Nkwanta but at the priest by his side. The stare was long. The priest had something like a scowl on his face to start with. As Damfo stared at him the scowl changed slowly. It turned into something almost shy, a sort of shamefaced smile. At the same time the look in the priest's eyes grew softer, as if he expected an answering smile from the healer opposite him. All this while no one spoke.

The healer Damfo did not return the priest Okomfo Tawia's smile. He simply continued to stare at him. In a while the priests's eyes began to water and he coughed. As if he had only been waiting for the silence to be broken, Damfo stopped staring at the priest, turned his attention completely away from him, and addressed Asamoa Nkwanta:

'Our conversations would be more genuine if you came alone.'

Asamoa Nkwanta lifted his head and looked frankly at Damfo, as if his words had just brought him back from a far journey.

'How so?' he asked.

Damfo suppressed a smile. 'If the pains bringing disease to the mind come from the past, healing means the mind must go beyond the past, travelling into the future as lightly as it can. In that case the past is heavy, a weight. It must be left behind.'

'I cannot forget the past,' the warrior said. His voice was gentle, and the words came out almost like a plea.

'There is no need to forget the past,' replied Damfo. 'But of each piece of the past that we find in our present, it may be necessary to ask: Will it bear me like a stepping stone, or will I have to bear it, a weight around my neck?'

'I hear you,' the warrior said, nodding.

'I will speak even more plainly,' Damfo continued. 'If there is anyone listening to your conversations before whom you would rather not say certain things, the conversations will not be genuine.'

'I said I hear you,' Asamoa Nkwanta repeated. He sat looking at Damfo, but neither of them spoke again that day.

On the day of the second conversation, Asamoa Nkwanta was alone. The great fighter, the warrior of the crossways, winner of a hundred victories, terror of the enemies of Asante, looked a wasted wreck. On his body the flesh was wasted. The skin hung loose on his limbs. His face looked as if he had inherited the skin covering it from one several times bigger, and the difference showed in long, deep lines. It was plain the man had suffered—the kind of suffering that comes from within. Strong men may resist pain inflicted from outside themselves. But against the pain that has its source inwards they are more helpless than the weak, because the pain borrows their own tremendous strength and pits it against them. Asamoa Nkwanta's body showed the results of a terrifying struggle. His eyes showed worse—that the struggle was far from over.

Asamoa Nkwanta's eyes had lost their natural colour. There was no white separate from the black of the pupil. Black and white, both had been overwhelmed by an angry, virulent red. The warrior's eyes looked at if they had spent a continuous month knowing no sleep, their owner chewing kola all the while, the juice colouring not his mouth alone but his nostrils and his eyeballs. The red of the balls was not the purest kind; it was dull, a sort of sick brown redness.

There were deeper reds. These ran in lines—a great multiplicity of little swollen pathways running up and down, across and athwart the eyeballs in thirty twisting directions, as if armies of red ants had passed over a distant field and left their mark indelibly stamped on it. What gave the eyes a weirder look was their dryness. They lacked all moisture, even a fugitive drop. It was as if the pain that had eaten his body had also sizzled up all Asamoa Nkwanta's juices.

Damfo stood by him a long time, but Asamoa Nkwanta stared ahead, his head and body motionless. He did not look as if he was taking breath, and his eyes seemed not to blink at all—so motionless was he. Damfo spoke to him as if he were merely continuing a previous conversation. He said the healer was only a helper. He would be impotent to help unless he, Asamoa Nkwanta, was himself ready to search for the way to recovery. He would be ready to discuss everything with him, and he would bring him the best of medicines he knew. Finally, he asked Asamoa Nkwanta to remember that medicine coud do nothing if a human being was making war on his own natural self.

That night Densu took a small bowl of juice prepared by Damfo to Asamoa Nkwanta. The sorrowing warrior, taking it without a word, drank it.

It had started as a quiet night, but past its middle the silence was lost. Asamoa Nkwanta did not wake from his sleep but he began a strenuous struggle with the demons populating his soul, and the struggle charged the air with urgent sound. There was the heavy, hissing breathing of a man determined to survive foes mightier than himself in combat. There was the manic laughter of the winner in his victory, ready for rest. Then protests and groans at the discovery the struggle was not over, had hardly begun, in effect. It grew fierce. The warrior's sounds sank from victory to defiance, defiance to fear, fear to panic, and from panic Asamoa Nkwanta's voice slid all the way down to a long, impotent wail shattering a great slice of time in the night: 'I'm coming. Yes, I'm coming. I'm coming!' The wail was endless, unvarying, and each repetition contained a well of sorrow.

Next day at noon, Damfo called Densu to bring a mat, and together they went and sat under the odum tree. As if Damfo had been waiting just for him, Asamoa Nkwanta came. Damfo made room for him on the mat.

The warrior looked more relaxed than he had looked the day before. But his face still looked drawn:

'The medicine you gave me was helpful,' Asamoa Nkwanta said.

'You slept well?'

'Better than any day since—since they killed him.'

'Dreams?'

'Nightmare, not dreams, like every day since.'

'Then you didn't sleep well.'

'I did,' Asamoa Nkwanta said. 'They didn't wake me up this time.'

'Who?'

'The nightmares.'

'They always woke you?'

Asamoa Nkwanta nodded.

'Why?' Damfo asked.

'You know, I always try to save him.'

'Your nephew?'

The warrior nodded. Something like a sigh escaped him.

'From whom?'

Pain contorted Asamoa Nkwanta's face. 'That's something I don't know. I can't ever see his killer's face. But I can feel the strokes cutting him. Not the pain, but the blows.'

'Do the blows hit you too?'

'No. I can feel the killer's arm in the act.'

'Struggling against you?'

'Not struggling against me,' Asamoa Nkwanta said impatiently. 'I don't see him, but I feel his strength in my arm, and I know I can stop him. I try to stop him.'

'You feel the killer and you are close?'

'The same.'

'Then why aren't you able to stop him?'

'I can't!' the warrior gasped, a man in pain. The admission broke some barrier damming the flow of his feelings, and without pausing he let go of a rapid stream of words. 'I can't help him. It's my own hand, but I can't stop it, I can't turn it against myself. Against the killer I can do nothing. I can't even see him. And the child is looking at me, needing my help. I watch him go, killed just like a slave.'

'That killing was the root of your illness then?'

'The root of everything,' he said hoarsely. 'They killed him like a slave.'

'Why?'

'What do you mean, why?'

'Do you know the reason for that death?'

'It's the custom.'

'Have you examined the custom that can result in so much murder?'

Asamoa Nkwanta's face gathered itself up into a puzzled mask of lines and shadows. His eyes narrowed, almost shut. Here was a man trying to master an idea still new to his ways of thought.

'Would you change the custom if you had the power?'

'No!' This was also vehement.

'Would your nephew have died if there hadn't been any such custom?'

'But I tell you the custom did not kill him.'

'I hear you. You say it was an accident, not a necessity of the custom.'

'Yes. It was an accident.'

'My question is, may not such accidents be prevented if . . .'

Asamoa Nkwanta finished for Damfo: '. . . if the custom is abolished?' Those eyes of his looked so tired. 'What kind of world would it be then? A world without slaves?'

'Precisely,' said Damfo, calmly. 'A world without slaves.'

Asamoa Nkwanta had been ready to say something, but now he paused. He looked at Damfo's face. Then Asamoa Nkwanta laughed, even in his sorrow.

'A world without slaves! You might as well wish for a world without kings.'

'Yes, no slaves, no kings.'

'No slaves, no kings,' Asamoa Nkwanta repeated to himself, incredulously. 'What would there be then?'

'People. Human beings who respect each other.'

The laughter left Asamoa Nkwanta's face. 'You think impossible thoughts, healer. Our people have always had kings and slaves.'

'Not always,' Damfo said.

'When have the Asante not had kings and slaves?'

'Are our people the Asante only?'

'What do you mean?'

'The Asante are part of the Akan. The Akan in turn came from something larger.'

A brightness came into Asamoa Nkwanta's eyes. He lowered his eyes, when he raised them again the brightness was gone.

* * *

For days Asamoa Nkwanta said nothing to Damfo about the idea of the Asante people being only a part of the Akan, and the Akan themselves belonging to something much greater. It was as if he had forgotten it entirely. But one day, with no preparation, he threw the subject up again:

'It is a disturbing matter to think about,' he said.

'What is?' Damfo asked.

Asamoa Nkwanta looked a bit unbelievingly at Damfo, as if Damfo had forgotten something said just a moment back.

'Who we are,' he said grudgingly. 'The Akan, and the black people being one.'

'What is disturbing about it?' Damfo asked.

'I also know the idea, but it goes so far into the past,' Asamoa Nkwanta said, 'a mind going after it may get lost in the past.'

'Minds don't stay in the past,' Damfo said. 'They can find the truths of the past, come back to the present, and look towards the future. That's not getting lost. The present is where we get lost—if we forget our past and have no vision of the future.'

'If I let my mind go so far into the past,' Asamoa Nkwanta said, 'the journey confuses me. The Akan were all one people before. The black people were all connected before. But we are not now. What will it profit my mind to run back after things that are no more?'

'If the past tells you the Akan and the black people were one in the past, perhaps it also tells you there is nothing eternal about our present divisions. We were one in the past. We may come together again in the future.'

Asamoa Nkwanta shook his head: 'Thoughts like these paralyse me. They make the present look shabby and unbearable. They take away all energy.'

'Yet these same thoughts, followed into the future, may give us greater energy for work.'

'Perhaps,' Asamoa Nkwanta said. 'Perhaps.'

Conversations with the General

The fourteenth day:

'What I want to understand, but can't, is the connection between these thoughts I have in the day and the nightmares that come to me at night,' Asamoa Nkwanta told Damfo.

'Must there be a connection?' Damfo asked him.

'I feel there must be. Something disturbs me, a lack of understanding. I feel the disturbance should end as soon as I understand the connection,' Asamoa Nkwanta said.

'What are these daytime thoughts?' Damfo asked.

'You know them,' Asamoa Nkwanta answered. 'They're about divisions. I've spent my life fighting to make Asante strong. If the past was a time of unity, then must I see my entire life as wrong?'

'And the nightmares?'

'They are many,' Asamoa Nkwanta said, 'but they are always the same. I see myself walking outwards from Kumase, along the Subin Valley. I reach the Swamp of Death, where the corpses of executed slaves are thrown. I see no corpses there at first. What I see is my nephew alive again. He is playing happily, and it seems he has the power to run above the swamp without sinking in it. The games he plays are games I taught him when he was a child. Games for a warrior. He hides perfectly behind the smallest tree stump. He shoots two guns at once, and his aim with both is perfect. I stand amazed at the edge of the swamp, lost in admiration, dreaming of the future he will grow up to.

'When I look again I become anxious. My nephew is getting shorter, and I can't see why. I go towards him with my arms outstretched. He keeps sinking, and though I try to move fast, I can't reach him.'

Here Asamoa Nkwanta paused as if he had run out of breath. Then he opened his mouth to speak, staring at Densu as if he were seeing him for the first time. After that he lowered his eyes and continued telling Damfo of his nightmares.

'I lean far into the swamp. I can almost reach him. My fingertips feel his. But beyond that I have no power to do anything. He sinks into the Swamp of Death, and I watch him go. The last part is the worst. It's so slow. His neck goes, ring after ring. I see his mouth. The swamp takes his nostrils, his eyes staring at me, his eyebrows, his forehead, his hair. When he disappears completely there's nothing left. Not a ripple on the swamp.'

'Is it that you feel guilty you didn't prevent his death?' Damfo asked Asamoa Nkwanta.

'I don't know what I feel,' the warrior said, his voice eloquent of defeat. 'If I could have prevented his death I would have, but how could I have known such a thing would happen to him?'

'There would have been no way to protect him from being killed—as long as people could be killed that way. The guilt isn't yours,' Damfo said.

'But the feeling of impotence is bitterer than guilt. He was so good. He was quick. He shot as if his mother had brought him into the world with a gun in his hand. He would have surpassed me. But Boache Aso took his life.'

'Tell me,' Damfo said, 'does the memory of your nephew's death take you only into that past?'

'Yes,' Asamoa Nkwanta said.

'In that direction you will only lose energy,' Damfo said.

'What do you mean?' Asamoa Nkwanta asked.

'As long as you concentrate on the event that brought loss, your mind will take energy away from you.'

'What else could I concentrate on?'

'Ways to make such loss of life impossible.' Damfo said.

'But it has happened already,' Asamoa Nkwanta protested.

'To one person, your nephew, yes. But if that's all that's important to you, your soul will remain trapped in contemplation of that loss—in the recent past. Have you thought of the future? The past steals energy from your soul because it forces you to think of a loss you're impotent to prevent. The future may bring you energy—if it can show you ways to work against that kind of loss.'

Asamoa Nkwanta did not answer. He looked tired again, and his eyes indicated his mind was far away.

The thirtieth day:

Damfo spoke first: 'You look different.'

Asamoa Nkwanta replied promptly: 'I am different.'

'Is that good or bad?'

178

'You should know. The medicines you give me at night don't just make me sleep at night. They make me eat like a hog,' Asamoa Nkwanta said.

'Like the man you are,' Damfo said. 'When you came you used not to eat at all. Like a ghost.'

'I didn't have an appetite,' Asamoa Nkwanta said.

'You didn't want to live.'

'It's a burden, life.'

'But sometimes you have strength enough to carry it,' Damfo said. 'Have you had any more nightmares?' Asamoa Nkwanta shook his head. 'It's turned into a dream. Very strange.'

'Is it also a recurring dream?'

'Four times I've had it so far.'

'Similar to the nightmares?' Damfo asked.

'In a way,' Asamoa Nkwanta said. 'It's in the swamp again. But I see three men. They are tall and lean, so tall they tower above the trees behind them. They are solemn in their walk. They walk towards me in such a way I know it's me they're looking for. But when they come close they turn round so I can't recognize their faces.

'The way they talk is surprisingly gentle, for men whose heads reach so far up into the sky. They're talking to me, not ordering me or scolding me, but pleading with me. They ask me a question I don't understand:

' "What has the army done to you?"

'I ask them what they mean by such a baffling question. They tell me I have abandoned the army and placed a curse on it, so that it has been suffering. I say I have placed no curse on anyone. But they ask again, as if it were a song: "Why have you abandoned the army? Is the army the court?"

'Then at last they turn their faces towards me. They are smiling. I recognize them all. The one on the right is the old man Kwamen, he who gave himself up to be sacrified in place of the criminal Boache Aso. In the centre is Okomfo Anoche himself, smiling, smiling at me. The third person is my nephew.

'I could not see where they went. They simply disappeared from my sight. But in my ears their words remained: what has the army done to you? Is the army the court?'

Damfo looked at Asamoa Nkwanta.

'You live very close to the desires of your soul,' he said.

'I used to,' Asamoa Nkwanta said. 'Why do you say that?'

179

'It's your dreams that tell,' Damfo answered. 'When people build their lives close to their soul's desires, their dreams can be extremely direct, like yours. Their nightmares too.'

'I live far from my desires now,' Asamoa Nkwanta said.

'Have you thought why?'

Asamoa Nkwanta nodded. 'The army has been my life. I do not remember a single unhappy day as a warrior. I wanted to spend my life fighting for Asante, and after my life I wanted my blood to continue my work. My nephew . . .' he did not go on.

'What has happened to the desire?' Damfo asked. 'It's too strong to have died.'

'It didn't die,' Asamoa Nkwanta said. 'It cannot die in me. But there's a feeling in me that paralyses my will. When I think that the result of all my work, the best that is in me, is simply to give power to people who know only how to waste power and waste life, my arm grows weak and I feel all the forces of life and will deserting me.'

'You do not feel like serving royalty?'

'It never was my aim just to serve royalty,' Asamoa Nkwanta said. 'I like men who think well and can act strongly for a good purpose. I respect them. If I find such men among the royals I respect them.'

'Do you find such men among the royals?' Damfo asked Asamoa Nkwanta.

Asamoa Nkwanta hesitated, a man searching his head for answers, before replying: 'Osei Tutu was such a man.'

'Certainly,' Damfo said. 'But what of the royals today?'

'They have inherited royal power,' Asamoa Nkwanta said. 'But the unfortunate thing is they have not inherited the skills and strengths of personality that made their uncles fit to be kings.'

'So you would say the first kings did serve the people well?' Damfo asked.

'Certainly. Of the likes of Osei Tutu and Obiri Yeboa, I shall always say that,' Asamoa Nkwanta said.

'Is it possible that what paralyses your will is a sense that the royals no longer serve the people?'

'The royals these days serve only themselves,' Asamoa Nkwanta said, sadly.

'If that is true, what is the army you have built your life around?' Damfo asked.

'A plaything the royals indulge themselves with,' Asamoa Nkwanta said calmly.

'You know the source of the conflict that's sapped your energy then,' Damfo said.

'I can't name it.'

'Division,' Damfo offered. 'Division in the soul. You live to work for the army. You don't want your life's work wasted. But you see the royals wasting everything. So you can't decide whether to continue working for the army or stay out. Your mind races from one idea to the other. You get exhausted without moving forward.'

'I may see the conflict,' Asamoa Nkwanta said, 'but I can't see a way to end it.'

'Have you examined the possibilities? All of them?'

'I've tried,' Asamoa Nkwanta said. 'But I only see problems, no possibilities.'

'Look more closely,' said Damfo. 'First of all listen inwards, to your own soul. What does your spirit say do?'

'My spirit always says the same thing,' Asamoa Nkwanta said. 'Fight, and teach men to fight. Work for the army, the people.'

'Good,' said Damfo. 'It's always good to have the soul speak clearly. Can you see any way you can obey the voice of your soul without being at the same time a plaything in the hands of royalty?'

'That is the connection that escapes me,' said Asamoa Nkwanta. 'At times I have the feeling I see a way. But when I try to grasp the feeling it flies away.'

'Let's begin with the feeling itself. Even an image will do to start with. What is it about?'

'War, of course.'

'A war you've fought in before?' Damfo asked.

'No.'

'A war you've heard about?'

'No.'

'You baffle me.'

'I first had the idea long ago. Ten years ago we heard a white army was coming to invade Asante. The royals were indignant. But all I felt was a definite pleasure.'

'Why pleasure?' Damfo asked. 'Would you welcome a white invasion of your own land?'

'I looked forward to fighting the whites. I know the whites, I know their strength. They have tremendous strength as far as weapons are concerned. After all, where do we get our own weapons but from them? So I did not dream of confronting them weapon against weapon. That would be fatal. I knew their strength.

'But I also knew their greatest weakness. A warrior needs to know his enemy's weaknesses. I saw the weakness of the whites. It wasn't military at all. It was a weakness of the spirit, the soul. The whites are not on friendly terms with the surrounding universe. Between them and the universe there is real hostility. Take the forest here: if they stay long in the forest, they die. Either they cut down the forest and kill it, or it kills them. They can't live with it.

'So I would like to fight an invading white army, not with guns but with the natural environment. I would fight them by bringing them deep into the forest and letting the forest wrap itself around them, sucking the life out of them.'

Damfo was leaning far forward on the mat, and his face was very close to Asamoa Nkwanta's. 'That is the clearest idea I have heard in a long time,' he said.

'The royals won't agree to it, however,' Asamoa Nkwanta said.

'Why not?'

'It would mean a long war. An extremely long war. At home,' Asamoa Nkwanta said.

'Does that matter?' Damfo asked.

'I see I have to teach you now about war,' said Asamoa Nkwanta. 'What is a king?'

'A leader of a nation,' said Damfo, smiling.

'Precisely,' Asamoa Nkwanta said. 'He could be called any other name, but the thing is that he leads the nation. What is a general?'

'He leads the army,' Damfo said.

'Don't you see the possibility of conflict between the two, the king and the general?' Asamoa Nkwanta asked.

'I see it,' Damfo answered.

'Wars away from home are good for an incumbent ruler. They keep the leader of the army far from home. His leadership doesn't clash with the leadership of the king. But all kings fear a war that comes home. This is not just a fear of the invading foreigner and the harm he can do. That fear is nothing compared to the royal fear of the defending army and its leader, the general.

'This is what I meant when I said I'd teach you now about war. We know this principle: when a war comes home it changes the whole nation into a battlefield. That means it changes the whole people into an army. Now the general is the leader of the army. If the whole nation gets turned into an army, the general becomes the leader of the whole nation. Do you see?'

'I see what your soul sees, Asamoa Nkwanta.'

The look the warrior gave the healer at those words was quick, like a sharp instrument exposed in a flash and immediately withdrawn.

Damfo looked steadily at Asamoa Nkwanta. Then he asked him: 'So does it seem so impossible for you to do what your spirit says do and at the same time avoid getting wasted by royalty?'

'If there was an invasion by whites, no. But these petty wars in which the army gets sent to fight other black people are a waste.'

Damfo nodded: 'There may be a white invasion, after all. There's talk of that on the coast.'

'I don't know any more,' Asamoa Nkwanta said. 'Someone at Oguaa used to send me reliable news, but no longer. I want to know what goes on at the coast among the whites and their black helpers. But I can't think of a way to find out.'

'We shall see what can be done,' Damfo said.

5   Recovery

Ajoa was the first to notice the change. It was evening. She had given Araba Jesiwa her liquid food for the night. Damfo, Densu, and Nyaneba, having eaten, had all come to keep the silent Jesiwa company. They talked a bit, then having nothing more of importance to say, each sat in silence.

It was in this almost total silence that first one, then another of the others noticed Ajoa was crying. Damfo and Nyaneba looked at her, looked away, and said nothing. Densu looked at her and could not take his eyes off her face. She was crying, but there was something odd in the way she cried. Her eyes were bright in the gathering darkness. Around her lips there was no suggestion of depression.

Densu was about to ask Ajoa what the matter was, when the conflict between her tears and her almost happy appearance became open. Ajoa laughed a joyous laugh; but at the height of that laugh her voice shook the way only deep sorrow can make a voice tremble.

'What is the matter, Ajoa?' Densu asked her.

She shook her head and wiped her tears. 'Can't you hear?' she asked.

'Hear what?' Densu asked.

'Her,' Ajoa said through her tears. 'Listen to her.'

Densu and Damfo and Nyaneba fell silent, but none of them heard anything.

'I don't hear anything,' Densu said.

'You're not listening,' Ajoa said. Her voice was close to exasperation.

'I have listened, Ajoa,' Densu said, 'but I heard nothing.'

'She's talking,' Ajoa said. 'She's been saying something all this evening.'

Damfo looked at Densu, then at Nyaneba. All three looked at Ajoa.

'Did you hear words?' Damfo asked Ajoa.

'No,' she shook her head. 'Not words. Just sound. How can she talk words all at once?'

'It's a good sign,' said Damfo. 'All the animals with broken bones have walked. Araba Jesiwa's bones should be healed by now. If she's finding her voice again, that's welcome news indeed.'

For almost a week only Ajoa heard Araba Jesiwa's voice. Then one night shrill, harsh shrieks tore the healers' sleep to pieces. The shrieks began before dawn and did not stop before sunrise. They came from Araba Jesiwa. When Damfo, Densu, and Nyaneba went in to see her they found Ajoa by her side. Jesiwa's face was streaming with sweat. A violent, fearful struggle must have taken place in her mind. It had affected her body, and even though it was over its results were plain to see. The cast on her right leg had cracked at the knee.

Damfo looked closely at the crack and said: 'It's time to free her limbs. They're strong enough now.'

Damfo cut a number of deep lines into each cast. Into the lines he poured water and let it soak steadily into the clay and cloth of the casts. He worked slowly, taking extreme care not to disturb Jesiwa's body or her mind. By the afternoon all the casts had been softened and removed, leaving only one thin layer of cloth around each limb. Araba Jesiwa's bed was moved so that the incoming rays of the afternoon sun fell on her body but her head was in a cool shadow.

184

The last thin layer of cloth was removed on the third day. Araba Jesiwa's skin had turned pale, a sickly whitish colour like old, wet ash. But in a few more days, exposure to sunlight brought back the colour of life to her limbs.

Now she was able to eat porridge, half-solid fruit like ripe pawpaw, bananas, and plantains, and even yam mashed fine and mixed with ground spinach stewed in palm oil. But meat made her vomit, so it wasn't given her.

*　　*　　*

Strength returned to Asamoa Nkwanta. Sitting irked the warrior's spirit, and soon enough he made it his habit to go hunting, bringing back so much venison that the healers had to ask him to spare the animals.

Asamoa Nkwanta spent a lot of time watching Densu, just staring at him.

'Does he remind you of someone?' Damfo asked Asamoa Nkwanta one day. The warrior's face darkened, as if he had been surprised in some secret pursuit. He didn't answer there and then, but later that same day he himself returned to the subject of Densu.

'This your Densu,' Asamoa Nkwanta asked, affecting a casual tone, 'can he aim a gun at all?'

'Ask him,' Damfo said.

Asamoa Nkwanta pointed to an orange tree down the hind path from the healers' compound. Only one fruit was ripe, but it hung close to a green cluster. .

'Try that one,' Asamoa Nkwanta said.

Densu took the gun offered by the warrior, checked to see it was loaded, aimed it, and pulled the trigger. The green cluster shook, then steadied itself. The ripe orange had disappeared.

Densu laid the gun down and walked to the orange tree. When he came back he had the ripe orange in his hand. He gave it to Asamoa Nkwanta.

The warrior took the fruit, stared at it, and looked again at Densu. 'I thought you were going to hit it.'

'Well, then I failed your test.'

The warrior laughed a long, convulsive laugh, and tears came from his right eye. 'Will you hunt with me?' he asked Densu.

Asamoa Nkwanta told Damfo of a new recurring dream. In this dream the great Asante priest Okomfo Anoche came to him alone, in the middle of an endless battlefield. Apart from the two, no one else was there, even though the field of battle stretched on every side as far as the horizon.

The ancient priest came to the warrior riding in the middle of a thick cloud of gunsmoke, as if a castle cannon had fired him. There was no sound, however, only the thick smoke.

When he reached the warrior he took his hand and led him into the air, and the wind bore both of them up, though they had no wings. The priest showed Asamoa Nkwanta the bones of thirty thousand dead warriors. There was not a shred of flesh left on any skeleton, but looking at the skulls Asamoa Nkwanta recognized each of the thirty thousand dead warriors. He recognized also the fleshless faces of three hundred of the captains he himself had trained. He could not believe they had died in any battle, so many of them, and no alien bones anywhere to be seen. But there they all lay on the battlefield stretching endlessly around him.

A voice called out to him. It did not call him by his name, but by a new name which sounded like the sweetest name Asamoa Nkwanta had ever heard: 'Srafo Kra! Soul of the Army! Where are you? Where have you been?'

Asamoa Nkwanta couldn't answer the questioner in his dream. He looked around him trying to find out from where the voice came. It sounded as if it came from every point around him. His companion held him gently by the right hand and together they came down to earth, gentle as leaves. Then the priest left him.

'That is another clear dream,' Damfo said.

'How clear?' Asamoa Nkwanta asked.

'You miss the army,' Damfo said.

Asamoa Nkwanta showed no emotion.

'You'll go back to the army,' Damfo continued. 'You'll be violating your soul if you don't. One thing only baffles me about you.'

Asamoa Nkwanta took a long time succumbing to the urge to ask Damfo, 'What?'

'You're waiting for something,' Damfo said. 'I wonder what it is.'

6 The Warrior of the Crossways

The first to come seeking Asamoa Nkwanta were three ordinary warriors from the Asante army. They made a weird little group, these
three men. They told a story wilder than their own wild eyes, about
an army destroying itself because it had no one to take care of its
welfare. Asamoa Nkwanta listened to the warriors, asked for food for
them, then as gently as he could reprimanded them for having broken
from the army just to search for him. The warriors returned whence
they had come.

The next to come were not just warriors. They were seven war
captains. They told a more definite tale of waste and despair ravaging
the Asante army. The army had crossed the Pra and descended south-
ward like a flood of fire. Nothing in its road had stood against it, till it
reached the coastlands. There the fiery flood stagnated, burning
aimlessly, eating its own energy up, wasting itself utterly. The captains' story was a long dirge of disasters with no meaning, death for no
reason, destruction with no end in sight. No one, it seemed, could see
the cause of such misfortunes clearly, but all the captains agreed they
had started when the Asante army lost the leadership of Asamoa
Nkwanta.

Now the army had gone down to the coast, but its commanders did
not know what to do. An army doing nothing rots: disease, not
fighting had sickened the spirit of all the army's warriors. The captains did not want to talk about the leadership of the army's present
commander, except to say it no longer existed. They were sure the
only salvation for the army lay in the return of the supreme commander they were all waiting for. They asked Asamoa Nkwanta a
final, impatient question: 'When?'

It was plain to all the captains Asamoa Nkwanta was moved. His
eyes were red, and his jaw was tense. But he spoke to them calmly. He
reminded the captains the command of the army was not any single
person's to take or give. If the royal council thought the army needed
Asamoa Nkwanta, surely the royal council knew ways to let Asamoa
Nkwanta know. If the royal council did not think the army needed
Asamoa Nkwanta, would it not be sheer usurpation for Asamoa
Nkwanta to think himself needed?

The seven war captains were angry as they left, but for Asamoa Nkwanta their only emotion was clearly love. They told him they had heard terrifying rumours of unnatural omens. They feared a great disintegration of everything was coming. On the coast they had also heard about the coming invasion of a white army. Some had seen signs that this time the white invasion would not be a joke.

Asamoa Nkwanta's dreams of the priest Okomfo Anoche and the endless battlefield came more frequently, then stopped. In their place came a conscious obsession: an intense need to know what was going on down at the coast. He talked to Damfo and told him it was important for him to find out somehow what the whites were planning.

'We also need to know something more definite,' Nyaneba said when Damfo told the healers. 'If there's going to be war, we'll have a lot of work ahead of us. We must know what the whites intend.'

'Is there no one at Cape Coast?' Kwao Tweneboa asked.

'We have Ama Nkroma,' Damfo said. 'But she's old.'

'I could go,' Densu offered.

'It's dangerous, isn't it?' Ajoa asked.

'It needn't be,' answered Damfo. 'What you need is to find out what the whites are planning. You can stay with Ama Nkroma and go to the town when you need to. It's a short walk along the beach.'

'Shall I need a disguise?' Densu asked.

'It's best to be what you really are,' said Damfo. 'The less disguise, the easier. You won't waste thought trying to remember what you're pretending to be. If there's an unexpected problem, you have free mind-space for solving it.'

'I know little about medicine.'

'You know enough. Take only one kind of medicine—something those you want to move among are sure to want.'

'Don't the royals want all sorts of things?'

'That they do, individually. Everything imaginable. But of all the earth's herbs and barks they prize one most. That's what you should take.'

'You have it?'

'Some.'

'What is it?'

'Bediwona.'

Densu laughed in sheer astonishment. 'Is that a name, or a nick-name?'

'A real name,' Damfo answered, also laughing. 'It's an aphrodisiac, after all, and it works.'

'But to make men want their mothers?'

'Some mothers look very good,' Damfo said. When he stopped laughing, he got up and went out. He returned in a short time, carrying a closed pot. He set it down on the floor with both hands, opened it and took out a piece of bark. The light from the doorway caught it as Damfo lifted it, and he held it steady in the light. Densu moved closer to examine it.

The piece of bark was the width of three fingers, and about twice as long. The bark was not smooth. It had a thin outer cover of scales, greyish in colour, under which the wood was hard and brown. Something attached to it shone brightly in the sunlight, and Densu touched it, then smelled it.

'It's just gum. The bark bleeds when cut,' Damfo said.

'Smells like some kind of oil.' Densu said, thoughtfully. 'How is it used?'

'It has to be ground to powder first. I haven't had time to do that. Didn't think we'd need it, really.'

'Is it eaten by itself?'

'A fellow could chew it, or eat the powder alone, but that's a bit desperate. It's easier to take it with drinks or food. Advise your clients to do that.'

'But how do I let people know?'

'You won't have to cry out loud. The drug has many names. Just a discreet whisper: medicine for manhood. The repairer. The harried husband's hope. Saviour of his frustrated wife. Keep a serious expression on your face. You'll see. The people you want to find will come searching for you. Or they'll send for you. Be careful. But if anything goes wrong Ama Nkroma will help. You can depend on her. She's the healer who lives at Bakano, across the lagoon from the town.'

In the evening Ajoa pounded a handful of the bark in a mortar, then ground the small pieces to a fine powder. She put the powder in a bag that had a holding string, and gave it to Densu. Densu slept early.

In the morning he took the food Ajoa had prepared for his journey, an extra cloth, and the bag of medicine. Ajoa and Damfo walked with him along the path towards the river, Ajoa helping him carry his bundle.

'When you come to Manso, Jukwa, Abakrampa, and Mpeasem,'

Damfo added at the river's edge, 'leave the road and take the first path east of the village. You'll find signs to lead you to healers living nearby. Show them this.' He slipped a ring off the little finger of his left hand and gave it to Densu to wear. 'Then tell each of them we're waiting for them at Praso, and that there's work for all of us.'

'Be careful, Densu,' Ajoa said.

A small canoe was waiting on the river. Ajoa untied the rope holding it and threw it to Densu. There were two oars in it. Densu took one. He raised it high in a farewell gesture, then dug into the water with it. The canoe rode across the river.

'Return soon,' Ajoa called after him.

PART SIX

⟨⟨⟨ decorative band ⟩⟩⟩

1   Cape Coast

The tiredness he had felt from his journey left him on the evening of his second day at Bakano. He had not known how tired he really was at first. He had wanted to go directly to the centre of the town the day he arrived, to look at the area around the castle, to try and find out what he could. But Ama Nkroma, his healer hostess, had dissuaded him.

'Rest,' she said. 'You're tired, but you're too young to know it. Besides, what you want to know I can tell you perhaps. I was there just yesterday, the whole morning and a good part of the afternoon, before you came. You'd be surprised how much an old woman gets to know in that town. There's always something happening.'

'Has there been a ship out at sea recently?'

'One.'

'With many whites?'

'I saw some come ashore. Thirty, perhaps forty.'

'Any idea, who they were? Soldiers? Traders?'

'Soldiers, definitely. One seemed the leader; the guns were shot for him, and the black soldiers from over there made lines for him to pass through, so he must be big. But no one on the beach knew anything, and the white men went directly into the castle by the sea gate. It was funny, the chiefs had come to the shore to have their hands shaken by the new white men, and they were just ignored—left standing there like a heap of fools. You should have seen the big chief Ata. He was out under his big red umbrella. On my way back here there was the sound of drums all over the town, and I heard they were getting ready for a great meeting on Saturday.'

'Tomorrow?'

'Yes, tomorrow. The new white man must be in some hurry.'

'Where's the meeting?'

'Their usual place—the open area near the castle. It's not far. You can walk there along the shore—if you like the breeze and don't mind sand underfoot. I'd go with you, but I must meet a healer who's been on a long journey to the west, to Nzema, and give him your message from Damfo. Tell me what happens when you come back.'

The morning was quiet. The breeze blew seaward and Densu walked with it. By the time he reached the shore the breeze was no longer strong. It wavered, then died into a calm, total stillness.

Densu walked along the west side of the lagoon. The green surface of its water was constantly getting broken at many small points all at once, as if the drizzle of a gathering rainstorm were hitting the lagoon. But the breaks came from below the surface. Occasionally a fish actually jumped clear, a dull silver flash curving its way back into the water as soon as it had left it.

A great dune of yellow-white sand separated the lagoon from the sea. It rose higher than the surrounding beach, and Densu could not see beyond it till he climbed up to its crest. He heard the song almost the same moment he saw the soldiers. They were coming along the beach, trotting in single file. They came in a long line, their uniforms and their skins making a stark contrast with the pale sand below and behind them.

Densu kept walking steadily as they drew near him, and they passed him with only a few among them casting curious sidelong glances at him. The song they were singing was a simple, monotonous one. But its very simplicity and monotony gave it a sort of massive, irresistible, stupid force, a strength that made Densu think of the castle out in the distance. The song said:

> We're going to war,
> We're going to war.
> We're going to kill,
> We're going to kill.
> We're going to die,
> We're going to die.

Then a great, fantastic shout to end it:

> Yeee! Yeeeee!
> We're going to die!

Trotting at the same speed in the sand, shouting their happy song of impending death, the soldiers went down the beach going west. Densu sat down on the sand, looking at the sea, waiting for the sun to rise higher in the morning.

The walk along the beach did not tire Densu. It cooled and refreshed him. The sand under his feet was not yet hot, just pleasantly warm. The sunlight was strong, but there was a new breeze blowing a bit uncertainly, and the combination of moving air and sun felt pleasant to the skin. It was a day clear as if the entire world had been washed, even the sky above. At first Densu saw only the white form of the castle in the distance, growing larger as he approached it. In a while he saw the gun-holes and the cannon in them not as confused black patches in the white wall but as clear, separate things. From the distance ahead he began to hear the mixed sound of drums and a confusion of royal horns.

An outcrop of large rocks overgrown with bushes blocked his view of the low-lying field below the castle. When he came to the rocks he thought of skirting them by turning left and walking away from the shore. But he looked at the rocks and decided he could climb them. He saw a jutting piece of stone large enough for him to hold on to with both hands. He pulled at it to test its firmness. It held. He swung his body upward, and his feet found a safe ledge half his height up the rock face. The climb was easier after that, because higher up the rocks were rough with many platforms, cracks, and hand-holds.

At the top he could see nothing at first. Thick bush shut off the view ahead. But now the music of horns and drums was very clear. Densu had reached the meeting ground. He parted a soft clump of bushes, carefully skirted a thorny one and found himself looking down on a scene of extraordinary commotion.

Two tents stood in the centre of the field facing each other. Between them a tall white pole had been planted, from which the flag of the whites fluttered in the breeze from the sea—streaks of red, white, and blue. From where he stood Densu could not see what was under the tents. His eyes did not have liberty to search. The loud competition of royal noises in the field was an echo of dizzying movements surging around the tents, centering on them.

From the castle side a large procession led by drummers and horn-blowers was making for the tents. In shape it was a procession much like a python freshly fed. The head and tail were slender, but the line spread out monstrously in the middle around a large red umbrella with a gilt carved figure topping it. The sun hitting the golden figure came off in a sharp glare that made it impossible for Densu to see what shape the figure was. Huge as the umbrella was, it was whirling with a kind of mad, happy speed in the air, turning round and round so dizzyingly that Densu involuntarily closed his eyes after the third circle. In the dome behind his eyelids everything became green.

When he opened his eyes again he made an effort to keep them off the dazzling red canopy, but it was hard. Again and again the thing, bouncing and turning, its yellow fringe of tassels flying up and down with the bearers' motion, caught his unwilling eyes. But he freed his gaze and saw below the manic red umbrella a wild crowd bulging at the sides. On the outermost fringes were little children, many naked, dancing to the drummers' music, moving forward with the umbrella without missing a beat, and very often in their ecstatic dancing occupying the forward path of the group under the umbrella so completely the whole procession was forced to halt. That this caused some irritation was plain. At every such forced halt a huge attendant ran out from beneath the umbrella, pushing and scattering the children dancing in the procession.

The attendant's appearance should have been enough to frighten children anywhere. His chest was completely bare, but the skin of it was hidden under a thick growth of hair. His trunk down to the waist was also uncovered. He wore a piece of calico, half rolled up around his waist, the remainder of it reaching down to his knees. The calves below the knees were monstrous in size. They made the attendant look as if large round gourds had been attached to his legs.

He carried before him an enormous belly. Behind him his buttocks billowed outwards. His arms were thick, the muscles knotted in permanent tension. The muscular upper arms were covered with dark brown leather bangles. The shape of the man's head was altogether odd. It was a head longer than it was high. The forehead projected forward, and the back of the head reached even farther back so that his head seemed shaped in imitation of the line his paunch and buttocks made.

The procession was half-way across the distance to the tents in the centre of the field when it was brought to another forced halt. The drummers, whether commanded by their leader or under some spontaneous impulse of their own, began to play faster and much louder. The change affected the dancing children. They had spread out all around the group, but when the music rose in intensity they surged forward like warriors and completely overwhelmed the procession's front, dancing with vertiginous energy.

The heavy man whose job it was to keep the path clear burst rushing out from the procession's rear and charged at the children. He was carrying something in his hands—a long, thick, cudgel, and from the way he advanced he looked ready to use it against the dancing children. The children saw the coming terror, but they did not stop their dancing. As the heavy man came near them, they each stepped nimbly aside, leaving him isolated in the middle of the circling crowd. Anger seized the man then, and he made a sad mistake. He swung in savage fury at the child nearest him, and hit him. The blow might have done real damage, but the boy had seen it and started dancing away. At the moment when the cudgel made contact with the boy's buttocks he was at the beginning of a light final jump. The blow caught him with a loud smack, and the boy fell. The heavy man moved menacingly upon him.

However, the fallen boy's companions, far from being intimidated by the heavy man's fierce approach, closed in on him as he swung his club at another boy on his way to the one on the ground. Before he had had time to regain his balance from that last swipe, a swift knot of children dashed towards him. Their aim was not the man—it was his club. A great number of little hands seized it from the end opposite the heavy man. He tried to wrest it free, and he did succeed in jerking the children forward a step or two. Then they tightened their hold on the club, and broke into a quickening backward run. For all his weight, the heavy man was unable to resist the children's pull.

Their speed increased, and the huge man's efforts to stay on his feet grew frantic. The children had reached a peak of enjoyment, and were running fast now. So fast the heavy man finally lost the fight to keep up with them. His feet flew off the ground, and for a moment he hung suspended in the the air like some monstrous wingless bird. Then he crashed to earth upon his belly. The belly was a sufficient cushion, so that no other part of his body touched the ground. The legs stuck out behind it, and in front his head and arms were raised. For some strange reason he still held on to his cudgel. The children were still pulling it.

The children whirled round with their victim as if they meant to recross the field. But now the drummers and horn-blowers had abandoned their instruments and were running to save the heavy man. Before they could reach them, the children wrenched the cudgel from the fallen man's hands and ran towards the town, scattering in all directions.

The musicians helped the heavy man up. He was most subdued. He said nothing, and on his way back to the huge red umbrella his walk was that of a defeated man, robbed of energy. The group returned to the umbrella but the musicians did not resume their playing. The procession, much smaller now that the children had deserted it, went forward slowly and in silence. Near the entrance to the tents the umbrella stopped. A solitary horn blew praises into the air. The umbrella whirled faster and faster; the tassels bordering it curled upward and flapped high in the air. The group under it waited a few moments, then as if at some signal Densu had not seen, they found places on the ground and all sat down.

Now other groups, other processions were arriving and crossing the field towards the tents in the centre, each under its bright umbrella, each flowing forward to the beat of great drums and the wail of horns. Here was an umbrella of blue and yellow stripes with red tassels; there another bright orange with white borders. There were huge green umbrellas and a dozen multi-coloured ones.

As for the music, there was such a coming together of different sounds that all the air was soon vibrating with the power of three hundred drums and a hundred royal horns. Between the umbrellas the spaces began to fill up—men, women, and great hordes of children.

Densu decided it was time for him to come down from his position above the field. The red umbrella that had attracted him first was the closest to the tents. He made his way towards it. It was not easy moving through the great crowd. Children ran across his path at almost every step, and adults stopped him to ask him what medicines he carried. He greeted people but did not stop to talk of the medicines he was carrying.

All around him the dust rose like steam from the confused motion of thick crowds. It made breathing hard, and Densu moved as quickly as he could through the mass of moving bodies. There was less dust as he came closer to the red umbrella. The crowd under and around it was no longer in motion. Most of the people there were seated, and those not seated were standing calmly, waiting expectantly for something to happen.

Densu searched for and found a twisting path through the seated people. It brought him close to the group directly underneath the red umbrella, and he recognized the heavy man who had so recently lost his battle against the children in the field. The man was standing dejectedly, looking downward at a spot three steps ahead of him. In all that crowd, he looked completely lost, alone.

Directly under the umbrella a man—the king—was seated on a royal stool. The curved seat was supported by a carved elephant whose feet stood firmly on the oblong base. In front of the stool a skin had been placed—the hide of a leopard with the head still attached, the yellowed fangs bared fiercely even in death. The king's feet, almost lost in a pair of enormous flat leather sandals, their upper thongs encrusted with intricate gilt designs, rested on the leopard skin. In front of the king, to one side of the skin, a young man sat cross-legged, holding two ceremonial swords slanted across each other. Over the king's right shoulder stood a grey-haired man with a black staff at the head of which a parrot with its beak open had been carved.

Densu's eyes returned to the heavy man just at the moment when he lifted his lost face from the ground and saw Densu looking straight at him. Densu did not look away. The heavy man shifted uncomfortably, as if standing still had cramped his muscles. Then he began to walk aggressively towards Densu. Densu stood his ground.

'Out of the way, you standing there!' the heavy man shouted. Densu only looked steadily at him. The heavy man upon reaching him, stretched out a hand to push Densu. Densu shifted his left foot backward to steady himself against the push. The heavy man pushed hard, with no result. The day was growing hot, and this new exertion brought fresh sweat to the man's face.

'I'm telling you to move!' he shouted again. Densu said nothing. The man looked around him in desperation; then, with the resolute step of someone who had found a solution that could not fail, he walked over towards the seated king. The grey-haired man with the parrot staff— the spokesman of the king—stepped smartly between the advancing heavy man and the king.

'What is it now, Kotu?' the spokesman asked in a slow voice.

'That man!' the heavy man pointed towards Densu.

'Yes, what has he done?'

'He looks like a witch-doctor.'

'Perhaps he does, Kotu. But what of that?'

'I don't know him.'

'You don't know all the medicine men in the world.'

'He has come to bewitch the king,' the heavy man said. He had intended this as a whisper, but it was audible enough.

The spokesman smiled: 'How do you know?'

'I feel it,' said the heavy man with great conviction, smiting his chest three times. 'He brings evil.'

'We shall see,' the spokesman said with a sigh. 'Tell him the king wishes to speak to him. Go!'

The heavy man walked with all the consciousness of his importance as the bearer of heavy messages. He began talking before he had quite come up to Densu

'You with the juju bag. The king wants you.'

Densu was ready. Calmly he turned and walked towards the red umbrella. The spokesman was waiting for him.

'You come from far away, young man,' the spokesman said.

'Not too far,' Densu answered.

The spokesman smiled affably.

'What is your work?'

'Healing.'

'What is in your bag?'

'Medicine for my work.'

'Such a small bag?'

'I'm only carrying one kind of medicine today.'

'What is it?'

'I will have to whisper the name to you,' Densu said.

The grey-haired man's eyes sparkled. 'Oh, oh. A name demanding whispers. This I must hear.' He shifted his trunk closer to Densu's, and tilted his head to the right, so that his left ear was raised upward. 'I hear better with this ear,' he said. 'Now let me hear your whisper.'

Densu leaned till his mouth almost touched the spokesman's ear.

'Bediwona,' he whispered.

The grey head perked upright so fast it would have bumped against Densu's face had he not anticipated the movement and pulled back his head the moment he pronounced the word. The spokesman gaped incredulously at Densu. He blinked three times, closed his eyes and took a deep breath. When he opened his eyes he asked a question:

'Is this a joke?'

'I am a healer.'

'And you have medicine bearing that name.'

'I do.'

'I have heard the name, but I've always thought it was a joke told by ruffians. Is it true?'

'Is what true?' asked Densu, all innocence.

'Will the drug make a man do that?'

'In a manner of speaking, it will. All power comes from nature, of course. But what I have here does one thing: it removes those obstacles in a man's feelings which block the full thrust of his power.'

'You amaze me, young man. Something tells me I should be slow to believe you.'

'You need not believe me at all. There are ways of finding out what's truth and what's a lie.'

'Are you suggesting I should try the drug?'

'If the spirit so moves you.'

The spokesman chuckled. 'Do you not see my grey hair, you disrespectful child?'

'I see it. It is a sign of great experience and sometimes of wisdom.'

The spokesman now laughed out loud—a great hearty laugh that startled the king into looking upward interrogatively. He did not speak, but his eyes told the spokesman what he wanted and the old man leaned low to hear his master's whisper. The spokesman whispered something in return; and the king covered his mouth with his left hand, his cheeks flared sideways under the hand, and his eyes watered. He whispered once more to the spokesman. The latter straightened up and stepped towards Densu again:

'Go nowhere yet, young man,' the spokesman told Densu. 'The king wants you to stay.'

'Does the king want my medicine?' Densu asked. The spokesman's expression grew severe. 'Understand, young man,' he said, staring at the ground, 'that the king has no need of drugs. His power is sufficient, more than sufficient. It is not for himself that he wants your drug. Not for himself, but for an unfortunate friend.'

'Quite so,' said Densu.

The spokesman smiled once more. 'Come and sit near me,' he said. 'And tell me your name.'

'Densu. What may I call you?'

'Nsaako.'

Densu sat near the standing spokesman. Looking over his shoulder he saw the entire field packed with people, the royal umbrellas doing their wild multi-coloured dance above the whole, under a sky now fierce with sunlight, almost white.

By degrees the music stopped. It was replaced by a sort of whisper, which rose to a murmur, then a shout. Densu looked around for the cause of the commotion. At first he could see nothing. The crowd behind him was straining forward to see what was there; the few ahead had all turned and were craning their necks, looking backward as if whatever was coming would come from there.

The white men came from the front, between lines of black soldiers with long rifles. Their leader wore tight trousers and a tight coat of smooth red cloth with golden ropes and numerous shiny pieces of metal on his chest. Close beside him, but a shade behind, walked a tall, unsteady-looking fellow, also dressed in the manner of white soldiers, but he wore only one rope. This man's face was pale and blotchy, as if he suffered from some leprous, disfiguring disease. He carried under his left arm a thick book, and in his right a pad of papers. The other whites—there were more than thirty dressed as soldiers, and about ten wearing different clothes, four, like the leader's companion, carrying pads of paper to write on—marched stiffly to the tents and took their positions on chairs arranged there on a long platform. In the rear of the group came a black man dressed like a white man. When he reached the platform he stood below it, near the middle. He too carried paper and also had a pen to write with. The black soldiers took up positions all around the tents. The crowd, at first excited by the arrival of the white officers, grew quiet now that the general curiosity had been satisfied, and prepared itself to listen to the leader of the whites.

The white man rose from his chair and stepped forward. He was not a tall man, but the way he held himself he gave the impression of wishing the world to take him for a giant, straining to scrape the sky itself with his forehead. The one with the leprous face also got up and stayed close beside the leader. He gave the leader some papers, and the leader began to read a speech to the assembly below him. He spoke his words not all at a time but in separate pieces. After each piece he waited, and the black man dressed like a white man, standing below his master, translated what he had said:

'These are the words of the powerful white officer you see in front of you,' the translator said, 'the renowned Sir Garnet Wolseley, commander of armies greater than any ever seen in this land or anywhere else. Hear his words.'

Each time the white man spoke, the crowd was dead silent. Then the translator explained what he had said and a murmur rose from the listeners, dying down again after the white man began once more to speak:

'The great white man says he is overjoyed to see so many kings and important men here, all good friends of the greatest among the whites, the English nation. The great white man comes from a great white queen, powerful beyond all kings on earth. This queen—her name is Victoria—has ears that hear everything that goes on everywhere in the world, even here. She has heard how much damage the Asante armies have done against us on the coast. She has therefore sent us this powerful white man, out of the kindness of her heart and the fullness of her might, to help us drive away the Asante armies and defeat them thoroughly, so they will never rise again.[1]

This last was greeted with sounds of great disbelief, but the translator had stopped, and the white man talked again. The translator continued his work: 'The white queen is all powerful, but like God, she only helps those who help themselves. Therefore we shall have to recognize that the war against the Asante armies is our war. We are to remember how often the Asante royals have said they have no quarrel with the whites, only with other black people, like us.' Another pause. This time the murmurs came more subdued:

'The powerful white officer says the whites have their castles,' the translator pointed towards the huge fort, 'against which the Asante armies, even if they numbered a thousand thousand thousands, could never hope to prevail. Were the white queen selfish, she could let her people stay safe in these forts. But she is kind. She does not want us to suffer.' Loud cries of approbation came from under several umbrellas at this.

'That is why she has decided to help us. She will help us by giving us guns, with officers skilled in war who will advise us. She will even give us food. But the fighting we shall have to do ourselves.' More murmurs, loud but unclear in meaning, followed this.

'The powerful white man wants to know from each chief how many men he can put in the field ready for war, and when. He wants all our warriors to assemble at Dunkwa. Every chief must personally be there with his warriors, until the war is over.'

The murmur could have been a protest beginning this time. The white man spoke quickly, and the translator spoke even more quickly:

'Hear the powerful white man. He says no chief should fear to be doing all this in vain. The powerful white man will give the huge sum of ten English pounds, ten English pounds, let me say it again, ten English pounds, the white man's real money, the powerful white man

201

will give this money every month to each king who brings a thousand warriors to Dunkwa.

'The powerful Sir Garnet Wolseley will give each king all the guns and powder and bullets he will ever need. In addition there will be rice to the measure of one pint each day, and meat, delicious salted meat to the measure of one pound every four days, for every fighting man. All this will be available at the castle.

'The food is on its way here from England. While we wait for it, the powerful Sir Garnet Wolseley, out of his own pocket, will pay each chief four whole pennies and another half every day for each fighting man.

'Even after the food is here, there will be a payment of three pennies per man, paid through the kings and chiefs.'

This produced a swell of contented talk.

'The powerful Sir Garnet Wolseley, to ensure that everything goes well, will send one of his white men from among these you see here, to be with each king. That white man will be an adviser, and he must be obeyed, because his advice will be merely for our own good. Disobedience will be punished.[1]

The enthusiasm that had greeted the previous statement was gone now. A vague confused murmur was the only response.

'The powerful white queen, whose ears are everywhere, has heard that some of our kings still kill prisoners and cut off the heads of people killed in battle. She orders us to stop this.

'The powerful Sir Garnet Wolseley is a busy man. No one should disturb him with petty troubles and requests to speak with him. If he wants to talk to any king, he himself will send for that king.

'The powerful Sir Garnet Wolseley wants to know without delay, how many men each king will bring. He says the kings may now go and put their heads together.'

At the end of the interpreter's explanation of what the white general Garnet Wolseley had said, a kind of silence fell upon the listeners. It was a while before voices began asking each other discreet questions, talking, arguing, till their noise rose as on a market day.

Then the spokesman from underneath the red umbrella stepped towards the platform, and the crowd was again hushed. The spokesman said what he had been told to say on behalf of the kings, and the interpreter turned his words into English for the white officers.

The kings, said the spokesman, had heard the white general's words. Those were the sweetest words ever uttered since creation began. So

202

sweet were the words, the spokesman continued with the most serious expression, that had the kings been centuries dead and buried they would nevertheless have woken, broken open their overgrown graves and come with the single purpose of tasting those words. It was the burning desire of all the chiefs to co-operate most warmly with the general. They hoped for only one thing: that in his dealings with them he would tread firmly in the footsteps of the brave and generous Governor McCarthy, he who had died so bravely in battle at Nsamankow fifty years back.

The spokesman looked over his shoulder and smiled at someone under the red umbrella when he made that last statement.

2 The Kings

Again the attentive silence gave way to whispers, which rapidly grew into a general commotion, and the drum beats took over the air again. The kings and their followers began to move out of the field, each group going back the same way it had come, all making way for the red umbrella to pass first.

The spokesman, having regained his place under the red umbrella, turned to Densu as the procession ambled forward: 'You must come with us to the palace. The king has important business to attend to. When it's over he will talk to you.'

'I shall have to return home before dusk,' Densu said.

'Home where?' the spokesman asked.

'Beyond the lagoon.'

'That's not far at all,' the spokesman said. 'Walk here, by my side.'

Densu walked beside the spokesman, behind the king, who tried at first to walk instead of riding his palanquin. The royal sandals, being flat and several times wider than the king's feet, made him walk slowly, with great difficulty, raising each knee high under his rich cloth, then taking a half step forward before repeating the process with the other foot. So when the carriers brought the palanquin he sank into its softness, a gratified look spreading over his face. Four men lifted the palanquin on their shoulders, each taking one corner with its jutting pole. The horns began the praises of the king, and the drums took them up in turn. The red umbrella was lifted again.

The procession marched forward, the crowd ahead opening a path for it. Densu was baffled to see that the route followed was a twisting one. He asked the spokesman why.

'We're passing by the other umbrellas. The king must greet the other kings and invite them to the palace,' the spokesman explained to Densu.

The procession stopped a while at each umbrella. The king nodded to the other king under it, a spokesman stepped forward to exchange whispers with Densu's friend, and the procession moved on, turned and turned again till it found another umbrella and the pattern was repeated.

All the way to the palace the streets were full of people. Some stood on the flat rooftops of houses, their legs hidden by the grass growing there. When the procession reached the palace most of those who had followed it turned back at the gate. Some more were driven forcibly away by servants from within. The king was taken to the steps in front of the largest building in the courtyard, and then he stepped out of his palanquin and went gingerly inside.

The spokesman took Densu's hand: 'You will come with me,' he said. Without waiting for an answer he walked into the room with him.

It was a huge room. The floor was entirely covered with reed mats. Drums of different sizes and shapes stood along each wall. In the centre stood three heavy-looking tables made of dark red wood. On each table stood two boxes of plain white wood, bearing numerous marks on every visible side. All round the room, in a sort of huge rough circle, stood large stools.

The King Ata sat on the stool farthest from the door, but the spokesman, after he had seen the king to the stool, turned round and went to stand at the door. Densu went with him. As soon as he reached the door he saw another procession come to the gate. It too shed its train of followers, and the king in the palanquin was brought to the door. An aged man, trim and dignified in looks, descended to the ground. As he stepped out, the spokesman went forward to help him up the three steps and into the room. The new king took the seat to the right of the host.

'That's Nana Edu, from Mankesim,' the spokesman told Densu when he came back. 'He will want to take you with him when he hears about what you've got.'

His chuckle was interrupted by the arrival, simultaneously, of two kings. One was a strange-looking man, who walked unsteadily, like a toddler. He had a ludicrous-looking crown, a small shell cone which sat insufficiently on top of his head. It was gilded, but the sunshine only made it seem even more undignified. It was not age that made him so shaky on his feet, however, because he did not look old. Certainly he was nowhere near the spokesman's age. At his second step he actually tottered. Densu jumped forward, fearing he would fall. But before he got to him, the second king who had got down from his palanquin had already reached the unsteady king, and laughing, propped him up. The other laughed too, heartily, as if the joke had been at another's expense, not his own. As he passed up the steps into the room on his companion's arm, Densu glimpsed the cause of this king's instability: his eyes were red as daylight blood, with the kind of redness lent by hot spirits too freely drunk.

'He's so unfortunate,' said the spokesman.

'Who is he?' asked Densu.

'Nana Kwesi Kyei, king of Denchira. The Asante armies have driven him out and sorrow has turned him into a forgetful drunkard. But the other is his good friend—Nana Amoonu, from Anomabo. He tries his best to keep him happy. Twice he has stopped him from killing himself. But he's doing it with drink, slowly but certainly.'

Other kings came in so rapidly that all the spokesman had time to do was to tell Densu their names: 'Nana Tsibu, from Assen,' he said, nodding towards one still to reach the steps. This one had glistening hair and skin of such smoothness it was hard to think of him as a grown man and not a large pampered baby.

Another king, whose age showed in a bald pate surrounded on the sides by a crescent of white hair, the spokesman named King Solomon, from Dominase.

'That is not one of our names,' Densu said.

'It's a name borrowed from the whites. Among the royals that's the new style. Look, there is Opanyin Bentsir, from Gomoa. Only these days he likes to call himself Bentil. Mr Bentil, Field Marshal. It is a great title among whites, I hear.'

The Field Marshal wore a bright red coat, cut in the style of white men's clothes, but unlike anything Densu had seen on a white man.

Next came a giant, Nana Amfo Otu, of Abora. Then a confusion of incredible names: Blankson, Moore, Thompson, Robertson, each wearing a strange assortment of white men's clothes.

The room was now lively with the laughter of the kings. No one else came through the gate, but the courtyard was filled with the attendants who had brought their kings. The spokesman ordered water to be brought for everyone. Then, taking Densu by the hand, he entered the room and stood beside his king, leaving Densu a step behind himself.

One of the kings—the unsteady one, Nana Kwesi Kyei of Denchira—had begun struggling to open one of the boxes on the tables. He not only failed, but almost brought the whole box crashing down on top of himself. Respectfully, the spokesman persuaded the unsteady king to wait till some servant could be found with enough skill and strength to open the boxes. Then he asked Densu to step outside and call for a servant:

'Shout for Buntui,' the spokesman said.

Densu recovered quickly from his surprise. Going out into the yard, he cupped his hands to his mouth and yelled out Buntui's name.

Before the echoes of his name had died out, Buntui came bounding in like a happy buffalo. He was singing a song. His voice was not the sweetest in the universe, but what it lacked in sweetness it made up for in loudness and enthusiasm. The song was something Densu had heard before, just that morning. It was the song of the new army recruits—monotonous, irresistibly stupid. Only, Buntui had had the brains to change the words, so that the song was now about himself alone:

> I am going to war,
> I am going to war.
> I am going to kill,
> I am going to kill.
> I am going to die,
> I am going to die.
> Yeee, Yeeeee! I am going to die!
> Bueee, bueeeee! I am going to die!

The spokesman hushed Buntui as he entered the room, still singing happily about his coming death.

'Shut up, Buntui. Can't you stop singing that fool song for just one moment?' The spokesman shook his head. 'It's hard to teach an idiot; harder to make him forget the bit he manages to learn.'

The giant stopped singing and stood grinning before the spokesman. 'Open those boxes,' the spokesman said.

As if he had been born opening such boxes, Buntui went to the one the unsteady king had failed to open. He looked for a space between the slats of wood, found one, inserted the fingers of his right hand, and wrenched the slat outward with sheer brute force. The slat came loose in his hand. Taking the loose slat, he used it to lever the others free.

The kings had been laughing at the unsuccessful attempts of their red-eyed brother. As the first box was opened they fell quiet. Bottle after shiny green bottle came out, and the laughter of the royals became first a gasp, then a lively conversation about what kind of drink the bottles might contain.

The king of Denchira, reeling forward again, snatched a bottle from the open box and thrust it at the interpreter. The interpreter, with an air of great wisdom, studied the writing on the bottle's white label, turned the bottle round, searched for further inscriptions, returned to the label, stared at the words again, and shaped his mouth to pronounce the liquor's name. He was not able to bring out the sound. While he had been studying the bottle, the king of Denchira had grabbed a second bottle. Unable to contain his thirst or even to wait for the bottle to be properly opened, he had banged its neck violently against the edge of the nearest table. The wood was hard. The bottle-neck broke off and splintered on impact against the floor. King Kwesi Kae did not even look at the mouth of the broken bottle so left in his hand. He swung it upward to his lips and sucked hard. He took a long swig, and when he removed the shortened bottle from his mouth his eyes were no longer dull. They were red still, but now they were also bright with joy.

'Gin!' he declared triumphantly. 'And strong!'

The bottle flew back to his lips. He sucked desperately, like a famished baby at a mother's breast. When he released the bottle a second time, a trickle ran down his chin, and carelessly he reached up with his left hand and wiped at the trickle with his palm. On the hand's way down again he glanced casually at it, and the bottle of gin in his hand dropped to the ground, shattering into a thousand tiny fragments.

What King Kwesi Kae had seen was his own blood.

'I am wounded, brothers,' he shouted, real consternation on his face. The motion dislodged his crown. The fragile shell hit the ground with a crack, and rolled unevenly towards the door.

One of the kings, seeing his distress, bounded from his stool, scooped up the wayward crown in mid-stride, crossed the room and in a moment was by the king of Denchira's side. It was Amoonu, king of Anomabo. First he replaced the crushed crown on Nana Kwesi Kae's head. Then, with his right arm over the wounded monarch's shoulder and the other supporting his left elbow, King Amoonu steered his friend back to his seat.

'It isn't very deep, your wound,' he said consolingly.

'Now they want to bleed me to death,' the king of Denchira said. 'They've taken away my land, and they're still not satisfied.'

'It will not prove fatal,' said King Amoonu. 'Only a slight cut.'

'We have a healer here with us,' the spokesman said in a loud voice.

'Bring him here,' Amoonu ordered him.

Densu went forward. He was asked to look at the wound. He told the smiling kings it was nothing to worry about. 'Let me have clean water to wash it. After that the only medicine the king will need for it will be the salt and pepper he eats.' Everybody laughed, except the morose king of Denchira himself.

Densu had taken a swift look at Buntui even as he tried to make sure Buntui would not recognize him. But their eyes did meet. Buntui looked away at once, then turned his head sharply to look again at the young healer. Slow doubt clouded his face. Belief struggled with incredulity. A few moments of this mental tension exhausted Buntui's capacity for thought, and he turned his attention to the remaining boxes. Now came the serious business of sharing the drinks. The good humour with which the kings had begun their discussions died. In its place there was grim earnest bargaining.

'Let's count the bottles, and divide them equally,' said Chief Robertson, standing up to speak, his hands stuck importantly into the pockets of his European coat.

'Heh, heh,' the king of Denchira laughed dryly through his swollen lips. 'That would not be wise. After all, we are all kings, but there are kings among kings, heh, heh.'

The remark produced a strange silence. For a while no one seemed able to think of anything to say. Then King Edu, the old one from Mankesim, cleared his throat.

'Hear the old man from Mankesim,' the spokesman said. The others turned to see King Edu:

'It is true there are kings and there are kings,' he said, smiling complacently. 'But let us think also of the host.'

There were nods of agreement, and small whispers were exchanged in little groups of two and three. King Ata called the spokesman and whispered urgently to him. The spokesman moved from group to group, all round the room, saying a few words to each, then bowing to listen. He stood in the centre of the room after he had spoken to each of the kings:

'There are twelve kings here,' the spokesman announced. 'The bottles number one hundred and forty-four.'

'One hundred and forty-three now,' corrected the young king, Amoonu of Anomabo, with a smile.

'There are one hundred and forty-three bottles to be shared among twelve kings. It has been suggested the wisest way to share the bottles would be ten to each king. That would leave twenty-three bottles. Of those it has been suggested we let the father of kings, the king of Mankesim, have ten to add to his ten. That leaves thirteen. Twelve of these should go to the host . . .' There was a dissatisfied gasp here, spurring the spokesman to speak with smoother speed. '. . . to the host, who of course will only use it for the present entertainment of those here today.'

The gasp of dissatisfaction grew subtle. It turned into an approving sigh.

'The thirteenth bottle will be a libation to our departed kings,' the spokesman said.

'And those yet to come, don't forget,' the king of Mankesim said.

The spokesman smiled, nodded, and said: 'And to those yet to come.'

The meeting of kings agreed that the division of the white generals's gift of drinks was just. Cups were called for. Servants brought them in a great brass pan. Each cup was filled to the brim.

The spokesman waited till each king held a cup ready in his hand. Then, taking the thirteenth bottle, already opened, he moved solemnly to the centre of the room. He tilted the bottle an instant. A single bright white oval of liquid dropped from it.

'Nananom,' the spokesman called in a far-off voice:

Nananom,
The children of Oburum Ankoma greet you,
the children of Odapa Djan greet you,
the children of Oson greet you.

The spokesman's eyes were closed, but his blind gaze was directed at a spot just in front of him as if with his closed eyes he could see the departed to whom he was now called upon to talk. The oval drop of gin was succeeded by several, then all turned into one thin line of clear liquor descending gently to the floor:

Nananom,
this is not a festival we're holding for you.
This is a heavy time
and we're crying to you for help.
The Oyoko enemy,
the Asante thousands
for whom war is love
have risen against your children
again.

In times past we have called to you
in our need
and you did not fail us.
You did for us what was in your power,
in the power lent you
by the dependable one,
the trustworthy one,
the repairer,
the keeper,
the owner of a thousand praises.

You did all that was possible
and though we didn't prevail against the enemy
we survived his fire.

Nananom,
Now the Oyoko enemy,
the Asante thousands,
the prickly porcupine quills
for whom war is love
have risen against your children
again.

This time
you have sent us help,

the help of the white strangers
from beyond the seas,
from beyond the horizon.
Help them help us,
Nananom.
Help them help us drive the Asante thousands back
and keep them in their own lands
so we can have peace.

Nananom,
Ask this for us,
ask it of the almighty one,
the creator of beings,
the unbending tree of life,
the beginning of all things,
the end of all things

The spokesman finished speaking before the bottle was empty. He did not open his eyes, but continued pouring the drink until it was all gone. When he opened his eyes they were red, and there were tears in them. He did not try to keep them from falling. He ordered Buntui to take ten bottles to each king, and place them behind his stool. The kings began to drink. The king of Denchira was audibly the first. He drained his cup at one heroic go, and announced this feat to the world with a great, powerful belch loud as a cannon shot going off at night.

'Gently, brother,' the young King Amoonu said softly, 'gently.'

'Ten pounds!' declared the bald man with a ring of white hair around the shiny pate, King Solomon of Dominase. 'That is money.' He chuckled.

'Not so much,' said the one in the red coat, 'if you consider what we are told to do. Ten pounds for one thousand fighting men. That is not enough. I, Bentil, Field Marshal of Gomoa, know how difficult it is to gather even a hundred warriors together. One thousand men! The white man is crazy. We should get a hundred pounds for each thousand men we can persuade to fight.'

'But the ten pounds are for our own use only. The whites will give food to the fighters, and pay them. Everything.' This was the big, quiet King Amfo Otu, the one from Abora. 'And who knows, if all the food and pay and ammunition are to be distributed by us, we may find ways to end up with considerably more than these ten pounds.'

211

'Yes,' agreed the host, 'I think we'd be wise to accept the ten pounds, at least to start with.'

The Field Marshal from Gomoa spoke again: 'Did you count how many men the white general brought with him? About thirty.'

'Fifty,' said the interpreter.

'So let it be fifty. We don't need fifty. What can fifty white men do against the thirty thousand warriors from Asante?'

'The whites are to help us with guns, food, money, and advice,' the interpreter submitted.

'That's not enough,' the Field Marshal said heatedly. 'They have always supplied us with those, and we've always been defeated.'

'Not always,' challenged the giant Amfo Otu.

'Almost always, then,' the Field Marshal continued. As he talked he played distractedly with the bright yellow buttons lining the front of his scarlet coat. 'When the whites merely advise us, they take care not to give us the latest guns. What do they care if a thousand of us die? But if they had whites fighting here they'd bring the best guns ever seen in this world. The only thing that will defeat Asante is an army of whites.'

'We can't make them bring such an army. The whites are afraid of that,' said Solomon.

'Why do they fear? They have better weapons than the Asante.'

'It isn't the Asante alone. They fear the forest. White men don't last long in the forest. The fever catches them and they die.'

'Even if they weren't afraid, this Sir Garnet Wolseley is not so powerful among the whites. He has not got the power to send for white soldiers.'

Here a look of displeasure came violently upon the interpreter's face. 'I must ask pardon to speak like this, but what has just been said is not quite true.' He cleared his throat and looked around suspiciously, but seemed to make up his mind there was no harm in continuing. 'Because of the work I do, I overhear a lot the whites say to each other. This man I work for is powerful. The only person in the world more powerful than he is the Queen of England, and to tell the truth, from what I hear he and the Queen are like this!' He brought his index fingers together, hooked them around each other, and pulled hard to demonstrate how impossible it would be to tear them apart.

'This man I work for, whatever he wants from England, he will get. Now I heard him ask the old governor, Sir Harley, and the other whites who were here before him, if he thought there would be a black army able to invade and conquer Kumase. They said no.'

'Good,' said the host. 'At least the white men know we're not suicidal fools, to go and die so stupidly.'

'This man I work for, Sir Garnet Wolseley, then revealed to the others that he had the power to ask for two thousand white soldiers, but only if all the fighting can be done and over before the rains start.'

It was as if all the kings had decided to take in a deep breath at the same time. Silence fell.

'That means only six months to go from now.' said King Tsibu.

'Five,' corrected the Field Marshal.

'The whites fear the rains more than they fear the Asante army,' said King Ata.

'I don't blame then. They die rather fast when they come here, and here we're not even in the forest yet. Remember what happened ten years ago? They sent an army to Praso to frighten the Asante king. The army came back half dead. It hadn't fought any battles, except against the rains and the diseases that came with them. The whites have good reason to fear.'

'But,' asked Amoonu, 'if they can't fight more than a few months, why not bring more than two thousand men?'

The drunken king of Denchira answered him: 'They don't have so many men. Don't you know? The white women have a hard time giving birth. They don't like it.'

'Now how do you know? Have you had any white women?' asked the Field Marshal from Gomoa.

'I haven't, but I know,' answered the king of Denchira.

'Two thousand white soldiers are too few for fighting against Asante,' Amoonu repeated. 'And if they actually hope to capture Kumase . . .'

'But have you seen the guns these two thousand will be carrying?' Amfo Otu asked.

'No one has seen them,' said Ata.

'I have,' Amfo Otu said. 'I've seen one in action. The bullets shot from it travel more than twice as far as any Asante gun can send bullets. And faster. That's not all. I hear, confidentially, that the whites want to bring a gun here that can shoot a thousand bullets into one small space in a few moments.'

'Is that possible?' asked King Solomon.

'It is not merely possible,' said a voice so full of conviction it had to be listened to, 'it is certain.' The voice belonged to the interpreter, and it did not stop. 'But all this you will see with your own eyes in good time. Besides, I can assure you there will be more than two thousand soldiers marching against Kumase.'

'Will there be another white army?' asked King Solomon.

'And where will it march from?' asked the Field Marshal.

'No,' the interpreter said importantly. 'There will not be another white army marching against Kumase. But a white man almost as great as my general, Sir Garnet Wolseley, is raising an army in the east, on the right bank of the Firaw river. I can even tell you that white man's name: Glover. This white man Glover is raising a huge army of all the peoples east of us: Ekuapem, Krepi, Ga, Awona, Ada, even people from beyond Dahomey, from Bonni and Alata and Opobo.'

'When is this great army supposed to move against Kumase?' the Field Marshal asked.

'I have yet to hear a definite time given,' the interpreter said. 'All I know is everything must be done before the big rains start to fall.'

The conversation of the kings settled into a kind of reassured buzz interrupted frequently by the tinkle of cups against bottles. Again the interpreter cleared his throat to speak.

'Pardon me, but I must remind you General Wolseley expects a message from you confirming your agreement to his plans. Also, may I remind you to inform all the kings who were not here today?'

'That is no trouble at all,' said Ata. 'Write it down for us. We agree. We'll inform the others. We only hope this white general, being so powerful and rich, will be generous when the time comes for rewards.'

The interpreter wrote down the message. It took him plenty of time, and several different frowns passed over his face. The spokesman beckoned to Buntui, who had been standing near the empty boxes staring vacantly about him. Buntui went to him. The spokesman examined Buntui's hands. They were dirty. He ordered Buntui to wash his hands in the water Densu had used to wash off the blood from the drunken king's lips. When Buntui had wiped his hands dry, the spokesman took the letter from the interpreter and gave it to Buntui.

'Run all the way to the castle,' the spokesman ordered him. 'When you've given this to a white man, come back at once. You have to take a message to Esuano tonight.'

214

This seemed to bother Buntui. He looked helplessly at the spokesman. The spokesman suspected the cause of his dismay.

'You'll have enough time to rest before you go,' the spokesman continued. 'You won't have to start till the first gun sounds from the castle after dark.'

Buntui looked relieved. He took the note and walked briskly out. As he passed by the door, Densu stepped back into the shadow, away from the bright light in the doorway, and turned his face away. Buntui, hesitating at the door, searched for the face hidden from him.

'What are you waiting for?' the spokesman demanded, harshly.

Buntui jumped down the three steps into the courtyard. In another moment he had disappeared beyond the gate.

'A good messenger,' the spokesman said, shaking his head, 'but he should have been born with a bigger brain. Very strong, though, and he'll do what you tell him—if he remembers. He's a stranger here, really from Esuano.'

'How long has he been here?' Densu asked.

'He used to come and go. His master sends him here when he doesn't want him around there. He gets into trouble, I should think, on account of having too much strength and too little sense. Since his master Ababio became king at Esuano he's been here all the time. That suits us here. He's an excellent messenger. Not afraid to go anywhere, even at night. No wonder. He can defend himself. Who would want to waylay such a giant? He'd break his neck.'

The kings sat listlessly, waiting for the messenger to return.

'I don't think we should have agreed so readily,' the Field Marshal said. His voice was low, as if he were talking to himself. 'The white man respects a tough bargainer.'

'We were wise not to risk offending him,' said Ata. 'After all, we don't know him yet.'

'Ata is right. We don't know this Sir Garnet Wolseley yet. He may really help us,' Edu said, pensively.

'Not the way McCarthy helped us—getting himself killed,' said Kwesi Kyei with a laugh.

'I wouldn't laugh at his memory,' answered Edu. 'He is remembered as one white man whose words were sincere.'

'That may be the reason they killed him themselves,' Amoonu said. The others looked startled.

'But wasn't it the Asante who killed him? Didn't they chop off his head and make his brain pan a drinking bowl for their king?' asked the Field Marshal.

'Yes,' said Edu. 'But the Asante found him dead already. He had shot himself.'[1]

'The question is why?' Amoonu said. 'He had no intention of killing himself when he started out for Cape Coast.'

'That he hadn't,' Edu agreed. 'But what would you do if you opened what you knew was a barrel of gunpowder, needing to use it in the heat of battle, and found it wasn't that at all but food? What would you do?'

'Asante magic,' Kwesi Kyei growled.

'Not Asante magic,[2] Amoonu said. 'I've heard only two reasonable explanations of what happened to that good Governor. The first: the whites, in spite of all their power, are stupid enough to make such mistakes. Maybe because they have so much power, not in spite of it. The second: the whites don't like sincere people. They are glad to put such men in situations which destroy them. McCarthy was a sincere man. Too sincere.'

'At any rate, we can continue drinking to his memory,' said Kwesi Kyei.

It did not seem as if anyone had a stomach for continuing to talk of the dead McCarthy. The kings drank in silence.

There was a loud noise at the gate, and before anyone could ask what it was about Buntui burst into the room.

'Hey, learn not to enter places like a hurricane,' the spokesman said, taking the letter Buntui carried and handing it over to the interpreter. The interpreter translated it:

'The white man I work for, he says he thanks you, he hopes to see you all again on Monday, day after tomorrow, and he will certainly reward you as befits your courage in the war to come—after the war is over.[3]

King Ata of Cape Coast sighed: 'After the war is over, he says.'

Now that Buntui had done his work, he looked at the spokesman. The spokesman reached up to put an arm on his shoulder, and steered him into the doorway. Densu stayed where he was, in the shadow within.

'You may go and rest now,' the spokesman told Buntui. 'Come back here as soon as it's dark. You'll be taking a message to your master at the first night gun. Make sure no one sees you, and go as fast as you can. Understand?'

216

Buntui nodded, then went off as fast and as noisily as he had come in.

In the room the earlier liveliness was gone. A king was nodding fitfully on his stool. It was Solomon of Dominase. Kwesi Kyei was actually snoring, no longer on his stool but propped comfortably against the hind wall, a cup and a bottle beside him, both empty and overturned.

The spokesman looked around uneasily and went to whisper to King Ata. Then he came where Densu was and said: 'The king wishes to know how to use the medicine—so he can tell his friend.' He led Densu toward the king.

'It is not difficult,' Densu said, putting down his bag and taking a pinch of the powder in it between thumb and forefinger. 'It may be sprinkled on your food. Or you may wish to put it in water. Do not mix it with alcohol. They don't go together. And do not take more than this quantity, just a pinch at a time. That is quite enough. Taking more will not increase the power of the bark. It may diminish it instead. That is all.'

King Ata's eyes were almost closed by now. The spokesman quietly asked for leave to take the stranger away, and walked into the courtyard with Densu.

'You must come home with me,' he said. 'I know you're in a hurry, but I haven't had a chance to talk to you, and you look hungry.'

'I am,' agreed Densu, 'but I must hurry back.'

'Eat something at my house. It will give you strength, and your journey will be quicker.'

The spokesman's home was a short walk from the hall, near the entrance to the palace courtyard. There was a bowl of food ready in the middle of the outer room, and a stool next to it. The spokesman pointed out another stool in the far corner, and Densu fetched it and sat on it. As if she had been watching them unseen, a woman came in with a bowl of water and placed it beside the food. The spokesman washed his right hand and Densu did the same. Then they ate.

'Your wife cooks well,' said Densu after the meal. 'The fufu was soft, and the soup—I bit my tongue twice.'

'Yes, Bosoma cooks well, but she's not my wife. She's a relative of the wife I lost. Fifteen years it's been. I did not think I would live. But fifteen years is a long time.' He closed his eyes. Densu, feeling this sudden sadness of his new friend, was silent. 'Now I won't keep you any longer,' the spokesman said. 'But promise me you will come to me, as my guest, whenever you return to this town.'

'That I will gladly do.'

The spokesman walked Densu to the gate and beyond it into the town.

'One day,' he said, 'when you come back, I shall tell you many things, and you will tell me about your life. Farewell.' He took his hand from Densu's shoulder, looked up at his face, shook his head twice, and turned to go.

Densu crossed the town in a hurry. The evening had been bright, but dusk was descending and he had work to do in preparation for the coming night. By the time he reached the lagoon the sun, still visible but only barely so, had turned a dark orange. It disappeared altogether as Densu reached the entrance to Ama Nkroma's house under the coconut trees.

'You've been away long,' Ama Nkroma said by way of greeting. 'Did you succeed?'

'Better than I had reason to hope,' Densu answered.

'But you lost your bag.'

'No. King Ata wanted it, with everything it contained.'

Ama Nkroma chuckled. 'When he sees what the drug will do, he'll search the whole earth for you. But have you eaten? There's food.'

'I have eaten. I met a friend, the spokesman Nsaako.'

'Ah, so Nsaako found you. I wish you had had time to talk the whole day with him. He has a wise head, and a good heart. I have always called him a healer pretending to be a spokesman, and he has always laughed at me. Is he well?'

'Very.'

'You're restless.'

'I must go to the Esuano road tonight. I have work to do.'

'At night? What kind of work?'

'It will take time to tell. When I return here, I'll tell you. I must hurry now. Do you have any rope?'

Ama Nkroma pulled a length of rope from beneath the thatch of the roof and gave Densu a knife to cut the length he needed.

'Keep the knife,' she said. 'You may need it, going like that without a weapon.' It was a good, sharp knife.

3   Encounter

Densu walked quickly through the thickening darkness. He had not heard the castle guns go off, but he was anxious. Weird possibilities occurred to his mind. Perhaps the plan to send Buntui to Esuano had suddenly been changed. Perhaps he had gone much earlier. Perhaps he wasn't going at all. Densu made his way to the Esuano path, cutting through the brush going away from the town, keeping the faint lights of the castle on his right and slightly behind him. The brush began to thicken into real bush. Bushes ran together in thickets, and soon vegetation cut off sight of the lights from the castle and the town. The moon was beginning to shine, feebly.

The path had led northward, away from the sea. Now it took a sharp turn left. At the same time it took a dip into a long slope. Densu searched for trees near the path and found two suitable for his purpose. Working on the first, just to the right of the path, he cut a notch around its bole about the height of his own navel, then worked it into a groove. He inserted one end of the rope so that it rested securely in the groove, and tied a fast knot to keep it in place. He led the rope across the path, and dropped it below the second tree while he carved a groove in that also.

He hesitated, wondering if he should hold the loose end of the rope himself, waiting till he actually heard Buntui coming along the path into the rope trap. But he knew no one else was likely to be travelling to Esuano, and as for anyone making the journey from Esuano so late at night, that was impossible. Densu finished the groove in the second tree. He stretched the rope taut, tied a triple knot to secure it, and reinforced the knot with a stick. Then he sat down in the shadow of a tree three steps down the path, leaned his back against its trunk, and waited. Above him the foliage cut off the sky almost entirely. Only in places was the faint moonlight able to pierce the covering of leaves, like tiny starpoints in a black sky. On the ground below the darkness was thick, but along the path and near it there was a sprinkling of faint light points. The forest was silent. There was no sound at all, not even one sound from a forest creature. When the boom of cannon from the castle sounded it took complete possession of the calm air, a great violent sound carried on the air, moving away into the invisible distance ahead.

Densu waited. He tried to gauge how long it would take Buntui to reach him where he was on the path. That brought back all the troubling, anxious questions he had already pushed out of his mind: what if Buntui wasn't coming after all? What if he'd gone already? A new worry added itself: what if he was travelling with a group and not alone? Again Densu made the effort to free himself from these anxieties. He noticed his body had tensed itself up. He closed his eyes and let his head reach gently back till it rested against the tree trunk behind him. He took a deep breath of air and was surprised there was nothing of the sea's salt in it.

He heard steps coming down the path. Heavy steps, but rapid. They were not walking steps. They sounded like the steps of a man trotting. The steps came nearer. They grew louder, as if whoever was making them intended deliberately to crush the earth at every step. The man was not just trotting: he was humming a phrase, the same one over and over again from the training song of the castle recruits. Densu got ready. The humming grew louder, then expanded into real singing, words and all:

I am going to war, yee, yee!
I am going to kill, yee, yee!
I am going to die, yee, yee!
Yee! Yee! I am going to die!

The singing came to a brutal stop. The carefree voice was cut off in a hoarse gasp. A long, heavy object shot through the darkness, its flight more audible than visible. It smacked violently against a tree on the other side, bounced back across the path, hit a stone with a crunch and slithered to a stop. Densu reached out for it, and saw at a glance he had a rifle in his hand, so new it shone even in the scanty moonlight. He had never held one like it before. It was the same as the guns of the white general's guards.

A heavier sound followed the rifle's fall. There was first the cracking of undergrowth, an angry grunt, then the massive thud of a giant body against hard earth. Densu had jumped up from his hiding place. Holding the rifle, he stood in the path, looking down at the prostrate form before him. The form's head was invisible in the darkness. Its trunk was half hidden in the foliage it had crashed through. Its legs were spread awkwardly apart, and only the feet really touched the clear path.

The fall had evidently hurt the giant. He took some time doubling up into a kneeling position beside the path. Then he shifted into the centre of the path, where there was some light. He peered confusedly upward.

'Buntui,' Densu called down to him.

The effect of Densu's voice on the giant was swift. It was as if he had at the same moment realized there was a human being present with him, and that this human was responsible for his fall. The shout that rose from the huge throat was eloquent of brute anger. The giant leapt at Densu. Densu had not expected the attack. The way Buntui had looked on the ground, he had seemed too hurt and confused to put up any resistance, much less fight. Densu barely had time to step back, avoiding the giant's thrust. He turned the rifle butt forward and smashed it hard down against the huge mass that had leapt at him.

The blow was harder than Densu would have made it had he had time to prepare himself. In addition, Buntui had leaped forward with tremendous momentum. Stopped by the hard wood of the rifle, he collapsed again on to the ground. Densu leaned over him and examined him. He felt no blood on the head, but the giant had been stunned, and lay unconscious now. Densu dragged the limp form off the path into a broad clearing to the left. He laid the giant down on the grass. He found a pouch of cartridges tied to a belt around his waist. He took it. Then he sat beside the unconscious giant, waiting.

It did not take Buntui long to come to. When he did, he made a violent effort to rise, but the effort seemed to make him dizzy, and he stopped in a sitting position. The moon was shining more brightly now, and Densu could see Buntui clearly.

'I have your gun,' Densu said. 'I have no intention of using it. But if you force me to, I will.' Buntui said nothing in reply. 'I want to ask you some questions. If you answer me, you can go on your way. If you refuse, I'll keep you here till you change your mind.'

'What do you want?' asked Buntui.

'You know who killed the prince Appia,' Densu said.

Buntui was silent.

'I know you know,' Densu continued. 'That person will be hanged, just as soon as the truth is known.'

Buntui swallowed audibly, but said nothing. 'The only way the killer can save himself is if he can prove he was obeying someone else.'

'Why are you keeping me here like this?' Buntui asked. His voice was a compromise between defiance and a whining entreaty.

'You know who killed Appia,' Densu said again.

'I don't.'

'But I've been told you killed him.'

'Who . . . who told you?' Buntui was afraid.

'Ababio. Who else?'

'Ababio told you?'

'Ababio told me.'

In the silence that followed, the confusion that ravaged Buntui's dull mind was audible in his heavy, staggered breathing. At last he sounded as if he had accepted defeat and given up the attempt to think his way out of a maze too complex for him.

'But why did he tell?' he asked, a genuine question.

'Think of it,' Densu said calmly. 'The killer will hang.'

'He made me do it,' Buntui said, peevishly.

'Who?'

'Eja Ababio himself.'

'He did not force you.'

'He wanted me to do it. He said all the powerful people wanted me to do it, and I would be rewarded.' Buntui paused for thought. 'And he didn't even let me keep the jewels.'

'What jewels, Buntui?'

'The jewels!' Buntui said vehemently, as if emphasis was the best explanation he could think of. 'She had jewels.'

'Who had jewels?'

'Herself. The prince's mother. She had the jewels, and I took them, but my master took them from me.'

'What did he do with them?'

'He hid them.'

'Where?'

'He forced me to bury them myself. In his room.' Buntui sighed.

'What happened to the prince's mother?'

'Eja Ababio hadn't told me about her,' Buntui said, shaking his head sadly in the moonlight. 'He just said I was to wait till a man fell in the trap, and then I should go forward and break him. I heard the man in the trap and went and started to break him. Then the woman came to me. I thought I was fighting a witch.'

222

'What did you do to her?'

'Nothing. I took her hands and broke them. I broke her arms. Then I broke her legs. She fought all the time. I had to break and break them. Then she was quiet.'

'You were going to kill her?'

'No. Master hadn't said I should kill her. He said nothing about her. That was annoying. The woman grew quiet and still. I left her there. I had to tell master I had done it, and ask him about the woman, what to do with her. But when I told him he got angry and later took my jewels away from me.'

'Did you return?'

'Where?'

'Where you killed Appia.'

'We went both together,' Buntui said. 'It was terrible. The woman had flown away, I swear upon my master's foot. She was a witch. Do you know, my master refused to believe me. He was angry with me, as if I had given the witch the wings to fly away with. I had never seen him so angry. Now he has sent me to this town. I don't know why. I like Esuano. But this place isn't really bad.' Now he sounded happy again. He stopped and cocked his head, listening. A sound had come on the air, but Densu had paid no attention to it, so engrossed had he been in what Buntui was telling him. The sound had come closer, and Buntui had finally heard it. Deep male voices sang the harmony, and the heavy tramp of soldier's feet on earth gave the beat.

> We are going to war,
> We are going to kill,
> We are going to die,
> Yee, yee, we are going to die!

Buntui rose up on his feet. Densu thought he saw an expression of benign contentment on his face. Before he had shaken off his astonishment at the sudden change in the giant's mood, Buntui was crashing his way through the undergrowth, heading in the direction of the soldier' song, towards the path.

Densu did not shoot. He did not even feel like threatening the happy fool. He simply took the precaution of moving away from the place. He went forward parallel to the path, as fast as he could without making a noise. He stopped before he got entirely out of earshot.

The giant had forgotten entirely about him. In his flight he had been less a man running from danger than a man rushing to meet some object of his desire.

The singing stopped. So did the tramp of running feet. In their place, only a confusion of voices.

'Kai! Here's a beast!'

'He's the one who tied the rope there!'

'Shoot him!' Several voices shouted.

'Don't shoot me!' Densu heard Buntui howl. 'I'm no beast. I'm Buntui. Ekow Buntui.'

'Hey, the beast talks. Listen to the beast.'

'Shoot the beast! Shoot the beast!'

'Don't shoot me. I'm Ekow Buntui.'

'Catch him!'

'Silence!' a strident voice said.

There was a sound of blows, shouts, grunts.

'The beast is big.'

'But he's a weak beast.'

'He can't fight.'

'Let the beast speak.'

'He's saying something. Listen!'

'Silence!' shouted the strident voice again.

There was no silence.

'When I say silence, I want silence, do you hear?' the strident voice said.

The soldiers kept quiet.

'Now who are you?'

Buntui's answer was inaudible.

'What are you doing here?'

A long interval. Then several men laughed, and a voice from among the soldiers said: 'The beast is mad. He says he was captured by someone just now.' There was loud laughter.

'Silence!' the strident voice howled. The laughter died. 'So show us where this strange man with the gun is!' the strident voice commanded. There was the noise of men crashing heavily through bushes, breaking twigs and snapping branches.

'Where is the man with the gun, beast?' the strident voice asked. The others laughed, and one shouted: 'The beast is a dreamer. He sees strange men when the moon appears.'

'Silence!' the strident voice said. 'This is no beast. He is a spy.'

'I'm no spy,' Buntui shouted angrily. 'Let's go to the palace and ask if I'm a spy.'

'All right, beast,' the strident voice said. 'We'll take you with us on our way back. If you're a spy telling us lies, you'll see.' There was a shrill order. The soldiers started their song again. Their feet stamped the earth again, and they continued trotting down the path, away from the town.

Densu waited till their voices were faint in the dark distance. Then he picked up the gun from the ground where he had rested it, and crossed the path. He walked as far into the forest as he could go without undue difficulty, then he stopped to wait for the soldiers on their return. In a short time they came rushing back up the path. He could hear them singing—a different song, unfamiliar to him, but just as brisk as the first. He let them go completely out of earshot before he regained the path and walked the distance back to Ama Nkroma's house.

She had been waiting for him.

'What kept you so long?' Ama Nkroma asked Densu. 'I was afraid something had happened to you.'

'I had to meet an enemy,' Densu said.

'How mysterious. And he gave you a gun. A generous enemy. Who was he?'

'A fellow called Buntui,' Densu answered. 'You wouldn't know him.'

'Anyway, you seem to have got what you went for.'

'More,' Densu said.

'You have to be tired,' Ama Nkroma said. 'Eat something before you sleep.'

'Not food at this time of night.'

'There's fruit.'

Ama Nkroma talked to Densu as he ate. She told him of her conversation with the healer Ezua, who had just come from the west. She had told him of the coming meeting of healers at Praso, and he'd said he'd go and had promised to take another healer with him.

'I wish I could go myself,' Ama Nkroma said, 'but look at me. Old age is defeating me, and I have to stay here. You will all come back here and see me, will you not? You must.'

Densu slept a deep, dreamless sleep that night. He woke up with a sweet taste in his mouth and a great head of energy throughout his body. As soon as he had washed himself he took the gun and headed into the brush. Once there he did not have to wait long. A solitary antelope came to drink at a nearby stream, and Densu brought him down with one shot. The rest of the morning he skinned, cut and smoked the meat for Ama Nkroma. Then he cleaned the house and the area around it. After that he ate and rested.

When the sun went down he was ready to return to the healers' village at Praso. Ama Nkroma made him promise again to return, gave him greetings to take to Damfo and Nyaneba and every other healer. Then she said farewell.

4 Reincarnation

The first person Densu saw on his return to Praso was Araba Jesiwa. The morning was young, and she was sitting outside, leaning easily against a wall. Densu had an impulse to speak to her, but he checked the impulse. She looked steadily ahead, taking no notice of him. Ajoa came out of the house.

'Does she walk?' Densu asked her.

'Not yet,' Ajoa said. 'But she moves more freely now. She should walk soon. Welcome back.' She ran forward and took his bundle from him. 'Who gave you the gun?' she asked.

'I took it from Buntui,' Densu said.

At the sound of Buntui's name something happened to Araba Jesiwa. She gave a cry like a whimper, almost inaudible. Tears sprang to her eyes and flowed down her cheeks as if they had been dammed up, awaiting release. It seemed she was straining her neck and mouth to say something. But the effort was too much for her, and she collapsed where she sat, leaning sideways, sliding against the wall.

Densu threw down the gun and caught Araba Jesiwa before she fell.

'Let's take her in,' Ajoa said. They put her on her bed and took her inside. Ajoa held her head up and gave her a drink, and soon she was sleeping peacefully.

Ajoa gave Densu cool water, and looked at him as if he had been absent for years.

'I dreamt of you every night,' she said.

'Nightmares,' he said.

'Dreams, real dreams.'

'Only me? Or all your suitors?'

'I have no others,' she said. 'It's you I have to worry about. There's someone who will want to take you away from me.'

'But there's no other woman here your age.'

'Does it have to be a woman, and my age?'

'You like riddles.'

'This isn't a riddle. Everybody knows. The Asante general shouted your name in the middle of a dream two nights ago.'

'Asamoa Nkwanta?'

'Yes.'

'Did he say what the dream was about?' Densu asked.

'Perhaps he told my father,' Ajoa said.

In the evening, after supper, the healers came with Asamoa Nkwanta to hear what news Densu had brought from the coast. He told them what he had heard and seen. The healers were quiet, pensive. Asamoa Nkwanta asked him a great number of questions. Something about the white general Wolseley fascinated him.

'What does he look like?' Asamoa Nkwanta asked. 'Is he the tallest of the whites?'

'He's not the tallest,' Densu answered. 'He's a small man. But he carries himself haughtily, and the white men around him seem to respect him, some even to fear him.'

'Does he look strong?' Asamoa Nkwanta asked.

'In what way do you mean strong?' Densu asked.

'In every way. The way he moves, the way he expresses his will, the quickness of his mind.'

'His will and his mind I can say nothing about, though I heard he'd travelled over the whole world fighting wars, and had everywhere won victories,' Densu said. 'His body is not strong. It may have been in his youth, but now one leg is lame. He tries to hide it, but he limps badly when he walks.'

'What of the second white man, the one supposed to attack us from the east? What is his name?' Asamoa Nkwanta asked.

'They call him Captain Glover,' Densu said. 'I heard nothing said about him, except what I've told you: he's collecting a black army along the river Firaw.'

'What I need to know,' said Asamoa Nkwanta, 'is which of these two white men is more important than the other. Who has the greater power? That is the important thing.'

'That I wasn't able to ascertain,' Densu said.

'I have to know exactly what that other white man, the one called Glover, intends.' Asamoa Nkwanta repeated the sentence, over and over again. Tiny drops of sweat appeared on his nose. 'And I have no one reliable there on the Firaw.' He turned his head and looked into Densu's face. On the great warrior's face there had come an expression strangely close to entreaty. 'Have you ever been as far east as the Firaw?'

'Not yet,' Densu answered.

'Could you, would you go, for me?' Asamoa Nkwanta asked, an embarrassed softness in his voice. It was as if he felt vulnerable, afraid the answer might be no.

'Yes,' Densu said.

The answer seemed to have taken the warrior by surprise. Asamoa Nkwanta repeated the question. Only when Densu repeated what he'd said did he appear satisfied that he had heard him correctly.

'When will you be able to go?' Asamoa Nkwanta asked.

'In a week or two, I think.'

5   The Watergazer

In the time before going east to the Firaw, Densu began watergazing. He ate nothing the whole day. He stayed indoors, gazing into the water in a wide clay bowl placed before him by Damfo. At first Densu saw only water in the bowl. He tried to see beyond the water, but the strain on his eyes produced tears. By the third day, however, he was able to keep from blinking, and there were no tears. His eyes had become accustomed.

He saw an image of his own face. It was a confused image, and he wanted to give it a sharper definition. He failed. Frustration tempted him to stop gazing for the day. He looked up, intending to tell Damfo he did not feel like going on. But Damfo had gone out silently and left him alone. He hadn't even noticed. Later, the vagueness of the water image didn't matter to him. He looked steadily at the image. The image looked back at him. Then the sight of the image dissolved and became thoughts, and it was as if the water in the bowl were no longer stagnant, but flowing. He was not sure now if he was seeing images, or just giving images to his thoughts.

He saw a person in the water, not just a face as at first. The person was not whole, and he seemed to be searching for completion. Others passed by him in the water. They beckoned to him, invited him into spaces they had prepared for him. But it seemed he knew the kind of space he needed, and he could not find it among any of those offered him. The still water threw up a question in Densu's mind: what was this space he was looking for? Why a specific space?

An answer came: the search could not end until the need was stilled. And the need was not for just any relationships with others. It was for a definite kind of relationship that would be possible only with people moving in the same direction. There was a strong urge to examine the difference between the people actually available for relationships and those the seeker sought. A vague fear said the people in the seeker's mind did not exist, but Densu thought of his own reality, and the fear lost potency at once. There was Ajoa. There was Damfo. There had been Anan. They were not an absence, a hope only.

The others available were many, of course. The impression they gave of something stable, undisturbed, came from their accepting the existing world as satisfactory. But what deep-eating blindness could make any soul see its satisfaction in such warped realities? The only problems the others saw were two: to find a personal place in the given world; and having found that space, to keep it. But his need was for relationships with people for whom the existing world was not perfect, not even reasonably satisfactory. These would be people whose place in the world was something yet to be created because their real world was not yet entirely present. People to work with.

A hurtful thought arose. Suppose the need for completion was merely a disease? A second thought took the hurt away: the search would not be any the less natural for that. In the water the gazer saw a world in which some, a large number, had a prevalent disease. The disease was an urge to fragment everything. And the disease gave infinite satisfaction to the diseased because it gave them control. There were those with a contrary disease, an urge to unite everything. If that was a disease, the gazer thought, so let it be. But there would be nothing to keep him from choosing it for his own disease, and following its natural course, reaching for its natural aim.

By the time the gazer was ready to take his eyes off the water it was afternoon. The world was warm. He felt a great need for water, water inside his body, water outside him, water covering him entirely. So he went to the nearest stream. He left his cloth on a rock overhanging the stream where it made a pool, and plunged under the water. He didn't swim. He just let himself sink into the water. He closed his eyes and let his sense of direction go, not trying to hold on to anything.

When he came up for air he kept his eyes closed and lay on his back upon the water, letting the sun bake him. In a while he felt his face burning. He opened his eyes, swam till he was directly beneath the overhanging rock, jumped up and grasped the end of the rock with both hands, and pulled himself up on to its surface. He looked for his cloth. It had disappeared.

There were no marks on the rock, but where it dipped under soil he found the grass lightly crushed. He followed it. He had to look carefully—whoever had passed that way had passed lightly. The trail of disturbed grass ended abruptly, yet ahead there was still fresh grass. Densu did not look up into the tree under which the trampled grass had ended. He sat under it to rest. His cloth was thrown down to him, and it fell in a soft bundle on his head, unravelled itself, and covered his face. While he was taking the cloth off from his face someone dropped beside him from the tree above.

'You're a good hunter,' Ajoa said.

'You're a good temptress, leaving me naked,' Densu said.

'I've given you back your cloth,' she said.

'I'll also give you back yours,' he said, reaching for her waist band. She stepped backward, but he held it fast and it came loose. She was still trying to free herself, so he pulled her against himself, bent her backward till she fell, and he fell with her.

'Be careful. You'll hurt me,' she said.

He shifted so as to lie on his side, and pulled her so she was no longer lying on her back but on her side, facing him. He opened out his cloth with one hand and spread it out on the grass there beside him. Rolling her on top of himself, he turned and brought her to rest again on the other side, on top of the cloth. He reached for the unused half of the cloth and pulled it over both of them.

His right leg searched for space between her legs, and she made way for him.

'I thought you'd begun watergazing,' she said.

'I have,' he answered.

'You aren't supposed to want women while you're searching for your soul,' she said.

'That's not what the water told me.'

'So what did it tell you?'

'The water said to the gazer: sometimes the only way you see your soul is in one other person,' he said.

'Does that one other person have to be me?' she asked him.

'Ask the water that,' he said. 'For me it's never been a question but an answer.'

'I'm the same way,' she said. 'But tell me truly. What did you actually see when you gazed into the water?'

'I saw a secret.'

'Even from the other part of your soul?' she laughed.

'I'll tell you, since you want to know,' he said. 'When I gazed into the water I saw Ajoa stark naked.'

'I can always tell when you're lying,' she said. 'I watch this vein in your temple.'

'What does it do?'

But Ajoa couldn't answer. She couldn't even remember what the question had been about.

'Don't get out of me,' she said when both were quiet.

'I shall have to, sometime,' he said.

'Something isn't right, about all this,' she said.

'I don't see that.'

'I see it,' she said. 'When it begins, you want to get in so badly you have to fight me to let you in. When it ends, I'm the one who has to fight you to keep you in.'

'We could stay locked together forever,' he said gravely, 'but people might miss us and come looking for us.'

'You've convinced me.' She gave a violent, forced cough, pulled herself back a fraction, and he was out. Laughing, she got up and ran to the water. He followed her.

They bathed their sweat away and afterwards lay down on the warm rock. It faced west, and was tilted slightly upward on the side overhanging the pool. When they lay on it, the afternoon sun streamed directly into their faces. Both closed their eyes.

'Do you see what I see?' Ajoa asked Densu.

'I don't know,' Densu said. 'What do you see?'

'What's the colour behind your lids now?' she asked him.

'Saffron now. It gets paler if I pretend I'm opening my eyes. Do you see rainbows when you look through your eyelashes?'

'Peacock feathers,' she said. 'But close your eyes completely. I want to ask you something.'

'Ask. I'm ready.'

'Look hard,' she said.

'I can't look when my eyes are closed,' he protested.

'You think you can't,' she said. 'But have you tried?'

He tried.

'What do you see?' she asked him.

'The same saffron background,' he answered.

'What of the foreground?'

'There's nothing there.'

'Look closely,' she said.

He looked. 'There's this long, transparent thread. It keeps the same shape but never stays in the same position. It keeps trying to slip out of sight behind my eyelid.'

'Which way is it trying to go now?' she asked.

'Down.'

'Look up. It'll follow your look,' she said. Then she asked him: 'Did it?'

'It did,' he answered. 'Did yours have little knots in it?'

'Many,' she said. 'I thought I could count them, but I see that's impossible. The whole string is made up of knots. Small, transparent knots.'

She groped for his hand under the cloth, as if both of them were blind. She found it and held it, pressing it. They lay there in silence until she asked: 'What happened to the sun?'

'The great python swallowed it, didn't you hear?' he asked her. 'Why do you ask? Don't you see it behind your eyelids any more?'

She pressed his hand with an urgency beyond playfulness, and that made him open his eyes. He saw the sun partly hidden behind the head of a man standing barely a step away from them. The stranger was not alone. The stranger had a large gold plate hanging from his neck. The chain holding the plate was also made of gold. He was totally bald, and his pate was oiled and shiny. His companions stood in a curved line behind him, as if they had come down narrow pathways and had not yet noticed they were in the open. Densu looked at Ajoa. She already had her cloth round her body. He stood up, adjusting his cloth, and greeted the man in front of him, as well as his companions. The companions only nodded in reply, but the one with the gold plate spoke.

'We are looking for the way to the village of healers,' he said.

'With whom do you have business there?' Densu asked.

'As you see,' the man said, pointing to the gold plate on his breast, 'we are royal messengers. We carry a message from the king at Kumase for the general Asamoa Nkwanta.'

Densu and Ajoa led the envoys to the village. Ajoa brought them water to drink while Densu went to tell Asamoa Nkwanta of their arrival. The general showed not the slightest sign of surprise. It was as if he had been expecting just such a mission all day.

'Bring them to me,' he said to Densu, 'and tell Damfo also, so he can come if he has time.'

6 The Call

Asamoa Nkwanta's meeting with the royal envoys was short. Asamoa Nkwanta asked them what news they brought. The envoys said they had come with a simple message: the Asante people needed Asamoa Nkwanta; the Asante army was perishing in the absence of Asamoa Nkwanta; the Asante royal families were asking for the counsel of Asamoa Nkwanta. They would listen with an understanding ear to any further terms he might want to state before he would agree to return to the head of the army he had abandoned because a grievous wrong had been done him. The envoys said this was all; they had been told to return to Kumase the moment they got an answer from Asamoa Nkwanta.

Asamoa Nkwanta gave the envoys his answer with no pretence at hesitation: he would go to Kumase to listen to the royal council there. The envoys did not even stay to eat. They took the road back to Kumase as soon as they were sure they had heard Asamoa Nkwanta's reply right.

Asamoa Nkwanta himself went to Damfo and told him the news.

'That's something you've been hoping for, isn't it?' Damfo asked him.

'I just didn't think it would happen so soon,' Asamoa Nkwanta answered.

'They need you,' said Damfo.

'Asamoa Nkwanta tried to suppress the smile that came to his lips. He failed. 'I came to ask you a favour,' he said.

'What kind of favour?'

'I'd like to take Densu with me when I go back to Kumase,' the general said.

'Why?' the healer asked.

'I think you know already,' Asamoa Nkwanta said. 'Densu does something for me. I don't understand it, but I know I need it. When they murdered my nephew, something left me. It was like my blood flowing to waste. But now I can look at Densu, the way he talks, the way he moves, everything he does reminds me of my nephew, but the strange thing is the memory isn't painful when Densu brings it. Do you understand?'

Damfo nodded. 'Still, he is no warrior,' he said.

'Only because he has no desire to be one.' Asamoa Nkwanta said.

'Whether he goes or not depends on himself,' Damfo said finally. 'Have you mentioned it to him?'

'I shall,' Asamoa Nkwanta said.

PART SEVEN

1 The Eunuch

When Asamoa Nkwanta asked him to go with him to Kumase, Densu agreed. Asamoa Nkwanta timed the journey so that by the time they reached Kumase it was dark. Near the city they passed along the edge of a depression whose outlines were dim in the darkness, but whose stench made Densu retch.

'What is that?' he asked Asamoa Nkwanta.

'Subin, the Swamp of the Dead,' Asamoa Nkwanta said. He remained silent for the rest of the journey.

Asamoa Nkwanta's entry into the city was quiet. On the first street two night guards, their hair long and wild, brandishing their long spears in the general's face, challenged the travellers. Asamoa Nkwanta did not answer their challenge. He simply stood there and let them come all the way up to him and see his face. The night guards' behaviour changed at once. One stood aside, his spear pointed at the earth. The second offered to accompany the general home. Asamoa Nkwanta laughed a dry laugh and said he would make his own way home. The house Asamoa Nkwanta went to was not one of the great ones of the city. There was no one there to meet him.

'This is where I used to come whenever I wanted to be in a quiet place but couldn't go outside the city. There's just one room,' Asamoa Nkwanta said.

There were several thick reed mats propped up against the far wall. Densu rolled out one for Asamoa Nkwanta. He himself felt like sleeping outside. The journey had made him hot, and there was a dankness to the air inside the unused house that made him uncomfortable.

Densu could hear Asamoa Nkwanta's breathing coming to him from within the house. It was not the even breathing of a man at rest. It was irregular, fidgety. From time to time the general uttered a small cough, as if something were irritating him, something insignificant but persistent. But after a while the general's restlessness gave way

235

to complete silence, and not long after Densu heard him snoring.

Densu felt exited, but not in any wild, agitated way. Here he felt he had entered a place entirely new to him. He did not know what the morning would reveal to his eyes, but his ignorance did not upset him. Knowing he would be seeing and hearing things he had never before in his life heard nor seen gave him a keen, anticipatory thrill. So though he didn't sleep, his body was not tense. It felt sharp, alert, ready for whatever the morrow would bring.

A noise caught the edge of his attention. He held his breath and listened. The noise had not come from within the house, yet it had sounded close by. The next time he heard it it was even closer, almost right on top of him. Then Densu saw a form. In the darkness all he could make out was that the form was human, and it was enormous. It was advancing slowly forward, making its way towards the door to the house in which Asamoa Nkwanta was sleeping, moving at an eerie crawl. To reach the door the form would have to pass over Densu.

Densu rolled sideways off his mat, suspending his breathing to keep from making any noise at all. The form had not seen him. It was advancing as stealthily as before, with no change in pace.

Densu lay still till the form reached the mat. He could not see whether the form was armed. He lay dead still. The form took a step that brought one foot on to the mat, steadied that foot, then lifted the other foot. At that instant Densu grasped the mat's edge with both hands and yanked at it with all his strength. Even as he fell, the intruder managed to remain silent. From the sound his body made as it fell there was no suggestion he carried any weapon. Densu jumped upon the fallen form, reached for the head, and put a tight arm lock on the neck.

The form put up a sort of struggle, but it was not full-blooded. In a while Densu began to feel there was something strange. The man under him was huge. He could have exerted some strength had he chosen to. But he seemed only remotely interested in fighting him. Densu had reached for his arms to pinion them. He had found only one—and, that arm was held in an attitude far from any suspicion of violence. The other arm he could not reach at first. Persisting in his search for the arm, he realized the man under him was keeping it deliberately covered with his massive body. Densu had thought of rolling his captive over forcibly. But the man's passivity made him change his mind.

'Who are you?' Densu asked the man under him.

236

'I should ask you that,' the man said. He spoke in a small whisper. Densu realized he was still afraid of discovery.

'You have to tell me who you are, and what you're doing here,' Densu insisted.

The man was silent for a spell. Then he whispered: 'I'm looking for him.'

'Who?' Densu asked.

'The general,' the man said resignedly.

'Do you always visit people in this style?'

'What do you mean, this style?'

'Creeping up on them at dead of night.'

The man underneath was not amused. He spoke in a much louder kind of whisper now, even though he wasn't addressing Densu any longer. He said: 'The world is full of fools to waylay us.'

Densu was wondering what response to make to the man's words when he heard Asamoa Nkwanta's voice:

'What's the noise about?' the general asked.

'I have a creeping giant trapped here,' Densu said. 'He claims he's looking for you at this time of day.'

The man beneath Densu sucked his teeth in sheer irritation. 'He thinks he's funny,' he said.

'Is that Oson's voice I hear?' Asamoa Nkwanta asked. In his voice there was pleasure, riding above surprise.

'His very own,' the man said softly, 'but persuade this your hangman to unwind his lean arms from my throat. I'm a man of peace.'

'That you are, Oson,' Asamoa Nkwanta said. 'Densu, let go of him. He's a friend, the best of friends. Sometimes he has his own way of doing things, but that's no fault. Bring him in.'

Densu released the fallen man and went inside with him.

'We don't need light,' the man panted

'I know,' agreed Asamoa Nkwanta. 'What brings you at this time, though?' How did you know I was here? You know they would kill you if they knew, at the palace.'

'There are times when I think that would be better,' the man said. He sighed. 'I don't have time. The guard Amfom told me. He's a friend. I've missed you, Osajefo Asamoa.'

'Did you risk the daylight dance of death to come and tell me that?' Asamoa Nkwanta asked.

'I brought you this,' Oson said. He had been holding something in his left hand. Now he opened the hand in front of Asamoa Nkwanta.

Even in the dark there was no room for doubt. The thing gathered in itself all the little light there was in the darkness and shone with it.

'A diamond,' Asamoa Nkwanta said, surprised. 'What have you become, Oson?'

'Peace, Osajefo,' Oson said. 'I'm still what I am: a simple eunuch, the same you saved from total death. How can a man made a eunuch become something else?'

'Where did you get this?' Asamoa Nkwanta asked.

'Peace,' Oson said, 'I never stole a thing, and never will. This I found at the source of the river Tano. I went there with a group of priests while you were away. There was something the queen-mother needed to ask about.'

'You know the law,' Asamoa Nkwanta said, somewhat sternly. 'All treasure so found goes to the king.'

'I know the law,' Oson said. 'But I hear a different voice. Osajefo, how could I give such a gift to anyone but you? I've dreamed so long of giving you not one gift but a universe of gifts. Have you already forgotten what you gave me once? I never was able to give you anything in return. What has a slave got to give, and a eunuch on top of being a slave? At the source of the river Tano I found this precious stone. Just a stone, and my soul and all my blood cried out your name. I could not disobey my soul. I disobeyed the law. I had no idea where you were. The royals were saying you'd gone mad and disappeared. I was in despair. But I kept the diamond and hoped. It was dangerous. Just when I thought I couldn't keep it any longer, you came. Now I know my soul was right to tell me to keep it for you. Take it, Osajefo.'

Asamoa Nkwanta closed his right fist over the diamond. 'Thank you,' he said, 'but Oson, don't ever risk your life to please me again.'

Oson laughed out loud at the general. 'Is there anything I can do for you, Osajefo?' he asked.

'Yes. Keep yourself from getting killed. If they find you out . . .'

'No one will find me out,' Oson said. 'Even an elephant can move discreetly if he has this.' He tapped his head audibly. 'Forgive me for waking you up, Osajefo. I'm going. I suppose I'm obliged to say farewell to this your hangman also. What's his name?'

'Densu.'

'All right, farewell, Densu,' Oson said. 'If you see my neck swollen one day, know it's your fault.'

Then he disappeared into the night, as silently as he had come.

2 Omens

The third day after Asamoa Nkwanta's coming to Kumase, the royal council met to hear him. It was not the full royal council. Many kings had not had enough time to come to Kumase, and the King Kofi Karikari himself said it would be better to have a small council. Secret matters were to be talked about.

So the kings present were these: from Juaben there was Nana Asafo Adjei. From Mampong came Nana Kwabena Jumo. There was also the chief Kwamen Ajapong. The chief of Bantama, Amankwa Tia, was there. So was his rival, Edu Bofo.

The last to enter the council hall was the queen-mother herself, Efua Kobri. She, the elegant brown one, came wearing silk robes as usual, her skin soft as a baby's. Seven female attendants followed her—she was travelling light today. The last of her train were three fat men—eunuchs. Among the three Densu recognized one form as surely as if he had seen Oson in broad daylight before. But in the council hall Oson gave him not the slightest sign of recognition. He did not make any special gesture even towards Asamoa Nkwanta himself.

When Efua Kobri, the queen-mother, had sat, the meeting began. First the queen-mother talked of Asamoa Nkwanta's personal sorrow. Then she talked of the sorrow of the Asante nation. She talked subtly, with infinite grace, and she made her message clear: let Asamoa Nkwanta forgive past wrongs. Let him exact whatever further price he thought himself entitled to. But let him not abandon the Asante army, leaving it to bleed itself and the nation to death.

Others spoke. But neither in substance nor in style could any of them improve on the queen-mother's speech. Then it was time for Asamoa Nkwanta to speak. What the great warrior had to say was startlingly brief. First he said he was ready to dissolve his personal sorrow and forget it in the greater pain of the nation. But he needed to know one thing:

'What do you want me to do?'

The royals did not whisper long among themselves before Efua Kobri answered Asamoa Nkwanta:

'Save the army, Osajefo Asamoa Nkwanta. At present, it is seeking a way home, but it is lost, without a guide. Give it your guidance again.

239

'That,' said Asamoa Nkwanta, 'is not a heavy task to accept.'

'There's more,' the queen-mother said. 'There are signs and sounds of a white army preparing to invade Asante. Some have even heard talk of the white men dreaming of conquering Kumase itself.' Here one chief laughed. A second swore an oath against the presumption of these whites. Others were content to shake their heads in sheer incredulity. 'No one,' the queen-mother continued, 'no one among us has any idea how to counter these threats from the whites. The usual comment when people talk about the matter is this: if only Asamoa Nkwanta were here. If only Asamoa Nkwanta were here.

'You are here with us now. Already you have earned the name Osajefo for what you have done with the army. Only one title is higher than that: the title Srafo Kra, Soul of the Army. Osajefo, even that ultimate title is within your reach. Reach out your hand, and it will be yours. We are calling to you. Return to the army. Give our warriors the spirit they need.'

Asamoa Nkwanta accepted the call. As for the return of the army, there was nothing to say about it. All that remained was to do it. But thought would have to be given to the reported plan of the whites to invade Asante and to capture Kumase.

'I hope the whites are brave enough to come,' Asamoa Nkwanta said.

Quite audibly, the statement took away the breath of several kings.

'Some of us do not understand that hope,' the queen-mother said.

Asamoa Nkwanta had a well-thought-out plan. He explained it:

'I have seen our brothers on the coast, those at Edina, trap fish,' he said. 'When they begin, they never oppose the motion of the fish. They lead them into the net. Only then do they close up the end of the net. There's no way out. The fish are trapped.

'So let the whites invade Asante. I shall select a place good for fighting a battle. When the whites reach that place, they will be fish facing the forward wall of the net. Let our centre regiments be that wall. Let the left regiments turn on the white troops in the forest and harass them to death. And let the regiments of the right wing circle round the whites, come up from behind them, and block up the end of the net.

'The whites have better guns than we have. In fact we are dependent on them for our weapons. But the whites fear the forest, because they know the forest fights for us, against them. They may plan to invade Asante, but they cannot plan to fight a long war here in our forests.

240

The clearest way to defeat the whites is to oblige them to stay long in the forest, fighting a long, long war. Then when we have trapped them in our net and they cannot retreat, all we need do is to hold them till the forest finishes them.'

The silence that followed Asamoa Nkwanta's speech was deep. When it was broken, it was broken by praise. The royals were competing with each other to sing the great warrior's praises. He himself sat listening to them, once more silent as a wall.

Densu looked round at the royal faces. In their ostentatious happiness he saw here and there a suspicion of pain. When he took a closer look at two of them—the King Kofi Karikari and Nana Asafo Adjei of Juaben—what he saw was something like a sourness, a deep chagrin only poorly hidden under the glad noise. As for the queenmother, she sat wrapped in a cold silence, like a mausoleum. There was no judging her reaction from her secret face.

After Asamoa Nkwanta had told the royals of his plan, the royal council approved it and immediately gave him leave to go and take command of the army on its way back to Kumase. As the general and Densu left, they saw that everyone else in the council hall was being turned out, except the royals themselves and the three eunuchs, Oson among them.

The journey back to the Pra river was swift. Asamoa Nkwanta walked with a happy, eager energy, and Densu was infected. At Praso they spent the night at the healers' village. Early in the morning they said farewell and crossed over to the left bank. Asamoa Nkwanta led the way along a faint path almost parallel to the river. The path led to a kind of simple hunter's shelter in the forest. Seven men were waiting there, war captains from the Asante army. The captains greeted Asamoa Nkwanta and Densu greeted them.

'He's my helper,' Asamoa Nkwanta told them.

The captains led the way along a circuitous route which ended suddenly in an open space only recently cleared. In the centre of that space there were three huts. The captains went into the one in the middle. Asamoa Nkwanta and Densu followed. Just before Densu bowed to enter through the low doorway a small movement high up in a tree in front, behind the hut, caught his eye. He straightened up to look. It was a warrior with a rifle, his back to the clearing, who had moved.

Inside, Asamoa Nkwanta began asking questions almost before he sat. He asked each of the captains how many men they had gone out with, and how many were now left. When did they plan to have the army reach the Pra? When had the envoys arrived with the king's circle of beads to recall the army home? What were the present obstacles in the path of the army?

The captains' answers made Asamoa Nkwanta grim. Part of the army was almost at the river already. There was no means of getting the soldiers across, however.

Densu searched for Asamoa Nkwanta's eyes with his own.

'Speak,' the general said.

'The army has canoes ready for the crossing, surely?' Densu asked.

The captains looked at each other, somewhat perplexed. Asamoa Nkwanta looked at the captains.

'Won't you answer him?' he asked softly.

One of the captains shook his head. For a while no one said anything. Densu asked another question.

'Does the army not have craftsmen skilled in carving canoes?'

Again the captain shook his head.

'I know something of the craft,' Densu said. 'If carvers can be found in numbers and brought here with their tools, I will work with them to make the canoes the army needs.'

'That will be done,' Asamoa Nkwanta said. He looked at the captains. 'Which of you will find the carvers?'

One volunteered.

'Who will find men to fell the trees to be used?'

Another volunteered.

'Meanwhile I'll go down south and bring up the farthest regiments,' Asamoa Nkwanta said.

The re-crossing of the Pra river began on a Thursday. The first group to reach Praso was impatient and impetuous. There were four hot-eyed captains with the group, and they said they did not want to wait for the canoes being carved. Two of them crossed over in an old canoe with fifteen warriors. The other two stayed behind on the left bank with the remaining warriors.

The four had formed a plan. They had seen two huge silk cotton trees standing opposite each other, one on the left bank, one on the right. Why not cut down both trees in such a way they would fall into the river? Their branches should meet in the middle of the river, and the warriors could go across the river on them. The trees were felled. Their branches almost met. Almost, but not quite. It was difficult to judge whether the gap between the fallen giants of the forest could indeed be leapt over.

One brave warrior tried first, and being lucky, made it. He hung trembling on a frail branch, from which he was able to pull himself forward and to safety. Several warriors jumped after the lucky first one in an impatient rush to reach the right bank. Few made it. Most did not even leap far enough to touch the frailest twigs at the tip of the opposite tree. In a short while the branches of both trees were loaded with limp bodies. In the distance they looked like some uncommon kind of fruit.

Now the warriors' impatient urge to cross the river gave way to the patient acceptance of the necessity of work. By day and by night the carvers hacked out canoes from the massive tree trunks. Soon the canoes were ready, and the re-crossing began.

It went smoothly, thirty warriors crossing over in each canoe. Only once did disaster strike again. One group of forty, sacrificing safety to speed, packed a single canoe. It capsized in mid-river. Only the rowers were swimmers. By the time darkness descended on the greatest of days, Saturday, the Asante army had crossed the river. The warriors were home again.

But what a sad homecoming this one was for the army! What a terrible accounting faced the nation! A procession of warriors passed through Kumase, Kumase the virgin capital, Kumase the impregnable stronghold, Kumase the evergreen garden. But this was no proud procession of victory. Those who came out of their houses to welcome their returning warriors saw only a slow, sorrowful march of survivors whose every step cried a single message: to death alone belonged the victory in this war.

Tongue-tied were the singers of victorious songs of praise. What could they sing of? And for whom to hear? Those who had looked forward to the cruel pleasure of taunting long lines of captives brought back from the battlefields grew sad. Here were no captives to be taunted and insulted. Here were only bereaved survivors. Nephews in all the strength of their youth had gone to this war with forty companions. Now they returned alone carrying forlorn bundles to remind those left alive of beloved ones whom death had swallowed away from home.

Bones taken from old war skeletons were brought out to show the credulous that Asante was still strong in battle. But trickery merely dirtied the face of truth; it was impotent to hide it. What new deceit could royalty invent to explain the absence of three hundred proud war captains who had set out in full view but were nowhere to be seen among those coming back? What new deceit could sweeten the bitterness of kin who had packed bundles for seven brothers to carry and now had to be content with welcoming only two?

Hold your stricken tongues, singers of royal praises. Your work is done. You who sent thirty thousand marching south against forgotten brothers, didn't you know your songs of pride and joy were mere preparation for the long dance of death?

Death has done its work. Now comes the time for the singers of slow dirges. Make room for their voices. Let the air be cold and clear. Let them sing of the thousands dead. In the middle of their dirge, if you happen to run out of tears to accompany their singing with, why, you can call upon the overflowing Pra for more water. Or you could even ask the sacred Tano. It would help you remember your dead.

At Kumase the survivors returned to homes silent with sorrows too heavy to wail about. What could they do? When they were able at last to open their mouths, they tried bravely to talk of matters other than death. They retold all the great stories about Asamoa Nkwanta. They retold how, hearing the Asante regiments on their way back home were trapped between the deadly waters of the Pra, the fatal fury of disease, and the hostility of the armed enemy brother, Asamoa Nkwanta had pushed his own long sorrow down and taken his place once more at the head of his pupils the generals. They told of the difficult crossing of the Pra, and added it would have been a total disaster but for the wisdom and the careful work of Asamoa Nkwanta. Then they told how in sheer gratitude the rulers of the land had given the great warrior the greatest of titles among fighters: Srafo Kra, the Warriors' Soul.

But when all the brave words had been exhausted there were still the gaping wounds left in the people's spirit by unexpected loss. There was still the terrifying emptiness left in people's minds, an emptiness that left the nation wide open to every strange new conjecture.

Could it be true there really was an army of white soldiers, a ghostly army actually marching against Kumase the never violated city this time? Kumase the queen-mother of cities, Kumase the beautiful green one, Kumase the city that had never once allowed any hos-

244

tile foreigner to penetrate her? Could it be true? And could it be true the king himself had begun swinging like a helpless puppet between fear and hope?

Why should it not all be true? This was the time of omens and strange stories. A flood of evil imaginings and happenings overwhelmed the senses and minds of people who had lived too long with the fear of disaster. All the events talked about were extraordinary but in these days of fear they became the common currency. All these reported happenings were incredible, but all were swiftly, eagerly believed. All were frightening to think of, but even the most cowardly were numbed into open-eyed contemplation of unspeakable horrors.

This was the time of omens, and the first omen was this. At a time when no rains were yet expected a bright day had suddenly been changed to menacing night. Huge clouds had come to choke the air and fill the sky. Lightning flashes split the clouds like fierce messengers of death looking for something to destroy. As for thunder accompanying the lightning, the sound of it alone was enough to shake buildings that had stood a hundred years against flood and rain. Throughout the remainder of the destroyed day the clouds hung threateningly immobile over the earth. They stayed far into the night. At midnight the clouds mumbled like an ill-tempered giant and then parted to precipitate on the astonished earth not rain, not water but a flood of hard stones. One was so large it crashed through a roof and broke the skull of a child six days old, dragging him back among his ancestors.

Next a story came floating on secret whispers from Bantama, the sacred burial place of kings. A royal eunuch had seen a porcupine, the Asante beast himself, slowly crossing the open place before the principal mausoleum. The eunuch had called the attendants of the burial chambers to come and admire the symbolic beast. Scarcely had the porcupine reached the centre of the open space when the beast that had put him to flight appeared crawling behind him—a great huge silver python. The eunuch and the attendants of death, fascinated, stood watching the unfolding encounter.

The porcupine turned to face his hunter. His quills shot out, stiff, rattling fiercely against each other. But the python flowed just as smoothly forward. When he reached the porcupine, without first throwing his coils on him, without attempting to stretch his prey, he swallowed him whole—quills and all. Having thus fed, the python did not move on. He coiled himself in a pile of circles, laid his head on the highest coil and began the sleep of days.

The eunuch and the attendants sought a priest. The priest feared something terrible would happen if anyone touched the full python. So the snake was left to lie there. He lay a whole week undisturbed. Even the ants of the earth did not go near him. The wonder was not over. At the end of an exact week the python began to excrete, one after the other, porcupine quills to the number of thirty. That done, the serpent disappeared, never to be seen again.

At Kumase the king, the whispers said, agitated by the news, asked the court priests what they understood by such a portent. Not a single priest opened his mouth to give an explanation, though none of them was dumb. In all their eyes could be seen the shifty light of unwanted understanding. Who did not know it was forbidden to tell evil news to the king of Asante?

A story reached Kumase from Ejiso. A year back a woman, barren till that time, had inexplicably conceived. The ninth month came and went, and the tenth, and the eleventh. The pregnancy continued to grow, but yielded no child. Then when a precise year had passed, a child was born to the woman, exactly in the blind middle of the night. As if there hadn't been enough wonders already, this strange night-child commenced to talk as soon as he had freed his head from his mother's womb. The child spoke like an old man, one who had eaten barrels of pepper and salt in a long life:

'What a place you have brought me to, my mother. And what a time you have brought me into, my mother. But, my mother, why have you brought me here at a time like this? Did I tell you this was where I wanted to come? The home I'm coming from is peaceful. I'm going back there, my mother. You here will never see me again.'

With that the wonderful child disappeared. The mother, dazed by so many unbelievable events and words, crawled outside the house, intending to call back the child. She could find no trace of him. In defeat she returned to her house. But she could not recognize the place she had left just a moment before. The whole house was covered with grass and thick bush, as if for two seasons no human being had lived there.

The priests at Ejiso also kept quiet when asked what meaning such an event could have.

A story reached Kumase from Bekwai. A pregnant goat had roamed all round the town for three days, uttering a loud and pitiful bleat. From time to time the goat was unable to stand on her thin legs, so heavy was the weight she carried in her belly. Children pelted her with stones. The goat did not attempt to run. She turned to face the children and looked straight into their eyes. She looked at them as if she pitied them, like a mother sorrowing for wayward children losing themselves irretrievably in spite of all her care. The goat looked thus steadily at the children; then, in plain view of everybody there, she shed a tear and turned to go away. Among the children one who had been most active in the throwing of stones, a small, nervous, active boy, began to tremble just as if the shaking disease had been upon him three days running.

As the boy stood shaking helplessly, the goat began to give birth to a kid. It was a strange birth, starting with the legs. Two legs appeared. The body followed. But just a short distance, maybe a hand after the first two legs, a second pair of legs appeared. The head was now expected, but it did not come. Instead, after a while two more legs appeared, making six.

The watchers began to say here was an animal made of two joined together. But the whole kid descended, and it had only one head. A single goat with six legs. The beast lay wet and vulnerable beneath its mother on the sand. Then, before it was dry, it stood up on its wobbly legs, all six of them, and began to walk after its mother, quite placidly and slowly.

The mother goat led the kid with six legs on a deliberate tour around the town centre of Bekwai, staring straight up into the eyes of all the assembled watchers. In this way the two animals completed three circles round the town centre. Then, as if she had remembered something at last, the mother goat lay down and suckled the monstrous kid. When the kid had drunk its fill it started to run. The mother followed it. The two disappeared into the bushes below the town. No one saw them again.

A story came from Mampong to Kumase. A man had, without much effort, made his wife pregnant, this for the seventh time. It was this man's habit to lose interest completely in his wife from the moment he knew she was definitely pregnant till a hundred days after she had delivered a baby. This seventh time the man lost not only interest in the woman, but sympathy for her as well.

The woman, as was her custom, was bearing her lonely burden as patiently as she could, but the man would not leave her in peace. Every day, every morning stretching on until evening, this man would hang around the overloaded mother just to burden her with gratuitous insults. He would stare deliberately at her, fixing his gaze upon her belly, then suddenly and violently, spit. The woman would continue tranquilly doing whatever she was busy doing. But her calmness only angered the husband. Without being asked to give any explanation for his fierce disgust, he would offer one himself: he found his wife's belly ugly. He wondered aloud if the huge belly contained a baby really, or was it just the result of greedy eating? And why, he asked, did the woman have to spit so frequently? He spat again in disgust. And then who was going to find food for all these children she was producing, like some sow? Besides, the brats would all disappear from home and go to their uncles when they grew up, after having sucked their father dry.

For six months the wife listened to these insults and many more. At the beginning of the seventh month she told her husband she was tired of his insults and warned him to stop or else . . .

'Or else you'll do what to me?' the man asked sarcastically. He asked the question thirty times, and the woman still refused to add a single word to her threat. Angry as a young flame, the man hit his wife, beat her up until she was unconscious, then strode away from home to go and drink palm wine to cool his temper. He did not return home till the end of that month, the seventh of his wife's pregnancy.

The woman welcomed her husband quite calmly, as if nothing at all had happened; as if, in fact, he had merely stepped outside a moment to relieve himself, and had then come back. The man was hungry, so he ate a huge meal. He had brought some palm wine with him; he drank that also. Night fell. The man sank into a deep, contented sleep. In that sleep he dreamed his wife was standing above him, smiling down at him and asking him if he would please do her a single favour.

'And what sort of favour would that be?' the man asked in his dream.

'Just to hold our baby a moment,' the dream wife said.

With that the wife took the full belly in front of her and fitted it on to the front of her reposing husband. Then she flew out through a smoke hole in the roof.

Morning came. The husband woke. He tried to stretch himself and found it hard. Something heavy was impeding his movements. He looked down at his belly and realized with some chagrin he could no longer see his penis. A mountain of flesh had grown where his stomach used to be. The disdainful husband was pregnant. His wife never returned from her night flight. Secretly, the man sent for priests and begged them to help him. But they could not help him. They, the priests who should have had answers to give him, kept asking him: 'What is happening these days? What is happening in this land?'

Another story reached Kumase from Bonwire, home of the royal weavers. A woman had gone to her farm in the forest. At the edge of the farm the woman bent down, stooping with her back to a tree in order to pull up some weeds from a mound she'd made for yams. She felt something enter the space between her thighs, from behind. She looked over her shoulder. There was no one behind her, only the tree. She continued weeding, but then the sensation between her thighs became unmistakable. She made an effort to pull herself away, but the tree held her fast, with what power she was later unable to explain. She did not lose consciousness. She was not hurt in any way. The tree released her gently after it had done with her. She turned to look, and saw the tree really had genitals.

The woman came home to Bonwire and told her story. Together with some helpers, she went back to the farm to search for the portentous tree. They found nothing, not even a trace of the tree. Yet all concerned swore that on the woman herself all the signs were plainly visible.

In Kumase itself, for the first time since the world began, a white male child was born. The child was born to two of the white captives brought by the general Edu Bofo at the end of his fruitless raids against the Krepis to the east. The parents were priests in the service of the white people's god. Why Edu Bofo had captured them, no one really knew. It was said his lack of success in war had angered him. It was said he wanted to do deeds his rival Amankwa Tia had never done, and in his folly he imagined the bringing of white captives to Kumase would be just such a deed.

But the captives had only brought uncertainty and dissension to Kumase. The whites on the coast begged for their return. The royals were of conflicting minds. They waited for Edu Bofo himself to decide what was to be done. Edu Bofo said he wanted money in exchange for the captives. The whites haggled, but in the end they paid the money. Edu Bofo changed his mind, and the captives remained at Kumase.

The white captives did not lose hope. The birth of a son was such a strong indication of their trust in their god and the future, that some of the royals at Kumase grew afraid. The old prophecy of the Moshi to the north was remembered: 'When the first of the whites appears in the land, the nation will die.' And the question was added:' If the first sight of a white man means a nation's death, is not then the birth of a white son here the nation's burial?'

Finally, there was an omen of the last days, coming after all the stories and all the other omens. Even if all the stories of omens and portents reaching Kumase were false, what happened at Kumase itself, the capital city of Asanteman founded under the kum tree by the great priest Anoche and named by him, what happened at Kumase was true. It happened plainly for all to see, so that there was not the slightest possibility of doubt. The kum tree, planted at the nation's birth, a tree supposed unshakable, huge giant of trees, the kum tree fell.

In the time before the Oyoko clan of Asante became a force to be feared in the land, in the time before the Asante nation grew to be the greatest power in the land, in those beginning days the founders did not know where the seat of power, the capital of the nation they dreamed of, should be placed. Here again the genius, the priest Anoche, was asked what ought to be done. Okomfo Anoche said two trees should be planted, one at each of the possible sites. The two kum trees were planted.

One died. Where it died a small town grew, a home for some of the Asante, but not the home of homes. The other kum tree lived. It lived to be a giant among trees, fitting symbol of the mighty Asante family with its wide spreading branches.

The tree stood in the centre of the capital. The dire prophecy was not even whispered that said the fall of the kum tree would be a sign that the power of Asante had reached its ordained end. Now this tree had fallen in plain view of all the citizens of Kumase the great capital, Kumase the virgin, Kumase the beautiful green one.

There had been no warning. No branches had dried up. No disease of bark or branch or root had given a single signal of impending decay. They great tree simply fell of a sudden. It was as if a hand, enormous yet unseen, had plucked it whole from the earth and dashed it in anger against the stones of the ground. A tree fallen, even in a hurricane, breaks in a few places at the most. Here a branch twists upon itself. There another splinters, and its pieces hang broken from the joints. But the kum tree did not fall like that. The great tree fell and was shattered into tiny pieces—a thousand and thirty fragments—as if whatever force had brought it down was not content to break it, but wanted to pulverize it completely.

People heard what had happened, but at first they were unwilling to

250

believe the news. They made their way slowly to the site. There they saw the incredible had indeed come to pass. So they moved on, their tongues clinging to the roofs of their mouths. Fear kept all who saw the fallen kum tree from going close enough to touch it.

The Asantehene called the priests of the Asante nation together. He charged them to tell the truth, even if the news was bad. What did this omen mean? The priests heard the king. But none among them wished to be the direct bearer of the terrible understanding they could no longer hide. So they found a cruel, devious way to say what they knew. They ordered two slaves selected for sacrificial deaths. The two were brought.

They were so young, these human beings chosen to be destroyed. One tried desperately to save himself from death. He pleaded with his tormentors. He asked for the protection of the king. He invoked all the names of the royal ancestors of Asante, from Oti Akenten to Kwaku Dua. He begged the queen-mother as a mother to save a son. To stop his pleading tongue an executioner drove a short arrow into his left cheek and through his tongue, until the iron barb at the arrow's tip came out through the right cheek.

The second victim knew he had no hope of being saved. He stared with full understanding at those about to kill him. He offered them no prayers, no pleas. He made no noise even as the iron barbs of the sepow arrow were driven through his cheeks.

The priests told the king the nation's hopes would depend on the way the two slaves died. If they died quickly, within a day, that would mean the ancestors had accepted the sacrifice with pleasure, and the Asante armies would win a great victory against the white invaders. If the victims took a long time dying, say three days, that would mean the time had come for the nation to learn to sing the long dirge of defeat.

So the victims were taken away from the town, into the forest near the Swamp of the Dead, with the iron barbs skewering their cheeks. Thus bleeding, they were tied fast to two trees and left to die at their own speed.

The first day passed. Both victims stayed alive. The second day passed. Both victims stayed alive. The third day passed. Both victims still lived on. Not only that. The second victim, that proud one who had never once whimpered for mercy from those killing him, had a smile in his eyes from that day on—a smile that terrified the priests who came to see him every day, hoping to find him dead.

251

The first victim did not die until the sixth day. The second victim, the calm, proud one, lived beyond the seventh day and the eighth. He died serenely on the ninth.

*　　*　　*

Densu rested for three days after the crossing and the re-entry into Kumase. Then he set out for Ada. He took enough food for ten days' journey—dried fish and salted meat, kenkey, and, for the first two days, a little quantity of dried plantain. The journey took much less time than planned. He did not force himself to go on when he was tired, but he did not sleep more than was necessary to restore his strength either. He travelled all day, and as a rule was up again not too long past the middle of the night. The countryside changed as it came to meet him. He had never seen such hilly land, such sharp crags and stones as he found going east. The day before he reached the great Firaw river he had to climb up a hill so steep it made him light-headed and his eardrums popped gently near the top—a queer sensation. At the top he thought he could see the huge, broad river ahead of him, but it disappeared as he hurried down the cool, stony slope, and he did not see it again till he came to it the next day.

He met few travellers the way he had chosen, but those he met all knew the way to Ada and told him he was on an unusual path, but a true one.

'Do not go to the town when you arrive,' Damfo had advised him the night before he left. 'Search for the highest hill to the left of the town, close to the river. Go round it, upriver, then turn right towards the river. There's a village, Atike, not really a village, just a few houses. Only healers live there. Ask for Duodu. Show him our signs, and tell him you come from here. Greet him for us, and tell him why you've come. He's a friend of a king near there, Sakity, so he will know what goes on, and together they will help you.'

Densu found the collection of houses with ease. The healer Duodu was there. He seemed unwell and his voice was weak, though he was greatly pleased to welcome Densu and asked a full flood of questions about the healers on the Pra. Densu told him why he had come. He listened thoughtfully, and after Densu had finished, he was lost in thought.

'Sakity would have been most helpful,' he said, shaking his head. 'Damfo was right about that. But you won't find him. He's been taken to the white man's prison in Accra. They say his hot temper got the better of him at a meeting with the one called Glover. It seems this Glover has a lot of money and alcohol and guns, which he gives in large quantities to the kings who promise to fight for him against Asante. The kings have no intention of going to fight in Kumase, but they like Glover's alcohol and his money and his guns. So they agreed to give him all the promises he wanted, take his gifts and abandon him to his dreams when the time is ripe. Sakity alone said that was a childish, dishonest, cowardly way to act. He talks like that. He refused to swear allegiance to Glover. He said he owed no white man anything, certainly not allegiance. Of course the other kings feared he'd make them lose all that wealth. They wanted to kill him. Glover imprisoned him. Just like a white man, he was glad to say he was only imprisoning Sakity to protect him from the fury of his own black brothers.'

'Is there anyone else who might help? Like Sakity?' Densu asked.

'No one, I'm afraid,' Duodu answered. 'That man Sakity is the strangest of people. A king who values honesty. Your healer Damfo used to call him a healer pretending to be a king. You know, Sakity respects Damfo more than anyone in the world. With good reason. Damfo saved him from madness. Not once. Twice.'

'So there's no one else I can contact?'

Duodu creased his brow. But his memory yielded nothing new. 'Nobody,' he said with finality. 'You'll have to go a different way. Do you know the white men's language?'

Densu nodded.

'You could go to the white man, yourself. As a soldier, or a servant.'

'A servant would be better,' Densu agreed. 'I'd be around him. And I wouldn't risk being asked to kill for whites.'

'I don't know this Glover,' Duodu said. 'But everybody talks about him. From what I hear, his greatest quality is vanity. The fool thinks we black people cannot resist loving him. That we'll do anything for him. He likes to be called the Great White Father of the blacks, the protector, the friend. You know he's foolish like a king, and just as hungry for praise names. The broadest road to get to him would be through this vanity of his.'

Densu nodded, and smiled.

Duodu smiled back at Densu. 'I see you're no child,' he said. 'When will you be ready?'

'Even tomorrow.'

'What's today? Wednesday. Glover himself is not at Ada. He started to go upriver on Sunday. He hasn't returned. We'll know immediately he gets back. Those ships of his make some noise. You can rest, and I'll show you the land, and maybe you can help me bring home some herbs and tell me more about Damfo and the other healers.'

The white man Glover did not return to Ada that Wednesday, nor the next day. But on Friday his two huge boats came down the river like uncertain monsters, turning and twisting to find the deepest part of the shallow river.

Duodu had heard the boats approaching before they came into view.

'Can you read the things written on the ships?' Duodu asked Densu. Densu had to wait till the boats drew closer.

'Names, I think. The first one says it is the woman of the waters. The other is a person's name, perhaps. Gertrude.'

'Does it mean anything?'

'I don't know. I've never heard it before.' Densu said.

The two sat there on the hill and watched the ships make their way slowly to the makeshift landing. The ships were brought close to the shore. Almost before they had come to a stop men came down from it carrying bundles and heavy crates. Three white men jumped ashore. At that distance it was difficult to see clearly how each looked.

The watchers had eaten nothing since morning; their bodies demanded food and rest. They walked down to Atike, bathed, ate and talked, mainly about Glover, till night began. They went to sleep early. Densu woke before sunrise. He lay on his back in the darkness, thinking of what he would have to do before the day was over. He felt a kind of excitement rise in him. He struggled against it, trying to reach a steady, unshakable calm before it became necessary to act. Shortly after sunrise he washed and went up to the hilltop to see what was happening downriver. At Ada people were already up and busy at work at Glover's camp. Densu returned to Atike.

'Are you ready?' Duodu asked him.

'Yes.'

Duodu gave him an old rag to replace his cloth. Densu tied it around his waist. He said farewell to Duodu.

'You may have to be there a long time before you find out what you need to know,' Duodu said. 'Did they say when you should return?'

'I'm to stay as long as necessary, but the moment I get what I came for I'm to rush back.'

'You could be there for months,' Duodu said.

'I hope it won't be necessary,' Densu said.

He ran twice round the base of the hill before his sweat began flowing freely enough to satisfy him. Then he ran, taking long, steady strides, towards the white man's camp at Ada.

As he came down the last rise before the camp, he saw clearly in which direction he must go. There was one white man who moved back and forth across the camp with more energy than anyone else. He would go to one group of men putting stakes in the ground and, taking a hammer from one of them, would do the hammering himself, in the way of a man teaching others how best to do a thing. Immediately he would hurry to another group piling stones in a heap, and instruct them too. Elsewhere he would find people cutting bushes. He had a lesson for them too. Glover was everywhere, doing every little thing himself, or telling the doers how it should be done.

Here indeed was the white man in action. Glover the godlike, Glover the white man descended among the black people to do magical wonders. The white man looked immensely happy, fulfilled this Saturday morning. Why should he not be? Here he was a god, a god among mere men, a beloved father-god among infant-men.

Here he was, the white man who was known to have travelled through the lands beside the river even greater than the Firaw, the lands of the long, immense Kwarra to the east. Here he was, the man who had gone along the mysterious Kwarra and done what no mortal white man had ever hoped or dared to do even with help from thousands. Here he was, the man who knew himself a true magician when it came to getting black people to fight other black people for the profit of white people. Here he was, the one white man who could boast he could tell black men to do anything, no matter how difficult, and they would do it immediately out of love for him, Glover. Here he was, Glover the father of the Hausa fighters, protector of loving slaves. Here he was, Glover, he whose word was alone sufficient to inspire thirty thousand black men to rush delirious into the open jaws of death. Here he was, Glover the glorious, boastful one, Glover for-every-five-black-men-any-other-white-man-can-raise-I-alone-will-raise-hundreds. Here he was, the great white man. No need for the searcher to tire himself searching. Glover was visible as the sun this Saturday morning.

255

Was it men still unloading crates from the boats? Glover flitted like a wasp between the river's edge and the growing centre of his camp, making sure nothing would go wrong, that everything would be as perfect as the fantastic plans in his own head. Were men pitching new tents on the expanding outer reaches of the camp? Glover was there like a shot of lightning, giving them the most correct instructions about the proper tautness of each rope. Was it another line of men arriving from the river with bundles on their heads and shoulders? Glover was there, to show them which tent to put each bundle in. Glover was everywhere. Glover was the great white father, Glover was the omnipresent, omniscient god.

Farthest from the river, out where the partly cleared ground was flattest, men with long cutlasses were at work trying to clear more space. Glover strode out to them and they stopped to learn his wishes. He measured out for them the exact dimensions of the new area they should clear.

Just behind Glover, about a hundred men in blue tunics and blue shorts, carrying guns, came running, stopped, gathered together, and began going through the vigorous motions of military drill, obeying a leader in front of them. On his way back from marking the extra ground to be cleared, Glover paused a few moments, watching the drill. Then he bounded with impetuous energy towards the drill leader. First he snatched the leader's gun from him. Next he demonstrated the proper way to hold the gun, to charge, to retreat, to turn left, to turn right, to wheel about, to do everything. His motions, exceedingly vigorous, should have exhausted him. Yet each new spurt of effort seemed to leave him not tired but recharged with enormous amounts of fresh energy.

After each new involvement Glover paused slightly merely to look around him, to see where else the flow of his energy could go. Visibly, he seemed eager to discover which new hole in the arrangements and events surrounding him called for him to fill it.

Glover was recrossing the camp, making for his tent, when a young man, lean but strongly built, running at great speed but with obvious ease, broke into the camp. The runner was headed straight for Glover, and did not begin to slow down till he was only a few steps from him.

There were several men around Glover, trying desperately to keep up with him. Some were waiting upon him for instructions. Some were staying close to him because they formed a sort of guard for him. Some were hanging around him because they had perhaps come with messages for him.

Among these men around Glover some, seeing an unknown runner rush upon Glover, this white sun, this magic god, this centre of their lives, turned suddenly alert and jumped to block the runner's path. But the runner was no mediocre runner, easy to trap. Turning his body and straining it visibly so it seemed his intention was to move heavily to the right, he caused those trying to block his path to move that way. Immediately, in just one swift spring he had jumped left and forward, and between him and Glover there was nothing.

At that moment Glover's face, till then red with all the exertion of the morning, turned white. Glover took one step backward, and his hand sought something at his waist. But this Saturday morning Glover had stepped out of his tent in forgetful confidence, taking neither sword nor gun.

There was no cause for Glover to fear a premature end to his fantastic plans, however. As he reached Glover the runner bent his body so that it took on an attitude far from any suggestion of aggression. By the time he was actually within touching distance of Glover the runner was on his knees. His arms were held out in a suppliant reach. His hands were seeking contact with the white man's shoes.

The white man Glover could not be counted among the tall men of the earth. But on seeing the runner kneeling before him he drew himself up as if he were the giant Asebu Amamfi himself, he who was so huge and strong he used to mix his roast corn with rocks to make them pleasanter to chew. The redness of the morning's excited work returned to colour Glover's face.

Those who had attempted to stop the runner from reaching Glover and failed had by now recovered from their surprise. The special aggressive zeal that follows humiliation now animated them, and they tried mightily to hustle the runner away from Glover's presence. But Glover himself, now once more confident, Glover the benign, Glover the father of the tribes, Glover the god, Glover ordered his men to leave the suppliant runner alone and let him have his say. The grovelling runner had in fact begun to speak. One of Glover's black men translated for him.

What did the runner have to say to Glover?

It was a kind of praise song to the white man. When the men around Glover let go of him, the runner turned his eyes upward from his crouching position and directed a fulsome look of gratitude at

Glover. First he called Glover redeemer of the enslaved, hope of the oppressed, true friend of the unfortunate. As each praise name was translated to him the white man Glover acknowledged it with a solemn nod.

After calling Glover by several praise names the runner spoke of his humble self. He was, he said, a pitiful wretch, a homeless fugitive escaped from a cruel Asante master. He had long known of Glover—who on earth did not know his fame? He had long wished to find him. Finally he had worked out a way to escape, and had come running days and nights through the forests, seeking his saviour.

Glover let the suppliant talk till he ran out of breath. Then he ordered the interpreter to ask him what precisely he wanted from him. Single and prompt came the answer:

'Let me be your servant. Let me see your face every day, every moment. Let me do whatever you need done. That will be my happiness.'

Glover tried to maintain a certain fitting sternness of countenance. He failed. There was nothing he could do to stop the happy smile that came to his lips. He had adopted a steadier stance now, putting his left foot forward half a pace ahead of the right. In that position he was more comfortable while the suppliant beneath him continued to grasp his foot. His left hand, doubled into a fist, rested at his waist. His right he had thrust into an opening in his jacket, between buttons, at about the level of his heart. Glover was pleased with this running suppliant so eager to be his servant—that was plain.

Glover ordered the interpreter to ask the fugitive his name.

'Densu,' the fugitive answered.

Glover stared fiercely down at Densu. Densu looked up smiling a somewhat bashful smile.

'Do you speak English?' Glover asked with ferocious suddenness. On Densu's face the bashful smile did not change. The interpreter, laughing uncontrollably at the idea of such a poor wretch speaking English, translated the question for Densu. Densu looked immensely puzzled. It was clear the strangeness of the question had rendered him speechless.

'Well, well, Den Soo, my boy,' Glover smiled, 'you will be my servant.'

Densu was given new clothes and work to do assisting the chief personal servant of the great white man Glover. It was not heavy work. He took care of clothes, seeing that after they were washed, they were well ironed and cleanly kept. He swept out Glover's tent and served his meals. Glover loved to watch him run. Some evenings he would set Densu to run against the best of his soldiers, boasting proudly of his servant's speed as if it were his own. Densu did not let him down; he won all the races. The days passed into weeks. From the first Glover talked with abundant freedom even when Densu was around. He talked about his plans—fantastic plans all of them, and even more fantastic methods for making them come true. Densu saw more money handled than he had ever seen before in his life, money, drinks, and guns.

Every day kings came to visit Glover. Some came smiling, drank, and joked with the white man, took their gifts and went back where they had come from. The gifts were many—large bottles of gin, often given in whole cases; bright new guns and powder and bullets to go with them, and always the coins that could make the angriest king break out into smiles.

Densu watched the white man and heard him in his most secret moods, but for weeks and weeks he could not find out what he had come to learn: of Glover and Wolseley, whose power would override the other's? Who was under whose command?

What Densu did find out surprised him. In spite of all his manic energy during the day, the white man Glover was at night a morose, solitary being. Sometimes he talked with one of the other white men, but most often he drank alone in his tent, bursting out with angry words when he could control his pain no longer. Often when he slept, he would hold long arguments with invisible people, telling them they knew he was right and would succeed, if only they would stop blocking his path at every chance they got.

To his friends Glover complained that the money he needed to give the kings was not enough. He said he knew the blacks thoroughly. 'Give a black man gifts,' he used to say to one thin white officer with a long, black, oily moustache, 'and his soul belongs to you. He and his people will fight for you. But think, Sartorius, how can I get my allies to come over when I'm given so little money for them?'

Glover complained he had been cheated by his own people at Accra. He had bought drinks to bribe the kings so they would bring their men to fight for him, but the drinks which should have cost four shillings a case were sold to him for eighteen.

Glover complained he had ordered four thousand five hundred guns and not got them. He needed silver coins for little gifts, and these had been withheld from him. He had bought some big guns, but the ammunition to go with them was the wrong type. Glover complained he had only one doctor to heal the wounds of all the thousands he wished to invade Asante with. And his ship was not whole—something was wrong with it, and it hampered his plans.

The kings, in order to get Glover's money and his alcohol and his guns, had filled Glover's head with wonderful promises. They had promised to bring him thousands upon thousands of virile men to work, fight, and die for him. Glover had measured out camping space for fourteen thousand Krepi warriors—the Krepi king had promised him that number. He had measured out space for twelve thousand men from Accra to Ada, seven thousand from Ekuapem, and seven thousand from Krobo. From Akim he expected at least four thousand fighters.

Sometimes at night Glover spoke these figures aloud, and seemed to be commanding such numbers in great battles which he won with ease. In his waking conversations he occasionally talked of the kinds of honours he would be given when he returned home, together with his officers, after an unprecedented victory. He spoke of the ease with which he could get black men to fight against black men for white men's purposes.

Glover's conversations with the kings became more frequent with the passage of weeks. Soon it became plain to him that what he had taken for a union of ambitions—the black kings dying to die for him—was no union but a sly collision of selfish desires. The conversations between Glover and the kings became encounters of men with big mouths and tiny ears.

'We march against Kumase!' Glover said.

'We must first strike our enemies on the other side of the river,' the kings told him.

'What enemies? Aren't my enemies your enemies?' asked the sly Glover.

'Yes, yes,' answered the sly kings, 'and our enemies are your enemies.'

'We go west,' cried Glover.

'We go east,' cried the kings.

Glover continued to dream. He dreamed of a time in which he could satisfy his slippery royal friends by making a few swift marches to the east across the river, then leading a huge army of pleased allies into Asante. Glover continued to dream of a great triumphal march to Kumase and after that a voyage at the end of which endless praise songs would be sung to him, a conqueror among conquerors, he who had had the wisdom to win an empire for the white people without the shedding of white men's blood.

Glover continued to dream, but then a fatal week came for him. Between Densu's sixth Saturday with him and the seventh, reality pierced his dreams. Reality converted the sweetness of dreams into unbearable bitterness. The exulting hero crashed from the heights of imagined glory, and fell down a laughable clown. Glover the magnificent, Glover the omniscient, Glover the father of the Hausas, Glover the redeemer of slaves, Glover I-can-call-forth-a-thousand-black-men-where-any-other-could-scarcely-raise-five, in that swift week Glover the white saviour came down from the inflated mindsize of giants and dwindled to the mindsize of a dwarf. His nights became almost entirely sleepless. In the few moments of restful darkness he tried to steal from pain, unwanted voices called out to him not songs of praise but mocking epithets. Glover was no longer the great white man. He had become, even in his own eyes, merely the gross white buffoon.

What brought the high one so low?

The third Sunday after Densu had reached Glover's camp, as was the custom among the whites and their slaves, nothing much was done. The Monday after that there were important messages to be sent to the other great white man, Wolseley, at Cape Coast. There were also hurried, earnest consultations with the kings at the camp. This was a restless day, filled more with anxious fidgeting than with real activity.

The next day, Tuesday, day of the sea, was a day of action. Glover was manic. He spoke to the chiefs again, and after that he was a thundering deity, sending flaming missiles across the sky against the Awona people living on the Firaw's other bank. After the flames had done their work, fighters were sent across the river, under the tall white officer with the oiled moustache, the one called Sartorius. There they had a swift victory, and at the end of the day Glover was a happy man.

The next day, Wednesday, Glover rested. But on Thursday his appetite for war returned, and he indulged it with such energy that the following day he and his men needed to rest all day. It was the same Friday that was destined to bring stormy news.

Messengers had come to the main camp from Cape Coast, bringing messages from the white commander there, Wolseley. Not finding Glover at the camp, they crossed the Firaw and found him on the left bank. The messages they brought blasted Glover's peace of mind. From that moment his nights, all of them, turned a pitiless, blazing white with sleeplessness.

The next day, Saturday, greatest of days, Glover, he who had hoped to do so much with such ease, Glover the great white father, called a hurried meeting of the kings who had promised so many thousands to fight and die for him in return for gifts of guns, money and alcohol. Trying to speak with a firm voice in spite of all the troubles preying on his mind, Glover told the kings assembled at Adidome the heavy news.

First, Glover reminded his listeners there was another great white man at Cape Coast. His voice broke when he pointed out that the ways of white power were such that it was now necessary for him to obey that other great white man.

That white one who must be obeyed, Wolseley, had sent a message ordering Glover, with his Hausa fighters, with his Yoruba soldiers, and all the thirty-thousand and more he had said he would take against Asante, to march towards Kumase at once. Glover was not to go to Kumase directly, but to march to the Pra. On the banks of that river, at Praso, the two great white commanders would meet, each with his army.

Glover told the assembled kings all this with tears in his voice. He no longer spoke with the confidence of a hero sure of his destiny. He looked towards the kings and reminded them they had pledged loyalty to him. He asked them to cross the river with him, and, with their men, follow him on the march to the river Pra, and to Kumase.

It was hard to say which feeling was strongest among the listening kings: puzzlement, consternation or indignation. In sheer incredulity the kings asked why they should stop fighting on the east bank of the Firaw. Why should they stop now that they had their real enemies in their power, to go chasing after other people's enemies? Why should they go to attack the Asante before they had exterminated the Awona people?

So this Saturday Glover knew only bitter failure. He tried to coax the kings into crossing the river back to the camp with him. The chiefs added salt to the wounds of Glover's frustration. They told him, smiling, that they would go willingly to attack Asante, they would go even to the centre of the earth with him. But they would not move across the Firaw until they had wiped out the last of the Awona people.

Sunday followed. Glover found no rest. There was work to do in preparation for the forced journey ahead. The great white man acquired a new habit: tearing his hair. He stalked furiously inside his tent, cursing Wolseley, calling him a wild stream of names: a jealous, envious, cowardly traitor.

Densu stayed silent and immobile just within the entrance to the tent while the great white man raged like a youthful tempest. Glover sent for the messengers again. It was as if he could still not believe they had actually brought him such bad news. Glover wanted to question all of them who had come from Cape Coast: the messengers as well as the guards.

As the first messenger entered Glover's hut, he looked to his left just inside the entrance and saw the still form of the silent Densu. Perhaps in the sudden change from the bright sunshine outside into the dimness within the tent, the messenger mistook the form he saw for that of someone other than a servant. At any rate, the first messenger gave Densu a respectful bow before going forward into Glover's presence. In imitation of the first messenger, the second repeated the bow. So did the third.

Six guards followed after the messengers. They came in single file, their line so arranged that the smallest came first and the last was the tallest and most massive. All gave the small salute of respect to the man at the tent's entrance, and this amused Densu.

The tent was not a small one, but it was not meant for a crowd of messengers and guards. The last of the guards could not find space near Glover, in the centre. They therefore had to stand nearer and nearer the door. The last, the hugest of them all, stood just within the entrance. The distance between him and Densu was a forearm's length, no more.

The huge one had also greeted Densu when he came in from outside, as carelessly as the others, with a most awkward motion of his hand. Then he had stood heavily in the doorway. Because he stood in the light, Densu saw him plainly and the sight made him calm his heart and look straight ahead. Out of the corner of his right eye he examined the giant again, though he did not need a second look to confirm what was so clear to him. The massive body, the broad, thick neck rising from the shoulders like the buttresses of the odan tree, and the small, blunt head—all of this Densu recognized at once. The last of the messengers was none other than Buntui of Esuano, the brutal, mindless one.

It took Buntui a long time to adjust to the darkness within the tent. In that time Glover had begun asking the messengers questions and listening to the translations of the answers they gave. Glover wanted to know in what kind of mood the messengers had found Wolseley just before they left Cape Coast. He wanted to know if any of them recollected the sound of his words. Was he laughing as he gave them the message? Had any new white visitors arrived at Cape Coast recently?

Glover's questions were many; the messengers' answers were few. He even questioned the guards who had come with the messengers. The less information Glover got, the higher rose his fury. The translator, to calm him perhaps, explained the guards' position: they were simple soldiers. In the ordinary course of their work they never came near the white officers, at least not near enough to hear their private conversations. Besides which they understood no English.

Buntui, standing at the tail-end of the line of guards, and rather baffled by the long discussion going on ahead of him, spent his time looking this way and that now that he could distinguish objects in the tent with some clarity. He looked upward, forward, to the right, and he looked left. His eyes repeated the cycle, but they reached the end quite fast the second time. Then they did not, or could not, move from their final focus.

Buntu looked at the figure to his left and blinked. He looked again. On his face curiosity was replaced, slowly, by doubt. In its turn doubt yielded place to certainty, then fear. In sheer surprise, Buntui opened his mouth. Without warning a huge cry like a bellow burst forth from the giant throat. The noise was so unexpected that Glover, who was restlessly fidgeting with a baton in his hand, dropped the stick. He looked up angrily towards the source of the noise, but the light in the the doorway was strong and against it he could not see the offender clearly. 'Bring the fool here!' he screamed.

The other guards, surprised by Buntui's strange outburst, were confused by the sudden order from Glover. While they hesitated, Buntui, the veins of his neck swollen to bursting with excitement, poured out a stream of words so fast his listeners did not even make an attempt to understand him. He was telling the white man that Densu was from Esuano, that he had escaped on the night of the ordeal, that he led a charmed life, that Ababio said he was a sorcerer, a spy for the Asante

264

army and a child of the devil and his wife, and many other things besides.

The white man Glover understood no Fantse. All he could hear was a wild cascade of sounds issuing from the ugly figure blocking the doorway of his tent. He repeated the order he had given. Buntui, still pointing accusingly at Densu but not daring to move towards him, put up a struggle when the guards closest to him moved to lay hands on him. But against all five his resistance did not help him.

'Get him out of here!' shouted the enraged Glover. The guards dragged Buntui out of the tent. From the howls he uttered it was plain they were doing more than just taking him out—they were beating him, and he kept asking why they had so easily forgotten he was their own companion.

The disturbance Buntui had created had aggravated Glover's mood, already fouled by the recent unexpected developments. He looked at everything with an angry eye, and for no reason at all he began to scold the interpreter and the three messengers.

'Get out!' Glover shouted at the baffled four. 'Get out, all of you!' They went out. The tall white officer with the oiled moustache came in. Glover looked at Densu standing by the entrance. He had never spoken harshly to him, and even now he hesitated—only one brief moment. 'And you too,' he said, 'what are you waiting for?'

Densu did not need urging twice. At last he had found out what he needed to find out. He was eager to return to Praso. Leaving the tent, he walked away from the centre of the camp. On the edge of the camp farthest from the river he could see the five guards around their past comrade and present victim Buntui. They had made a ring around him. All of them had obtained ropes, which they were now using as whips on Buntui's bare back.

Densu avoided the sweating group. He walked over to the servants' hut and picked up a gourd there. Then he crossed the camp in the direction of the river. A little short of the river there was a leftward fork in the path, going downriver. Densu turned along that path, and increased his speed. Far below the camp the new path reached the river. There was no ford, but the river was narrower at that point than anywhere else within sight. The current looked rather swift but it flowed directly leftward with no sign of dangerous whirls or eddies in it. Densu placed the gourd on the bank and slipped into the river.

The river was muddy, but its water felt cool and refreshing. Densu did not struggle against the current. He swam in the general direction of the right bank, but let the current carry him as far downstream as it had strength to.

He did not wait to let the sun dry his clothes when he reached the right bank. He made his way swiftly, walking and running, to Atike. The healer Duodu was at home.

'Welcome back,' Duodu said quite casually as if Densu had only been gone a day or two. He gave him water. 'Did you succeed?'

Densu nodded. 'I want to thank you . . .' he began

The old healer interrupted him: 'Don't start saying farewell yet. Rest a few nights with me. I haven't finished asking you my questions. I haven't even begun, really.'

'I have to go today,' Densu said. 'The white men plan to move on Kumase in a few weeks.'

'I see,' Duodu said. 'You must come back here. I'm not strong enough to travel, these days. But you will come? Promise me that.'

'At the first chance,' Densu promised.

The old healer gave him food, and made him rest until the food had gone down. Then he walked with him a short distance, and left him on the western road.

Densu got an eager welcome from Ajoa, from Damfo, from Nyaneba and the other healers, and from Asamoa Nkwanta. From Araba Je-siwa he got the happiest surprise of all: he found her walking gently in the open space in the centre of the healers' village. She seemed to recognize him, because she stopped and looked at him. But she said nothing. She could say nothing.

Ajoa brought him water, but he told her the food could wait. The healers had assembled together with Asamoa Nkwanta to hear the news Densu brought. He went directly to them as soon as he had washed himself.

They sat silent, no one interrupting as he told them all that had happened to him, all he had seen and heard. Afterwards Asamoa Nkwanta needed reassurances:

'This Glover receives his orders from the one called Wolseley?'

'He does.'

'He has been ordered to advance towards Kumase?'

'He has, and he's not pleased. He says his allies are not ready. They have refused to march with him to Kumase.'

'If he obeys the order, how large an army will come with him?'

'No army at all,' Densu answered. 'A thousand men at the most. Those he brought with him from farthest east. The men from Bonni and Opobo, and the Hausa slaves.'

'And they're to reach the river Pra by the middle of next month?'

Densu nodded.

A happy smile softened Asamoa Nkwanta's face. 'Everything will be perfect,' he said musingly. 'This Glover brings only a thousand from the east. Asafo Adjei need not have nightmares about the safety of his capital, Juaben. He can leave a few thousand men to protect the town. All the rest of his army will then be available to close the trap into which the crippled white general Wolseley is marching with his white army. The important thing is to slow the white army down.' He turned to Damfo. 'How has the healers' plan been going in that respect?'

'Well enough,' Damfo said. 'So well the whites say their main problem is the desertion of carriers and labourers. Some of our men have been captured in the course of their work. You know two of them: Kwao Tweneboa and Kojo Mensa. There were here not too long ago.'

'What exactly do you healers do that so frightens the whites?' Asamoa Nkwanta asked. 'I fail to understand why they fear unarmed women and men more than they fear us warriors.'

Damfo smiled: 'The white army is heavy. It is an army of things, depending on the weight and force of things. The whites cannot carry anything for themselves. Their heavy guns, their food, their medicines, even water must be carried for them. Without carriers they cannot move. All we healers do is to hold conversations with the carriers. We greet them, and ask: "Brother, why do you sweat so? Do your people have such a great quarrel with other black people that you must become a beast of burden for the whites? Would you do this if you were allowed to choose? Or are you doing this so some chief can grow a bit fatter than he already is? When last did you rest? When last did you eat? And the pay you were promised, have you received it?" That's all we do. We talk with people. We remind them of who they are. We open their eyes to what is happening to them. Sometimes they just drop their burdens and disappear. Often.'

'Only one great difficulty faces us. At times the carriers agree with us, but say the choice is between being slaves of the Asante kings and being slaves of the whites. Then we can't give them the answer we would like to give, because we healers also see what they see: the royals of Asante do not wish the unity of black people all over this

267

land. All they know is Asanteman. Of Ebibirman they are totally ignorant. Wilfully so. That is the sad thing.'

Asamoa Nkwanta sighed: 'I wish I could tell you what the royals
are up to, but I can't. I have a man I trust at court, Oson. But these
days I can't find him. I just hope he's alive, and well.'

At the end of the meeting Damfo took Asamoa Nkwanta's right hand
in both of his and said farewell.

'You're leaving?' Asamoa Nkwanta asked in a startled voice.

Damfo nodded. 'You're well, and it's time for me to go back down
south. Araba Jesiwa walks now. All that remains is for her to talk. In
some ways that will be the most difficult part of her healing. I've
examined her body. It is whole now. The inability to talk doesn't
come from the body. If she's to talk, we'll need to do a lot of work,
and she'll have to have the calmest surroundings. There's such a lot of
activity here. And my medicines, many of them, I've left in the south.'

The warrior was sad, tongue-tied. When he found his voice again,
he asked the healer in what way he could express his gratitude: 'If
there's anything you and the healers need done, let me know.'

'We shall,' Damfo said. 'And we shall wish you luck and good fortune in all your days.'

The warrior swallowed, and the healer asked him if there was anything else he wished to say.

'I had hoped to have Densu with me in these coming days.' He
looked at Densu. 'What he does for the peace of my soul I dare not
speak of. And he's more than a helper.'

'He's the same to us all,' Damfo said. 'But let him decide. Ajoa will
be there to help me.' He looked at Densu. 'What do you want to do?'

Densu looked at Ajoa. Ajoa smiled.

'I can wait for you,' she said. 'But don't be too long.'

'I will join you later then,' Densu said.

Asamoa Nkwanta left, and a change came over the meeting of
healers.

'Is it true you're leaving, Damfo?' two healers asked at once. Their
unison startled even themselves.

'Yes, I'm leaving,' Damfo said.

'But why?'

'I came to Praso to help cure Asamoa Nkwanta. That work is done.
He is whole again, and doing the work he loves. I am returning to

Esuano. The work of healing Araba Jesiwa is unfinished. I need to finish it.'

'Are we not losing our way now, we healers?'

'How?' Damfo asked.

'It is a part of our work to heal individuals.'

'The smaller part,' agreed Damfo.

'It is another part of our work to seek the healing of our people, the black people.'

'The greater part,' said Damfo.

'In coming to Praso our hope was to move towards the greater healing work.'

'That was so,' agreed Damfo.

'In leaving Praso now,' Nyaneba asked, 'are you not abandoning the greater work of healing for the lesser?'

'You speak well, Nyaneba,' Damfo said. 'I have considered the matter. Often I have wondered whether Asamoa Nkwanta was just a sick individual needing healing, or something more: a force for the healing of our people.

'So I have looked steadily at Asamoa Nkwanta while he's been under our care. I have listened carefully to him, and I know a little of the nature of his soul. Asamoa Nkwanta is a good man. He is also a valuable man, one of those highly skilled in the pursuit of a vocation. But all his goodness has been spent in the service of Asante royalty. Among our people, royalty is part of the disease. Whoever serves royalty serves the disease, not the cure. He works to divide our people, not to unite us, no matter what he hopes personally to do.'

'Is there no possibility of a man like Asamoa Nkwanta, trained to serve the disease, changing and putting himself into the service of healing work?'

'Let's think of it,' Damfo suggested. 'Say Asamoa Nkwanta wishes the healing of our people now, the coming together of all black people. But he must work within the royal army, under royal command. We know that to the royals the healing of the black people would be a disaster, since kings and chiefs suck their power from the divisions between our people. How can Asamoa Nkwanta do healing work while remaining trapped in a group serving the disease?'

'Could he not turn the army against the disease?'

'He, the single individual?' Damfo asked slowly.

'Yes. Asamoa Nkwanta.'

'I don't believe so,' Damfo said, 'and I will not allow myself even to wish so. Healing is work, not gambling. It is the work of inspiration, not manipulation. If we the healers are to do the work of helping bring our whole people together again, we need to know such work is the work of a community. It cannot be done by an individual. It should not depend on any single person, however heroic he may be. And it can't depend on people who do not understand the healing vocation—no matter how good such people may be as individuals.

'The work of healing is work for inspirers working long and steadily in a group that grows over the generations, until there are inspirers, healers wherever our people are scattered, able to bring us together again.'

'You are saying our time is not now?' Nyaneba asked.

'I am saying this is seed time, far from harvest time,' Damfo said.

'But,' said another healer, 'is this not our perennial shrinking from power? Is it not possible we healers are suffering from a disease—the fear of power—that will keep us forever impotent, because even when we have a man like Asamoa Nkwanta willing to help us, we fear to grasp him and use him to lend our good aims strength and power?'

The silence was heavy. And Damfo's voice, when he spoke, was subdued:

'That would be our misfortune,' he said, 'if we did have a disease, a blind fear of power. But I do not see us blindly fearing power. We healers do not fear power. We avoid power deliberately, as long as that power is manipulative power. There is a kind of power we would all embrace and help create. It is the power we use in our work. The power of inspiration. The power that respects the spirit in every being, in every thing, and lets every being be true to the spirit within. Healers should embrace that kind of power. Healers should help create that kind of power. But that kind of power—the power that comes from inspiration—can never be created with manipulators. If we healers allow the speedy results of manipulation to attract us, we shall destroy ourselves and more than ourselves, our vocation.'

'I hear you,' Nyaneba said. 'But I am old now. I have seen my generation come near the completion of the half-circle of life, and the hopes of healers have not moved one single step closer to realization. What is left of my life is nothing to me. It will be a waste no matter what I do. I am curious about the opportunity Asamoa Nkwanta has shown us. I shall wait to see what comes out of it.'

So there was a division among the healers. All understood Damfo when he asked: 'Are we forgetting that for healers the meaning of the span of life takes in our whole people, not just our single separate lives?' It was a hard question that was let pass. All understood Damfo, but almost all sympathized with Nyaneba's ultimate tiredness with the slowness of work.

Damfo went south. The other healers waited. What was their hope? It was not articulate, but it had to do with a possibility of Asamoa Nkwanta becoming the ultimate power in Asante. And if in such a time of momentous change he needed help . . .

*   *   *

At Kumase men hoped that the white man Wolseley would be unable to march an army to Kumase. Their hope shaded into doubt when they saw he had caused a broad road to be built from Cape Coast all the way north to the river Pra. If he crossed the river he would be in Adanse. And what was Adanse but the entrance to Asante?

The labour that went into the building of this road was strenuous and cruel. Wolseley had sent his white officers to the chief towns of the land to hunt black men for use as labourers. One called Hearle was sent to Denchira. One called Filliter was sent to Dominase. One called Cochran was sent to Asebu. One called Pollard was sent to Dunkwa.

The white men went to the kings with more bribes and alcohol, and the kings accepted both. Almost all the kings repeated their generous promises, but when it came to the keeping of promises, the white men found the kings worthy to be their own kin in the slippery arts of hypocrisy.

Bribes and alcohol failed the white men, but violence did not. One of the white officers became famous, his genius for destruction exciting immense wonder. This man roamed over the land burning villages at night, threatening towns with destruction, capturing hostages and terrifying populations—if they did not provide labourers for the white road. His name became something to frighten children with: Colonel Colley.

At Cape Coast the whites sent soldiers into homes to capture men. Priests supposed to be saving souls of believers in the white god turned their followers into the white man's labourers. This was another time when even the most credulous understood the purposes of the Christian god were not so mysterious after all. They were whatever white men decided they should be.

The road to the Pra was not built by willing men. But it was built.

Even after the building, the anger of those forced to build it some-times made itself visible. Piles of refuse appeared mysteriously after dark, blocking the road. Wide holes not made by nature destroyed the smoothness of its new surface. Two hundred and thirty bridges had been built across rivers and streams so the white general Wolseley would not have to wet his feet on the march to Kumase. Men pulled up the wood and wrecked the bridges. But the whites forced others to rebuild what was torn down. Men ran away when they were sure the white man's guns were far away. But the whites forced women and children to take their places. The road moved forward.

The road, broader than two tall men laid on end, moved forward past the Fosu Lagoon, past Siwdo, Pedu, Kakomdo, Nyame Bechere, Kube Kor, and neither desertion nor destruction was able to halt its progress. It was not the road alone that had to be built. At intervals along it, the white soldiers needed stations, places where they could rest before moving on. The forest was cut down beside the road. Where only small villages had been, new towns now sprang up.

Large storehouses grew out of the ground from forced sweat. Big houses had to be built hastily, measuring ten tall men in length and three in width. The branches of a thousand palm trees had to be dragged long distances to roof the new houses. Bamboo stakes were cut and split for making beds all along the sides. Smaller huts were built with four beds to each. Then there was always one special hut set aside for Wolseley, the great white general.

At Nkwabem the news was that those willing to work on the white man's road would be paid a shilling a day, their leaders two shillings and sixpence. The news did not bring crowds. The soil was hard. In addition to the houses, wells had to be dug, and a huge machine set up to purify water for the whites, always fearful of disease.

At Ekrofor, and at Fantse Nyankomase the story was the same. The whites feared the forest. Even its cleanest running water they would not drink.

The work at Manso was heavier than at Nkwabem, Ekrofor and Fantse Nyankomase together. A huge space was cleared and beaten flat. The houses were bigger. The work had to be done with greater care than at the other stations. Rain fell and dissolved a great part of past labour. Along the road ditches had to be added to drain the rush-ing water. In all the rain the labourers were forbidden to stay in the areas they had worked to clear. To fatigue in the daytime the white men added discomfort at night and disease in after days.

At Nsuta there was a change. The slippery red soil worked treachery on the tired workers. The large machines to purify water for white throats could not be taken there, but the water still had to be purified. Men were set to work piling strange basket filters on each other.

At Assen Nyankomase the whites stood enchanted before the fresh beauty of the Subin stream, a stream so clear the sand at its bottom was visible, grain from grain. At Assen Bereku the Brupae stream worked the same magic, and that was the last of the stations before Praso.

News came to Kumase from the coast, bringing anxiety. One Saturday the white general Wolseley left Cape Coast, travelling on the wide new road, heading for the Pra. The anxiety of those who heard the news at Kumase was lightened when one of the royal messengers, Kwamen Owusu, said confidently that it meant nothing. Wolseley, after all, had left Cape Coast on a Sunday afternoon exactly two months before, and had not reached Kumase, had not even reached Praso. Fever and madness had forced him to go back, sick as a dog, to Cape Coast for healing. He would have to go back once more.

But the happy Kwamen Owusu was proved wrong. Scouts watched Wolseley's progress and brought the news to Kumase: the white general had not turned back, and was expected to reach the Pra on Friday. At the court anxiety turned into real fear. The unthinkable—an army of strangers entering Kumase—began to seem not so unthinkable to some.

'Something must be done, and quickly.' This was the opinion passed around in grave whispers at the court. But what? No one was sure, till another opinion brought relief.

'We must find ways to delay the white man at the Pra, while we consider what to do.'

So an embassy was sent to Praso. The clear-voiced court crier Osei Kwaku went with it. So did Koranche Safo and Kwamen Owusu. There were nine others, four of them guards, four carriers, the last not being really part of the embassy but a servant of the half-white man from Cape Coast, the interpreter called Dawson. Robert was his name, though he was a black man.

The twelve reached the north bank of the Pra on Friday. A white officer crossed over with soldiers and took them across the river to the white soldiers' camp. Osei Kwaku told the white men he and his friends had been sent to see the white general Wolseley and to give him letters from the king. The answer was swift: the white general

273

would speak to no one less than the king himself or at the very least a close relative. So what could Osei Kwaku do but agree to let others take the letters to the white general? Meanwhile the envoys waited to receive an answer to take back.

The waiting angered Kwamen Owusu.

'We shall make this proud white fool eat dung,' he said.

'Be quiet, Kwamen, and control your anger,' Osei Kwaku said.

There was nothing the envoys could do but wait. A new day came, Saturday. From the whites there was only an enigmatic silence. Nothing happened to advance the work they had come to do. But they saw much at the camp, not enough to make Kwamen Owusu quit predicting doom for the white invader, but enough to make his tongue somewhat slower.

New groups of soldiers entered the camp that day. Two hundred were black, two hundred white. The whites were the strangest soldiers ever seen. They walked like drunkards, lurching from side to side. They sang like drunkards too, with red faces and great energy. Yet it was clear they were not drunk: though rolling from side to side, they moved in straight lines and even their lurching and their singing were done together to a pattern.

On account of these new arrivals the Asante envoys were subjected to humiliating discomfort. They were all moved to a different, smaller house to make room for the soldiers. After that they were left alone for the rest of the day and night.

The next day, a Sunday, did not bring the long awaited message either. The envoys grew restless, especially Kwamen Owusu. In the afternoon their anxiety was lightened: a call came for all the king's messengers, and they felt sure the message was at last ready. But when they met them the white officers said nothing about any message. Angry beyond control, Kwamen Owusu spoke out of turn and asked about it.

The whites answered there was no need to worry: the general would send his answer with a white man to Kumase when it was ready. At this statement Kwamen Owusu laughed with that contemptuous arrogance for which he was famous. Before Osei Kwaku could check him he spoke fierce words:

'The white man who goes to Kumase will never return alive!'

Koranche Safo silenced Kwamen Owusu with a stern look, but said nothing.

The white men had not called the envoys out for nothing. They had called them so they could show them a little game of theirs. The game turned out to be a preparation for the dance of death.

There was a strange new kind of gun there at Praso. The white men when they talked called it a Gatling. Occasionally they also called it Rait's gun. This was no gun to be carried by one man. To move it, the white men had to take it apart, and the pieces were carried forward by strong black men, those the whites always called the Hausas.

The white men and their Hausa helpers had the greatest trouble positioning the gun for their game of death. But in the end they succeeded in putting it down in such a way that its mouth pointed straight up the river. There was a lot more trouble when the white men tried to get the gun to work. Kwamen Owusu smiled a bitter, satisfied smile and told again the joke about the great new engine at Cape Coast that was supposed to take the captured Entwi to Praso, so Entwi could return to Kumase and tell about the white man's wonderful power.

'The engine fell apart at the first hill, right there at Cape Coast,' Kwamen Owusu said. 'What do the whites know about power? They can't even command their own machines. How can they dream of conquering Asante?' He spat. Koranche Safo told him to hold his peace.

Then whatever trouble the whites had been having with their strange new gun came to an end. All at once they stood apart and made three noises, sudden, surprising yells. Many then went running to the one who had seemed to know most about the gun and hit him several times on his back, laughing happily and calling out his name: 'Rait! Rait! Rait!'

The gun began to fire. Ah, Kwamen Owusu, what a terrible pain it was, to watch a horribly new instrument of power, see its conquering devastation, and know that this monstrous tool of power was not for you and yours but against you, against the power of your beloved king! How far could the most powerful weapon available to the Asante army throw its stone seeds of death? Three hundred lengths? Four? Five hundred? Here was a terrible new gun hurling heavy death-metal up the river a thousand lengths and more. A fraction of that flight and all the force behind any bullet from any Asante gun would have been exhausted. But even after such long flight the metal from the white man's new gun was potent with death. Kwamen Owusu, how your blood turned cold when you saw the way the metal hit the water as if its furious intention was to murder the eternal Pra itself! Nor was this the haphazard flight of bullets shot forward in mere hope. The white man in charge of the gun, the one they called Rait, had an art to choose exactly where the seeds of death should fall. He made sure the Asante envoys could see plainly he could make the hot metal pierce the water in a narrow circle or a wider one. And he could also choose the speed and frequency at which death flew through the shrieking air. That was what the white men showed the envoys that Sunday.

The envoys and their guards returned to the house set apart for them. Koranche Safo turned to Kwamen Owusu and spoke, not in anger, but sadly:

'There was no need for you to threaten the white men, Owusu. Besides, what you said was untrue.'

Kwamen Owusu sat in a heavy mood. He looked like a creature unexpectedly bereaved. All he seemed able to do was to shake his head in mute acceptance of his own guilt. Osei Kwaku also looked long at Kwamen Owusu. He did not talk of guilt or of broken vows.

'I too,' Osei Kwaku said, 'I too have often laughed at the very idea of an army of white men coming to attack Kumase. But I find the desire to laugh has left me today. How can I laugh, after seeing what we have just seen?'

The silence of ultimate defeat hung over the envoys in the room. Night came. But half of it went before the last of the envoys from Kumase found sleep.

Sleep was snatched again from the sleepers, violently. A gun was fired, so close it awakened everybody in the room. It was not just the noise that woke people. It was above all the felt force of the explosion's violence. Those who got up first rushed to the door wanting to know what had happened. The apprehensive guards outside pushed them back in. Lamps were brought. In their light it became plain the gunshot had not come from outside. The weapon had been fired from within.

Kwamen Owusu had fired the gun—against no foe but his own self. He had put the muzzle of the long gun under his chin. He had pushed the trigger down towards the butt with his toe—the toe was still caught, twisted in the trigger-space. The explosion had burst his head open. The wall beside him was spattered with matter from his brain, mixed with blood and hair.

Soon a number of whites came into the room to look. In the lamplight their expressions were not of surprise. They looked immensely excited, as if there was some tremendous event in their future, and their anticipation of it was getting too sweet to contain.

The following day was Monday. A cold harmattan wind blew from Kumase and beyond. Black men shivered; the whites rejoiced. A burial casket was made for Kwamen Owusu's body and the remaining bits of his head. In the daylight the corpse was rowed over to the right bank of the Pra, the side closer to Kumase. There it was buried. The companions who crossed over to be at the burial each said his farewell to the exulting one now sunk so low, with a handful of earth. In the boat going back to the white men's camp Koranche Safo looked at Osei Kwaku and shook his head.

'A bad way to go,' he said.

All night it rained. But the white men's soldiers could be heard singing hoarsely and felling trees, labouring to build a bridge across the river Pra.

Morning came. The white general's message was at last given the envoys. When the time came to cross over the river, this time they went walking over it, on firm, dry wood all the way. The white men had finished their bridge. Not only that, within sight of the envoys, they had marched a portion of their invading army over that bridge, towards Kumase. On their way the envoys overtook groups of ten soldiers, some still marching forward, some digging for a camp, some just resting on their journey.

When the envoys reached Kumase, to their eyes—eyes that had seen the new camp at Praso, eyes that had seen what Kwamen Owusu had seen to break his brash spirit—Kumase looked such a different city. As the time came to tell the assembled royals what they now knew, neither Koranche Safo nor Osei Kwaku for all their long training and their art, could keep the truths on their minds from shaking the timbre of their voices as they talked.

* * *

The envoys returned from Praso and delivered the letter from Wolseley. Koranche Safo and Osei Kwaku told the royal listeners, as calmly as they could, the things they themselves had seen. The royals sat quiet as stones while the envoys talked. Kofi Karikari, the Asantehene, was there. From Juaben the stubborn Asafo Adjei had come. Kwabena Oben, the Adanse king, was not present. He sent a message fiery as his temper, saying the time had come for men to fight, though women and children could continue to sit and talk. He added also that even if the other kings of Asante had not the powder or the courage needed for fighting the advancing white army, he, Kwabena Oben, had enough of both. Kwabena Jumo came from Mampong. Kings were present also from Bantama, Hemang, Kokofu, Ejisu. The queen-mother was there too—Efua Kobri.

After the envoys had talked Kofi Karikari dismissed them. He sent messengers to bring the half-white man Dawson, and also the white captives. Dawson was told to read the letter from Wolseley, and after that he translated it. Wolseley's message was this: he was sending not one, not two, not even three armies but four whole armies to invade Asante and capture Kumase. With the arrogance of one who already sensed himself a victor, the white general pointed out the roads by which his armies would arrive. The first would come along the Wassa road, from the west. The second would come along the Assen Praso road, from the south. The third would come along the Akim Praso road, from the south-east. The last could come from the Firaw river in the east, through Begoro in eastern Akim, through Juaben, and meet the other three armies at Kumase. These armies were coming not to negotiate, but to force the king to obey the white man, and his white queen over the seas.

A silence, the silence of old graveyards, greeted the reading. Karikari turned to the white captives and asked them to check the letter, and tell him if all Dawson had said was true. In their slow speech the ones called Kuhne and Ramseyer, the priests, confirmed everything Dawson had said. The king sent Dawson and the white captives away.

The meeting of royals was quiet as the grave until the strangers left. But immediately they were left to themselves the heavy weight of what they had heard broke down their silence.

The Asantehene Karikari looked nervously around him, searching for signs of hope and strength from the faces he saw. He started from his mother Efua Kobri, searched every face and ended with hers again. But he did not find what he needed from anyone. So he reached for strength in the safest direction he knew—from the past.

'From the time of Okomfo Anoche and Osei Tutu, from our very beginnings,' he said, 'no one, black man, white man or monster, has ever invaded Kumase. And since that time we have obeyed no one.'

The words were meant to inspire confidence, but the voice was hollow. There was fear in the Asantehene's face, and even his mother saw it.

'What you say may be true,' she said sadly, 'But this is not the time of Osei Tutu, and Okomfo Anoche died so long ago. This is not our beginning. It . . .' The other kings looked at Efua Kobri in alarm and she looked down at the ground, lost in her own thoughts. She did not pick up the thread of her words from where she had dropped it. 'Ever since we began, we have depended not only on our strength, but on the help of the great one, Odomankoma Kwame, God of all creation. When our cause has been just he has given us victory. But what cause have we been fighting for these days? We have done so many things to bring the curse of God on our own heads, and God is punishing us. Why in the first place did Edu Bofo take our armies to the east to fight? What was the result? Did we really have to fight so long just to bring these miserable white prisoners here? What help has their presence here been to us?

'The whites wanted to ransom them. They paid the ransom Edu Bofo wanted. But the captives were not released.

'Why did Amankwa Tia have to take so many men down towards the sea? Did we hear it was to subdue the Fantse people once and for all, and to bring peace and prosperity? But what was the result? The army did not reach Cape Coast. Asante warriors fought with their usual courage, but something was wrong. The army was not turned back by guns. It was defeated not by men but by God. How else can we explain the death of so many thousands by disease? Even the Pra, sacred child of God, snatched lives from us going as well as coming. These were signs sent to us by God. Signs we've been doing evil things. I shall say nothing about the wrong done to Asamoa Nkwanta. Perhaps we can save ourselves. But let us return the white prisoners to their own. Their presence here has been the presence of evil among us. So many signs have appeared these days. All of them point in evil directions.'

The queen-mother's voice was clear. It was not an angry voice but a sad one. Her words produced another awful silence. The king spoke:

'Shall we then give up the hostages? It was not my desire that kept them here in the first place, as you know.'

'Perhaps they should be given up,' said Kwabena Jumo. 'But carefully. If the people see that, they will lose heart. They'll say the king fears the white men now.'

The Asantehene made as if to speak. But he said nothing.

'We must prepare to stop the white armies,' said Asafo Adjei. 'Who says we need to fear anyone? Kumapem Asante! We have men who know how to fight!'

'They have scattered,' Efua Kobri said, 'since Amankwa Tia stopped drinking long enough to gather the remnants, and since Asamoa Nkwanta brought them back.'

'They can be assembled again,' Asafo Adjei said.

'I shall send messengers to all the chiefs of war, immediately,' said the Asantehene.

'What of bullets for them to use?' Efua Kobri asked bitterly. 'Have we not wasted all during these wars that brought us nothing?'

'We can buy more,' Asafo Adjei said.

'With what?' asked Efua Kobri. 'The gold goes out from Kumase, but somehow it doesn't find its way back from the kings and chiefs any more. Why? And besides, even if we had the gold, where would we go to buy bullets, or even lead? From the white man on the coast?'

'The slaves will break ironstone and shape it into bullets,' said Kwabena Jumo.

'I shall send messengers to tell all our houses to put their slaves to work,' said the Asantehene. 'Immediately.'

'Where will the armies gather, though?' asked Asafo Adjei.

'Here,' said the Asantehene. 'Where else?'

Asafo Adjei hesitated, then said: 'It worries me. There'll be a white army attacking Juaben. If all the warriors come to defend Kumase, what will happen to the other places?'

Asamoa Nkwanta rose to speak: 'I sent someone east to find out if there is any truth in the white general's threat to send another army against us from the east. What he found out was this: that invading army exists only in the fevered head of one white man, the one called Captain Glover. There's nothing to fear from that direction. All we need to do is keep to our plan. We shall let the white army from the south approach Kumase, but slowly. When the time comes to strike, the Juaben army under Nana Asafo Adjei will circle round the whites and cut off their escape route. We shall destroy their bridges, and oblige them to stay in these forests and fight till death. The whites fear the forest. They will not survive—if we keep to our plan.'

In Kumase all the large households obeyed the order to find and break ironstone to make bullets for the coming war. Messengers bearing royal plates of gold left the capital to call upon all the chiefs of the land to assemble their men again for war.

The king decided to release the first of the white captives, the sick priest Kuhne. Kuhne was to go away carrying royal gifts: gold-dust and a rich silken kente cloth. In order not to infect the people with fear, the white priest was not released till long after dark. Even then, when only the long-haired night guards walked the streets carrying their sharp spears, the white prisoner was first taken secretly to the royal village of rest, Kaase. There the king himself came to visit the white prisoner. The king asked him to plead with the white general and to repeat to him that the king had no quarrel with the whites, and only desired to fight against black people, without involving white men. And there at Kaase the white priest was released for the journey to the Pra, where he would be carried in a hammock borne by four men. With him the king sent messages begging the white general Wolseley to stop where he was, and await peaceful negotiations.

The king waited to see if the white general, on receiving his messages of peace, would halt his advancing army. The white general did not stop. Every new message Wolseley received only convinced him the hour had come at last to strike a blow against Asante power, and he urged his men towards Kumase.

In desperation the royals asked their priests if there was anything the spirits could do to help the Asante nation in its hour of danger. The priests said the spirits first needed blood—animal blood and human blood generously spilt.

What did the priests not try in order to stop the inevitable advance of the white army, this force they could not understand? It was known the white army had stretched a line on poles from Cape Coast to the Pra. The priests explained this was nothing but a powerful juju. They knew how the power of the white man's line could be made to work equally for Asante: they caused a piece of white string to be tied between trees from Kwisa up to Fomena. Now, the priests said, the white army would be stopped by the power of the high string.

But still the white army came towards Kumase.

The priests announced with confident joy they had found a powerful charm against the invaders. The white men's power lay solely in the power of their guns. The priests had images made of guns. Knives—real knives, not mere images of knives—were stuck into the carved guns. This was an infallible way, the priests explained, to break the power of the advancing white army, which was after all merely the power of the white man's gun. Carved guns with knives stuck into them were placed along the road along which the white army would have to come: at Kwisa, at Fomena, at Dampoase Nkwanta, at Bojawe, at Kwaman, at Edwinase, at Amoafo and Bekwae. The guns pointed down the road, away from Kumase. Their broken power, the priests explained, would force the white army to turn round, going back the way it had come from the river Pra.

Still, the white army pressed on towards Kumase.

And then how many people suffered untimely deaths to feed the spirits the priests claimed to serve!

'Do not kill only the weak, do not kill only the sick and the children!' the priests exclaimed. 'The spirits deserve the youngest, the healthiest, the strongest sacrifices. Do not deny them the best offerings!'

The bodies of victims were mutilated, not to please the spirits who only wanted their blood, the priests explained, but to frighten the advancing white soldiers into turning back, away from Kumase. The bodies were placed along the road, at every junction, at every great turning, to stop the white invaders.

Still the white army pressed on towards Kumase.

The day after the royals had met again and sworn to fight the invaders to the death, scouts of the white army were seen at Fomena. That was a Sunday. The Tuesday following, early in the morning the white general crossed the Pra and himself joined the advance towards Kumase. On Wednesday more white soldiers crossed over. On Thursday more crossed over. On Friday yet more crossed over.

The royals tried again to halt Wolseley with words and belated gestures of peace. The king wrote more letters to the white general Wolseley. He released the remaining whites: the trader Bonnat, the priest Ramseyer and his wife and child. The envoys sent with the letters did all they were sent to do. As emphatically as they could, they told the whites again and again what the king had bidden them say: his quarrel was not with white men, only with black men.

But still the white army pushed on towards Kumase.

*   *   *

In the time left him Asamoa Nkwanta tested the warriors who answered the call to gather and prepare for great battles. Time and

282

despair had made the warriors slow, but it did not take long for every group to regain its accustomed speed, and to regain its ability to slip through the forest unseen, unheard.

The system used was old, tested, and found true. There would be three lines of warriors on every front, one line behind the other. The first was the firing line. The second was ever ready to replace the first, as soon as the first had fired. The third was the loading line.

Endlessly Asamoa Nkwanta encouraged the warriors to repeat the sequence: the first fires, replacing the last; the second runs forward, replacing the first; the last loads, replacing the second—a cycle constantly renewing its motion.

Asamoa Nkwanta ranged over the land he knew so well, looking for perfect places to place his trap of warriors. He found it between Edwinase and Amoafo.

The road north from Edwinase dips low into a wide valley at the bottom of which flows one of the arms of the Aprapong stream crawling westward to become the Dankranang and then the Oda river. Rising towards Amoafo, the road lies below a semicircle of high ground, a perfect position from which to command the road. Asamoa Nkwanta chose the curved ridge. There he placed the front end of his net: the centre regiments of the Asante army.

The white army appeared on a Saturday morning. The day was hazy. The light of the sun was hidden under a heavy, grey cloud, and the air was sullen. It was as if the sky were gathering rain.

The first of the white soldiers moved down into the valley and began to climb up the high ground, marching to their weird, whining music.

Asamoa Nkwanta gave the order when the white marchers came within range, and the old thunder of the Asante army was heard again. It was a long, continuous roar. The last became the second line, the second became the first, and the first became the last, cycle after cycle throughout the morning. All around the valley and the hills above it the forest shook. Branches broke and fell, cut through by bullets as if by an axe. Smoke rose endless from thousands upon thousands of guns fired incessantly, and the morning turned to night with no connecting noon, afternoon or evening.

It was not Asamoa Nkwanta's intention to make a final stand there below Amoafo. All morning he waited to hear news from the white enemy's rear. The warriors from Juaben, under Asafo Adjei, were expected to circle round behind the whites and bring up the end of the net. Asamoa Nkwanta waited for news, for a sign that the closing of the bottom of the net had begun.

But from the south, the enemy's rear, all Asamoa Nkwanta heard this Saturday morning was the deep, gloomy silence of a universe grown indifferent to his hopes. He waited, hoping what he feared would prove to be untrue. But from behind the white lines no sound came to reassure his still grieving soul, and he saw no sign.

Instead, what Asamoa Nkwanta now saw brought back the deepest bitterness of his long sorrow. The great guns of the whites began to sow their seeds of death up the slope. What a harvest death claimed this Saturday! Where there had been a line of men loading guns one moment, the next moment there was no life, only corpses, bones, torn flesh and blood spattered over scorched leaves and twigs.

The whites had made no ground at all before the great new guns began their devastating work. But now the only way the Asante warriors had open to survival was retreat. The guns that had driven the arrogant Kwamen Owusu to suicide spoke their harsh language, and after each round of carnage the whites moved forward into the breach cleared for them by death. By the middle of this strange, sunless day Amoafo had fallen to the whites, and there was no counting the dead of Asante.

Asamoa Nkwanta had not planned that Amoafo should be the last battle. The net would retreat before the white invaders, bringing them deeper into the Asante forests. Then the end of the net would close in upon the cut-off army of whites.

After Amoafo, Asamoa Nkwanta still hoped there had merely been a mistake. He sought to find those among the royals who might know why Asafo Adjei and the warriors from Juaben had failed to do their promised work. But all he heard were bizarre stories of a huge white army said to have attacked Juaben.

Asamoa Nkwanta ordered a retreat to Odaso. There too the terrain would be favourable—if he could find Asafo Adjei. He searched like a demented seeker and yet he found no one, heard no reasonable news.

In the absence of Asafo Adjei and his forces from Juaben, Asamoa Nkwanta was obliged to change the plans so carefully made and agreed upon. His aim remained the same—to delay the white army in the forest until time, the weather, and the power of the forest itself wasted the invaders completely. But Asamoa Nkwanta changed the means.

He knew the land well, but he went over the territory between

Odaso and Kumase again, almost as if he were a total stranger seeing every hill for the first time in his life. He walked restlessly; his every step had an extra charge of energy. He seemed in great need of some vehicle faster than legs able to carry him forward at a speed matching his mind's. Before midday he called his war captains and gave them their positions for the battle he expected to begin the next day.

Asamoa Nkwanta explained the whole plan to his captains. When he was sure they had understood every detail of it, the restlessness that had possessed him all morning vanished. In its place came a bottomless calm. On the general's face the look was peaceful, and he was smiling.

In the afternoon scouts came to Asamoa Nkwanta with news: the British army had reached the river Oda and seemed bent on building a bridge across it. Even as the scouts were turning to go, the noise of axes ringing against wood came from the distance, wavering with the afternoon breeze. The noises of wood breaking, trees falling and, occasionally, men shouting to each other, lasted well into the evening.

That day was sunny, but in the night a heavy rain fell. From across the river the Asante warriors could hear curses from the white soldiers. Asamoa Nkwanta thanked the clouds and wished for numberless such days ahead.

Tuesday found the white army wet after a sleepless night. The soldiers brought their big guns forward, using them to clear a safe passage for each small advance.

Asamoa Nkwanta had had some remnant of hope in the morning. Perhaps the regiments from Juaban had been delayed the day before. Perhaps they would come now. But the day wore on. The big guns of the whites hurled incessant death up the road towards Kumase. The ambushes were carefully laid, but even the strongest of them had to break apart, unless Asamoa Nkwanta was willing to make many more thousands food for vultures.

Asamoa Nkwanta called together the closest of his captains. He was asking them what was to be done, and telling one to send more runners to find out what had become of the Juaben forces, when three hot messengers came down the road from Kumase.

The messengers recognized Asamoa Nkwanta. They did not have to say they were from the king. One wore the golden plate of royal messengers on his breast, and the last of them simply drew close to

Asamoa Nkwanta and placed in his palm the circle of beads—the sign that the royal council wanted the Asante army to cease all fighting and withdraw.

'What does this mean?' Asamoa Nkwanta asked, his eyes full of fire. But he knew finally what it all meant.

'Mine was only to bring the message,' the messenger said. 'I know nothing of meanings.'

'You're right,' Asamoa Nkwanta said. 'Your work is done. Return.'

Asamoa Nkwanta went down the lines of soldiers, and he thought bitterly of the net that could no longer close. The white army would drive right through the bottom of all his well-laid plans. But what had happened?

He sought out his captains, and as he came to each he gave him the incomprehensible message: 'Stop your fire.' He did not pause to explain what he himself could hardly understand. He now searched the lines for signs of Densu, but could see no sign of him. Several captains shouted after him: 'We want to fight on!' But he did not stop to listen to them except once, when he answered tensely: 'We'd only end up massacring each other.'

Something sent a brilliant flash up into his eyes. When the reflection was gone, he saw down in the valley a man with a gold plate on his chest, a royal messenger, walking in the direction of the British army. He was not alone. Beside him was another carrying a large white flag in his right hand. In the other hand he held something pale. It looked like a letter. The two were walking slowly down the valley. One of them kept shouting a plaintive plea for peace and, straining to hear the shouts clearly, Asamoa Nkwanta thought he recognized Osei Kwaku's practised voice.

Around him everything was so quiet that the noise of someone running close to him startled him. He turned and saw Densu, breathing hard, frowning and smiling at the same time. His gun was smoking.

'Something strange is happening,' Densu said before he had come to a complete stop. 'The whites are marching on, and everybody is just looking at them.'

'Your eyes are better than mine,' Asamoa Nkwanta answered him.

'What is happening?' Densu asked.

'I don't know.'

'Then who knows?'

'That I don't know either,' Asamoa Nkwanta said, a bit irritably.

'The king has given a sudden order. We must stop fighting the whites and withdraw. I must go back and find out what is happening.'

'May I come with you?' Densu asked.

Asamoa Nkwanta took his hand but said nothing, as he took the quick path towards the city.

3 The Fall

Evening had not yet come when Asamoa Nkwanta and Densu reached Kumase. The general led the way directly to the palace. There were warriors in the streets, and in spite of the general's furious speed some came to him and asked him why he had given the order to cease fighting. He did not answer anyone. The questioners, baffled, shook their heads and turned to look after him.

Asamoa Nkwanta walked directly to the palace. He passed through every connecting courtyard; he went upstairs and downstairs looking for someone in the place to whom he might talk. The rooms were empty of human beings. Only a few stray cats, remnants of the king's pets, ran here and there through the rooms.

While Asamoa Nkwanta and Densu were there a small group of palace servants arrived. Quickly they set to work collecting jewels, bundles of cloth, and other possessions precious to the royal household.

'Where has the king gone?' Asamoa Nkwanta asked the leader of the servants. The man stared in fear at the general and at Densu, and could not open his mouth. As for the other servants, they turned their eyes away and bent to the work they had come to do.

The energy that had urged Asamoa Nkwanta on during the rapid journey to Kumase left him when he saw what had happened at the palace. He said nothing, but his eyes had the redness of a mourner's eyes. As he left the palace his step became unsure, weak. Densu had to hold him at one point to keep him from falling when he had stumbled against a stone.

'Where do you want to go?' Densu asked.

'The little house, where we were last time,' Asamoa Nkwanta said.

The little house was not far. On entering it, Asamoa Nkwanta went directly to take a mat, unrolled it and lay down heavily.

'Shall I bring you anything?' Densu asked.

'No,' the general said. 'Leave me here. Go and see what is happening. Look for Oson if you can, and bring him here.'

Darkness hung in the air. Only a little remnant of faint light was left from the wasted day. Throughout the streets of the town, loose crowds flowed slowly, aimlessly about. It was as if they had all come out of their houses to await some extraordinary event.

The extraordinary event was the entry of the white invaders into Kumase, the never-violated city. As the sun dipped down in the west the white general Wolseley came riding—the cripple—on an ass, surrounded by his officers and red, sweating soldiers. Densu heard a familiar voice: it was that of the sweet-voiced crier Osei Kwaku, telling the people in the name of the king not to touch a single white man in anger.

The whites went along the central streets. From the palace and the houses of chiefs they found gin and brought it out, so that in a little while the air around was loud with their happy sound. Once they gave three weird shouts all together.

Night came quickly. Densu searched for Oson all through the town, but nowhere could he see the eunuch's enormous frame. He saw white men moving like so many ghosts in and out of the palace. They had black servants carrying loads behind them—they were plundering the palace. As the groups bearing plunder from the palace passed Densu on their way to the houses the white officers had chosen to stay in, the sound of another crier's high voice came floating on the air again. Its message had changed: whoever stole anything would be punished with a quick, painful death. Near Densu a voice from the shadows laughed.

'Funny, these whites,' the laughing one of the shadows said. 'They themselves are busy stealing. But they tell us stealing is a crime and we shall die for it.'

A group of black soldiers commanded by a single white man entered a house across the street from Densu. Two of them bore torches, and in the shaky glare Densu saw a form he knew well. The group did

288

not stay long in the house. They came out carrying boxes on their heads. Densu searched again for the form he had recognized, but the form was missing.

He waited till the soldiers had disappeared up the street, then he went into the house, making no sound. He passed beyond the front courtyards and came to the last row of rooms at the end. A sound to his right attracted him, and he saw one of the doors was still open. Gingerly he looked in. In the darkness the form was at first hard to make out. But in a while Densu was absolutely certain.

'Buntui,' he called out softly.

The giant leapt up with a cry strangely like a whimper.

'Don't shout,' Densu said.

'Who are you? I haven't done anything!' Buntui said vehemently.

'Perhaps not. Those whites will be looking for you. I wouldn't stay here if I were you.'

'Who are you?'

'Densu.'

The giant was quiet. Only his heavy, irregular breathing was audible.

'I find you everywhere,' he said.

'So do I,' Densu chuckled.

'What do you want?' Buntui asked.

'To talk to you,' Densu said.

'Of what?'

'The future.'

'What of the future?' the giant asked.

'Have you decided you want to die for Ababio?'

'What a horrible question!' the giant exclaimed.

'Answer me. Have you?' Densu persisted.

'No. Why should I want to die for Ababio?'

'Because he's decided you'll die for him.'

'Me?'

'You.'

'But why?'

'Think of it,' Densu said. 'He ordered you to do something. You did it. Only you know how he was connected with the crime. He has no more use for you. You're dangerous to him. If he can arrange to get rid of you, permanently, he will. All he needs is to get you tried for murder.'

The giant was very quiet.

'Are you sure of what you're saying?' he asked at length.

'I'm certain.'

'What can I do?'

'It depends on whether you want to live, or die for Ababio.'

'I must live,' said the giant solemnly.

'Live, then,' said Densu. 'When you return to the coast there will be a trial. Will you tell the truth, all that you know? It's the only way you'll save your life.'

The giant did not answer.

'Think about it,' Densu said. 'And if I were you I'd get out of this house fast, leaving everything.'

The giant chuckled as Densu made his way out.

As Densu came to Asamoa Nkwanta's secret house he saw something disappear around the back. He walked to the front, taking care to make his footfalls loud. Then, silently, he went round towards the back. He recognized Oson the instant before he collided with him.

'It's me, Oson,' Densu said.

'Were you born to scare me to my grave?' the eunuch asked in exasperation. 'Where is he?'

'Inside,' Densu answered.

They went in. Asamoa Nkwanta was silent, but he was wide awake.

Oson wept. 'I looked for you, Osajefo. I looked for you so long. But I couldn't find you to tell you. They kept me away from you.'

'To tell me what?' Asamoa Nkwanta asked.

'Everything, Osajefo,' the eunuch said, the tears shaking his voice. 'That day you told the royal council of your plan, the way you wanted to fight the whites . . .'

'The royals all agreed,' Asamoa Nkwanta said.

'While you were there,' Oson said, 'while you were there, Osajefo. But you went away, and there were only us eunuchs and the royals, and the royals said what was on their minds. If only you had known, Osajefo. But how could I find you when they watched me day and night?'

'What happened? What did they say?' Asamoa Nkwanta asked.

'When you had left, the queen-mother asked the king and Nana Asafo Adjei if they were such children as to believe that you, Asamoa Nkwanta, had forgiven them. She said your plan to fight the whites was a clever one, because it was also a plan to avenge yourself on the royal house.

'The king asked if she believed your way was not the only way to stop the whites from reaching Kumase. Her answer was yes. But then she asked the king if he would rather be king of a violated kingdom or be nothing in a virgin nation.

'Yes, she asked him that. She said if Asante followed Asamoa Nkwanta's plan and resisted the whites, there would be nothing to stop Asamoa Nkwanta from becoming king of the inviolate nation. She said the wisdom of a king lay in knowing at all times what to do in order to remain king. If what should be done now was to yield a bit to the whites, better that than to lose all power to an upstart general.'

The general took in a deep breath.

'And what of Asafo Adjei? What did he say?'

'He saw wisdom in everything the queen-mother said,' Oson replied. 'It was he who asked what remained to be done.

'The queen-mother said: "Let Asamoa Nkwanta set his trap for the whites, the thing he calls a net. His success depends on your closing the net from behind the white army, Asafo Adjei. Is it your ambition to help Asamoa Nkwanta to the Asante stool?"

' "What can I do?"

' "If I were you," the queen-mother said, "I would go and protect my own seat. Go to Juaben, and leave Asamoa Nkwanta to do his fishing with half a net." '

The eunuch had stopped weeping. 'Osajefo,' he asked, 'did you hear me?'

'I heard you, Oson,' Asamoa Nkwanta said. His voice was hoarse, so he kept quiet. Then he said, 'Leave us a while, Densu.'

Outside, Densu walked into a world gone wild. A man ran like a hurricane past him, going in the direction of the palace. The man smelled of gin. In his right hand he held a flaming torch, trailing it behind him so the sputtering bits of flame would not scorch him. Densu watched him run up to a house just next to the palace. Arriving in front of the house, he tossed the flame through a doorway and turned back, still running, howling like a man possessed by demons.

Along the main streets almost every other house was on fire. The flames lit up the sky and gave the night an eerie yellow lucency. Densu walked towards the palace, not yet touched by flames, and beyond it.

A small crowd came towards him, moving in the direction of the central square. In the middle of the crowd was a man with a rope around his neck. One of the black soldiers serving the white army held the other end of the long rope. Four soldiers with guns prodded the captive forward from behind. A sixth soldier rolled a barrel behind them all. Densu was about to go closer for a look at the man, when the man gave a loud, plaintive shout, a bellow like that of a bull bound for slaughter. That voice would stand out anywhere. The man with the rope around his neck was Buntui.

Densu felt a sharp pang he could not even understand. He had never found anything to like about Buntui, but to see him led away like a beast brought a disconcerting taste of pity into Densu's head. Buntui was pleading loudly and desperately with his captors.

'Don't kill me! I didn't take anything. I have returned everything!' he shouted, over and over again.

The only answers he got from the soldiers behind him were repeated jabs in the ribs with rifle butts. The group, with the crowd of onlookers it had attracted in the lurid night, stopped when it came to the central square. A huge wawa tree with great horizontal branches stood there. One of the soldiers, the leading one, climbed the tree, holding his end of the long rope in his teeth, and sat on a strong branch. The sixth soldier rolled his barrel to a stop directly under the branch. There he stood it on its end. That done, the remaining four soldiers lifted the giant Buntui bodily and placed him standing on the barrel, with the rope still around his neck.

Buntui fought desperately, but the four soldiers had been selected for their strength, and their brutality overpowered him. The first soldier up on the tree pulled his end of the rope, wound it around the branch, and pulled it taut. As soon as he had done that he shouted fiercely: 'Now!' The four soldiers below kicked the barrel from under Buntui's feet.

Something snapped. The giant's heavy body dangled a brief moment at the end of the rope. Then a horrendous voice broke from Buntui's constricted throat:

'Don't kill me!'

The soldiers below him laughed and mimicked his terrified cry:

'Save me! Help me!'

The soldiers only laughed and laughed.

As if he had understood he was alone, and would get no help from anyone on earth, Buntui raised his hands above his head and grabbed the rope hanging him. He pulled on the rope, and the rope between his neck and his hands loosened. The four soldiers stopped laughing and watched the struggling man. As soon as Buntui's throat was free, he resumed his bellowing pleas:

'Don't kill me! Somebody help me. I'm dying! Please help!'

The soldier in the tree had not yet descended. He untied his knot and loosened it. The rope brought Buntui's body heavily down to earth. Buntui fell, but in a moment he was up, struggling to throw off the rope.

He failed. The four soldiers threw themselves against him. Holding him still, they slashed off a piece of the rope with a sharp knife, and bound Buntui's hands together behind him. When that was done they threw the rope-end up again to their companion in the tree. He made it fast again while they brought the barrel and forced Buntui to stand on it. Again they kicked away the barrel. Buntui opened his mouth to shout for help. Only the first syllable came out—a hoarse, cut-off growl. Then there was silence, except for the laughter of the soldier up in the tree.

They left Buntui hanging and went away. Densu saw them disappear. Going to the hanging corpse, he slipped a lone bangle off its arm and turned away.

4 Witch Hunt

When Densu returned to the little house he found Asamoa Nkwanta alone. Oson was gone.

'What was all that noise?' Asamoa Nkwanta asked.

'Someone I know died. One of the police from Cape Coast. The whites had him hanged.'

'What did he do?'

'He was imitating the whites, stealing the property of the departed princes of Asante,' Densu said.

Asamoa Nkwanta sighed. There was light coming in from the fires outside, fluttering in intensity but never going out. Densu saw the general's face. It was strained.

'Oson told me something I hadn't known,' Asamoa Nkwanta said. He paused, as if uncertain. Then he said: 'You have to go back to the healers, Densu.'

'When?'

'As soon as you have rested. Can you go tomorrow?'

'Yes,' Densu answered. 'But what is it?'

'The royals think you healers captured my soul, bewitched me, and tried to use me to overthrow them. They think that what healers want is to make themselves into a new kind of aristocracy to replace the old.' Asamoa Nkwanta chuckled dryly. 'I can see Damfo strutting around this city in royal robes!' He stopped laughing. 'You see there's no time to lose.'

'Do you think the royals intend to attack the healers?' Densu asked.

'Of that I am certain,' Asamoa Nkwanta said. 'Unless the healers can be warned.'

'I feel I should go at once,' Densu said.

'Rest first,' said Asamoa Nkwanta. 'You haven't had any rest today. Oson brought food. Have some. Then I want to give you something for Damfo and the other healers.'

After Densu had eaten, Asamoa Nkwanta put something in his hand.

'Look at it,' he said.

Densu recognized the diamond Oson had brought Asamoa Nkwanta.

'It was a gift to you,' he said.

'I can't keep it. They'll kill Oson if they get to know. And I do want to let Damfo have a small sign from me,' Asamoa Nkwanta said. 'Tell him I shall look for him, and I shall find him. But now I have work to do here.'

'Will you be safe?' Densu asked.

'I will be safe,' Asamoa Nkwanta answered, 'as long as I have strength, and the will to live.'

He said nothing more that night.

*   *   *

A heavy rain fell all morning, but Densu did not wait for it to end. The journey from Kumase back to Praso was longer than it should have been. The road was crawling with groups of skirmishers, stray remnants of the now confused Asante army. Densu had to make long detours to avoid collisions with them. When he reached Praso, night had already fallen.

As he crossed the clearing to reach the house he'd used while there, a movement in the bushes ahead of him caught his attention in spite of the darkness. A shadowy form had flitted across a gap in the vegetation, and then disappeared. Densu stood flat against the wall he'd reached and watched. A second shadowy form crossed the same gap. A third followed.

Moving as fast as he could without making any noise, Densu opened the door and entered the house. He didn't need light to find what he needed. Going to the left wall, he groped for and found three rifles. He took them and loaded them. Then he went out again. It was his intention to go to the other healers in their rooms and wake them up. But before he had taken seven steps he saw a figure run across the open space towards the house Damfo had lived in. The figure carried two flaming firebrands.

When the runner reached Damfo's house he hurled the firebrand in his right hand up on to the roof. He was transferring the second firebrand from his left to his right hand for hurling, when Densu aimed at him and fired. The man fell at once on top of his remaining firebrand. With a sizzling sound the flame weakened and died. But the runner had not been alone. Even as he lay there by Damfo's house, a small crowd of other night-figures rushed out of the surrounding bushes. Each carried two firebrands. From the way they moved they seemed to have divided up the healers' houses among themselves. Three ran up to each house and tossed their brands up on to the roof. Then the whole lot of them retreated into the bushes they had come from, shouting an eerie chant:

Fire oooooh! Fire!! Fire oooooh! Fire!

Densu aimed the second gun and fired. One of the runners, who had reached the edge of the bushes, fell without a sound. Densu fired again. Another yelled: 'I'm hurt!'

In the cover provided by the house he'd come from, Densu knelt to load the guns again. The loud commotion had woken the healers who were coming out of their houses, seeking to escape the intensifying heat. In the heightening glare each was starkly visible.

'Be careful!' Densu shouted.

Too late. Whether it was the burners themselves who had turned snipers, or whether they had had the snipers with them all the time,

Densu couldn't tell. All he heard was a fast peppering of bullets in the burning night. The healers were easy targets for their hidden hunters. There was no possible cover for them. Behind them were raging fires. In front, to the left, to the right, all round them, came the whine of bullets seeking flesh.

Densu saw Nyaneba stagger out of her house. Frantically he called to her, telling her to lie down and crawl. But she did not seem to hear him. She walked like a sleepwalker, making for the other burning houses. Thus walking, she ran into a storm of bullets. She did not fall at once. She came down in a sitting position, her body turned round so that she was facing the doorway she had come from.

How many of the healers had been overcome by fumes before the bullets got them? How many had been torn to pieces by the unseen killers' bullets?

Densu saw there was no chance of saving any healers. He crouched low and ran into the bushes, carrying his guns with him. He searched the bushes and saw the outline of one of the snipers there. He fired. The sniper fell. There were many with him, and after he fell Densu could see their movements more clearly. He shifted his position and shot again.

One shouted in panic: 'They're all dead. But some demon is killing us!'

'Let's go back!' came an answering shout. It became general.

Densu thought of pursuit, but something else pressed on his mind more insistently. He went to look at the fallen healers to see if there were any still alive. But those who had been trapped in their houses had turned to ashes. Those shot outside had been pierced by too many bullets and all their life's blood had been wasted. There was nothing he could do for them. They were past all help.

He was turning away from the destroyed village when he heard a groan. It came from somewhere near Damfo's house. Densu saw the form from which the groan had come, and went towards it. He turned the face up. It was vaguely familiar, but he had to think hard before he recognized it. The dying man was the priest who had accompanied Asamoa Nkwanta when he'd first come to the healers. At first Densu thought the priest had recognized him and was calling out his name, but he was only asking desperately for water.

All Densu could say to the priest was: 'Why?'

The priest understood him and answered him, but his voice was far gone. 'Those healers,' he said, 'they bewitched my Osajefo. They turned him against me and all the other priests. They should all die. All of them. All! Water. Give me water.'

The priest was near death. The bullet had hit him in the forehead. After his fierce words he no longer had the strength to hold his head up from the ground. Densu left him where he lay.

5   Confrontation

The road south was dotted with abandoned villages and burned houses. Where there had been farms before, the landscape was now stripped bare, leaving only stumps and dead leaves. All along the road there was the stench of unburied corpses. Sometimes Densu walked off the road he was following, his mind having wandered off the sense of his destination, his soul ravaged with knowledge of the unrelenting waste around him. A week passed before he reached the eastern forest. It was Ajoa who found him wandering aimlessly along a path there, like a lost stranger. She led him home.

When Densu regained a sense of where he was, he told Ajoa and Araba Jesiwa and Damfo all that had happened, about the fall of Kumase, the disappointment of Asamoa Nkwanta, and the massacre of healers at Praso. Damfo did not hide his tears. Ajoa wept, and Densu knew Araba Jesiwa had understood him even though she still could not talk, because she too wept.

The days that followed were filled with bitterness and illness. There were times when Densu felt there was nothing in him capable of holding on to life. But he was surrounded with love, with care. Days passed, and his blood flowed with increasing strength. Throughout his illness he heard an inner call potent and rhythmic as blood itself. It was not something he could decide to heed or not to heed. It was like the beating of his heart, like the rise and fall of his lungs. He had seen so much destruction around him.

'And Jesiwa is still destroyed,' he said disjointedly to Damfo, more than once.

Though strength was returning, in the middle of all the waste he'd seen, Densu's soul tired of all escape and a pull like despair took over his energies. The direction of that pull was back—back towards places and days and pains left behind in space and time but never finally overcome in the soul.

'Why can Jesiwa not talk?' he asked Damfo once.

'I don't know,' Damfo answered.

'Was her throat also wrecked?'

'There's nothing wrong with her body now,' Damfo said. 'For her to speak, all that is necessary is a desire in her strong enough to overcome the body's massive fear, and the loss of the habit of speech after she saw Appia killed.'

Once, Densu wondered if fear would stop him in the end. But as he took the path to Esuano, going alone, he realized with a piercing clarity that long ago he had become used to living beyond fear.

It was night again when he reached Esuano. The town was the same. Why had he expected to find so much change? He walked through the town, past houses he had been in and out of as a child, past Anan's home, past the house in which the white trader Collins and after him his compatriot the Christian priest Warner had lived. Then he came to the palace.

A guard at the palace gate stopped him without recognizing him. Densu had with him the bangle he had slipped off Buntui's arm as he hung from the tree in Kumase. He took it and gave it to the guard.

'Give this to Eja Ababio,' he said.

'Nana Ababio,' the guard corrected Densu. 'He's the king.'

'Since when?' Densu asked.

'Since Nana Kanto died,' the guard replied. 'What's your business with the king? You'll have to wait till morning.'

'Show him this bangle,' Densu said calmly. 'Say to him the man who brought it comes alone, and has a message for him. He won't forgive you if you wait till morning.'

The last statement decided the guard. He went into the palace. In a little time he came back with another guard, a huge man who never once opened his mouth. It was this mute giant who led Densu to Ababio's room, now the main one in the whole palace.

Ababio lay comfortably sprawled on a great brass bed under a canopy of red silk. He looked fatter; his skin looked oilier, and somehow he seemed to have grown balder, though that should have been impossible. A large mirror stood at the foot of the bed. Several torches burned in the room. When the mute giant presented Densu, Ababio stared at him. The stare was a long, puzzled one, but it ended in a high, hysterical laugh

'I expected Buntui,' Ababio said.

'Buntui died in Kumase one Wednesday night,' Densu said.

Ababio actually laughed.

'You sound relieved,' Densu said.

'I am,' Ababio said, yawning. 'I am.' He paused, stared again at Densu as if he hadn't really seen him yet. Then he said: 'But if I live to be thirty thousand years old, I'll never understand you. The duiker that fled the trap set for it has returned. Why?'

'Why what?' Densu asked.

Over his shoulder Ababio pointed with his thumb to the giant body-guard: 'He hears nothing. And even if he could, he'd never be able to report what he heard. His tongue has been cut out of his head. So save your spittle. Don't ask clever questions, seeking to draw me out and make him your witness. You're alone, Densu, in this great new world. Quite alone.'

'You don't have to worry,' Densu said. 'It wasn't any kind of hope that brought me here.'

'That's clear as rainwater,' Ababio said, smiling. 'What did?'

'I thought you'd know that also.'

'Pride, I think,' Ababio said. 'And curiosity.'

'Let's consider curiosity,' Densu said.

'About what now?' Ababio asked.

'Why did you kill Appia?'

Ababio laughed. The laugh was genuinely happy. But all the same he lowered his voice. 'You mean you can't see for yourself?' He stretched himself full length on the bed, let his head fall back, and looked at the ceiling as he talked. 'You've always been slow to comprehend reality. Let me describe it for your benefit. This is a new day in the land. The whites are in control. They recognize those who have helped them. They recognize me, Ababio, as king of Esuano. Whoever goes against me will have to take on the whites. They protect me. They look after me. Whatever I want from them, I can ask for it, and I'll get it.'

'Was that worth killing a relative for?' Densu asked.

'Appia was not really a relative of mine,' Ababio answered. 'You

299

ought to understand royalty. Your father did—so deeply, unfortunately for him, that he loathed all contact with them. That was his undoing. A man does himself harm when he puts a distance between himself and power.

'If you didn't know it before, know it now. Every royal family is also a slave family. The two go together. You don't get kings without slaves. You don't get slaves without kings. My family has been a part of this—at first the lower part, the slave part.

'My grandfather was a slave at Kumase. It was a miracle he wasn't castrated. He served in the queen-mother's household then. Some say he was so faithful the king trusted him perfectly. Some say he was so ugly there was nothing any man could fear from him, as far as women went. Others say his behaviour was so congenitally mild he was considered quite impotent. At any rate, the king decided to leave his testicles alone.

'My grandfather knew how to be a grateful slave. He served his king well. As a reward he was given away to a white man, as a gift. You know how royalty is. The white man didn't need him. It was he who gave him, again as a gift, to the then king here at Esuano.

'Habits learned at the larger court at Kumase stood my grandfather in good stead here. He knew how to talk, and he did not make the mistake of wasting his eloquence in honest talk. He used his tongue profitably, only for flattering the powerful. His loyalty was unquestioning; so it became unquestionable. Once, my father told me, this my grandfather lay down in front of the king, in public, and shouted:

' "Spit into my mouth, O King, so a little of your infinite wisdom may pass on to me!" '

Ababio laughed—a laugh hard as metal. 'The king accepted the invitation. He spat. His aim must have been excellent. The spittle fell into my grandfather's mouth, all of it. And my grandfather swallowed it. To his eternal credit and to the immense profit of his decendants, he didn't retch.

'Do I still need to tell you I know everything there is to know about roads to power? The knowledge is in the spirit my grandfather passed down mixed with the blood of our mothers. I can show you the quickest of the roads to power: blind loyalty to those who already have the greatest power.

'After that heroic swallowing of the king's spittle, it didn't take long before it became impossible for anyone to see the king without first being forced to pass my grandfather's scrutiny. I ask you, Densu, what firmer foundation for power can there be than that?

'My grandfather began the long climb from powerlessness to power. Look at me now and tell me. Have I betrayed his dreams? Or have I been a worthy successor to him? Who now ever thinks of calling Ababio a slave? Ababio is royal. Ababio is a king.'

'And a murderer,' Densu added, softly.

'Use your big brain, Densu,' Ababio said, almost purring the words. 'How can a king be a murderer? If a king wants a man killed, that man becomes a traitor. And traitors are not murdered. They are executed—for the benefit of the people.'

'Buntui told me . . .' Densu began.

Ababio cut him short: 'Buntui is dead. Who listens to a dead witness?' Ababio rose to a sitting position. He let his legs dangle over the edge of the bed. 'It's such a pity we had no chance to complete your trial. It was such an exciting happening. What happened to your friend, Anan? He was another just like you.'

Densu gave no answer.

Ababio continued: 'Now we'll have to arrange another trial. It will have to be different, of course. A civilized trial. The whites keep telling us we used to do things like sleepwalkers in the past. Now they say they've opened our eyes. We're civilized. No more ritual trials with the drug of death. This time we'll have a proper court. A whole white man will come from Cape Coast to see to it that everything is done properly, in the new, civilized style. You'll get a chance to talk in defence of yourself. Then you'll hang, Densu.'

Ababio made a sign. The giant guard came forward. Before Densu was taken away he turned and told Ababio: 'You need fear nothing. I've no desire to escape. Not any more.'

* * *

The trial was held at the palace. The reception hall was cleared of all its drums, stools, and skins. A high chair made in the style of the whites was brought from Cape Coast and placed at one end of the hall. Long benches were provided for people to sit on. Before the trial began, ten West Indian soldiers marched into the hall and formed two lines, one on each side of the judge's chair.

The judge was an old white man. His hair was white. His face was red, the reddest part of it being his nose. It was he who sat in the high chair, and he ought to have been comfortable. But for the greater part of the trial he looked acutely distressed. He had beside him a large flask of some dark silvery metal. From this he took a drink whenever his irritation with the goings-on in the court seemed likely to overwhelm his patience. Whatever the drink was, it helped: it improved the judge's humour, at least for several moments after each swig.

First, the case against Densu was announced as soon as he had taken his position in front of the court between the judge and the audience. A translator from Cape Coast told the judge what it was about: that Densu was suspected of having killed the prince Appia, heir to the stool at Esuano. The evidence pointing to Densu's guilt was plentiful. First, there had existed a knife-edged rivalry between Densu and the murdered prince. At the very end of this rivalry, during the games of the year just spent, Appia had proved the victor over Densu. Densu had come a disappointed second.

There was other evidence. Certain parts of the prince's body had been removed, obviously for purposes of ritual and magic. Those parts were the eyes, bits of muscle from the arms, and similar bits of muscle from the legs. The listeners were asked to consider why those parts alone were removed for magic. They were to bear in mind the following facts: Appia had proved superior to Densu in marksmanship—the sport of the eyes. Appia had been set to win the competition in wrestling, though his own kindness made him give up an easy victory. Hence the slashing of the arm muscles. Appia had also won the short races—the power of his legs was known. Further: after the games Appia had been fêted as befitted a true victor. Densu was ignored; at the time of the celebration of final victory he slunk off by himself, a solitary, brooding figure.

Witnesses were called. They said what they knew or had seen and heard. Of these witnesses the chief was Ababio.

Ababio remembered, with passion and for the benefit of the court, how he had been a guardian of Densu's for years. As a guardian he had been troubled from the earliest days by two strong traits his ward showed in everything he did: arrogance first, and envy second.

Densu, explained Ababio, had always been too arrogant to admit another's superiority to himself, no matter how manifest. Naturally, he was bitterly envious of those who proved themselves his betters. Of course he envied Appia. Envy grew to hate. Hate gave birth to murder.

When he reached this part, Ababio was overcome with sorrow and he stopped to wipe a tear from one eye. He paused. The pause was a long, dramatic one, so the judge profited by it to reawaken his spirits with something from the flask. Ababio had been facing the translator all the while. Now he turned his eyes from him, and raised them to look directly up to the judge.

As Ababio went on, his voice trembled with high emotion: 'Before I continue, I'd like to have another witness called. He too knows the criminal well.'

The witness called was Esuman, the court priest at Esuano.

Esuman told a harrowing story. Densu, he remembered, had sought him out some time before the prince Appia's murder to ask him a strange question. Densu had asked him if it was true a person could gain certain powers through eating selected parts of a creature known to possess those powers in some high degree.

'My answer was yes,' Esuman the priest said. 'Then Densu wanted to know if that would be so even if the creature was human. Surprised and alarmed, I asked Densu if he was planning to eat parts of a human body. At that question the boy just laughed a maniacal laugh. He didn't answer my question. Instead, he asked me how the parts, once obtained, were to be prepared for eating. I told him only a priest such as I could do that.

'The day after the prince Appia died, Densu came to see me. He came to me with these.' Esuman parted his cloth a little at the side and drew out a small pouch smeared with white clay. From the pouch he took out, one by one, two dried, shrivelled eyes, and four leathery strips of dried flesh.

'These are all human. They come from the body of the dead prince Appia. Densu brought them to me. I can say no more.'

Esuman the priest lowered his head and moved away from the front of the court. Plainly, he was overwhelmed by the sheer weight of so much evil.

Ababio added a brief sentence: 'I know about Densu's crime, not just because I heard of it from Esuman, but because the young man himself, in his agitation of spirit, came and confessed it to me.'

Densu looked around him. He saw the white judge on his high chair, drinking to overcome his boredom with these matters he could not understand. He saw the solemn Ababio and Esuman. He saw the people in the courtroom. There was so much distance between him and everyone he could see here. And everything looked small, as if the physical distance had also become huge.

Ababio was talking again. The court was hushed with shock. 'Densu himself came to tell me what he had done. He said he couldn't help himself. He said he'd not intended to kill the prince's mother Araba Jesiwa. But the woman, seeing her son trapped and savagely attacked, sprang upon the murderer. Densu told me the woman fought like an enraged leopard as long as even a single bone remained unbroken in her body. So he broke them all, and she died.'

When this was translated, the red-faced white judge interrupted with a question: 'Did the accused actually confess to killing both the prince and his mother?'

'Absolutely!' swore Ababio. 'He told me he'd killed both. What I could never get him to tell me was where he hid the mother's body.'

The judge showed signs of running out of patience. His flask was nearly empty.

'Anything to add?' he asked curtly.

Ababio did have something to add: 'The young man we have here on trial was my own ward. So it pains me to say this, but I would be shirking my responsibility as king if I kept quiet. He is a dangerous person. An insatiable urge to power pushes him to evil deeds. If he's left free to continue roaming the world, the crimes he's already committed will be nothing compared to the ones he will commit.'

The judge spoke sharply: 'That's enough. We've heard the case against the accused. Has he got anything to say for himself?'

Two of the West Indian guards pushed Densu till he stood, handcuffed, before the judge. The judge repeated the question. The translator translated it again. But Densu did not say a word.

'Is the nitwit dumb?' the judge sputtered. In his agitation he knocked over his flask, and the few drops of liquor left in it spilled out. The judge gave the flask an angry look and muttered something fierce under his breath.

Ababio sprang forward and volunteered an answer: 'The criminal is sound. Only guilt stops his tongue.'

'It is not guilt that stops his tongue, Ababio,' a voice said from the entrance to the courtroom. The voice had something uncertain about it. It was hoarse, and not very strong. But it was a voice infinitely sweet to hear, so beautiful it abolished at once the immense distance that had separated Densu from everything and everyone around him. 'It is not guilt. The boy is overwhelmed with astonishment. He is astonished to hear his own guardian tell lies to get him killed.'

It was a woman who spoke. She walked slowly, as if in great pain, towards the centre of the courtroom, leaning on another, young woman not long past girlhood. Araba Jesiwa and Ajoa reached the centre of the courtroom and stopped there. Behind them, Damfo stood just within the doorway.

The appearance of Araba Jesiwa in the courtroom seemed to have turned everyone there to stone for several long moments. Next, there was a fierce collective whisper, as if everyone were gasping at an incredible truth at the same instant. Then came a dead silence.

By now the judge was so angry he was changing colour from red to yellow, then back to red. He pounded on the arm-rest of his high chair.

'Who the bloody hell is that? Who is that woman?'

Like a zombi bound to translate everything, the translator translated the white judge's question. The answer came in a confused hubbub from the audience, many people speaking at once: 'Araba Jesiwa herself! The mother of the dead prince!'

The translator had to lean towards the judge to tell him the answer, so great was the commotion. His words had a strange effect on the judge. They woke him up thoroughly, and for the first time he showed a lively interest in what was going on.

'By Jove!' said the judge. 'This is the very first time I've heard a voice from the dead. Let the lady speak. Goddamn it!'

Araba Jesiwa spoke. She did not lift a hand to check the flow of tears running down her cheeks.

She told of her gratitude to Damfo the healer, and the infinite reason why. She described the journey she took with the most precious of sons. Then she talked of the sudden trap flinging the son upward, reducing him with all his strength to impotence. She talked of the brutal giant Buntui springing from behind a tree to attack her son, and of the speed with which the son, thus trapped, was destroyed. She had tried to help her son. But, unused to such violence, unprepared, paralysed with fear, what could she do?

'The giant Buntui broke all my limbs. I think then I saw a great fear in his little eyes as he looked at me lying at his feet, as if he didn't know what to do. Pain overwhelmed my senses, and while Buntui was still looking at me, I lost consciousness.

'When I came to, I was in a place I couldn't recognize. Around me everything was pitch dark. I thought I was blind. I couldn't move. I could barely breathe. But I could hear. I could hear movement somewhere near where I lay, and the sound of voices in a violent quarrel.

'I knew the voices. Ababio was quarrelling with Buntui. The quarrel was about Buntui having left me to disappear. Ababio said Buntui had ruined everything. He forced Buntui to search everywhere around. But Ababio was afraid people would find them there when the day grew brighter. So they had to leave and return to Esuano without finding me. I lay there alone a little longer, then I passed out again.

'A voice woke me up, I think after a long time. A familiar, welcome voice, his voice.' Araba Jesiwa turned and pointed to Damfo. 'Damfo gave me a drink that drove away all pain and put me to sleep again. I slept for ages, a dreamless sleep, and woke up in the village of healers in the eastern forest. I was for a long time unsure whether I was alive or dead. But the healers cared for me. Gradually they drove the spirit of death away from my body. Here I am.

'I know who killed my son and almost killed me: Buntui. I know also who sent Buntui to do the killing: Ababio.'

The white judge, quite unable to contain his excitement, turned to look at Ababio the new king. Ababio had become a shrinking, sweating figure. His friend Esuman could hardly stand for trembling.

Without waiting for anyone to question him, Esuman began exonerating himself.

'I didn't want to say anything,' he pleaded, pointing at Ababio. 'He forced me to lie. I knew nothing about Densu and the eyes and the flesh. Ababio brought them to me himself. I had nothing to do with them.'

The white judge looked highly amused.

'Damn it, it looks like we've got the wrong native on trial,' he said. 'Let's free the dumb fellow and take these two rogues to Cape Coast.' In a loud voice, he added: 'Free the prisoner!'

A West Indian soldier stepped forward, took a bunch of keys from his belt, and opened Densu's handcuffs. He turned and saluted the white judge.

The judge said to Densu: 'You may go.'

Densu turned to go. The translator hadn't said a word.

'God damn it!' he heard the judge say. 'The dumb fellow isn't deaf. And he actually understands English. I'll be damned!' All his anger and boredom spent, the white judge cackled gaily as he rose.

6 The New Dance

A crowd surrounded Damfo, Araba Jesiwa, Ajoa, and Densu. These same faces had been impassive before. Now they had become the faces of relieved well-wishers, enthusiastic, ready to celebrate the prisoner's liberation.

Araba Jesiwa was the first to break away from the crowd. The other three went with her. Jesiwa walked round the changed palace, nodding with incessant comprehension. She visited the rooms, now graves, of Kanto and Esi Amanyiwa the old queen-mother. She visited her own room, Appia's grave.

When she came out again into the courtyard, she saw people had brought a lamb ready for slaughter, a ritual sacrifice of purification. Araba Jesiwa stopped them.

'Let the animal live,' she said. 'It isn't a lamb's blood that can clean the dirty souls of men.'

Food was brought from outside the palace, and the four accepted it, and drank after eating. In the evening the eldest age group came to Jesiwa. They asked her pardon for the whole town.

'What for?' Araba Jesiwa asked them. 'You did nothing.'

'That's precisely it,' said the man who acted as spokesman for the group. 'We did nothing when we ought to have done something.'

'There's no call to ask pardon now for that,' Jesiwa said. 'Peace is what you wanted. That's what I wish you too.'

The elders were too embarrassed to put their next question directly. But by indirections they circled their way towards it. It was an astounding question, addressed to Densu. Would he accept the kingship at Esuano?

Densu looked at them sadly. Then he shook his head. He had no need of words.

The elders left. The four took the way back to the eastern forest.

* * *

Ababio's trial was to be on a Thursday, in the castle at Cape Coast. Damfo, Araba Jesiwa, Ajoa, and Densu reached Bakano the Tuesday afternoon before the trial. They found Ama Nkroma and stayed with her.

In the morning Ama Nkroma asked if they had slept well. They had.

'The say the white general leaves today,' she said. 'You might find it amusing to see him go.'

She led them east along the beach. Near the castle she turned left and inland, then right inside the town and right again, till she brought them to the bay east of the castle.

A ship stood out on the ocean. On the shore ten huge surf-boats lay ready at the boundary between sea and land, each with a crew of maybe thirty barebacked rowers standing ready by it.

A great noise announced the arrival of the white general. He rode in a wicker cradle carried on poles on the shoulders of four strong men, and they put him into the leading surf-boat without his feet once touching the sand. The king Ata of Cape Coast was there, under his red umbrella. His was not the only royal umbrella. The sound of horns split the air. The general said something, but his air was brusque. West Indian soldiers had come with him to the bay, with their guns and musical instruments. When the general Wolseley had finished his short speech there on the beach, the crewmen of his surf-boat pushed it into the water against the high surf and, rowing furiously, breasted the last big wave before the calmness of the open sea ahead. Other boats followed, their crews singing praises to the white conqueror.

General Wolseley was lifted up on to the ship out on the open sea. In no time the ship was chasing the horizon, taking the lucky conqueror home.

The West Indians had played solemn music to send the white general off. But once the ship had disappeared, their playing changed. The stiff, straight, graceless beats of white music vanished. Instead, there was a new, skilful, strangely happy interweaving of rhythms, and instead of marching back through the streets the soldiers danced. Others joined them. The dancers did not go back to the castle. They passed it, veered right to go past the great open ground, and took their procession meandering through the streets of Cape Coast.

All the groups gathered by the whites to come and fight for them were there and they all danced, all except the whites who looked on, shaking their heads, bursting into laughter now and then, shaking their heads when some particular feat of a dancer baffled their imagination.

Here were Opobo warriors from the east, keeping at a distance from their neighbours from Bonni. Here were Hausas brought by Glover from the Kwarra lands. Here were mixed crowds with men from Dahomey, Anecho, Atakpame, Ada, Ga, and Ekuapem. There were a few Efutu men, and numbers of Fantse policemen in ill-fitting new uniforms. Here were tough, hardened Kru men from the west, Mande and Temne men from even farther west, and the fierce Sussu men inseparable from their swords of war.

All heard the music of these West Indians who had turned the white men's instruments of the music of death to playing such joyous music. All knew ways to dance to it, and a grotesque, variegated crowd they made, snaking its way through the town, followed by a long, crazy tail of the merely idle, the curious, and the very young.

'It's the new dance,' Ajoa said, shaking her head. She spoke sadly, and her sadness was merely a reflection of the sadness of Damfo, Araba Jesiwa, and Densu as they watched.

But beside them they heard a long, low chuckle of infinite amusement. It came from Ama Nkroma.

'What do you find to amuse you, you strange healer-woman?' Damfo asked her. 'Or is it just the well-known madness of all healers that's come upon you now?'

Ama Nkroma continued to laugh. 'It's a new dance all right,' she said, 'and it's grotesque. But look at all the black people the whites have brought here. Here we healers have been wondering about ways to bring our people together again. And the whites want ways to drive us farther apart. Does it not amuse you, that in their wish to drive us apart the whites are actually bringing us work for the future? Look!'

Together with Ama Nkroma's laughter, tears came to her eyes.

Dar es Salaam,
Saturday 13th December, 1975